John H. King

Supernatural

its origin, nature, and evolution Vol. 1

John H. King

Supernatural
its origin, nature, and evolution Vol. 1

ISBN/EAN: 9783337387044

Printed in Europe, USA, Canada, Australia, Japan

Cover: Foto ©Andreas Hilbeck / pixelio.de

More available books at **www.hansebooks.com**

THE SUPERNATURAL:

ITS ORIGIN, NATURE, AND EVOLUTION.

BY

JOHN H. KING.

IN TWO VOLUMES.

VOL. I.

WILLIAMS AND NORGATE,
14, HENRIETTA STREET, COVENT GARDEN, LONDON; AND
20, SOUTH FREDERICK STREET, EDINBURGH.
NEW YORK: G. P. PUTNAM'S SONS.
1892.

LONDON:

G. NORMAN AND SON, PRINTERS, HART STREET,

COVENT GARDEN.

CONTENTS OF VOLUME I.

THE SUPERNATURAL:

ITS ORIGIN, NATURE, AND EVOLUTION.

INTRODUCTION.

As the great abstract principles that regulate the inter-relations of the various modes of matter and the various forms of life become more and more cognizant to human thought, we become conscious not only of their affinities, but of their representative characteristics. As it is with the organic and the inorganic, so is it with the organic and mental.

Thus in the whole range of organic evolution no essential stage in organic life has ever been lost, special forms have perished, but organisms presenting every important stage in evolution continue still to exist with the same vital attributes that the first beings of their kind, so far as we can judge from paleontological evidence, possessed. Thus we now have representatives of the whole scheme of phylogenic evolution from the incipient exposition of the uncentralized plasmic group through all the ranges of unicellular organisms to the highest organic evolvement yet known—man. And while all the classes and orders of living beings still have their representatives, the one continuous unity of all life is still expressed by every organism in its ontological development, passing through the same essential stages as in ages past marked the evolution of its ancestors.

Formative laws of an equally persistent character have in like manner regulated the output of the mental powers, and no mental forms once manifested have ever passed away, and not only does the ontogenic mind pass through the stages of the phylogonic mind, but, as is the case with men, living men may express any form of thought, any habit of will, any diseased, aborted or undeveloped mental status ever manifested by any human beings. Body and soul may revert to any possible stage of living continuity.

Hence we have ever persistent in our midst men who are actuated by every form of emotion that savage and barbarous races present. Not only are the crimes they commit of the same nature as those committed by the lower races, but their sentiments regarding such are wholly influenced by the same undeveloped attributes. As with the moral attributes, so with the intellectual, and it is even so with their supernal sentiments. We have, in our midst, men brought up under the ordinary conditions of modern civilization who are influenced by the same class of supernal thoughts as are noted among the lowest races who fear ghosts, have faith in evil spirits and witches, who believe in luck, charms and spells, and expect immediate Divine assistance by praying to saint or martyr. On this subject Leland, in his *Gipsy Sorcery*, writes :—" A habit-and-repute thief has always in his pocket or somewhere about his person a bit of coal or chalk, or a lucky stone, or an amulet of some sort on which he relies for safety in his hour of peril. Omens he firmly trusts in, divination is regularly practised by him. The supposed power of witches and wizards makes many of them live in terror, and pay black-mail. As for the fear of the Evil-eye, it is affirmed that most of the foreign thieves dread more being brought before a particular magistrate who has the reputation of being endowed with that fatal gift than of being summarily sentenced by any other whose judicial glare is less severe.

"Not only is Fetish or Shamanism the real religion of

criminals but of vast numbers who are not suspected of it. There is not a town in England or in Europe in which witchcraft is not extensively practised. The prehistoric man exists, he is still to be found everywhere by millions, he will cling to the old witchcraft of his ancestors. Until you change his very nature, the only form in which he can realize supernaturalism will be by means of superstition. Research and reflection have taught us that this sorcery is far more widely extended than any cultivated person dreams. It would seem as if by some strange process white advanced scientists are occupied in eliminating magic from religion, the coarser mind is actually busy in reducing it to religion only " (p. 13).

But this survival of early supernal sentiments is not only the result of inheritance; it arises *de novo* in the aborted mind from failure in development. It is a well-known fact that there are human organic faculties withheld at the lower types that mark the standard of the quadrumana, quadrupeds, even reptiles; so in like manner the intellectual powers may be stayed, and the moral faculties held back. The son of normal elevated parents may be an idiot; the daughter of those purely chaste and morally refined may be sunk in lewdness, in beastiality; the offspring of the just and pure in thought and action may be a brutal coward, who lies from the very pleasure of lying. So it is with the expression of supernal sentiments; the worshippers of an abstract God who recognize the power of law and goodness in all mental and material manifestations may beget sons or daughters who cling to the lowest fetish powers and regulate their volitions by omens and charms, and suppose they can control the action of the elements and the souls of men by the most trivial spells worked with filth, rubbish, and the fragments of dead animals and men. Man individually may advance to the full standard of his race, or he may be held back at any ontological stage.

More, the advanced man may not always retain the

status to which his mental powers have once advanced him, he may degenerate, any faculty of the mind may retrograde, and without arriving at second childhood, he may descend to worship imbecile charms and cling to spells to save him from devils and witches.

Hence we ever have with us, and possibly ever shall, not only the maimed and aborted physically, but the maimed and aborted mentally, and among these arising from natural causes a due series of the worshippers of every form of the supernal. It is by a comparison of the respective status of these representatives of the various concepts of supernals that we are enabled not only to define the stages in the development of supernal ideas, but in many cases the feelings that led to the evolvement of such sentiments. In some cases we can, as in the history of magic, witchcraft, and ghost presentations, recognize certain historical data, but the universality of the theory of impersonal powers and the evidence thereof presented in all ages, seem to intimate that they are so grounded in human nature as almost to denote an organic origin, and we in one chapter show that the concepts of luck and ill-luck are presented in certain bodily states apparently without any mental volition. It would seem, as many affirm of the God-thought, that ideas of fate, luck and fortune, are inherent instincts in the mind.

With these organic feelings as the basis on which to form his concepts of knowledge and rules of conduct, man has to associate the three classes of perceptive ideas he conceives, the apparent, the seemingly apparent, and the ideationally apparent, and it is from the last two classes that all supernal concepts are derived. Primary man, like the infant of to-day, found himself more or less powerless in the presence of the natural forces, and he sought some means of protection outside his own physical powers. Then it was that the ethical organic impulses in his nature, acting through his seeming and ideational perceptions, taught him to realise the concepts of supernal protecting powers; these at first were the mere expositions of luck according as the objects or acts were associated with corresponding results.

Thus a series of false sentiments arise in the human mind induced by its special organic sympathies, the same as another class of physical and mental attributes become defined in special instincts. All human supernal concepts have the same primary source in man's organic sympathies, and the forms in which they find expression depend on his status in evolution. The mental and organic depression that ensues when men recognise their powerlessness in the presence of the real or the seeming induces them to seek in the unexplainable powers they affirm sources of protective influences. The first sentiment thus evolved in the mind of man is that of luck, fear of uncanny evil or the desire for canny good, and now the same class of sentiments predominate, in the lowest evolved minds and mark their appreciation of the supernal.

As with every other human faculty, so with man's concepts of supernal influence, we trace a gradual advance in the nature of his deduction, a fuller and more enlarged expression of power, and a greater capacity to work out details. Thus from the mere protective influence of chance in all presentations, man advanced to the recognition of supernal powers or virtues of an impersonal character present in objects and appearances, and thus he learnt, that by certain combinations, or may be, certain actions or words, he could at his will exercise maleficent or protective powers; thus arose the doctrine of spells and charms. The forms of these may vary, and the power once affirmed of a lucky stone or hazel twig may now be associated with the relics of saint or martyr. This phase of early supernal development takes form according to the bearings of local sentiments, and even now it represents a vast mass of the supernal concepts of men, not only rude barbarians, or rustic villagers, but those who deem they hold position among the *élite* in society.

As in the growth of society men assume certain duties or are set apart for certain functions, owing to their more especial attainments, so was it with men supposed to manifest special supernal attributes. There are men now, as there were men in the olden time, who indiscriminately practise and even invent spells and charms; but as the local groups formed clans, some more acute or neurotic men assumed or were accredited with greater powers in working the spells and charms, they became the medicine men of the local groups; and now, instead of each man working his own spell, selecting his own charm, he looked for protection in the occult skill of the shaman, the mystery possessed by the medicine man.

As every form of supernal protection denotes a distinct aspiration for the good and power to withstand evil, so it implies a special element of faith. We have seen that this at first was founded on chance-luck, then on the controlling power that gave occult virtues to things. After the working of these powers became the privilege of men supernally endowed. We have now to consider the evolution of a new supernal form of power, derived from the dream ghost and which in successive stages advanced from the standard of the vulgar apparition to the ancestral spirit, the chieftain, the tutelar god, until it culminated in the highest concept of divinity man has yet evolved. But whatever its anthropomorphic or spiritual status, it is always present to men as a form of luck, either as a protective god or malignant demon. Every form of faith is the worship of luck.

Each local group of men evolved their supernal ghost powers from their own race and their own surroundings, and the attributes they attached to these powers were in all cases derived from the status in evolution of their own or the neighbouring races. Men could only attach power to ghosts or spirits in accord with those present in the natural world, physical or vital; hence as men advanced in mental, moral and social aspirations, so did their gods, and in the attributes attached to the gods, we have the marks of the human social evolution. The transcendental attributes attached to spiritual manifestations were in all cases derived from ideal readings of natural perceptions.

The lowest doctrine of faith, the primary religion, is thus that of luck; the universality of its influence all will acknowledge. Under its conception powers and objects with sympathetic influences are present to the mind as denoting either good or bad fortune, luck or ill-luck, in harmony with the organic and mental status of the individual.

In the second phase of supernal concepts—the religion of charms and spells—the human mind has defined the good and evil presentiments it holds as classes of transcendental influences of a curative, protective, prophetic, and death or disease-producing character. Thus each individual conceives he can produce whatever result he wills by the uncanny resources he has learnt how to utilize; hence he protects himself with amulets, or influences himself and others by using spells and charms.

The third stage of supernal evolution is the religion of the medicine man, or magic, in which the ordinary mind conceives that some men possess greater occult powers than their fellows, derived from various sources, and are thereby capable of controlling for good or evil the mystic powers of the supernal. Under the influence of the medicine man, through acquired neurotic states and dreams, the ghost, and hence the spirit concept was evolved. Primarily the ghost power was only evil, and men had to buy off the spirit or spell-evil by offerings to the medicine man. Hence the faith in, or religion of evil spirit influence became a phase in the development of the supernal.

The origin of spiritual goodness, and the religion of ancestral worship, followed as a necessary deduction from men conceiving that the ghosts of their warriors and leaders after death manifested the same protective attributes as when living; more so when, through the social development, ancestral spirits were evolved and conjointly therewith the doctrine of totem descent which raised animals, trees, and all physical manifestations into spirit kin-protectors. These began their supernal expression in the individual, then the family, and after into tribal protectors, ultimately evolving into the religion of tutelar deities. The subsequent God-phases which have been evolved, pass from confederations of associate tutelar powers to the ascendency of a Regal deity, then to that of a Supreme Autocratic deity, and lastly to that of the Universal Abstract God.

We have to show that these various stages of supernal evolution are co-ordinate with human development or are due to the original mind-powers possessed by great thinkers. In the latter case they are only individual expositions, in the former they are tribal. But, as in the stratification on the earth's surface, there are local gaps, the coal measures being deficient in one tract, the cretaceous formation in another, so there are races of men who have failed to manifest the ancestral supernal stage, while with other races it has been persistent even when they have developed the higher tutelar and chieftain forms of divinity.

What we have undertaken to demonstrate is that the impersonal forms of supernal faith have preceded the personal, and that when the supernal personal powers were evolved by any race, they commenced with the lowest class of ghosts or spirits, and in advancing they proceeded in accordance with their own social development, to scheme the divine government on the standard of their own social state. Thus for instance when the Australian aborigine came to recognize headmen in his tribe, then he built up the theory of spirit headmen in the sky. So, generally among the lower races of men when chieftain rule was established chieftain gods were created. In no case was the concept of universal rule ascribed to a deity before the people were elevated to that sentiment by the human rule of a king of kings.

Our purpose is to show by the internal evidence contained in the supernal concepts of all the great races of men that they have graduated through the various stages of supernal development, and carry in their lower concepts of the supernal, the survival forms of the archaic impersonal manifestations as well as the more advanced concepts of evil and good ghost powers. Hence we considered that it was judicious to take in review the evidences of supernal progress that the great races of men have presented, holding that it was only by so doing we could demonstrate the universality of the laws we propound that denote supernal evolution.

More, in special chapters we detail the rarer instances in which certain races have evolved the concepts of Supreme and Abstract Deities; then one giving a general retrospect of the various forms of the God-idea now held by the highest as well as lowest minds among the various races of men. In conclusion we show that there have been men of original mental capacity in all times and countries, whose mental concepts have passed out of the limited *rôle* of their contemporaries and have advanced to the full appreciation of the oneness in nature—the united and universal Deity. This we demonstrate by a series of literary and historical records.

BOOK I.

THE ORIGIN AND NATURE OF SUPERNAL CONCEPTS.

CHAPTER I.

The organic tendency to evolve supernatural concepts.

THERE is a natural tendency in the human mind to evolve supernal sentiments. Luck and ill-luck have no existence in themselves; they are but forms of thought, and their special deductions are due to the physical condition of the organism. Men when organically depressed cannot help assuming the prevalence of untoward conditions, nor when healthily excited can they forego anticipating favourable results. Incongruous, unsympathetic objects or appearances which, without implying any definite danger or an active offensive attribute, excite in us feelings of revulsion or dread, vague concepts that bode us no good, we cannot account for these influences in any other way than as the result of certain mental and physical conditions, and according to the strength of the impression is our fetish concept of the ill-luck or good-luck supervening.

The portents that start the emotion may be in our feelings, in any sense-impression of our own bodies; they may glance to us from the sky, and any object in nature may seem to present other than its natural attributes. More, as misfortunes and other deleterious influences are often affecting us, and these may seemingly be connected in our minds with certain natural phenomena of time or place, we are apt to connect the phenomena with such results and thereby create sentiments of good or ill-luck. Thus, the fear of some pending evil may override the mental will and evolve uncanny influences, as with a shying horse creating the sense of dread ever presaging ill-luck.

The nature of these indeterminate sentiments of good or ill depend upon the previous impressions on the mind, and the special results thereof entertained, which, as in all human volitions and thoughts, have a tendency to be repeated on like lines until they become sentimental habits.

Of the tendency of affirmed emotions of good or ill to become chronic, Dr. A. B. Granville in his *Autobiography* avows himself not only as a believer in presentiments, but in the vulgar accredited forms of luck. He says, "I am alarmed at the spilling of a salt-cellar. I don't like to meet a hearse while going out of the street-door. I would not undertake a journey or anything important on a Friday; and the breaking of a looking-glass would throw me into fits. One afternoon I became suddenly depressed in spirits, and this endured till the succeeding day when the knife and fork, laid before me crossways, startled me." So he describes their appearance at the two following courses; then on looking at his calendar he found it was a Friday. In this case we have the predisposing physical depression—the sentiment of ill-luck—and the iteration of like deductions from trivial incidents associated with the sentiment.

Each distinct physical state produces its own forms of supernal conceptions, often widely different; imbecility, senility, the various forms of idiocy, are each distinguished by their supernal tendencies as well as the special loss of normal tendencies. There are men unconscious of moral responsibility, who have lost all preservative instincts, have no fear, no sense of time or distance, who cannot co-ordinate their own muscular powers—are incapable of education and exhibit mental reversions to the instinctive states of the lower animals; so in like manner some men are devoid of all supernal concepts, they know nothing of ghost or other forms of delusion; incapable of kindness, they could not conceive of a protective power, and equally some repudiate all forms of luck; they know nothing of God or spirit, and are never troubled by any of the feelings or sentiments those ideas imply.

To others the supernal is an ever present reality; they recognize its presence as distinctly as the natural world, and they obey its behests with the same direct affirmations as they accord to their relations with all things living.

We only know of the supernal through human thought. We see it expressed by others, we feel its sentiments in our own minds, and we may infer from their actions that like influences affect some animals. The bird, the dog, the elephant and other animals dream, but of the nature of the sentiments left in their sensoriums we are wholly in the dark. In the waking state animals exhibit the same dread and doubt, if not terror, as men. In the presence of anything strange, mysterious or uncouth, they manifest the same mental emotions as the savage.

The bases on which all supernal concepts are founded are the sentiments of Wonder, Fear, Hope, and Love; and these severally, according as they are evolved, give character to the supernal concepts to which they become attached. Under the general aspects of things there is a quiet accord between the mind of man and the phenomena of the universe, but should the condition of things lose its accepted normal character then influences of dread fill the mind, and, as in the presence of the eclipse or the meteor, if the dread is more than spasmodic, man doubts the stability of the universe. So it is even with less variations from the normal. It may be a feather, a leaf, a stone, or an animal which presents unknown characteristics and excites first wonder, then dread, and on his failure to recognize their status they become to him uncanny—they are not natural—and excite sentiments of erratic influence, of supernal action.

That more novelty may excite supernal sentiments may be seen in the following incidents. O. C. Stone, in a few

Months in New Guinea, writes: "A few years ago they had no idea of any land existing but their own, and when at rare intervals the sails of some distant ship were seen on the horizon they believed them to be a spirit or *vaaka* floating over the surface of the deep" (p. 86). Again, Gill, in *Gems from Coral Islands*, writes: "When Davida landed he brought with him a pig. Having never before seen any animal larger than a rat, the people looked on this pig with emotions of awe; they believed it to be the representative of some invisible power. The teacher did all he could to convince them that it was only an animal, but they were determined to do it honour; they clothed it in white bark sacred cloth and took it in triumph to the principal temple, where they fastened it to the pedestal of one of their gods. For two months her degraded votaries brought her daily offerings of the best fruits of the land and presented to her the homage of worship" (p 77).

A man may not be able to explain all the normal common phenomena that his senses present to him, yet in ordinary cases he feels assured that they accord with the nature of things; but when from organic defect, mental excitation, or vague perception his imaginative powers endeavour to correct the impressions presented to his sensorium, they become modified to the prevailing sentiments in his mind, and may assume any supernal characters that his memory reactions may induce.

The primary abnormal presentation only suggests the idea of the uncanny, and there is in the unsubstantiality of the perception a doubt or a fear of the nature of the object excited. This may be like an incoming presentation in a dissolving view entirely diverse from the full reality. So little are the new perceptions determinate in the mind, that the figures first accepted are regularly cast aside. We have this mental phase presented by Hamlet when Polonius accepts the semblance of a cloud as being that of a camel or weasel, "or very much like a whale."

But not only may the false reasoning result from the vagueness of the impression on the sensorium; the very presence of the object seen may be an unreality of the sense and only due to a morbid mental impression; a persistent idea from the arcana of the memory may seem a physical reality. Dr. Hammond, in his work on *Nervous Derangement*, gives the following illustrative case :—" A lady of a highly nervous temperament, one day intently thinking on her mother and picturing to herself her appearance as she looked when dressed for church, happening to raise her eyes, saw her mother standing before her clothed as she imagined. In a few moments it disappeared, but she soon found that she had the ability to recall it at will, and that the power existed in regard to many other forms, even those of animals and of inanimate objects. She could thus reproduce the image of any person on whom she strongly concentrated her thoughts. At last she lost the control of the operation and was constantly subject to hallucinations of sight and hearing " (p. 81). There are many ghost presentations that these mental phenomena may cover.

We may even carry the influence of the deceptive but accepted supernal power another stage, in which even unconsciously the organic powers act under the influence of the memory, not the judgment. In the *Journal of Mental Science* we read of a boy at school who had shortly before lost his brother, both belonging to a family in which psychical concepts were dominant. One day he "found his hand filling with some feeling before unknown, and then it began to move involuntarily upon the paper and to form words and sentences. Sometimes even when he wished to write, his hand moved in drawing small flowers such as exist not here, and sometimes when he expected to draw flowers, his hand moved into writing; these writings being communications from his spirit-brother describing his own happy state and the means by which the living brother could obtain like felicity. The mother tried if the spirit would move her hand with a pencil in it, but days and weeks passed without any result. At last her willing but not self-moved hand wrote the initials of the boy's name, then after a time a flower was drawn. Afterwards the father had the power of involuntary writing." (IV. p. 369, &c.) This, like the forms of supernal suggestion, shows how the memory, or even the organic parts, may evolve habits outside the influence of the sensorium, and which it accepts as denoting supernal manifestations.

Some subjective sensations, and therefore deemed by some persons of a supernal nature, are due to organic changes, and the individual receives impressions to which others are not amenable. Thus in epilepsy, before fits, there are subjective sensations of smell, and a scent resembling phosphorus precedes loss of smell, and injuries to the head cause all substances to have a gaseous or paraffin smell. (*Gower, Dis. of Nerv. Sys.*, II. p. 182.)

Hallucinations deemed supernal may affect any one or more of the senses and express any possible form of deranged activity, they may be wholly imaginative or a blending of the real and the ideal, and they pass from objective realities to subjective concepts, from concrete facts to supernal manifestations. Hammond describes a case in transition. A gentleman all his life was affected by the appearance of spectral figures. When he met a friend in the street he could not be sure whether he saw a real or an imaginary person. He had the power of calling up spectral figures at will by directing his attention for some time to the conceptions of his own mind, and these either consisted of a figure or a scene he had witnessed, or a composition created by his own imagination. Though he had the power of calling up an hallucination, he had no power to lay it; the person or scene haunted him. All these cases intimate that local powers may be mentally suggestive without the cognizance of the central judgment, and thus evolve ideas that of necessity seem supernal.

The effects of such supernal concepts are not limited to the recipient of the abnormal sensations, but affect the sentiment of the supernal in all who are cognisant of the case. To the perceptive individual they may be simply realities; and, however absurd or incongruous, he accepts them as perfectly natural, or he may recognize their subjective nature and, according to their characteristics, attach any supernatural qualities to their presentations. Those observant of the expressed hallucinations and ignorant of the causes that may induce such, ever recognize in them the output of powers not belonging to the natural world and are apt to accept any supernal explanation thereof that may be present to their thoughts.

The standard of natural perception is formed in each man's own mind, and consequently as these differ so does the perception or conception of the uncanny; every sense-power may be excited or depressed, may tally with the ordinary human scale, be deficient or extend beyond the usual range. Under various forms of physical disorganisation and mental alienation the sense-powers are often perverted and in most cases give origin to fetish concepts. Things not in existence may affect any one or more senses, caused sometimes by the misperception of real objects, at others the forms and feelings induced are all subjective. One may always smell turpentine, another the odour of fresh blood. One may always see a black cat before him, another be constantly conscious of a human phantom accompanying him. Voices may be heard by the disturbed mind-powers; they may speak in whispers, they may come from above or below, out of the sky or from the depths of the earth. Thus Lord Herbert heard a sound from Heaven.

That the physical state of the organism which presents the capacity to exhibit any supernatural state or power may be induced by various means, is a fact not only well known to the scientific observer, but is familiar to the medicine man in all countries. The prophetic state may be induced—the capacity to see visions, the power to affirm spells, even the belief in our holding transcendental attributes.

Naturally in certain organic derangements men exhibit mental and bodily phenomena which are conceived to indicate supernal influences, as forms of somnambulism, catalepsy, ecstatic states, and epileptic and convulsive abnormal conditions. These various symptoms being deemed of supernal origin, led to the inference that like conditions which could be induced by personal excitation of various kinds, and more so by toxic agents, were of the same character; hence it was the object of the rude medicine men who, in the early social state, took charge of such phenomena, to simulate by any means in their power similar abnormal states.

In the hunt for food substances men readily learnt to distinguish the various vegetal productions of their native districts, into those good for food, and those having baneful or exciting qualities, and from the latter the individuals naturally neurotic and therefore most strongly affected by toxics selected suitable materials to induce such states, when for various social purposes they required to manifest those special powers. The Australian aborigine found such a neurotic agent in the leaves of a native shrub, and when he obtained tobacco from white men that was chewed for the same purpose. The Thlinkeet medicine man produces a supernal delusive state by the root of a Panax and the Siberian Shaman by the infusion of a mushroom. Mediæval witches in like manner, for like effects, used preparations of nightshade, henbane, and opium. Boismont describes the old Italian sorcerers as making a cheese containing a drug which changed their nature. Greek inspiration was said to have been produced by inhaling mephitic vapours and various fetish drinks.

That infusions containing certain vegetal principles will

produce mental and bodily phenomena of remarkable potency is generally known, and herbs and berries having those powers have in all countries been esteemed as possessing supernal virtues. Among these aconite, datura, belladonna, and opium have ever held the highest status. Van Helmont, after tasting the root of Napellus, said he felt as if the power was transferred to the pit of his stomach. Dr. Laycock having once accidentally taken a drop of tincture of aconite, described the sensations that came to him as strains of grand aerial music in exquisite harmony, and most have read of the vast poetical imaginings that are induced by opium and hachsheesh.

The power of manifesting states of inspiration and prophetic powers was greatly enhanced when men learnt to make intoxicating beverages, and there are few races of men but have attained this knowledge. The mental phenomena presented under the effect of stimulants may be excited ideality, inspiration, the desire to prophecy, or to manifest any extraordinary gift; and under these conditions the wondering savage looks on and marvels, deeming the herb or fruit capable of inducing such effects of divine origin and those special manifestations the evidence of a supernal state.

Nor are the concepts of supernal action in man limited to attributes derived from infusions of leaves and berries. Like sentiments of the uncanny arise in various actions which simulate corresponding states in epilepsy and mania when men in dancing, leaping, rotating, and simulating various animal activities, continue their unnatural actions as if they would never cease, and seem to the onlookers endowed with more than human powers of endurance.

That men under these induced states should claim the possession of various transcendental powers as invisibility, that of transformation, the conquest of time and space, and special prophetic knowledge, is due to the mental presentations they have under such conditions, and as to the onlookers so much that is wonderful is present to them they are in the due mental state to readily accept such assumptions. Hence the wide belief in mystic principles and powers, in ghosts and spirits, in transformation, in the conquest of death and disease, in the assumptions of controlling the rain, the thunder, and modifying natural appearances. Hence the belief in dreams, and in reading dreams in charms and spells, and all the spiritual phenomena of the inter world.

The more extended knowledge of the properties of drugs has demonstrated that there exist natural associations and reactions between such principles and the various parts of the human organisation.   When we read that Podophyllum acts specially on the intestines, that Aconite diminishes sensibility and Chloral withholds it, that Digitalis influences the heart's action, Conium that of the nerves, that Bolladonna arrests the secretions and Cantharides stimulates the sexual parts, we trace a method in the medicine man's mode of proceeding.

These various facts real and assumed intimate that the human organism has a natural tendency to evolve supernal powers and principles, and that men duly constituted, either naturally or by drugs, can no more withhold expressing supernal beliefs than they can the use of their limbs for walking. Men take faith as they take disease, by internal change, by inoculation; and as forms of growth, we may even predicate the evolution of supernal symptoms by the phenomena of the heavens. That there is a oneness in the universal exposition of the supernal in fetish ideas, ghosts, magic and classes of Divine beings only, expresses the fact that all normal men hold the same organic and mental powers, and are amenable to the same external influences. A man can no more help believing in supernal manifestations when his system is in accord with such forms of belief than he can resist the influence of sense-perceptions on his mind; they may be real or illusory, but he must receive them and find their due place in his sensorium.

That there are great organic differences in individual men we all know. It is patent to us all that we have our own individual special affections, that we are variously affected by things. This is well shown in *Reynolds's System of Medicine*. He writes: "Six people take an indigestible meal and one of them suffers nothing, a second is troubled with dyspepsia, a third with asthma, a fourth has an epileptic fit, a fifth an attack of gout, and the sixth is disturbed with diarrhœa." (I. p. 7.) So it is with a mental presentation; with one it is a normal object, another rejects it as spurious, a third looks at it with wonder, a fourth with doubt, a fifth detects in it a special emotion, while the sixth is excited to rapture.

Nor is the influence once excited in the mind alike a continuous form of expression, it changes as the individual grows and is altered, and not only is the influence of normal things modified in the development of the being, but the spiritual sentiments, however attained, are liable to like variations, even though the habit of life renders their uniform concept the desire of the soul. Men fight against the rising sense of change, they redouble their devotions, they attempt to coerce the mind by bodily austerities, but nothing avails, and they become heretics, even self-excommunicated, and are cast off by self, earth, and heaven, unless, by a great effort of will, they can accept the new mental dispensation, and mould their lives to its dictates.

The distinguishing attribute of man is to attach abstract conceptions of relations to the objects that are perceived by his senses; hence, he readily draws not only general principles out of extraneous presentations, but he attaches to them special affinities and special powers, not intrinsic in the object, but resulting from his own mental assumptions.

These assumptions may be founded on the actual indices presented by the objects, and lead to the evolution of the natural laws regarding the nature and actions of objects, or they may be founded on imperfect concepts in things, or false interpretations of phenomena by imperfect perception, or they may be wholly ideal, and have no existence outside the conceptive mind.

To the last class, we hold, belong all the many sentiments which have built up the world of supernaturalism that not only in a great measure engrosses human thought, but tends so materially to excite, both mentally and socially, organic states exhibiting the greatest amount of both good and ill.

Sentiments of such importance, and so universal among men, cannot be due to accident or chance; there must be some inciting cause in the human mind or its physical organism to create such a wide range of assumptions, and produce the mental state that was enabled to evolve them. As an example of the organic tendency to form supernal concepts, we take the case of Madame Hauffe, the ghost-seer of Prevost, who at a very early age manifested a tendency to conceive transcendental presentations. When almost a child she had premonitory and prophetic visions. Blamed by her father for the loss of an article of value, she dreamt upon it till the place appeared to her in a vision, much in the same manner as Dr. Callaway describes the Zulu boys divining the whereabouts of stray cattle, and, equally with them, cases of unconscious cerebration. She showed great uneasiness in passing by churchyards and in old castles, and once saw a tall, dark apparition in her godfather's house. At one time she was confined by a remarkable sensibility in the nerves of her eyes, which induced in her the capacity to see things invisible to ordinary eyes. She was, after, subject to frightful dreams. After her confinement for a long time she could not endure the light. Then gradually her gift of ghost-seeing was developed;

she had prophetic visions, divinations, and saw objects and motions in glass, and spectral figures were commonly about her. Their presence, she said, was confirmed by the opening of doors, and no one present to do so, knockings on the walls, the ringing of glasses, and their moving, even in a strong light. Amongst her spectral visitors was a knight, whose coming was announced by loud noises and the candlesticks voluntarily moving. This spectre rehearsed one of the old ghost tales of murder, contrition, and the gallows moral, of conversion in the presence of death. Another spectre was a short figure in a dark cowl, also a murderer, and his discourses with her, or rather hers to him, in both characters, were heard by the residents in the house; and he, like the other spectre, became femininely religious, and desired to be present—if we may use the phrase—in his invisible state at the baptism of her child. We are not told whether he became godfather to it.

Later on she had visits by a tall female with a child. These were announced by a sharp metallic sound. This spectre was intensely religious; and when Madame Hauffe had taught her how to pray, the spectre appeared to her in a white robe, claiming to be one of the redeemed. Others, under her strong affirmation, declared they saw the same spectres visiting her, with the usual accompaniments of ghost tales, antique dresses, spots of blood, veils and babies. Later on her multiplied experiences, after a tendency for somnambulism set in, were most remarkable. Crystal put in her hand awakened her, sand or glass on the pit of her stomach produced a cataleptic state, the hoof of an elephant touching her educed an epileptic paroxysm, diamonds caused dilations of the pupils, sunlight induced headache, moonlight melancholy, whilst music made her speak in rhythm. On looking into the right eye of a person she saw behind her own reflected image that of the individual's inner self; on looking into the left eye she saw the diseased organ pictured forth, and was enabled to prescribe for it. Like those of the old medicine men, her prescriptions were mostly amulets, though occasionally homœopathic or old-wife herb remedies. She claimed to read with the pit of her stomach, but her reading only implied the conception of lucky or unlucky; so, if it was good news, she expressed its interpretation by laughing, if bad, by sadness. Her death dreams were of coffins and children, but they might not be realized for months. She affirmed that her spirit was in the habit of leaving her body and passing into space, like as with other mystics—even the Australian wizard. She was a strange blending of primary supernal concepts, with modern spiritual innovations.

Nor is it only our waking sensations and mental expositions that are influenced by our organic condition. It is the same with our perceptions and deductions in dreams. We dream most of what the mind is most interested in, or the state of the body most prominently presents to it. Hence, as Macnish judiciously observes, "The miser dreams of wealth, the lover of his mistress, the musician of melody, the philosopher of science, the merchant of trade. So in like manner the choleric man is passionate in his sleep, a virtuous man with deeds of benevolence, that of a humourist with ludicrous ideas." Deranged bodily influences in like manner give their special impressions in dream forms; "the dropsical subject has the idea of fountains and rivers and seas in his sleep, jaundice tinges the objects beheld with its own yellow, sickly hue, hunger induces dreams of eating agreeable food, an attack of inflammation disposes us to see all things of the colour of blood, and thirst presents us with visions of parched oceans, burning sands, and unmitigable heat."

Even self-willed thought to the ecstatic may not only present ideal concepts as realities; they may so affect the sensations as to organically affect the organism, and induce reaction by the special faculty. Thus Balzac alleged when he wrote the story of the poisoning of one of his characters.

in a novel, he had so distinct a taste of arsenic in his
mouth afterwards, that he vomited his dinner. (*Tait's
Intelligence.*)

So self-willing in certain neurotic states not only
conceives of prescient power, but itself affirms its own
wishes and deductions as prophetic declarations. Dr.
Hammond describes the case of a lady who thus would
promptly affirm as facts, not only the far distant, as present
to her, as the affirmations in second sight, but that of the
future. (*Mental Derangement*, p. 14.) Du Prel cites cases
of organic monitions in dreams, as Galen's case of a man's
leg being turned in stone, and in a few days it was
paralyzed. Macario dreamt of an acute pain in his neck,
yet found himself quite well on awaking; but a few
hours after he had a violent inflammation of the tonsils. So
many other cases of premonitory signs felt in the deranged
part, and not in the sensorium. There are many local
premonitory indications which by unconscious cerebration
reach the consciousness and seem to it prophetic.

CHAPTER II.

The supernal attributes in things conceived as due to impersonal powers, or spirit action.

Men almost universally recognize the existence of supernal objects and powers, as well as material objects and powers. As a general rule the objects and the powers of the material world convey like ideas of form, colour, and action to the minds of all men, however much they may differ in regard to their causation or origin; but while the general supernal concepts are not only varied and diverse, there are men who deny *in toto* the presence or powers of supernal agents, yet no one disputes the existence of his own personality, nor the presence of other things, or the forces present in wind, fire, and water. The facts in the material world depend upon the amount of knowledge an individual man possesses; the disputed concepts of supernals rather express the absence of knowledge, and that its duties are supplemented by mystic idealizations, and these take the special characters of the race and the time.

If we endeavour to follow the evolution of the various forms of supernal concepts, we find we are thwarted in the first place by the absence of all evidence of the original state of man and the rise of each subsequent supernal sentiment. In this direction we have no records. Neither is there at present in existence any tribes of men whose mental character expresses the primary type. But though we are thus devoid of historical data, we have other

resources that will enable us to classify and explain the
stages in the evolution of supernal ideas.

The scientific naturalist has been long familiar with the
fact that the ontology of the individual expresses the types
in the phylogeny of the race, and that if the mind or
faculties of an individual are from any malcause restrained
in development, the mind or body exhibits the reversionary
types of those stages.   As supernal sentiments are one of
the forms of mental evolution it necessarily follows that
living individuals may at all times express the inmature
stages of the supernal phenomena.   Hence to become
cognizant of the origin and progress of supernal sentiments, it is only necessary that we duly classify the
supernal ideas expressed by individual men.   To do this
we must be able to mentally form a scheme of supernal
evolution as a basis for our deductions.

There was a time, and that not long distant, in which it
was taken for granted that the assumed presentations of
supernal forms and volitions were considered as real as
those of the material world, and in which the differences
between the highest and lowest supernal natures but
marked the special standards of evolution; not essential
typical differences.   The old writers classified the supernal
beings and supernal states according to the standards of
supernal powers they were presumed to hold, and without
explaining the difference defined all supernal manifestations
as being due to ghosts or spirits or to the occult powers of
magic.

No doubt the old mystics confused and blended the
phenomena of magic with spirit manifestations, though
they often distinctly expressed the one as the inherent
virtue in things and ascribed the other class to the
willing volitions of spirits; but modern writers on the
nature of supernals, with the ghost theory prominently in
their minds, deduce all supernal manifestations as the
varied modes of action of ghosts and spirits.   With them

the beginning and end of all forms of supernalism are
deduced from, at first, the concept of the human ghost
through dreams, and the after evolvement of spirits in all
material things and forms of material power.

Dr. Tylor, in his *Primitive Culture*, has collected a vast
mass of local conceptions of spirits and their ghostly connection with humanity. These which represent the various
stages of the passage of the ghost into the higher spiritual
personality are, however, unfortunately mixed up with some
few of the many expressions of supernal power that have
nothing ghostly in their attributes. It is strange how
commonly the facts which present the influence of occult
virtue or power as an inherent quality in things, are mixed
up with the more advanced idea which conceives the power
to express a willing and selective mind. We recognize a
wide difference between the natural chemic powers in
objects and even their physical manifestations to those
presented by mental thought and will, and we never apply
the concept of self-willed thought or judgment to the
action of medicaments or the virtues in mystic stones.
No one prays to an amulet, no one treats the lucky stone
as having a will, no one supposes that the curative
material, whether a medicine or a charm, has any choice
in the matter. Yet all these impersonal powers or attributes are classed by Dr. Tylor with, and as, ghost manifestations. We know there are many objects in which we
perceive the active powers of selective animals—some in
which, according to vulgar conception, certain so-called
ghost or spirit-attributes are generally recognized; but
there are also various objects, the action of which on other
materials and the attributes they present to the human
mind, imply the presence of an impersonal passive power,
good or evil only to the one possessing it. More, the
same object may to one man convey the idea that it represents an impersonal attribute, while another man may
conceive that it expresses ghost or spirit-power. If the

force were its natural attribute it would express that character to all men, but when it is only supposititious it merely expresses the tone of mind of the beholder.

Among the incidents quoted by Dr. Tylor to affirm the general spirit is one from Rower in which a negress proposes to effect a cure by the suppliant killing a white cock, and then after tying it up place it at a four-crossway, or he was simply to drive a dozen wooden pegs into the ground and thereby bury the disease. Both these magic formulæ have no ghost or spirit-will, they merely present an impersonal charm-power. So the virtue in the Australian's bit of quartz has no necessary connection with ghost-action, though according to their advanced theory a spirit might use it; the actual boylya is in the mineral itself, and the same impersonal power may be used, as in the case he quotes, to conquer a spirit's evil influence. That similar boylya powers were once common among the Caribs and at the Antilles only implies that the impersonal occult charm-power preceded the concept of a fetish ghost-power, not that they are the same thing. We infer that the supposition of spirit or ghost making use of the charm-stone was long subsequent to the original magic use of it by men, and that by an after-thought when ghosts were conceived they repeated as in so many other things their actions when man, but in no case even now among races like the Australian aborigines have men worked out the concept of ghost or spirit-created evil, they only make use of the same impersonal powers as men. The Malagasy are in an intermediate state between the man who only knows a charm-evil, and the one who ascribes the evil to the personal action of a ghost or spirit. Thus we are told that they ascribe all diseases to evil spirits, but the diviner does not expel the spirit-caused disease by the will of a more powerful spirit, but calls to his aid impersonal charms, from which we infer that they were originally caused by charms for which afterwards ghosts were substituted, but

like the higher races of men they had not evolved the higher
god concept of exorcism; so impersonal charms in the form
of a faditir were employed to conquer the disease. No
doubt originally the Carib and the Malagasy saw the
origin of the disease as an evil spell and cured it by a good
spell, but as with so many other races of men they had
evolved the Bhuto or evil spirit but not the good or guardian spirit. So in the case of the Dyaks of Borneo, it is
not the evil spirit that has caused the injury either by its
active personal interposition or by the higher form of
possession, it is the impersonal fetish stones and splinters,
which through the magic of the spell have entered his body
and which the medicine man affirms by his greater boylya
he is able to extract.

Even the case of Dr. Callawny's Zulu widow, who affirms
she is troubled by her late husband's ghost haunting her,
not in her, and which the medicine man lays by certain
charm objects, not conquering it with a greater spirit
power, exhibits the same stage of evil-spirit injury and charm
cure. In like manner the Mandan widow talking to her
husband's skull hold that his spirit was present; the same
with the Guinea negro and the bones of his parents which
he prayed to; but in these cases we are presented with a
higher stage of supernal development, the power of good as
well as evil spirits. The same sentiment is manifest in the
very idea of penates, household gods, and tutelar deities.

In the instance of finding a thief quoted by Dr. Tylor
from *Rowley's Universities' Mission*, we have the contest of
the two principles—impersonal fetish and ghost evidence.
The medicine man affirmed the woman selected as guilty
by the spirit was indeed guilty, but the charm ordeal, wiser
than the spirit, absolved her and she was acquitted.

We now have more immediately to do with those
influences whether *pro* or *con* that express luck, curing
or protecting the wearer and presaging good or evil to him.
In no case do objects holding these virtues necessarily

express this power by ghostly or spiritual influence. Ghosts may in some cases be affirmed as the inducing causes, but we hold when such is the case that originally the sentiment was impersonal, and that the attribute, when the ghost became a power, was transferred to it. But not only among savage races, but among all classes of men who hold the doctrine of luck and the other impersonal attributes, we look in vain for any evidence that they hold the intermediate agent as a ghost or spirit, and we therefore demur to the tone in which amulets are mentioned in connection with the exposition of ghost sentiments. Neither the ignorant and superstitious, nor those more enlightened who consider their mysterious virtues as quaint survivals from the past, ascribe those virtues to an indwelling ghost or spirit, or even assert a personality in the object. They never affirm that the power is expressed by will in the form of choice or selection, but that the unconscious virtue serves its possessor the same as any other substance, and like a piece of coal it might lie inert in the earth to no end of time and only exhibit its active or presumed virtue when man utilized it. But amulets become idols when the man who possesses them esteems that they hold angels or demons, as in the case of the Dacotah who painted his boulder and called it grandfather and prayed to it; but we ought always clearly distinguish such personified idols from impersonal mystic objects. In the one series the power is ascribed to a mental activity, in the other to a mere passive, insensate agent.

Surely there is no difficulty in a man recognizing one form of power in a boiling crater, others in the lightning flash, the bursting of a torpedo, even in the ascent of warm vapour, the flowing of a stream or the inrolling of the sea. So in like manner flame has its own special virtue of burning, water of cleansing, stone of hardness, and these virtues act on diverse things in different ways. Besides, the stone or other object may have many like passive powers. So with the Indian imbued with fetish sentiments there was nothing extravagant in attributing to stones luck for crops, for women in labour, and for bringing sunshine or rain. We know these powers never were in the stones any more than the often iterated power of luck, or of curing disease or protecting from ills. These were all mental occult powers and only existed in connection with the stone in the mind of man, and men could only ascribe powers to objects which they did not naturally express by already having formed these concepts in their minds, consequently the power affirmed can only exhibit the same status as the mind of its exponent.

Dr. Tylor quotes several instances of charms which have no ghost or spirit attribute, as Pliny's statement of the ailment in a patient's body being transferred to a puppy or dock. This form of charming is common in fetish leechdom. So the Hindu's third wife having her husband first married to a tree was only a charm to keep away from her what she esteemed a fetish influence, and the father's trousers being turned inside out in China to save the babe from uncanny influences. These and many other presumed evil influences may and have been evolved into forms of ghost and spirit-evil, but in the stage in which Dr. Tylor puts them they only express impersonal occult evil influences, not spirit manifestations. They are like all the folk-lore spells and charms, simply prestiges of uncanny influences. He admits that modern folk-lore still cherishes such ideas, and he quotes instances yet does not appear to note that these admissions nullify his own theory that such evils and diseases are supposed to arise only from ghost and spirit powers.

In like manner with Dr. Tylor, Herbert Spencer ignores all the assumed powers of charms and spells, and from his statement of first principles we should not be led to infer that such concepts even now guide and influence the minds of the greater part of human beings. In his observations on fetish he sees the power, not as an attribute of the object, but resulting from the mental action of the spirit controlling it.   He appears to know nothing of the assumed impersonal powers in precious and other stones, and in all fetish objects, but conceives that these things represent the higher attributes of ghost or spirit-powers.   All the primitive magic supernal powers denoting luck and ill-luck, curative, protective, and presaging powers, are by him passed over without comment; he ignores the whole philosophy of the impersonal, it does not appear in his scheme of evolution.

Sir J. Lubbock, in tracing his concept of the evolution of religion, similarly ignores all the primary ideas on which the more developed faiths were built.   The beginning of religion with him is the birth of the ghost.   It is true he illustrates natural magic, and quotes a few cases of impersonal divination, but he fails to perceive that they point to other than ghost power.   The needles which floating designate living men, and the one sinking the dead man, and the mats of the Zulus which cease to cast the shadow, are considered as marks of ghostly intervention, not as presaging impersonal monitions.   So the sticks which indicate the living by standing when planted but falling when the personality they represent is dead, with him present not self-contained occult powers, but the direct action of ghosts.   The same ghost personality is attached to Father Merolla's experience of witchcraft.

Our inquiry into the nature and attributes of supernal powers intimates that they are all deductions from the forms of power in the natural world, the ghost is the type of mental power, human or animal.   But the forms of power in the natural world are not all mental: we have power as expressed by material physical force; we have power as presented by the chemical interchange of atoms; we have power as manifest in the action of the celestial bodies, the change of day and night, summer and winter; we have special powers as denoting the attributes of like

objects of the most varied character.   Now all these forms
of power have their supernatural as well as their natural
deductions in the minds of men.   It is from the supernal
concepts of human and animal activities men have deduced
the whole series of ghost and spirit manifestations.   So in
like manner from the physical forces the chemical transformations—the influence of the sun, moon, and stars, and
the general phenomena of the elementary bodies—men
have evolved all the lower phenomena of supernal powers.
We thus have two great series of supernatural forces : the
impersonal derived from the attributes of things, the
personal whose origin is seen in mental action—human or
animal.   These two series of forces are absolutely distinct
in the natural world, but it is a common thing to blend
their powers in human supernal concepts.   Hence, while in
the living material world we never lose the actual distinctions of the mental and the material, we are in supernal
relations always confusing and blending these distinct
powers.   Hence, a stone may not only have its own natural
attributes as a mineral substance, but it may have mental
characteristics, it may have volition, it may hear, talk,
manifest selective attributes and emotions, at one and the
same time being both personal and impersonal.   Hence we
can understand how it happened that impersonal attributes
were defined as ghostly manifestations, and the common
tendency to read material transcendental qualities as
spiritual manifestations.   We have already shown in considering Dr. Tylor's ghostly supernalisms how the two
powers are blended in the same series of supernal relations.

Many impersonal attributes, because they are attached to
objects that formed parts of organic personalities, are
supposed to be under ghostly influence, and their canny or
uncanny expressions are inferred to be due to the ghost
once connected with them.   That this is a false deduction
we infer in the case of parts of animals esteemed as amulets,
whether curative, protective, or denoting luck.   It is not

that the mind of the animal dwells in the bone, or claw, or
hair, or feathers; it is the special fetish power that the
claw or feather exhibited, and which was a power beyond
its own mental to the animal itself, and which continues
still in the bone or claw now that the animal ghost-
mind has gone out of it. This impersonal power was in the
claw or nail when it formed part of the animal and at the
service of the animal; and the same impersonal power is
devoted to its new possessor whoever he may be.

We are not aware that this aspect of the supernal
question has ever been propounded, or that those who
trace a ghost connection in the assumed supernal power
continuous in the claw or bone, ever realize that men at
one time affirmed special occult powers to the various parts
of organisms individually distinct and separate from the
mental powers that govern the general organism. It was
so with feathers and bills of birds, teeth and claws of
carnivorous animals, and generally expressive of the heart,
liver, and other internal parts. It was manifest in phallic
worship. We recognize its influence in the cannibal
custom of eating the heart of a brave enemy. In all these
instances a special power distinct from the ghost, soul, or
spirit manifestation is affirmed of an impersonal nature.

More, there are occult powers supposed to be widely
diffused, that by no question of gender, no characteristic
of origin, is it possible to affirm or denote a ghostly
nature. These mystic impersonal powers — active for
good or evil, curative or destructive — exist in days and
hours, in the position of the heavenly bodies, in forms, in
words, even in the direction in which objects are placed;
any of these characteristics may override not only the will
of an individual but that of thousands, as in war, or at
birth, or in connection with any individual or multiple of
individuals performing certain volitions. None of these
forms of occult power are due to the soul of any individual
or the person they affect. It may be due to the accident

of the hour of birth, it may result from neglecting to make
chalk marks on the wall of the room, as with the Jews in
which the child-bed woman lies; or the neglecting to affix
the sign of the bloody hand, as is customary with
Eastern races. These customs, or charms, belong to the
ante-ghost age, and their place was supplied at the
evolution of the ghost by the mental action of guardian
angels and evil demons.

It thus appears that there exist, or are presumed to
exist, many forms of supernal power; and our purpose is to
trace their origin and status, and as we have no historical
data to aid us, we are thrown upon the internal evidence of
such facts that they present; and it is from the examination
and classification of the various characteristics and their
special relations to men that we have deduced our scheme
of the development of supernal ideas.

There is one important deduction we would point out—
that is, all the impersonal forms of power may be accounted
for by natural deductions from physical states and symptoms,
while the supernal attributes of ghosts are either deductions
from the impersonal attributes, or have no explainable
origin. Thus the prophetic character which would seem
essentially a ghostly attribute, is simply an attribute that
arises as we have seen from the state of the organic
capacity; there are certain medicaments that produce it.

Colquhoun, in his *History of Magic*, also writes:—" The
delirium which accompanies certain inflammatory disorders,
especially of the brain, frequently assumes a prophetic
character. De Seze holds it to be undisputed, that especially
in inflammation of the brain and in apoplexy ecstatic states
occur in which not only ideas are acquired, but also
extraordinary powers are displayed of penetrating into the
secrets of futurity."   (I. p. 61.)

In the impersonal state all forms of curing are the result
of the inherent virtues that are affirmed as existing in
things or actions. In the intermediate state this is pre-

sented as due to certain actions in connection with the will of the agent after it is simply effected by the power of will, be it by a man, a ghost, or a spirit.

The various mental states, modes of sympathy and affinity, have their impersonal as well as personal attributes; the impersonal would be affirmed long before the personal were known.   This is exemplified in the special action of toxics, various infusions of material substances producing special bodily and mental states; thus alcohol from wine induced gay drunkenness, while that from grain induces furious intoxication.   The taking absinthe results in paralysis of the legs.   Cherry-laurel water taken by a woman produces a religious ecstatic state—the eyes are turned up, the arms slowly raised, the hands being extended to heaven; other symptoms are, falling on the knees, weeping in a state of prostration, and having religious transcendental visions.   These characteristics that are ascribed to spiritual possession in toxic states are due to special material substances, and the various transcendental expositions has each its own material origin.   Thus the cherry-laurel water holds in it two toxic principles—prussic acid, and the volatile oil of laurel.   The convulsions in the ecstatic state are due to the prussic acid, and hallucinatory visions to the volatile oil.   Thus the compound ecstatic state results from taking the two in connection, or either of its special manifestations may be induced by taking the special agent.   Other toxic agents are nitro-benzol, which produces convulsive shocks and visions, and Valerian induces violent excitement. (*Journal of Science*, VII. p. 730.)

Not only real but presumed mental states are affirmed to arise from impersonal attributes, as in all cases of assumed sympathetic relations.   Bacon, in his *Sylva Sylvarum*, writes:—"To superinduce any virtue or disposition in a person, choose the living creature wherein that virtue is most eminent, and at the time when that virtue is most exercised, and then apply it to the part of a man wherein the same virtue chiefly exists. Thus to superinduce courage, take a lion or cock and choose the heart, tooth, or paw of the lion and take them immediately after he has been in fight, so with a cock, and let them be worn on a man's heart or wrist."

All the transcendental qualities ascribed to ghost and spirit interposition equally exist in the impersonal attributes in things, and from which we esteem they were primarily educed. Of these we may specify the power in impersonals to give diseases to cure diseases, to rack and torture the body or the mind, to render men impotent, women un-fruitful, to cause injuries and death. So the power of transformation of permeating solids annihilating space and time are common attributes without the intervention of ghost. We doubt whether any first principle of a supernal nature has ever evolved from ghostly influences. All the characteristic actions of fetish, of magic, of devilry and spiritualism, are presented in impersonal attributes.

As the Australian aborigines are the lowest race of which we have anything like a full exposition of their supernal concepts, we will endeavour to find what of them are primary derivations from impersonal sources, and what are due to after-ghost theories. The fullest exposition of these senti-ments are those given by Mr. Howitt in his essay on the attributes of the medicine man in the *Journal of the Anthropological Institute*. The supernal power exists in the wizard himself, it is not derived, as we shall show, from any ghost or spirit, but evolves in his own nature by induced bodily conditions resulting from fasting, toxics, solitude, sleeplessness, and acquiring by fetish actions boylya from other men. In using this personal power he does not appeal to ghosts or spirits, but to the fetish attributes and powers in things. Thus, he by his magic propels the mystic quartz-stone into his victim as any other man by his physical power might do; it is the occult virtue in the stone itself that then works evil in the mind of the man, or rather we should affirm, that all is semblance; and the mind of the man, itself susceptible of occult influence, accepts the theory that the stone is in his body, and fetish fear brings about the presumed result.   It is the same impersonal power which induces action when the quartz crystal is placed in the victim's footsteps, or when the Casuarina cone exhibits its affirmed mystic power.   In the mixing the flesh of a dead man with tobacco, and the roasting of something fetish once part of a man, or that has simply touched him, the fetish is neither in the fetish object or in the dead man's part thus utilized, it requires the two or more objects to be united, and the uncanny influence of the dead man's ghost has no part in the affair any more than the ghost of the fetish animal gives power to the nail or claw charm.   The spell, as we have said, is in the purport of the object and had the same consistency when it formed part of the animal as when it affected the man's supernal concepts by possessing it.

In like manner the abstraction of the omentum fat was a mystic not ghostly rite, or a cannibal act under the supposition of presumed sympathetic relations.   So with the medicine man's transcendental claims they are not due to ghostly or spirit interposition; but powers, he presumes, he acquired through the boylya in him, that a supposititious impersonal qualification.   Such is his assumed invisibility, his power of ascending into the sky, of transforming himself into a kangaroo or even the stump of a decayed tree, and the clairvoyant power of telling who caused his death which he simply derives from knowing whose quartz crystal he takes out of his own or the victim's body, the same as men tell the nationality of a shot, a lance, or arrow-head by its make.

So the wizard's magic tool, the bone Yulo.   Its virtue has no connection with a ghost, but to its being a fetish combination of the fibula of a kangaroo with cords formed of strips of human skin or human sinews.   Rain-making and weather-making are simply magic done by magic songs or spells. The power in the throw-stick pointing to the sleepers, which falls when the fascination is completed, is equally impersonal as a spell as is the sucking to draw out the evil object in sickness; they never exorcise a spirit, but by fetish actions presume to withdraw the fetish cause of ill, they also cured diseases by charm songs and various manipulations.

The first intimation we have of personal supernal power being claimed by the Australian wizard is that of the ghost or soul of the living, not of the dead, going at night to look at his victim in the grave. Other imitations of a ghostly nature arise in the abnormal wizard initiations, as when the novice sees in the tiger-snake his Banjan, and when in his dreams he is present at a corrobery of kangaroos. When there is so little of the presence of ghostly influence in the whole range of the Australian's supernal concepts, we conceive it intimates either the very modern evolvement of the ghost theory in his sentiments, or may be its acquisition from without. Essentially his supernal concepts are limited to the religion of charms and spells, the ghost and evil spirit being forms of supernal power that are only now acquiring influence in his sentiments.

There are various instances given in which the mode of causing injuries or disease are defined as being personally done, not by a ghost, but by a living medicine man, whose possession of the enchanting power, or boylya, enabled him to fly through the air and, invisible, work his spells. A native in Sir G. Grey's *Journals of Discovery*, describes the nature of this power as possessed by living men. "The boylyas eat up a great many natives, they eat them up as fire would. They move stealthily, they steal on you, they come moving along in the sky, the natives cannot see them, they do not bite, they feed stealthily, they do not eat the bones, but consume the flesh" (II. p. 339). As an illustration

Sir George quotes the case of a native who injured his spine by falling from a tree; paralysis of the lower parts of the body ensued, and as so commonly occurs under such conditions, the man wasted away and died. The natives, however, holding their special concepts of the wizard's power, read the progress of the disease in the lines that theory presented. They affirmed that the wizard had obtained fetish power over the man by having obtained possession of his cloak—used it as the means to work his supernal spell, first he broke his back by causing him to fall from the tree, then disguised he attended him, and in his invisible state applied fire (inflammation) to the injured part to increase the potency of the charm; the wasting away of the body was due to the unfriendly wizard coming in the night and feasting on his flesh (II. p. 329).

That many writers ascribe to the Australian aborigines the full development of the theory of ghosts and spirits, we are aware. Oldfield speaks of the wizards working their evil designs by the aid of malevolent Ingnas, the same as the devil-workers of the Middle Ages, and of these ghost spirits haunting all sorts of places; but the deeper researches of such men as Howitt explain them as acting under a much lower class of influences. The white man commonly looks for a God, and devils; he anticipates the presence of ghosts, and every supernal exposition of savages, however low and incoherent, he refers to one or other of those supernal sentiments. If the statements of Mr. Howitt and many others are to be relied upon, the Australian native mind uninfluenced by white men has only the most meagre concept of a ghost or spirit, the idea special to the race is the acquisition of the power of enchanting through the boylya influence and working that power in the person of the boylya man by means of spells and charms which, though of the same character as among other barbarous races, are of local origin.

We may note in another race how the white man's

sentiment of the nature of supernal evil is suggested to people who know nothing of devils. Darwin in his *Journal* refers twice to the fact that the simple Fuegian who had been staying some time on the vessel and had thereby become inoculated with the devil sentiment, repudiated it as a belief of his people, and though he abused other tribes he did not conceive that their dead men became evil spirits. There was no devil in his land. All he appeared to dread was the fetish influence of the elements, and the mystic powers of the bad wild men.

The two chief charms that the Australians make use of, are simply impersonal spells; and these as the charm objects of other races are either drawn from animals, or vegetables, or stones, but in all cases their virtues are not due to ghostly influence, but to their own intrinsic powers. That so many materials used in spells are supplied by animals to produce spells, may be accounted for by their having presented vital powers of action; but we have no evidence that these powers were continued to be influenced by the ghost of the animal that once owned them; rather, as we have seen, these special powers are always esteemed to be at the service of the present owner of the fetish object. The Australian Yountoo is a charm to produce sickness. It is a small bone from the leg of one man wrapped in a piece of flesh cut from another man and tied with a string made from the hair of a third. This charm taken to the hut of the man to be enchanted, is placed before the fire pointing to him, then a small piece of the bone is broken off, cast on the victim, and afterwards burnt. The Molee is a piece of white quartz with a string of opossum fur gummed to one end; this also is pointed at the intended victim and then burnt. In either case to cure or destroy the spell, the wizard has to suck out the charmed bone or stone. (*Jour. Anthrop. Inst.*, XIII. p. 180.)

CHAPTER III.

Supernal concepts derived from natural appearances.

Many phenomena read as supernal are the natural in unusual conditions. Such was the colossal figure of an angel seen in the heavens at Florence, due to the special form of a cloud and the position of the sun, in relation to the image of the gilded angel on the top of the Duomo, and as the cloud slowly moved the reflection seemed hovering over the city. Ships have thus been seen, with their canvas and colours abroad, floating in the sky. Of a like origin is the "Spectre of the Brocken" and the "Fata Morgana." In the moving lights, as sometimes observed in the Aurora Borealis, the Icelander behold the spirits of his ancestors, and many have discovered armies and torrents of blood in the lambent meteors of a wintry sky. It needs but colour and faint gleams of light for the mind to conjure up definite idealisms.

A gentleman travelling in Scotland put up at a small inn. He found on retiring to bed that a pedlar had died in the room, and that from superstitious motives the people had declined to take the corpse through the doorway, but had removed the small window, breaking away part of the wall. The window had been replaced, but the irregular gap left. Full of this incident, he had a dream of a frightful apparition before him, and in his half-wakeful state the appearance still was before him, and he saw a corpse dressed in a shroud reared erect against the wall by the window. After a few minutes he passed one hand over it, but felt nothing, and staggered back. When he renewed his investigation the mental image was laid, and he found the object of his terror was produced by the moonbeams coming through the gap in the broken wall. (*Ferrier on Apparitions*, p. 27.)

In the ordinary inexpressive nature of things, there is no supernal—all are passive, inert, and excite no special emotion; it is only when there is a movement, be it in waves of light or colour, or sound, or in a pressure felt, the cause of which is unseen, that the sentiment of the uncanny arises. Smyth, in his *Aborigines of Victoria*, gives an illustration of this mental origin of the supernal. "In Victoria, where hot winds and other electrical disturbances of the atmosphere are common, the natives used to think that the ground was haunted, and that the swirls of dust so often seen in the summer-time were caused by demons passing along in the ground."

A remarkable illustration of vague optical perceptions becoming spiritualized, is seen in the following statement of Big Plume, a Blackfoot Indian. He said: "The souls of the Indians go to the sandhills east of the Blackfeet territory. At a distance we can see them hunting the buffalo, and we can hear them talking and praying, and inviting one another to their feasts. In the summer we often go there and see the trails of the spirits and the places where they have been camping. I have been there myself and have seen them and heard them beating their drums. We can see them in the distance, but when we get near they vanish. I believe they will live for ever. There will still be fighting between the Crows and the Blackfeet in the spiritual world." (*Reports, Brit. Asso.*, 1887, p. 387.)

The natural world is always the source of the supernatural, consequently a man's spiritual deductions harmonize with the phenomena of his geographical position. Does not the soul of Zerdusht in the opening chapters of the *Avesta*, dwelling on the double character of the surrounding scenery, with its arid deserts and richly-teeming fertile vales, find the same contrast of good and ill in the human soul as in his natural world? Heaven ever accommodates its attributes to the living conditions of its human creators. We know that the islands of the blessed could only have been conceived by those who in life had dwelt in an island world. The Polynesian, used to distant voyages, must needs cross the vast ocean to his soul land, but the inland red man saw in the misty shades of the far distant hills, with their many play of colours, the home of his spirit-fathers. The nature of this life ever proclaims the future aspirations of the living; he would only eliminate the physical evils he has learnt to dread out of his ideal paradise.

All the varying terrific or mysterious phenomena in the natural world have induced supernal deductions dependent for their forms of expression on the amount of information in the mind of the beholder. It is so all the world over in connection with comets, eclipses, meteors, thunder, the Maelstrom, and all unusual sights in the sky. These are ever portents dire and terrible, produced by fetish power or malign spirits, and they foretell war, pestilence, or famine. When an eclipse takes place, the Moslems in Syria, like the Chinese and the Red Indian, crowd together with gongs, rattles, drums, every noisy instrument they possess, to drive away by the hideous sounds they produce the evil monster who is devouring the sun or the moon. The Red Indian, in the black cloud out of which the thunderbolt is launched, beholds the dreaded thunder bird, and the Karen regards the thunderbolt as a living thing—it tears up the trees in the form of a hog with bat-like wings; when it utters its voice it thunders, when it flaps its wings fire is produced. (*Asi. Soc. Beng. Jour.* XXXIV., p. 217.)

Dorman reports in his *Primitive Superstitions* that the Indians hold that all sounds issuing from caverns were thought to be produced by their spiritual inhabitants. The

Sonora Indians say the departed souls dwell among the
caves and nooks of their cliffs, and that the echoes are
their voices.   When explosions, caused by the bursting of
sulphurous gases, are heard, the superstitious Indians
attribute them to the breathing of the manitous.   Dead
Mountain, at the head of the Mojave valley, is regarded
with reverence by the Indians, who believed it the abode of
departed spirits.   When its hoary crest is draped in a light
floating haze and misty wreaths are winding like phantoms
among its peaks, they see the spirits of the departed
hovering above their legendary dwelling (p. 302).   The
Chinooks thought the milky-way was produced by a turtle
swimming along the bottom of the sky and disturbing
the mud.   The red clouds of the rising and setting sun
were thought to be coloured by the blood of men slain in
battle.   (*Ibid.* p. 346.)

The man who has been under the influence of a toxic, or
noted others in that state, ascribes the weird influence,
whether produced by alcohol, soma, kava or pulque, to the
action of a supernal principle contained in the drink, and
all the betimes pleasing mental excitements they induced
are attached to a weird cause.   So when a man observes a
companion attacked by epilepsy or some form of neurosis,
or expressing strange mental hallucinations, he can only
account for the change by inferring that the spirit of some
man or animal has entered his body or he has been
enchanted by a spell, and that the strange actions, the
discordant sounds, the unnatural movements, are due to the
supernal influence.

As illustrating the failure of the judgment in the presence
of something not fully comprehended, we quote the following: "A maid-servant in the Rue St. Victor, who had gone
down into the cellar, came back very much frightened,
saying she had seen a spectre standing upright between two
barrels.   Some persons went down and saw the same.   It
was a dead body which had fallen from a cart coming from

the Hotel Dieu. It had slid down the cellar window or grating, and had remained standing between two casks." (*Calmet, Phantom World*, I. p. 252.)

Sounds heard at night high up in the air were formerly, and now are by some, ascribed to Gabriel's hounds, they were supposed to be the cries of spirits in the air, and were considered the foretellers of bad luck, or death, to those who heard them. They are now known to be caused by batches of widgeons or teals, and which usually migrate in the night. (*Notes and Queries*, 7th Ser. II. p. 206.)

Betimes certain natural phenomena resulting from various special combinations of the elements, inasmuch as they occur only at long intervals, are esteemed to be due to supernal action, and often a legend or myth is invented to account for the phenomena. In Jones's *Credulities* we have two such instances recorded. At Saltburne Mouth there is a small creek which empties into the sea under a high bank; sometimes the incoming tide produces a horrible groaning, and the people say it is the cry of a sea-monster hungering for men's carcases (p. 64). Again on the west coast of Scotland certain conjunctions of the wind and tide produce what is called a " bore;" this became evolved into a fetish personification as the "avenging ware," and was accounted for by a fisherman having there killed a mermaid (p. 25). In another instance in Canada, at Manitobah Island, in a lake of the same name, there is a singular sound produced by the action of the waves on a peculiar pebble shingle which rub together with an intoning voice. This occurs only when the gale blows from the north, and the Ojibbeway Indians say it is the voice of the speaking God (p. 101).

Humboldt has shown how much the ordinary expressions of nature build up the supernal concepts of the various races of men, and create tones of feeling that become embodied in the social institutions. We will quote a case in point as illustrating the influence of nature on the Upper Indus

in the development of the local supernatural. " The howling
waste behind, invisible from the village and rising into still
higher masses, affords a fitting scene for all the supernatural doings of the mountain spirits. The scenery which
inspires awe has made its mark upon the inhabitants.
These lofty solitudes are from their earliest years connected
with ideas of dread which shape themselves into myths.
The priest affirms that sometimes in the early dawn, while
performing worship, he perceived a white indistinct shape
hovering over the cairn, and this he said was the goddess
of the spot revealing herself to her worshippers. The
people believe that this demon keeps a special watch over
all their actions, and in a country where frequent accidents
by flood and field are almost inevitable, and where a false
step or a falling rock may cause death at any time, they put
down such disasters to the vengeance of the goddess for
the neglect of some of their peculiar customs." (*Asiat. Soc.
Beng. Jour.*, XLVII. p. 28.) Such are some of the false
concepts of the supernal which have their origin in mis-
conceptions of perceptive appearances.

CHAPTER IV.

The evolution of supernal concepts in dreams.

No subject connected with the supernatural has more engrossed the minds of men in all ages than those connected with mental presentations in sleep. These generally arise when some of the mental faculties are in abeyance while others are active; they may and do occasionally occur when the dreamer is almost in a waking state; then the impressions active in the memory take a perceptive form and appeal specially to the senses. By far the greater number of premonitory apparitions occur at this awaking state, their power enhanced by the dominant figure remaining as in Newton's spectrum after the inciting cause has been withdrawn.

Diverse circumstances induce dreams; some arise from special mental excitation through the memory of previous impressions, they are also induced by states of the organic functions, as by special foods or drinks and forms of disease, also by special sensations. A writer in the *Journal of Psychological Medicine* writes :—" A man after eating a supper of halibut had a dream of sliding down a cliff on the shore and being saved by holding his niece's hand; another after a hearty fish supper dreamed of poisonous serpents; a third, after partaking freely of cold roast beef and pickled onions, dreamed of being forced to eat of what he loathed. A lady having a slight cough put a piece of barley sugar in her mouth and fell asleep while sucking it. She dreamt

she was a little girl at an evening party, happy and enjoying
herself; she enjoyed all kinds of childish sports, and after
a long period had elapsed she awoke with a smile to find
the cause of the dream still in her mouth, and that only a
few minutes had elapsed, her daughter who gave her the
barley sugar not yet having left the bedside (XI. p. 579).

The cause of a dream delusion may be due to altered
sense-perception. A gentleman had fallen asleep with
weary feelings, arising from indigestion, when there arose
an apprehension in his mind that the phantom of a dead
man held the sleeper by the wrist. He awoke in horror,
and found that his own left hand, in a state of numbness,
had accidentally encircled his right arm. (Scott, *Demonology*,
p. 45.) Deceptive spectral concepts, even in the conscious
state, are often due to false mental deductions, and man,
under such conditions, is apt to mould the accusing form to
some subjective memory impression. Mr. Taylor was staying
at a large old-fashioned country mansion, and from his
room was a secret door leading to a private staircase. This
was both locked inside and out, yet its presence evidently
tended to suggest supernatural phenomena, even though
he had no faith in them. One moonlight night in June he
awoke about 1 o'clock, and discovered by the moonlight
a tall figure in white, with arms extended, at the foot of
the bed. Fear and astonishment for a time overcame him;
then he thought that it might possibly be a trick; so,
mustering resolution, he jumped out of bed, and grasped it
round, only to find it was nothing more than a large new
flannel dressing-gown which had been sent him in the
course of the day, and which had been hung on some pegs
against the wainscot at the foot of the bed. (*Apparitions*,
by J. Taylor, VI.)

Sometimes the presumed ghost is real flesh and blood,
its supernatural character a mere inference in the mind.
A lady, when on a visit to a Scotch friend, waking up in the
night, beheld a hideous, almost shapeless, figure sitting on

a chair between her and the fire. After lying in great fear for a time, believing it was a spectre, she stealthily crept from the bed, and hid herself behind the window-curtains ; then she saw the wretched ghost throw itself on her bed, and in that way the two passed the night. In the morning the lady motioned to a labourer in the garden to come up, when they found that the supposed wandering ghost was a simple lunatic, who in some way had got into the house when passing across the country. (E. P. Hood, *Dreamland*, p. 70.) The mental deception suggesting the supernatural may be a sound. A low muffled wail heard on the sea by a lady was taken by her for a telepathic indication of her son's death. It was afterwards found that the so-called monition was produced by an amateur ventriloquist for his own amusement. (*Phant. of Living*, I. p. 125.)

Simple errors of judgment and instances of false reasoning account for many ghost narratives, but there are others which the inquiring percipient cannot thus resolve, and which not only leave their supernal influence on the mind of the beholder but convey like impressions to others. To test such presentations all are not equally mentally prepared, yet there are a few test qualities that any may apply. But, first, we have to note the various conditions under which such apparitional appearances occur. A large number arise in dreams—some are continuous from the dream to the semi-waking state—and the presence of the mystic figure as a continuous image is affirmed to the waking senses. In some cases there is no memory of a dream-phase, the figure is simply present to the half-waking consciousness, which, when fully aroused, may still behold the object. From the continuity of optical impressions, under certain conditions, we know that it is possible an optical impression may continue after the object is removed from the sight. Now it so happens that by far the greater number of presumed apparitional appearances are seen in these conditions of the organic being; they are seen in the dream or the half-

wakeful state.   It is quite certain that the visionary—not
other people—is most competent to test the nature of the appearance.   If the illusion or vision occurs when wide awake,
men of the calibre of Nicolai, of Berlin, may be certain of
the subjective nature of the impression, note its origin, and
even optically prove that it exists only inside their own
sensoriums.   But both judgment and the powers of observation are only vaguely exercised in the half-waking state,
and the imagination most probably in an excited state from
previous dreaming is apt to jump to hasty conclusions, and
when subsequently the visionary describes the impression,
it may consist only of vague generalities.   However, if the
seer has so far mastered the details of the vision as to be
able to define specially, not generally, its characteristics, he
or she may be able to affirm its subjective nature.

In the old ghost tales the presumed supernal being came
in its shroud, or, according to the associate circumstances,
was accredited to come covered with wounds or blood, or if
drowned as naked and dripping wet.   Usually in such cases
no clothes are noted, only the wounded or wet body; now,
as neither in a fight or at a shipwreck is it customary for
the body to be stripped, the subject-nature of the impression
ought to be at once apparent.   One class of subjective
impressions is thus built up of some memory impressions,
modified by the imagination; others wholly arise from the
reawakening of past impressions.   Now, usually these memory
impressions of an individual are of varying character.   A
mother may dream of her son as a stalwart young man,
the same as when she last saw him, or she may dream of
him in his boyhood or as babe.   Usually in such cases
there is an endless series of types in the mind.   So with
an ordinary acquaintance, we may call him to mind as when
we first knew him or when we last behold him.   More,
there are not only the differences of age and features to
consider, but the clothing and ornaments, and other distinguishing attributes attached to the person.   Of course,

if the visionary detects no special details, neither distinguishing features, age or dress, and recognizes nothing but a vague impression, which it designates as a certain individual, we have no test appliances, and can only esteem the presentation as vague and unsatisfactory. But if the assumed apparition comes before the visionary clearly defined in features and wearing some special costume, we know these attributes denote a special individual at a special time. Consequently, when a lady beholds, as she thinks, the spectre of a gentleman, clothed as she had once seen him as a character in the *Corsican Brothers*, we are assured that it was no ghost, however ominous might be the words it said or its movements, but only a reawakened impression in her memory. So in the case of the apparition of Mrs. Matthews by Mr. Charles Matthews, the ghost came in her habit, as when alive. We know nothing of spirit fashions of dress in the other world, but we can scarcely suppose they wear crinolines, or have high-shoulder dresses. Hence, it could not have been her spirit he beheld, but a renewal of a past endearing impression.

Few persons are as capable of demonstrating the unreality of an illusion as the captain whose case is quoted in Sir W. Scott's *Demonology*. When in a depressed state, and therefore most susceptible of being affected by supernal ideas, he went to see his confessor, and was in great distress and apprehension of his death. The same evening, when retiring to bed, he saw in the room the figure of the confessor sitting on a chair, probably as he commonly saw him in life. Being of a strong mind, and self-assured of its subjective nature, he sat down on the same chair as the figure was on. He owned after that had his friend died about the same time he would not have known what name to give his vision, but he recovered, and hence he knew that it was both physically and psychically an illusion of his own mind (p. 37).

In all the cases of haunted houses in Mrs. Crowe's *Night*

Side of Nature we have not one that even bears the affirmation of having been definitely seen by two individuals who noted the dress and features of the presumed supernal visitant. All is vague, indefinite, and uncertain. In one case there are two ladies in bed. The one, only a child, fancies she sees an old man in a Kilmarnock nightcap. She was not the least frightened, and probably the indistinct appearance of drapery or clothing was in the half-light personified by her imagination into a grotesque figure. The various white lady ghosts are as vague as vague can be, not a detail but that of colour is given.

The most apparently definite case is said to have occurred at Sarratt, in Hertfordshire, where one individual of whom we have no credentials, and who is even nameless, is said to have seen the figure of a well-dressed man having on a blue coat with bright gilt buttons; his own clothes had partly fallen on the floor and he saw no head, the half-drawn curtain hiding that portion of the figure. We should say he saw only his own clothes as they had partly fallen from the chair, and as from the context we read that the house was said to be haunted by a headless gentleman in a blue coat with gilt buttons, we need not look far for the illusion.

In another case we are first prepared for the due feeling of dread and mystery by the narrative of an iron cage with an iron ring to which an old rusty chain is attached having a collar at the end of the same material. Necessarily after going to bed with such a preparation for a ghost strange noises are heard, then the girls say they saw a figure or something and hid themselves in the clothes. Later on this figure is more defined, it was thin with hair flowing down its back and draped in a loose powdering gown. How much they saw of it in reality, if they beheld anything but their own fears, may be noted from the circumstance that at first both the girls thought it was their sister Hannah: consequently the powdered gown was only in the imagination, and it was only when their mother told them it could not have been Hannah trying to frighten them that they considered his ghostship had appeared to them. We cannot feel surprised that after talking over these incidents brother Harry by the light of the moon should have seen a fellow in a loose gown at the bottom of the stairs. Once again one of the ladies after being very tired by a long ride on afterwards awakening by the light of a night-light saw again the mysterious figure in the powdery coat; she more noticed the thin pale face with its melancholy expression. But in this, the most circumstantial case, we not only have no names of persons, no references, we even do not know in what town it occurred, though one of the many publishers who have rehearsed the narrative thinks it comes from Lille.

Though the various ill-conceived and undefined narratives in Mrs. Crowe's collection are unworthy of being assumed as representing supernal incidents, surely we ought to place some confidence in the carefully considered and select cases to which the credentials of Messrs. Gurney and Myers are attached, recorded in the *Nineteenth Century* (XVI. p. 69).

In the first case presented a Mr. Rawlinson had heard two months before that an intimate friend was ill with cancer. How many times during the two months the image of his friend may have been present in his thoughts associated with his dangerous complaint we have no means of judging, and it is such thoughts that are apt to become vague monitions or subjective hallucinations. Yet because a vague presentiment of the appearance arose in his mind presumed to be connected with the possible time of the friend's death, but of this no proof is given, we are asked to accept it as a supernal telepathic manifestation.

The second case is equally devoid of consistency. A slight accident occurs to an individual on a Saturday in London. The mother admits writing an account of the affair on the Sunday, and on the Monday night the aunt in

Ireland dreams she sees a confusion of cabs and hears
"Maurice is hurt."   Our version of the spectral intimation
is that the letter was possibly written on the day of the
accident, or the aunt informed thereof by another relative,
or possibly the aunt's illusion occurred on Thursday not
Monday night. It certainly was no visual perception but
only the concept of something that might have reached the
aunt in a letter as the dream as stated occurred two days
after the accident.

The same comments apply to the case of the Duke of
Orleans, and it did not take place at the time of the
impression, and the narrator of the trivial accident writes,
"I am not sure of the day of the week," yet on these imperfect and desultory impressions we are required to accept
implied supernal incidents.

The incident described by Lady Chatterton is explainable
in the aptitude for a dream to be fashioned from external
impressions. In the half-waking state so favourable for
the reception of such impressions Lady Chatterton saw the
figure of her mother, the face deadly pale and blood flowing over the bed-clothes, she then rushed into her mother's
room and saw her as in the dream. The incident had
occurred hours before and could not have been a present
apparition as two doctors who had to be fetched had not
only arrived, but they must have been there some time as
one observed that all danger was now over. Such a vision
might have come in her reverie not suggested by her
mother's spirit or any telepathic impression, but by the
talk of the servants or the conversation of the doctors.
There was only a long passage between the rooms, and the
echo of the voices as they passed to the stair-head may
have easily reached her ear and conveyed all the images
presented in the illusion.

We might pause to describe the loose character of the
other narratives, but we will conclude this part of supernal
cases with that referred to a Miss Manningham.   First we

may note that this illusion is said to have occurred at an
entertainment; the place in one statement is described as
the Argyll, in the other as the Hanover Rooms. There
were also two diverse accounts of the apparition—in one the
features were hid by a cloth, in the other the face was
turned from her; both agreed in its being a naked corpse.
As the death occurred through the upsetting of a boat we
fail to realize the origin of the naked presentation even if
we admit that without being able to see the features it was
possible for her to recognize her naked grandfather, and it
is the first time in the natural history of ghosts in which the
ghost of the clothes refused to accompany the ghost of the
body. As we read the narrative we would observe that
even at concerts, as well as when at church, people betimes
are apt to doze and may dream dreams, and that in her case
she had only heard her grandfather was drowned, and the
naked corpse was her own inference that it happened when
he was bathing, when there can be no doubt he must at the
time have been fully clothed.

When in the ghost tale the particulars of dress features
and externals are specified we can often detect in the
narrative itself, the proofs that it is the revival of an old-
memory impression. We will quote a few of such self-
indications from Mr. Gurney's *Phantasms of the Living*.
S. and L. are both in one office in the city. S. is aroused
one night by the apparition of L. coming towards him as
was his wont of a morning, wearing a hat with black hat-
band, the overcoat unbuttoned, no doubt ready for its
customary removal, and having a stick in his hand. But
the ghost of L. who died at 9 P.M. and came after S. had
gone to bed was not likely to be walking about with his
coat unbuttoned and a walking-stick in his hand. S. might
or might not have heard of the death of L. before he retired
for the night; the figure was certainly a memory reminiscence,
and his absence through illness might well suggest the
possibility of his death (I. p. 210).

A lady in case 168, describing an appearance that was presented to her, infers that it could not have been a subjective impression, but a real apparition, forgets the fact that our mental presentations are made up, not only of what we see, but what we hear or read. There are few—especially ladies—who hearing or reading of the altered appearance of any dear friend by years or illness, do not visualize the change. More particularly when he was an old sweetheart, and she knew sixteen years had passed, and that the face had become modified by the growth of a beard and whiskers, as she writes to his mother. From this we may well infer she was in regular communication with his family, and as she refers to the change, what more likely than his changed appearance had been familiarly dwelt upon : hence it would not be his old but his altered physiognomy that she might recall (I. p. 426).

In several cases the ghost appears not as he would have been, wasted away and in his bed-clothes, but dressed in his old costume and hale and hearty. Again, there are cases in which we are told the dead man is seen the instant of death laying in his coffin, as if that indispensable adjunct had been ordered before-hand and the body put in it before the spirit had quitted its mortal tenement. Some of the apparitions are pleasing reminiscences of many like impressions. Thus, 195 is the case of a lady who sees the phantasms of her grandmother in the plaid cloak she usually wore, leaning on the arm of the lady's mother. She is presumed to have died at the time of the vision, when the old lady would have presented a very different appearance. The group as seen had, no doubt, often been pictured in her memory from a child. Case 202 is that of a lady who died after a short illness ; yet at the time of her death she is seen by the percipient riding in her own victoria. She recognizes the bonnet and the sealskin jacket as those she generally wore in winter; but it was in August she died, therefore it must have been a subjective impression.

As for the idea of her death, the lady knew she was ill (I. p. 544).

One of the most remarkable cases supposed to prove the presence of a ghost, actually, by investigation, proves the truth of its being a subjective hallucination. In case 213, an old woman is seen wearing a special duster-pattern check shawl. There was no monition in this case, for the old lady is not supposed to die—it was merely an hallucination of a familiar figure. The percipient, however, felt assured of its ghostly character, so he visits the house and inquires specially about this shawl. He receives for answer, "We haven't such a thing in the house;" but sure of the truth of his mental impression, they hunt behind a box near the bed's head, when the identical ghost-shawl is found. From her family forgetting the article, it is evident that special shawl had not been lately worn, and the ghost of a few days past could not have appeared wearing it. Mr. Gurney writes the shawl is an important detail; so it is, for it proves that the percipient's impression must have been subjective.

The ordinary perceptive and imaginative mental states so blend into each other, that we cannot draw an absolute line between the ordinary perceptive, imaginative, hallucinative and dreaming states. Perception passes into memory, and memory grows into the excitations of the imagination, recalling past impressions, and gradually presenting them with over-increasing intensity—at first, mere acts of the will, gradually advancing until they are self-projected into the consciousness, in the one direction passing through reverie into dreams, in the other, from mere illusive deceptions, to accredited perceptions, whether idealisms, dreams, or hallucinations, and they may appeal to the ego through any one or more of the senses.

Under healthy stimuli these presentations are more or less under the control of the will arising either from normal conscious activity or normally unconscious cerebration. These thought and self-presentations normally are more vague than the real perceptions out of which they were evolved, not so when due to the stimulus of abnormal causes; then they are after projected with a brightness, intensity, or power proportionate to the nature of the exalting force. Of the impressions thus observed, we have several cases in the *Phantasms of the Living*. Thus Mrs. Willert has vivid representations; they come with her eyes open, but more brilliant when they are shut. She sees all kinds of things in quick succession; never blending into one another, she could never recall the same picture. "Mrs. Macdonald is accustomed to see multitudes of faces as she is lying awake. They seem to come out of the darkness and develop into sharp delineation and outline—they fade and give place to others rapidly and in enormous numbers. Formerly they were ugly human but resembling animal monsters, latterly they have been beautiful" (I. p. 474).

In general the dream or the hallucination is but momentary, but like some ghosts they become persistent for a long time, or after intervals, reappearing again and again, in bad neurotic states. They are always present, day and night, ever urging their victim to some special act or influencing him by denoting some special fear. There are cases in which such hallucinatory objects or persons are only seen under certain conditions, or are attached to certain forms of thought. Thus the Rev. P. H. Newman "saw figures whom he recognized in church, though they were not there, and they seemed to occupy the same place during the service." (*Ibid.* I. p .475.)

Expectancy, self-suggestion, or suggestion by others, are prolific sources of apparitional presentations. For a gentleman to see the figure of his future wife draped in white, is a by no means uncommon appearance to an expectant bridegroom, occasionally by an exalted perception defined as an appearance to the half-waking vision;

in some cases the dream-image remains, like Newton's spectrum, for a time on the retina.

A very general form in which self-suggestion conceives of distinct and definite appearances, and moulds any object into the expected semblance, occurs in several cases. A Mr. Jevons sees, as he thinks, a friend walking among the trees opposite his house. He says, "I waved my hand to him to go up the road where we had frequently walked." (*Ibid.* II. p. 528.) So in case 203. A lady who knew her mother was ill, when seated in the schoolroom reading, sees the figure of her mother, wasted by disease, reclining as in bed in her nightdress.

Often the presence of appearances are suggested by others. A word, a name, an incident, appeals not only to the consciousness, but even to the more or less unconscious faculties which passively build up appropriate scenes and semblances. In case 408, a mother and daughter in India are infected by snake-fears, a not uncommon form of suggestion in tropical countries. The daughter, while undressing, fancied there was a snake in her room, probably by the rustling of her drapery; the sound of her and the servants' talk on the subject reached the lady in her bedchamber, who after dreamed her daughter was bitten by a snake.

Betimes we are told of two persons seeing the same apparition or dreaming the same dream; but these when analyzed may generally be traced to impressions being transferred from one to the other, verbally or otherwise. That such is the origin of duplicate dreams may be discovered by their want of identity. Thus in case 127 a lady and her friend, asleep probably in the same room, have dreams on the same subject, but these are not identical. In the one the corpse of Mrs. A. is laid out in the bed; in the other that lady's daughter is seen running along the shore crying, "Don't stop me! my mother is dying." The one dream might have been due to

verbal suggestion by the other in her dream state, or both
due to the intimation they had previously received of
the lady's dangerous illness. In case 299, a man, dying of
typhus fever in his sleep, when in port is attended by a
stoker belonging to the same vessel. In his delirium he
had most probably been raving about his wife and children,
a not unusual thing in such a state. The stoker was
personally acquainted with his family, and under those
exciting conditions he affirmed that he saw the wife,
mother, and two children on the other side of the bunk in
which the man was dying.

One of the most singular cases of a ghost suggestion, is
case 331. It begins with two ladies probably by the
preliminary suggestion of one of them seeing the figure of
a Captain Towns in a gray flannel jacket such as they had
been accustomed to recognize him by. Then a young sister,
most likely aroused by the exclamations of the percipients,
sees the same. Even the servant, roused by the excitement,
notes "the master;" then the butler and the captain's
body servant are both sent for, and they also declared they
saw the figure; and lastly the nurse is fetched, but she,
more sceptical than the others, advanced as if to touch it,
when the ghost, probably by the shifting of the curtains or
apparel, vanishes, and after all it was found to be no
apparition, though seen by so many, but a reflection on the
polished wardrobe, a sort of medallion portrait. In another
like case a girl was sent home from school unwell. The same
night one of her companions was put in the vacant bed. In
the dim light in the night the spirit of the absent girl is
seen by the half-waking dreamer. She arouses the other
school-girls asleep in the same room, and they also see the
appearance, yet it is admitted that a bed-hanging, a curtain,
suggested the image. (*Ibid.* II. p. 186.)

Particulars, both personal and general, may be conveyed
to other minds in sleep by means of words, and these may, as
in the cases quoted, become attached to either the conscious

or unconscious memory. Thus two ladies sleeping together had the same experience of the presence of an old and valued friend of the one, even to the special onyx studs he habitually wore. This, a dream from experience in the one person, became by verbal suggestion a fancy image in the other's mind. Things mysteriously known to another may be transferred from mind to mind in the dream state, and that not by thought-reading, but by unconscious talking. Thus a lady, through her husband talking in his sleep and thus rehearsing an incident of his early days, became conscious of his once having had a sweetheart of whose existence, in his waking state, he had never informed her. (*Phantasms*, I. p. 317.) There are many cases in which, consciously or unconsciously, indications are transferred from one sleeper to another, not only when in the same room, but when they are in separate rooms, as in cases 89 and 90.

CHAPTER V.

The inter-relations of the supernal powers.

The first result of the failure of the perceptive and reflective powers is to present to the mind the many objects and movements it cannot comprehend as a new class of presentations diverse from any present in the natural world.

One of the first supernal concepts is that the moving force in the organism is distinct from its substance, that it induces all the volitional actions of the organism, and that it is capable of existing outside the object it controls. This in man is his ghost. In the ordinary state this ghost is the life of the man: it is his mind, his spirit, his soul, and the body and limbs are but the inert material which the ghost utilises for its many purposes. Out of the man the ghost may act the same as it did when in the body, save that as its nature is distinct so are its attributes. Rude men cannot separate the spiritual from the material; hence the ghost is a shadow, a vapour, an attenuated entity, possessing in a low degree the same characteristics as mark the perfect man. It eats and drinks and sleeps, is amenable to injuries, susceptible to the effects of the temperature and local conditions. The sentiment of the extent of these relations may vary with different men, but we find them always present among savage races.

The ghost as a separate existence is not deemed wholly amenable to the same conditions as when it formed part of the man. Then it partook of the destiny of the body in which it resided, and might be appropriated by the spirit in the man or animal which devoured it. As an independent being it avoided these unpleasant consequences, and more, through the nature of its special supernal attributes it was endowed with new sources of power. Thus the wandering free ghost was not amenable to many material influences that affected it when forming part of a man. Its attenuated nature enabled it to insinuate itself in any hole or cranny, it could penetrate the solid earth and ascend into the sky, as well as manifest many other transcendental powers. The man was ever a match for his fellow-man, but the ghost to the man was ever an object of unspeakable dread. If that of a friend he may have been neglectful of certain rites that it expected to receive, and the man knows it has power to command other ghosts to control the elements to pour on his head disease and death. He knows it can enter his body through any pore.

What was possible in his own nature, man also esteemed as possible in the nature of other beings, other objects. What more certain cause could he conceive as marking the active life of all things than this ghost existence? But we should err, if in the lowest races we looked for the general expression of this element of supernal power in all things. The savage is too little of a philosopher to go beyond the objects that immediately interest him to search for general causes. He accepts the appearance of each individual perception on its own merits. Hence the lowest savage races only affirm the presence of the ghost-power in human and local animal natures, and in some few fetish objects that have excited their animistic sentiments. Men are much more considerably advanced when they reason out that there is a soul in everything, even in the objects their own hands have manipulated.

Undeveloped man, ignorant of the chemical and physical powers induced by the altered relations of material things, and only conversant with force as resulting from the voli-

tional movements of men and animals, conceives that all its
manifestations in nature are due to the action of like forces
in rock, water, sky, and earth. Thus the earthquake is
caused by the ghosts underground, or the huge earth supporting whale, elephant or tortoise, changes its position.
So, in volcanic action, they perceive the might of an ingua
or the dread Pele, and her myrmidons in their sports are
casting up fire. The water-spout is caused by a spirit
dragon, and eclipses by dogs hunting the moon through the
sky. The eddying pool was the writhing of a great snake.
All motion was life, and every living force was possessed
by its embodied ghost.

Each race of men create their own explanatory idealisms.
With the Andaman islanders shooting stars and meteors
viewed with apprehension are believed to be lighted faggots
hurled in the air by Eronchawgala. An eclipse is caused
by the sun spirit being offended. Storms are regarded as
indications of Pullanga's wrath; winds are his breath;
when it thunders he is growling, and lightning is a burning
log thrown in his wrath. In all this we have embodied a
savage man's fury as he quarrels round the camp-fire.
(*Jour. Anthrop. Inst.* XII. p. 152.)

There is not a presentation of power in the natural world
but the savage accounts for by this over-capable ghost-
principle. We may not infer that the vast mythological
systems invented to explain the many natural phenomena
at once sprang into being. It is much more reasonable to
infer that the primary savage, like most rude men, idiots,
and animals, only took notice of those forces that immediately affected their own volitions. Some men have only
seen great spirits in the sky-powers, others refer their
primary concepts of great forces to the snowy mountain
peaks or the great sea, and it is only among matured races
of men we find general expositions of all the varied natural
forces.

It would seem that the capacity to appear in dreams is

the source of the supernatural attribute in the inanimate as well as the animate. It is the ghost of the mountain, the waterfall, the rock, and the sea that the dreamer beholds. So the weapon has a soul—the dreamer saw the lance in the hand of the foeman, he even felt it penetrate his arm, yet when he attempted to seize it, it was gone, because it was a spirit.

This sentiment of the spiritual nature of the secondary accompaniments in a dream is far more general than is usually conceived. Mr. Gurney shows that not only are dream-objects accompanied with all the subsidiary attributes of things, but that even the phantasm of the waking vision carries with it all the necessary supernal appearances of the secondary objects that constitute the idealism. The waking eyes not only behold the human spirit but the spirits of animals, trees, land, and water, the spirits of clothes, carriages, weapons, and all kinds of diverse things. Even now, without reasoning on it, the spiritually disposed accept as facts, not only that the ghost of one drowned in India an hour before its appearance in England should be able to traverse the intervening space, but that the ghosts of its garments, of the drops of water, and other material substances could, at the same time, accompany it. If developed man in the nineteenth century can passively accept such sentiments, need we be surprised that the untutored savage mind accepts the incidences which occur in his dreams as actual facts. A young Macusi Indian declared to Im Thurn that he had been taken out in the night and made to drag the canoe up a series of difficult cataracts. Nothing would persuade him of the fact that this was but a dream. (*Jour. Anthrop. Inst.* XII. p. 364.)

We have seen that to the man-ghost through the sentiments of wonder and fear are attached mystic concepts of powers which endow it with a weird nature, so according to the natural aptitudes of animals are they endowed with fetish powers, and this too with and without the ghost-concept. A snake seen has not only the ordinary powers of a snake, but as men may die of fear without having been touched by it, it can kill with a look. So the Australian aborigine, knowing the timorous nature of the kangaroo, when he observes a group coming towards him driven by an advancing body of enemies, ascribes to them the possession of weird knowledge and friendly intents; they are coming to warn him of the advancing foes, and to affirm the spiritual association thus induced they have established the kangaroo kobong.

One of the most general deductions drawn by the savage who has worked out the problem of the dual nature in animals is to affirm from the actions of the powerful local animals that they are possessed by men-ghosts. We find that the range of this concept obtains so extensively, that it seems to be almost a natural deduction from the similarity of the mental characteristics in the man and the animal. Thus the Thlinkeets hold that the ghost of a man enters a bear. Miss Bird describes the Ainos as crying out: "We kill you, O bear; come back soon as an Aino." (*Unbeaten Tracks in Japan*, II. 98.) Of the various man and animal associations this sentiment has evoked we may refer to the Tiger-man of the Khonds, the Lion-man of the Zulus, the Jaguar-sorcerer of the Mexicans, the Hyæna-man of Abyssinia, the Negro, Leopard, and Alligator-men; and in Europe to the many expositions of wolf-men and dog-men.

The fetish concept of the animal's nature arises in the present day as in the past. The man riding on horseback evolved the centaur among the old Pelasgians, and the South American Indians in the days of Columbus, and but as yesterday it was a mighty fetish animal to the Andamanese. "Da Costa brought a donkey into the Zanzibar country; the people had never before seen it, therefore they were much disturbed lest they should incur its displeasure, to such an extent that they brought it corn in abundance, and asked all sorts of questions with regard to the animal's powers." M. Williams, in his *Religious Thought in India*, writes: "A man bought a piece of ground and sat down to contemplate it under a tree. Suddenly he heard a hissing sound of a snake in the branches above. Panic-struck he ran off, but never dared show his face on the ground again, being firmly convinced that the serpent was the indignant spirit of its late owner" (p. 320).

The ghost sentiment alone does not explain all the early concepts of savage man that intimate phenomena beyond the ordinary natural expression of things. The manifestation may be that of a personality, but now as ever there are concepts of vague influences that the utmost ingenuity of the mind fails to make out as being personal. Such are most fetish objects, many omens, and all simply fetish appearances of things which are often attached to ghosts, or which in themselves do not intimate a personal appearance. The vulgar notions of luck are of the same nature: they may apply to an object, as a horseshoe, a day of the week, an appearance, a position, even the relation of words with thoughts.

We infer that the concept of the uncanny preceded that of the ghost: it is certainly the first sentiment of the supernal in the mind of the child. Hence the first result of the sentiment of the uncomprehended is that of the uncanny; it may express doubt, ill-luck, fear; there is in the sensation received a something seen, felt, or heard that implies the inexplainable, the inconceivable. It may be due to the association of two or more objects, neither of which alone had any mysterious significance, but which, in combination, raise the sentiment of dread; or mystic words and actions, presented at the time the objects are combined, may stimulate the sentiment of dread. So, though there be nothing weird in the articles or words or actions in them-selves, the combination of them gives origin to a new principle that excites fear.

The two principles at first affirmed by the mind are to classify such impressions as good or evil, lucky or unlucky, and the response is the corresponding desire or dread. As all that are good are accepted by the child and the savage as mere matters of course, and excite no sentiment of personal gratitude or feeling of interest other than to self, but those implying evil according to their vastness or vagueness excite corresponding sentiments of dread. Presenting no personality to the mind it cannot be appealed to, cannot be resisted, and the soul crouches before the impersonal evil, be it ill-luck, disease, or some nameless dread.

Among the large class of fetish principles and uncomprehended impersonal powers affirmed generally by men we may specify all charms and talismans, all the fetish principles of sorcery, the power to transfer fever, ague, warts, to cure through some supernal virtue in things; to make rain, thunder, work miracles, the influence of rites on material objects, as the laying on of hands, incantations, and ordeals, chance, fate, destiny as impersonal controlling principles ; fasting, drugs as supernal powers, positions, and so forth.

These may be affirmed as virtues in the objects themselves, or they may be mere signs or tokens set up to represent ideal deductions ; they may be symbolic working by the imagined conveyance of special influences, as in the cases Dr. Tylor quotes of wearing iron rings to give mental firmness, or a kite's foot to endow with swiftness of motion.

A fetish power may be in a thing and it be accidentally discovered, or it may be associated with some manifestation of feeling, or some action occurring in connection with its presentation. Thus a fetish man, going on important business, as he crossed the threshold of his door stumbled over a pebble which hurt him. He inferred that the stone was a stone of power, so he cherished it, and ascribed his after good luck to its possession. So, in like manner, the fetish object causes rain, brings the salmon to the landing stage, strengthens its owner's heart, and confounds his enemies.

A stone, or other fetish object, is usually credited with only one special virtue: one may ensure luck, another cause rain, a third be good for the headache, a fourth to keep money in the pocket, bring kangaroos, or turn aside an assegai; others may be good for women at childbirth, youths at initiation, men going a journey by land or by water, or any special circumstance or state.

Often the fetish attribute is induced by the action of men, and results from no ghost-power, but a special mechanical combination of things. Thus, in Melanesia, stones could be caused to make rain or sunshine, and produce abundant crops of yams or bread-fruit. To make sunshine, if a very round stone was found, it was wound round with red braid and stuck with owl's feathers to represent rays, and then hung upon some high tree. (*Jour. Anthrop. Inst.* X. p. 278.)

The essential element in all supernal manifestations is faith. It was so in all the lower impersonal attributes in all forms of healing, be they by old rags, holy water, the laying on of royal hands, or as Plutarch informs us, the passing the royal great toe over the parts affected. Talismans were objects possessing fetish power, and there can be little doubt that faith in their virtues upheld many a warrior in the deadly struggle. Faith in the higher spirit manifestations is the necessary law of their cognizance.

BOOK II.

THE EVOLUTION OF THE SUPERNATURAL.

CHAPTER I.

Animal concepts of the supernal.

IT would appear that the concept of the uncanny, that is
the capacity to distinguish in the mind the natural from
what is conceived as supernatural, is the common attribute
of all sensible vitality. As a necessary result of having
perceptive powers organisms distinguish, and therefore
classify, objects present to the senses into three classes.
There are, first, those that imply luck and excite desire
whether for food or association; secondly, those objects
which imply ill-luck, danger, enmity; betimes objects of a
third character are present to the animal's senses; there
are things that neither appear as desirable or absolutely
dangerous, but those that present characteristics that the
judgment of the animal cannot resolve. Of course to all
forms of life there is a large class of objects regarding the
appearance of which the animal is absolutely indifferent.
According to the average nature of an animal's class of
perceptions are the emotions evolved; curiosity will desire
to investigate all, caution will regulate the nature of the
advance made, and if doubt supervene from a consciousness
of possible danger, then fear is excited of a more or less
exciting character. But when the perceptive presentation
is read as neither exciting indifference, desire, or simple
fear, but from its strangeness, want of harmony with previous perceptions, or holding to the animal incomprehensible

attributes, then it is uncanny, the degree of disquietude excited depending on the extent of the concept of the unnatural.

The permanent effect of the uncanny depends upon the influence of the perception on the mind of the animal. If the uneasy excitement only advances to dread, curiosity may induce special investigation and result in the nature of the object being attached to its natural class as being indifferent, desirable, or dangerous. If the investigation is unsatisfactory, or dread has given place to horror, the animal may become fascinated or excited to mad undistinguishing fury. What, then, may be the nature of the impression on the animal's sensorium we have yet to discover; it may represent the discordinate condition of madness, or it may attach supernal sentiments to the unexplainable mental presentations.

That animal perceptions of the uncanny may by experience be resolved into normal perceptions most used to animals must have become conscious. Dogs, cats, horses, cattle and other domestic animals often have objects or conditions presented to them which their reflective powers cannot resolve, they become uneasy, and by their looks and cries intimate the unsatisfactory state of their perceptions. If they can, they often by moving round the object determine its innocuousness. C. L. Morgan, in his *Animal Life*, writes : " A strange noise or appearance will make a dog uneasy until he has by examination satisfied himself of the nature of that which produces it. My cat was asleep on a chair and my little son was blowing a toy horn. The cat without moving mewed uneasily, and as he continued blowing the cat grew more uneasy and at last got up and stretched herself and turned towards the source of discomfort. She stood looking at the boy as he blew, then curling herself up she went to sleep again, no amount of blowing disturbing her further. Similarly Mr. Romane's dog was cowed by the sound of apples being shot on the

floor of a loft above the stable, but when he was taken to
the place and saw what gave rise to the sound he ceased to
be disquieted by it " (p. 339).

Mr. Vignoli describes the case of a horse that was at first
scared by a white handkerchief being waved before its
eyes; this after a little time he became accustomed to, but
when it was afterwards taken out and the same handkerchief waved before its eyes from a stick—but the man
waving it hid behind a fence—the horse was scared and
shied violently, and afterwards even in the stable it could
not see the handkerchief without trembling, and it was
difficult to reconcile him to the sight of it; he evidently
regarded it as fetish.   (*Myth and Science*, p. 59.)

That the same mental sentiments mark the psychic life of
the lower animal organisms has been noted by various
investigators.   M. Binet, in his *Psychic Life of Micro-
Organisms*, says: " There is not a single infusory that cannot be frightened and that does not manifest fear by a
rapid flight through the liquid of the preparation, fleeing in
all directions like a flock of sheep."

The effect of artificial light in producing the sentiment of
the uncanny in fish has been noticed by Mr. Bateson.   He
writes: " Soles and rockling stop swimming if a light is
shown, and the former bury themselves almost at once.
Bass, pollock, mullet and bream generally get quickly
away at first, but if they can be induced to look steadily at
the light with both eyes they gradually sink to the bottom
of the tank, and on touching the bottom commonly swim
away.   In the case of mullet effects apparently of a
mesmeric character sometimes occur, for a mullet which
has sunk to the bottom as described will sometimes lie
there quite still for a considerable time.   At other times it
will slowly rise in the water until it floats with its dorsal fin
out of the water as though paralyzed.   I once saw one
which remained in this odd position for some minutes after
the light had been turned off it.   Turbot are greatly affected

by the light of a lantern, they seemed to be seized with an irresistible impulse like that of a moth to a candle, and throw itself open-mouthed at the lamp. On one occasion a turbot continued to dash itself with such violence at the lamp that it wore the skin of its chin through till it bled." (*Jour. Marine Biol. As.* I. p. 216.)

All the higher class animals are in like manner affected by the perception of something out of the ordinary nature of things. Captain Gillmore, in the *Daily Graphic* (October 21st, 1891) writes of the lion : " This grand animal is in character the most wonderful combination of timidity and courage. Thus an unexpected noise, or sight of an unfamiliar object, will scare him; while, on the other hand, regardless of consequences he will charge home into a crowded camp and carry off his prey in the teeth of all opposition. A horse—the lion's favourite prey—I have known to wander for days in the vicinity of a troop of these beasts unmolested simply because it was blanketed and knee-haltered; while, on the other hand, the same family rushed right up to my companion's waggons, and in spite of guns, shouts, and fires, pulled down the same nag."

Thompson, in his *Passions of Animals*, quotes a similar instance in a beast of prey being withheld by like fetish influence from attacking what it would have esteemed desirable food. In South America a native was out shooting wild ducks; he had put the corner of his poncho over his head, and was crawling along the ground upon his hands and knees, the poncho not only covering his body, but trailing on the ground behind him. As he was thus creeping he heard a sudden noise and felt something heavy strike his feet. Instantly jumping up, he saw a large puma standing on his poncho. The man remained motionless. At last the creature turned away its head, and walking very slowly away about ten yards, stopped and turned again ; the man still maintained his ground, on which, probably deeming the object something uncanny, the beast made off (p. 120).

The uncanny may be something very small. Captain Basil Hall describes the terror of a tiger into whose cage a mouse had been inserted tied by a string to a stick. The royal beast jammed himself into a corner and stood trembling and roaring in an ecstacy of fear. (*Ibid.* p. 122.) Fascination may be due to hopeless despair, but in many instances it appears as the effect of fetish paralysis. Vaillant saw a species of shrike trembling as if in convulsions on the branch of a tree; below was a large snake with outstretched neck and fiery eyes gazing steadily at the bird, the agony of the bird being so great as to prevent it having the power to move away.

The concept induced by the presence of something strange may produce various emotions. At first caution, then doubt, fear of something strange, then dread of an unknown power, may be ending in fetish horror of the uncomprehended object. Thompson says: "Cranes in their migrations have been seen to be attracted by a fire and to hover round it with loud screams. Dogs are astonished at any change in the outward appearance of those they are familiar with, and at any strange object, encompassing it repeatedly and smelling at it to discover its nature. They cannot recognize their master in the water, but swim round him, astonished at hearing his voice without identifying him. A dog chasing a raven fled with astonishment as the bird faced it and uttered the words it had been taught" (p. 124).

As illustrating the effect of strange appearances on animals, Mr. Vignoli writes: "I have suddenly inserted an unfamiliar object in the various cages in which I have kept birds, rabbits, moles, and other animals. At first sight the animal is always surprised, timid, curious, or suspicious, and often retreats from it. By degrees his confidence returns, and after keeping out of the way for some time he becomes accustomed to it." (*Myth.* p. 58.) Of course different species of animals are variously affected by the presence of the unknown and therefore mysterious, and even individuals of the same species are differently affected, as is also the case with human beings. Mr. Romanes had "a Scotch terrier that had a curious hatred or horror of anything abnormal. For instance, it was long before she could tolerate the striking of a spring bell which was a new experience to her. She expressed her dislike and seeming fear by a series of growls and barks accompanied by setting her hair on end. She used from time to time to go through the same performance after gazing fixedly on what seemed vacancy, seeming to see some enemy or portent unseen by me, as if the victim of optical illusion. I could produce the same effect by doing some unexpected and irrational thing until she had become accustomed to it, yet the seeing of some form of phantom remained unabated." (*Mental Evol. in Ani.* p. 150.) That animals can see phantoms and exhibit the common mental illusions the same as human beings, and like aberrations of mania and melancholia, there are many indications. The rabies in the dog runs the same course as in the man, the horse and the bull exhibit the same wild and incoherent mania as the madman, and like causes produce corresponding effects on both. "Pierquin describes a female upo which had had sunstroke and afterwards used to become terror-struck by delusions of some kind; she used to snap at imaginary objects, and acted as if she had been watching and catching at insects on the wing." (*Mental Evol. in Animals*, p. 150.)

That most animals have the power to reproduce subjective impressions in their minds the many evidences of animals dreaming confirms. Thompson describes the stork, canary, eagle and parrot as dreamers among birds, and the elephant, horse and dog among mammals. The hound betrays his dream by a hoarse suppressed bark and by a convulsive movement of the limbs. Dogs are prone

to dream, and then they may be observed to move their
feet; they make efforts to bark, agitate themselves as if
hunting, or become excited till the hair rises on their
flanks and the skin becomes clammy. Birds, as ducks,
move their legs in their sleep as if in the act of swimming.
(*Pas. of Ani.* p. 81.)

We can only judge of the waking concepts of the subjective in the animal mind by its actions, as in the case of the
ape just quoted and Mr. Romanes' Scotch terrier. Lindsay,
in *Mind in the Lower Animals*, writes: "Delusions may
be studied in the horse. Those of sight in animals occasionally take the form, as in man, of phantoms, images of
ghosts, or apparitions of imaginary persons, animals, or
things" (II. p. 103).

"Spectral delusions," the same writer observes, "occur
in several forms of insanity among the lower animals, as in
the rabies in the dog, the sturdy in the sheep, and the sunstroke in the ape." Fleming writes of a rabid dog: "It
appeared as if haunted by some horrid phantom. At times
it would seem to be watching the movements of something
on the floor, and would dart suddenly forth and bite at the
vacant air as if pursuing something against which it had an
enmity. In another case the dog would throw itself against
the wall yelling furiously as if there were a noise on the
other side." (*Ibid.* II. p. 104.) Many nervous animals,
especially horses, are frightened simply by darkness, which
imagination apparently peoples with some kind of goblins.

Animals exhibit the presence of fetish concepts through
certain colours, as that of red to an infuriated bull.
Lindsay writes: "As instances of insurmountable anti-
pathies to certain marked colours, Pierquin cites the case
of a horse and some birds in regard to black. Baker
remarks on the obnoxiousness of white or grey colours to
the elephant and the rhinoceros. Rats are terrified or
scared by scarlet." (*Mind in Ani.* II. p. 222.) In like manner certain sounds are canny or uncanny to special animals.

Notes and tones cause the dog to howl in distress. Some, as Darwin said, tremble at music. Rossiter tells of a pet rabbit which, when a harmonium was played upon by a lady, flew frantically at the instrument and scratched the legs, but if she went to the piano bunny was as frantic with delight. Sir Everard Home found that bass notes in the lion excited a dangerous ferocity. Again, there are most clearly proved instances in which enraged snakes have been lulled to quiet by the music of the snake-charmers. (*Ibid.* II. p. 226.) A pet dog was so nervous and sensitive as regards sudden noises that a clap of thunder, the report of a gun, or even a loud sneeze, made her tremble for hours. (*Ibid.* II. p. 227.)

Of the true nature and the extent of the supernatural inferences in the minds of animals it is difficult to arrive at any satisfactory intimation; we can only note that they are of the same nature as similar human presentations by their being educed from like incidents by the fact that the animal mind is organized on the same basis as the human mind, and from the evidence it exhibits of being amenable to the same aberrations as the human mind. We have spoken of animals dreaming. Lindsay on that subject writes: "During sleep the dog exhibits movements of the tail and paws, and sniffing, growling, barking occur. During sleep the sporting dog has an imaginary pursuit of imaginary game, this gives rise to actual physical and mental excitement as to cause the animal to awake and be bewildered to find its actual position so different from that of the morbid fancy, but it speedily realises its error and becomes aware that it was dreaming." (*Ibid.* II. p. 94.) Somnambulism also occurs in certain animals. (*Ibid.* II. p. 97.)

The mental aberrations that occur in animals are those common to man, as apoplexy, paralysis, the delirium of fevers, delusional mania, and hysteria. Madness, apparently of the character of human insanity, has been described in the chimpanzee, the horse, the elephant, dog, cat, cow, and

bull, sheep, hen, and the ant and the bee. Rogue elephants
and beavers, known as idlers, are probably insane animals
driven from the herd or community. The gnu is said to be
subject to madness in South Africa. Pierquin describes an
instance of acute dementia in a parrot as the result of fright
during a naval action; it showed terror by cowering, and
became stupid. Puerperal mania occurs after parturition in
animals as with women. Lastly, natural idiocy occurs in
animals as with children. Houzeau tells the story of an
idiot dog pup whose mother had denoted its mental
inferiority to its brother pups, especially in its incapacity,
as with some human idiots, to supply itself with food.
(Lindsay, *Mind in Animals*, II. p. 29.)

Other instances of real objects exciting supernal concepts
as in the case Darwin gives of the parasol on the lawn being
blown by the wind, and Thompson's instance of a party in
India being saved from a tiger by a lady opening her
umbrella in its face as she saw it about to spring, are of
this nature. Mr. Romanes' terrier was capable of conceiving the presence of a power which men deem supernal.
Thus "the terrier was in the habit of playing with dry
bones, throwing them to a distance. On one occasion
Mr. Romanes tied a long and firm thread to a bone and gave
it him to play with. After a time, when it was at a distance
from the dog, he drew it away by means of the long invisible
thread. Instantly its whole demeanour changed, and it
approached the bone with caution, but as it continued to
recede his astonishment developed into dread, and he ran
to conceal himself under some articles of furniture, there to
behold at a distance the uncanny spectacle of a dry bone
coming to life" (p. 156).

In another experiment the same dog was taken into a
carpeted room where Mr. Romanes blew a soap bubble,
and by means of a fitful draught made it intermittently
glide along the floor. It became interested but unable to
decide if this fitful object was alive, cautiously following it

at a distance. Being encouraged, it approached the bubble
with ears erect and tail down, but the moment it happened
to move again it retreated. After a time the dog regained
more courage, and approaching one of the bubbles nervously
touched it with its paw. The bubble burst, and astonishment was strongly depicted in the dog. On blowing another
bubble he approached and touched it with the same result as
before, yet, though encouraged by Mr. Romanes, could not
be induced to approach another bubble, and on pressing ran
out of the room, and no coaxing would induce him to re-
enter. (*Mental Evo. in Ani.* p. 157.)

Our illustrations as yet have all been expressive of the
fetish as uncanny, yet it may be recognized under the canny
aspect, as in the instance the Abbe Huc narrates. A Mongol
herdsman had a calf die soon after birth, and to excite the
flow of milk in the cow the calf was skinned, stuffed with
hay, and placed before the cow. It was evident that the
cow saw something not exactly normal in the aspect of
the calf, as it at first opened enormous eyes, then smelt at it,
sneezing three times, then licking it with tenderness. The
parody was continued until, by dint of caressing and licking
the calf, the cow ripped it open and the hay issued forth.
The cow's sense of the canny had been satisfied, and it
exhibited no agitation or surprise, but proceeded tranquilly
to devour the unexpected provender, even though it
demolished its own calf; possibly it had accepted the
spiritual theory of incarnation.

An interesting problem that still requires solution is the
effect of these various mental states on the reasoning power
in the animal. Beyond the emotion, can any animal in the
first place form a definite idea that the object it believes it
saw was something out of the natural course of things, and
did it categorize the appearance as one of a distinct class of
presentations; in fact, had it evolved the concept of the
natural as distinct from the supernatural? If the dog, as
in the case quoted, on awaking and beginning to think

settles in his own mind that his dream chase was an illusion
and unworthy of further consideration, then the general
principle is solved, and the dog as we imagined has the
abstract concept of objects as natural and *outré*. It is
altogether another question to infer that recognizing the
supernatural it can draw the same mental deduction after it
has recognized its character as he is in the habit of drawing
from the presence of natural objects.

Every animal attaches the sentiment denoted as luck to
its acquisition of any article suitable for food, and that
would even be the case in the dream so long as it was a
dream, but when it recognized the nature of the delusion
would the objects soon have any abstract effect, or only
excite desire ?   We are all aware that human beings attach
the sentiment of luck, good and bad, to dream-objects; but
from the emotions exhibited by animals subject to dream we
cannot infer that like sentiments of luck are ever realised in
their minds, either in regard to natural or dream-acquisitions.
Naturally the food instinct is satisfied, but we want higher
confirmatory evidence than we yet know of to realize in
their mental expressions the concept of an abstract supernal
attribute.

More, it has been affirmed that "the dog engages
occasionally in rites similar to those of negro fetishism and
of the dancing and howling dervish.   The object of
worship is apparently selected because of its oddness and
unfamiliarity."   (*Mind in Ani.* I. p. 222.)   As no examples
are quoted, we may take the case of the dog playing with
the dry bone given by Mr. Romanes as belonging to this
class. We, however, infer that the same as the kitten with a
ball of worsted and many like incidents, it only implied
sportiveness, the presence of objects only considered natural,
and which by easily being volitional give play to the
normally excited spirits of the young animals.   Not so,
however, when an unknown to the animal, a seeming living
power is attached to the bone; then the object passes out of

the range of the animal's powers of thought, as when
Mr. Romanes attached a thread to the bone when the animal
admitted the presence of something it deemed, as we may
infer, supernatural, and whose unreadable attribute caused
it to fly and hide itself; it could not accept the presentation
as denoting either good or ill-luck.

We cannot resolve that in any case of delusion the animal
mind expresses any other emotion than that of fear. Lindsay,
who has most entered into this question, remarks that "the
dog exhibits practically a belief in the supernatural. It
expresses alarm at apparitions. It has been described as
regarding the owl as a ghost, and the same kind of ghosts
that are occasionally made use of in practical joking produce
the same effect on the dog. A fertile imagination frequently
leads the horse as well as the dog to be terrified at the
sight of perfectly harmless objects animate or inanimate,
especially when seen in a state of motion and in comparative
darkness. Bartlett speaks of a sense of mystery in certain
animals in the Zoological Gardens. In many animals awe
or dread of the unknown readily gives birth to not only a
feeling of mystery, but delusion." (*Ibid.* I. p. 223.)

The first effect of the concept of luck in an object on the
savage mind is the desire to possess it and thus retain its
good quality in himself, this independent of any idea of
ghost presentation, but all know that this mental concept
has left no practical result in the animal mind; no animal
ever wears an amulet, and as far as we can judge no animal
entertains any concept of luck as an abstract quality, and
luck, as we shall show, is the first concept of the supernal in
the developing human mind.

CHAPTER II.

The concept of the uncanny as forms of luck.

Men, like animals, are conscious of the uncanny; but, unlike, as with the latter, the sentiment educed is not restricted to forms of doubt or fear. In the presence of the uncomprehended, through their higher organic and mental powers, men are able to carry the inference of the possible out of the natural into the supernatural.

The first element of thought to the animal, as well as the man, in the presence of the uncomprehended, is to see if it can derive any material advantage from the presentation. If the reply continues to be dubious and fear is excited, the animal flies from the object; if not of sufficient force to excite any consciousness of dread it is treated with indifference. Not so with men when the attributes of an object are unexplainable; as natural signs he attaches to them some mysterious signification, and the mental powers enter into a new field of inquiry. The status of man's thoughts is not limited to a present advantage; he can realize in objects the capacity to be serviceable at some future time, and, more, he can see in their appearances those mental associations we term supernal.

As far as we can judge no animal has any idea of luck, or ill-luck, as abstract conceptions; certainly, no animal utilizes amulets, and whatever objects they may attach to themselves or their movements other than as food, certainly carry no mysterious attributes. It is only as something to play with, to work out its redundant muscular activity, that the dog bites and throws about the stone, the stick, or the bone; so with the kitten and the ball, and even the bower bird and its shell and stick objects of interest, we know, that ordinarily no supernal attributes are attached to them; but, as in the case of Mr. Romanes tying a thread to a bone, such objects may be made to induce an unexplainable sentiment of the uncanny in the mind of the animal, which has no result but to excite dread.

We have seen how fully the human organism is surcharged with natural influences that ever question the meaning of things, that no object is ever presented to it which it does not question on more points than its immediate influence. Man not only conceives the idea of its future relation to him, but more in the hopes and fears so strongly present in his nature, he attaches to things various sentiments of mysterious relation, and he conceives the possibility and the presence of occult virtues for good or ill.

These crude abstract conceptions seem as natural to the man as the perceptive relations his senses express, and they influence him in a corresponding manner. In the fact that like classes of occult presentations are common to all men, we must look to the inherent character of the human organism for their origin. A man, as ordinarily formulated, can no more withhold the sentiment of luck from an object than he can the image of its visual presentation.

That the power that educes supernal sentiments is an inherent organic, or if we will mental attribute, may be noted in the range of its presentation. The concept of luck is not limited to objects of perception; it equally applies to modes of thought and sensation, to abstract qualities, as numbers, days, and hours, and any combination of objects each normal in its nature, but which by combination obtain occult attributes, and these attributes ma;

be enhanced by forms of words. In other terms, not only objects, but all forms of thought have the power to express occult attributes.

As with all other human characteristics, the capacity to evolve supernal sentiments is progressive; it is phylogenetic, it is ontogenetic; and we may classify its presentations in a definite scheme applicable to men in every period of growth in all countries and in all ages.

The lowest phase of the supernal, that which, passing by immediate use, would find an occult virtue of consequent advantage, a power that passes even from mere natural presentation to self-induced association—that is luck. It may be good, it may mean bad; we may court it by a movement, by possessing an object, by altering the place of things, by muttering a word, by spitting, by any volition the human organism is capable of manifesting. Under these infinite modes of operating it is evident the causative power is in the organism which presents the thought, not in the object that primarily induces it, and, consequently, it may be attached to any form of thought the individual mind is capable of evolving.

Forms of luck, therefore, are the earliest germs of religion; they are the basis of all religions; the human mind can only extend, vary, and multiply the modes in which it conceives of possible good and evil, and as the field of thought is enlarged so are the indices of luck brought into more exalted relations. Here, it simply responds to a bodily sensation; there, its inciting motive is a visual perception; to another it is due to an ebullition of thought; in a third it may be incited by words spoken, or be the result of a long series of presentations, material or mental. There is not a movement of man, accidental or intentional or organic, but may evolve the sentiment of luck or ill-luck, and be ominous of good or evil; so with all natural appearances, all the phenomena of the heavens, light and shade, day and night, the forms and movements of the elements, life in its many presentations—animal and vegetal, all modes of thought and feeling, states of sickness, death and dead objects, in short, every phase of things or mind that thought can dwell upon.

How small a basis of induction may control the will we have exemplified in the common forms of luck accepted by not only savages but men in advanced communities, yet even these, according to their mode of origin, represent grades of mental powers. There are those who can never originate a single form of thought, they can only rehearse derived forms of thought; others are for ever seeking new outputs of the supernal, they would trace the sentiment of luck in every position and relation of things, with them the supernal overpowers the natural.

Of this class of people James Greenwood writes—"How many men are there who carry in their purse, for luck, a shilling with a hole it, or a crooked sixpence, which they would not part with for ten times its intrinsic value! There are men, and women too, whose turned-out pockets would reveal a tooth, an odd-looking bead, a cramp-bone, or some similar rubbish, turned to a state of high polish by constant carriage. Rough men playing cards or dominoes at a table will gravely turn the peak of their cap to the back of their head, or even in extreme cases turn the cap inside out and wear it so to woo a change of luck. They will, though they can ill afford to waste it, throw away the broken crust of a loaf that would bring them bad luck if they ate it. They believe in a lucky look from a person who squints. At Billingsgate Market, and at Farringdon Market, may be found any morning a silly boy who picks up many a halfpenny by diffusing lucky looks. Among the stall-keepers it is reckoned to be nothing less than ruinous to them to turn away the first bid for an article. It brings bad luck on the day's sellings, so it is better to get the hansel over, even at a loss. When he has taken the hansel money he would as soon think of throwing it into the road as putting it into his pocket without first spitting upon it." (*Graphic*, June 14th, 1879.)

In taking a general survey of the concepts of forms of luck prevailing among men, we may trace some that seem universal. These are of organic origin, and therefore common to all men, as when luck or ill-luck sentiments are deduced from their own bodily conditions and the effect of meteorological phenomena on them. We may trace the origin of others equally general, as the appearance of animals and birds and their various cries as denoting luck and ill-luck, from the influence of such cries and appearances to men as hunters, and the effect of such cries and movements as presenting indications of the presence or absence of game, of the vicinity of foes—as in the case of the kangaroos coming towards them indicating the vicinity of foes to the Australian aborigine. The mental condition at special times gives a distinguishing character to the sentiments then expressed; thus, being unwell not only influences the thoughts of good or evil in the mind of the sick person, but it predisposes those about him to manifest corresponding deductions, hence so many omens of sickness and the still greater number of death premonitions and signs. So darkness, and any alteration in the ordinary course of things in nature, universally induce concepts of evil, as eclipses, meteors, abnormal darkness, and various electrical phenomena.

While so many forms of luck are universal there are others that are specially local and even individual, for as any man may select his own fetish so he may evolve his individual sentiment of luck and new conditions, new ideas of nature and the supernal always tend to cause new forms of luck to be conceived, and those men who are most exposed to new influences and various conditions and risks are most prone, like soldiers and sailors, to conceive of various forms of luck. Besides any new associations, altered conditions, modes of life and thought by presenting new appearances, new lines of mental influence predispose and build up new ideas of luck. Hence, as Greenwood shows, there arise gamblers' forms of luck and costers' forms of luck; so we have thieves' forms of luck; even the professional Thug had his murder luck. Naturally the prevailing form of the religious sentiment among a people in all times and countries has widely influenced the local forms of luck. We might in confirmation refer to any race or faith, but from our known familiarity with the subject we will be content to refer to the fetish forms of luck attached to Christianity. No doubt many of those have been transferred from old pagan forms from Semitic, Hellenic, and Norse mystic associations, but even when borrowed they have been adapted to local sentiments. Thus sentiments of luck are attached to everything connected with the church, its structure, the graveyard, the bell, the various relations, ministrations, christening, marriage, churching, burials, to communion, attendance, the Bible, even to modes of action of the clergyman, and any special incidents occurring during the religious services.

New modifications of old ideas of luck may arise anywhere. Thus, in the United States at the present day, the inquiries into the forms of folklore have detected new forms of luck and new variations of old forms. The hand of a man dead or symbolic has ever been a sign of luck, the luck is in the hand itself, it is its special virtue and has nothing to do with his ghost or spirit. So like forms of luck are attached to the paws of animals, the claws of birds. In India the lions and tigers' claws express luck, in Northern Asia the bear's paw, in this country it was noted as the special virtue of a hare's foot, in America this power is a potent talisman more particularly in the rabbit, especially in one caught in a graveyard. Circumstances may attach special significance in an individual's mind to one taken under fetish or assumed fetish conditions. Thus, at an execution in America as the body was cast off a rabbit was roused from a hedge, then a chase of all present ensued until the animal was caught, when Judge Winn offered five dollars for one of the feet to keep it as a talisman of luck. (*Jour. of Amer. Folklore*, II. p. 100.)

The transferring of any complaint or disease has been, as a form of throwing off ill-luck, practised in many countries. Modes of operation for that purpose were familiar to the old Greeks. We read of them on Chaldean bricks; our ancestors evoked them from Norse customs and attached Christian symbols to them; so some of the descendants of the pilgrim fathers have acquired the art of working them through modern inventions. A gentleman walking down a street in Lancaster, Pennsylvania, noticed a clean white envelope lying on the pavement; it was sealed, but had neither address or stamp upon it. On his opening it there was a sheet of note paper with a penny folded in it; on the centre of the sheet of paper were three red spots in the form of a triangle, and below the ominous inscription "Wart blood." (*Jour. of Amer. Folklore*, III. p. 238.) Another equally important conception of a new luck-form dates from San Francisco. There the girls as well as the boys as they pass home from school take pencil and paper and addressing each passenger say, "Please give me a bow," which done the youngster marks it down and addresses in like manner others, and when he has obtained one hundred marks he buries the paper when no one can see him, at the same time making a wish. At the end of four days under like conditions he unearths the paper, and then they say they always get their wish.

Ideas of luck are due to attraction; they are founded in sympathy, they are seen in symbols, they are recognized by similitudes. These may be in form, in name, through sounds or words, by affinity, by the accident of time or place, in dreams, or by chance. Hence they are allied with looks, touching, making passes, with movements, with every form of sympathy, every symbolic appearance, every sign of similitude of shape, as with stones, knobs, rocks, roots, and so forth. A name may be lucky or unlucky, words are significant of good or evil, even the most strained affinity may mean luck or ill-luck. The accidental association of incidents or times or seasons, even the chance arrangement or misplacement of articles may imply luck or loss, as in shifting the cuff of the cap, putting on stockings or boots, going up or down stairs, opening an umbrella inadvertently, and innumerable other variations of usual habits.

Now it is an important question to resolve what is the nature of this mental concept, and what is the range of its application. We have been referred to the ghost theory for its inception, but though the conception may be attached to the ghost apparition, its expression has no more connection with a ghost than any other object or appearance. Every thing, form of thought, appearance, sound or attribute, real or imaginary, are equally amenable to express luck, be it conscious or unconscious, organic or inorganic, material or mental, sentiments of good or ill. The bird that warns of danger, the animal whose presence signifies luck, the meteor or eclipse that threatens unknown horrors are indifferent and ignorant of the thought or the power, they work out their special attributes in accordance with the powers they possess, of all ulterior effects or influences they are unconscious. There are attributes and assumed attributes; the attributes are qualities in the thing itself, and present to every consensuous power capable of regarding them, but the assumed attributes have no relations in the things or concepts themselves, they are only mental phenomena in the mind which educes them. So it is with the sentiment of luck; each mind creates its own forms of good or ill, and applies them in accordance with the nature of its susceptibilities, and these as we have seen arise from the character of its organic tendencies. The differences affirmed that constitute luck are only concepts of attributes, but all actual presentations, even though by ghosts express will. The attribute denoting a virtue or principle is always the same; the ghost presentation varies with the mental attributes of the mind that conceives it and manifests choice. The concept of luck might have existed had no ghost presentation ever occurred, no spirit sentiment been ever evolved, or the capacity to conceive the ghost theory been ever dormant in the human mind.

Luck is a form of thought as distinct in its nature as the concept of a ghost. It was the earliest form of presumed outré manifestation, and is the individual's response, mentally, to its own organic impulses. Luck never needs the help of medicine-man or priest, it is only a self-influence; it was so when the savage had no spiritual concepts; it is so now. The man who turns the peak of his cap, changes his seat, or calls for a new pack of cards, expecting thereby to change his luck, is his own high priest in the oldest faith in the world. Such men rarely conceive of ghosts, never see apparitions, and have no knowledge of the interposition of Providence. They conceive there is more virtue in a holy stone, a bent coin, the tie of a garter, even a chance fly in a glass, than in a fetish object, an incantation, a ghost presentiment or a seraphic dream. The capacity to conceive the attribute of luck represents a distinct mental state; it has its own code of laws, its special phases of presentation and inciting causes. It is the only form of faith that is essentially individual; it knows no church or priest, its only temple the mind of its presenter to which all things and all thoughts may be ministering powers.

How vast the influence of lucks, presentiments, on men's actions and thoughts may be gleaned from the following records of its powers over human sentiments and human actions. Jones in his *Credulities* writes that St. Chrysostom said: "This or that man was the first to meet me when I walked out, consequently innumerable ills will certainly befal me; that confounded servant of mine in

giving me my shoes handed me the left shoe first; this
indicates dire calamity and insults. As I stepped out, I
started with the left foot foremost; this, too, was a sign of
misfortune; my right eye twitched upwards as I went out,
this portends tears." Addison said, "I have known a
shooting star spoil a night's rest, and have seen a man in
love grow pale and lose his appetite upon the plucking of
a merry thought. A screech-owl, at midnight, has charmed
a family more than a band of robbers; nay, the voice of a
cricket has struck more terror than the roaring of a lion.
To one filled with omens and prognostics, a rusty nail or
crooked pin shoot up into prodigies."

The same writer says, "I have seen a Minister of State
turn his chair round at a whist table in order to avert ill-
luck. I have seen a warrior, to whom the safety of an
army has been confided, lodge an ivory fish upon a candle-
stick to procure its good graces. I have seen the most
prudent of attorneys call for fresh cards, and pay for them,
in the full confidence that he would be gratified by that
extravagant proceeding. I have known a venerable
divine lay his finger with indecent haste upon the two of
clubs, because, as he said, whoever first touches the two of
clubs secures a good hand." (*Creduli*, p. 475.)

Equally pregnant sentiments of luck influence all savage
people. Dorman in his *Primitive Superstitions* writes:
"Among hunting tribes, the cawing of a crow at night
would cause a large party of warriors to run for home and
give up an expedition. The Comanches said the wolf
warned them of danger: if one sprang up before them in
their journeys and barked or howled, they would turn aside
and travel no more in that direction that day. The
Ojibways believed much in omens. The barking of dogs
and wolves, the bleating of deer, the screeching of owls,
the flight of uncommon kinds of birds, the moaning of
a partridge were ominous of ill. The two last were certain
ones of death. The sailing of an eagle to and fro, and the

noise of a raven, were omens of good.   When the Mankawis, a species of quail, perched at night upon a cabin belonging to a Seminole, the inhabitants of that cabin prepared for death.   If a white bird sports aloof in the air, this indicates a storm.   If it flies in the evening before a traveller, it forebodes danger.   Among the northern tribes the march is regulated by a sorcerer, according to good or bad omens. If he has seen a spider on a willow-leaf, the army must turn back.   If they hear the howling of a large wolf when travelling, sadness is at once visible in their countenances; it is the medicine-wolf, and forebodes some calamity " (p. 224).

The capacity to manifest the sentiment of luck denotes a special phase of mental development, that in which the powers of ratiocination were at a low ebb, and idealisation almost dormant; the perception of the immediate present only admitting of crude, often unconnective, ideas of association.   This mental state is a common phase now of the human mind, and the vague indeterminate sentiment of luck, the unatural output of the supernal in the greater portion of human minds.   Baal had his thousands, and Yahveh his ten thousands, but luck reigns triumphant in the souls of myriads.   It was so in the past, it is so in the present, it is denoted in the attire, it is indirectly indicated in trifles, in amulets, in objects for seeming use, but really retained as bringing good luck.   The Moslem has his several formal daily prayers, the Buddhist announces unceasingly his chant of praise, but the worshipper of luck at morning, noon, and night, offers his devotions to the boundless, endless principle of power he adores.   On getting up in the morning, he is most careful to put his right leg out of the bed first, in due order to select and put on his garments, never crossing them, never showing inattention by putting on his stocking inside out, or putting the left slipper on before the right.   Not an article that he uses in his toilet but may be injudiciously applied or made to indicate ill-

7 *

luck by being misplaced. So at breakfast, at noon, at every meal, his sense of luck orders all that he handles, he touches, or beholds, and woe be to him if he unduly crosses his knife, upsets the salt, or in a way puts himself under the power of an omen of misfortune. He anxiously watches the door for luck in the hope that his first visitor will be a man or woman, young or old, dark or fair, according to the semblance that his own mental idiosyncrasy denotes as fortunate. Ever he is on the watch as to how he sneezes to right or left, how he stumbles, how he spits. He may save the mischance of having gone under a ladder, by returning and spitting through the runnels, but he is ever most wary to leave a room by the same door as he entered it, otherwise he would leave all his luck for the day in the room, and he had far better go home and to bed than risk his fortune on any transaction under such baneful auspices. We may not—we need not—recapitulate the multitude of misgivings of misfortune that accompany every action, movement, and word of the worshipper of luck till sleep once more withholds the power of thought. The most earnest devotee of a supernal ghost-power, never adores it so continuously as the worshipper of luck beseeches the impersonal principle on which his faith depends.

You may read a man's totem guardian by the tattoo lines on his face, or its insignia on his wrapper, or his wigwam; so you may detect a man's devotion to his luck-charm by the movements of his hands to it, whether a jewel, a stone, or claw, suspended from the neck or watch-chain, or fumbled with in the pocket. It is ever bright from handling, and exacts more of his attention than he likes to manifest; hence he mostly reads his luck in secret and alone.

The early output of the concept of things, and the condition of things governing and defining human destiny, is what we have now to define. There is a material difference in the thought that leads to a definite exposition of the occult results induced by the impersonal powers it conceives, and the mere excitement of wonder by the presence of a power invisible and incomprehensible, and it is that mental state which is indicated when man only recognizes influences of a mysterious and indefinable character. These indications of uncanny influences he attaches to vague indeterminate feelings in his own person, to strange mental manifestations that seem to counteract his own will in the outer world—he attaches an uncanny significance to all uncommon appearances in nature and abrupt presentations of life. His own actions, or the actions of his fellows outside normal habits, intimate the presence of a power not in their own natures, and, therefore, mysterious. In all these cases, man fails to define the influence, fails to control the principle, and, like the dog frightened at the presence of the uncanny, he either hides or stands paralyzed in amazed tribulation.

Personally, such sentiments may arise from sneezing, ringing in the ear, the twitching of muscles, a strange sense of weight on the chest, the fluttering of the heart, forms of pain of a new character, an uncontrollable impulse to sigh, to weep, or to act abnormally, as putting left foot forward first, or stumbling. All startling phenomena of the external world may raise ideas of the uncanny not yet reduced to cause and effect as strange appearances in the heavens, the abnormal or unexpected movements and cries of animals and birds and things singular in form, condition, or motion.

As illustrations of the organic and mental origin of forms of luck and other supernal semblances, Sir Humphry Davy in his *Salmonia* writes: "Omens of death-watches, dreams, &c., are for the most part founded on some accidental coincidence; but spilling salt on an uncommon occasion may arise from a disposition to apoplexy, shown by an incipient numbness in the hand, and may be a fatal

symptom, and persons dispirited by bad omens prepare
the way for evil fortune.   The dream of Brutus before the
battle of Pharsalia, probably produced a species of irreso-
lution; so an illustrious sportsman always shot ill after a
dispiriting omen."   A writer in *Notes and Queries*, Second
Series, remarking on the same subject writes : "The want
of nerve or temper is frequently betrayed by some little
incident, and luck depends upon personal self-possession
and conduct.   Thus, spilling the salt is unlucky; it is the
act of a nervous, hasty person, and, therefore, one not
likely to prosper.   So breaking a looking-glass denotes
carelessness, or being clumsy, and is equally ominous.
Unlucky for a bride ready for church to look in the glass;
this implies an excess of personal vanity, and not likely to
be followed by success.   One who makes a patch-work
quilt will never be married, the occupation unsocial, and,
therefore, denoting one not apt for courtship.   That the
bridesmaid who catches the thrown silver is likely to be
first married, may be fairly reasoned by the greater energy
she has manifested for that result.   Stirring the Christmas
pudding by all in the house introduces male and female
sociality, and thus aids in the customary fulfilment—so
eating mince pies in different houses.   Lucky to be
followed by a strange dog infers a genial disposition, which
brings luck.   So cutting the top of the loaf means
prudence, one name for luck.   To tumble upstairs lucky,
but unlucky downstairs, because in the first case it implies
determination, which results in only trifling injury, but the
other careless haste, and a possible catastrophe " (XII.
p. 400).

CHAPTER III.

The evolution of Charms and Spells in the individual mind.

WE have seen that man organically evolves impulses which formulate in his mind concepts of the presence of supernal powers in objects and states of being and the conditions that environ them; that at first these forms of power are indeterminate, and man like a straw in troubled waters is the mere child of this chance luck, having no control over his destiny. We have now to consider the relations of man with nature and the supernatural, when through the development of his mental powers he is able to read a purpose in such presentations, and realizes the will to control and classify them, and thereby from forms of thought convert them into principles of action. In doing so we recognize the presence of mind, powers we could not in the earlier evolvement perceive, for man has entered into a new mental phase and the supernal has been endowed with moral characteristics and seeming rational affirmations. As yet there is no concept of will or mental power, save in the application of the forces recognized in the human; the evolving sources of the supernal are more impersonal attributes.

To recognize a purpose however illogical, to assign a cause however *outré*, to every phenomena he observes, is the characteristic of man; in this state the seeming to him is as important as the real. More, it is only a form of the real, and consensus in time with him implies affinity in notion. The associations, therefore, that he conceives, and the forces he affirms, are to him as material as the substances they affect; he has not yet learnt to separate the supernal from the natural; they all belong to the same category, only varying in their modes of expression. Thus having faith in his sentiments of the characteristics that denote and modify things, he evolves the belief of his power by simulating the associative influences he recognizes, to be able to control the occult virtues in things, and the occult powers he recognizes by certain substances, actions, and cries. Hence he becomes conscious of a power in signs, a power in times, a power in words and forms, and these he applies to all the modes, actions, and purposes in life.

Next to his own personal actions and the actions of his fellows, the phenomena of disease and death claim his application of the occult influences he has recognized. The man who in many fights had withstood the club or assegai of his foeman when pierced by a weapon, transfers to it the power that injures him; it possessed a virtue or charm. So with disease, it was the occult power in something he had eaten, something he had touched that had entered him. Every change in his own body caused by growth or evolvement had a more or less sinister influence, those of women commanded forms of dire misfortune. So general are these mystic significances that there are no undeveloped races but ascribe occult dangers to the presence of women in their courses, or at childbirth even among the Chinese a woman for a month after childbirth may not cross another person's threshold or she would cast ill-luck on the occupants.

The actions of men and women that may convey mystic powers, both of good and evil, are most varied. Thus, trimming a house on Sunday, brings grief before Saturday. If you sell medicine bottles you will require them to be refilled. If you sing before breakfast you will cry before night. If you rock an empty cradle you will have more children. Unlucky to kill a cricket or take a swallow's nest. Clothes mended on the back bring want; and so on with innumerable other human actions, each of which carries in its performance some often most heterogeneous occult power.

Many of these actions, which carry a baneful charm, may have that charm controlled or altered by after presenting a counter charm. Thus you may avert the ill omen of putting on a stocking inside out by not changing it; by spitting through the rowels of a ladder avert the ill-luck of going under it; so the threatened mishaps of salt being upset are cast aside by throwing a pinch of it over the left shoulder. Again, should you meet a funeral the omen of ill-luck may be averted by politely taking your hat off to the defunct. The evil threatened in seeing one magpie may be controlled by crossing two straws; and that from meeting a squinting woman by the courtesy of talking to her. More according to the Chinese the evil inoculated into a house by a man having hang himself there may be averted by cutting the beam down and burning it and carrying away and casting into the river the earth or ashes underneath.

When one reads of the many ill omens that denote a death we are almost tempted to ask how it is then that so many people are still alive. Thus a corpse in the house over Sunday will cause another death within a week; and under similar conditions if you fail to cover the mirror you will die within the year; so if a grave is left open over Sunday there will be another death within the week; still more should the rain fall in the open grave, there will be another death within three days; and if the hearse is drawn by white horses another death in the neighbourhood in the month. White animals are death-warnings in Bohemia; death is said to be a woman in white, and for the sick man to dream of white clothes is ominous of death. Again, if

anyone comes to a funeral after the procession has
started another death in the house will follow. Whoever
counts the carriages at a funeral will die the same year;
and should a party of onlookers enter the church before
the mourners, one will die the same year. The person on
whom the eye of a dying person last looks, or the person
bearing the last name uttered by the departing, will be
first to die.

If three persons look into a mirror at the same time,
one will die within the year; so breaking a looking-glass
is a death-sign. Many careless or thoughtless acts are
death-omens, as hanging a cloth on a door-knob; scissors
in falling having their points stick in the floor; or
carrying a hoe into the house. It is a death-sign to
try on another's mourning, and there are omens of death
in countless little contingencies. If you shiver some one
is walking over your grave; if you have a ringing in the
ears that is a death-omen. A clock stopping and
commencing again forbodes a death, so does the ticking
of the death watch, or live sparks in the ashes of a fire
on the following morning. The coals may not fly out of
the fire, the candle burn blue, or the flames be dim, but
death is threatened; even a lady's hair-pin falling from her
head is a death-sign. Anything out of season is a death-
omen, as apples in flower and fruit at the same time, or
a flower opening at an unusual time. Death occurs in
couples, one death follows another in the same house,
night brings death, so does ebb-tide.   (*Jour. American
Folklore*, II. p. 18.)

Nor is it only in family associations and home indications
we take cognizance of death-warnings. It may be indicated
by a rattling at the church-door, by the heavy sound of its
bell, by the corpse not stiffening, by the thrice-repeated caw
of the carrion crow, or it may enter the house with a broom
in May; a snowdrop or flowering twig of blackthorn bring
death in a house; so the flame of the *ignis fatuus* denotes a

death, the screech of the owl, the croak of the raven, meeting a hare, a dog howling, and the fire burning black.

It were a more pleasing task to point out the omens of marriage, which are almost as varied as those of death, and certainly of a more pleasing character, but as these are so well known, and more as they often consist of long rhymes such as old John Gay once loved to rehearse, and dear Keats embalmed in an ideal myth, we will pass on to other forewarnings of occult recognitions. In most cases the omen is outside the human will and comes like destiny, unsought, but often it depends on the human will and the human choice, and the far-away mystic force responds to our appeal. We may court fortune by casting an old shoe over the threshold, by spitting on money, by whistling for the wind. The Finlander obtains a favourable wind by untying the charmed knots in a cord accompanied with a song or incantation. The Persian husbandman invokes a winnowing wind by scattering saffron in the air. Not a few ladies shut their eyes till they get in the open before they look at the new moon, and where is the farmer who has not nailed a horse-shoe over his barn-door. Some of these time monitions are favourable to early rising, as bathing the face in May dew, and being the first to open the house on Christmas day; so he who kills the first snake in the year will gain power over his enemies.

In the various occult powers man has discovered in things, times, and movements, and the means by which he has obtained control over the various mysterious powers in the world, we may trace their antiquity and discover the mental state of man at the time they were announced. Some carry us back to the early forms of thought; they are rude crude guesses of relations or indeterminate presentations without definite concept, and which only vaguely denote forms of luck. Some denote a more concentrated outlook; a deeper investigation of cause, and the concept of higher powers; but all imply that beyond the world of the seen, the felt, the known, there are innumerable powers and controlling forces to which there is neither time nor space, neither substance nor let; without sense, without thought, passionless and personless, knowing nothing of spirit or will, allwhere and everywhere, at all times under suitable conditions as soulless destinies they work their unchanging, unswerving potencies without power to heed, comprehend, or avert the influences they bear. Like the lightning's potency, like the glory of the sun, as the energy of the sea, they may kill or cure, protect or ravage. Like the great imponderables they overpower the ponderables, and prayer or praise, hate and curses pass them by scatholess, as is the granite mountain by the breeze.

Thus man evolved the religion of charms and spells—that is the capacity in things to manifest hidden powers, and the capacity in man to apply those powers intensified by his act of associating them together, or increasing their energy under the influence of special times, conditions, or formulated words. Such powers may be good or bad according to their associations; they may be curative or destructive, protective or avenging, denoting the past or prescient of the future. They may claim any personal transcendental attribute as if a living power, and all such attributes afterwards applied to ghosts have their origin in the virtues attached to the most incongruous objects. The charmed quartz-stone laid in a man's footstep is able of itself to penetrate his body, a root of garlic may defy the disease power to enter, and a model hand withstand all that is evil. A stone may render one invisible, a herb transform one; a man may be possessed by many natural objects. The life of a man may be attached to any natural thing, organic or inorganic. One drives a peg in the ground; when it rots, the man dies. Another burns a stick, in whose existence is the life of a man. A vessel of water leaks, and with it being spent is the individual's existence. Affinities of actions are boundless. Killing a toad causes cows to give bloody milk. A wood makes a man invulnerable, another taken in the body wards off the shot of the enemy. Killing a ladybird causes a storm. A curse lights on the ground on which human blood has been spilt; so a red campion brought into the house means that a death will come quickly.

The association of occult powers between man and animals or vegetals, are almost innumerable. The toad cures scrofula, a frog the thrush; passing under a donkey cures whooping-cough, and a wood-louse fits. A hedgehog is good for epilepsy, a mole for the ague, also a spider; even viper's fat cures its bite; and a slice of the liver of a dog that has caused hydrophobia cures it. So the mysterious powers denoted by the presence of local animals and birds are most voluminous, so is the mystic significance of their cries. The presence of a hare has stopped an army, and the cry of a bird has sent a stalwart man to bed shivering with fear.

Early man looked out for a power to protect him from the many mystic and natural dangers which surrounded him. At first, any strange, uncouth, uncanny object, more especially if first seen under seeming protective conditions, denoted a power to ward off danger, and was secured as a precious charm. In a higher state he depended upon the boylya of the medicine man; after, on the influence of ancestor spirits, angels, and saints; and later on, upon tutelar deities and supreme gods. In a like course he evolved curative and prescient powers, and all the mystic spiritual forces, and not least the power to control man, beast, and all things, by making use of the natural occult powers in days, words, and things.

There are no objects or modes of arranging objects that one seeking an occult protector may not, by him, be endowed with that power. Anything of a strange shape, anything rare, whatever excites curiosity or appeals to the sense of the mysterious, anything from the living, anything associated with death, hint at special powers and dormant attributes. One finds in a stone or root, the claw of a beast or bird, the bone of the dead man or the dead animal, the protecting agent his dubious mind seeks; here it is sought in a herb, a leaf, a fragment of wood, or an object denoting human skill or human intelligence. "Gold," as Jones (*Credulities*, p. 154) writes, " was a powerful amulet; infants and wounds were touched with it to prevent any evil spells affecting them. Both Greeks and Romans employed coral necklaces beads and figures of divinities; they were worn on the person, and hung on the jambs of doors, so that in opening they undo the phallus move and ring the bells attached to it." One who had slain a relation, cut off the finger or toe as a protective charm.

Stones at all times and in all places were deemed to hold protective virtues. In this country we read of flints with holes, elf-stones, adder-stones, toad-stones, mole-stones, snail-stones. The toad-stone was preserved to prevent the burning of a house and the sinking of a boat. A commander who had one of them about him will win the day, or all his men will fairly die on the spot. The raven-tree was good for both man and beast. The sea-nut rendered the owner fortunate and secure, and the possession of some indefinite root promised the attainment of the owner's wishes. Laurel was a preservative from epilepsy, and the sea-nut blackened if evil were meditated against the wearer. (*Dalyell*, p. 130.)

Leland writes: " We find in many forms spread far and wide the belief that garlic possesses the magic power of protection from poison and sorcery. This comes, according to Pliny, from the fact that when it is hung up in the open air for a time it turns black, when it is supposed to attract evil into itself and, consequently, withdraw it from the wearer. The ancients believed that the herb Mercury gave to Ulysses to protect him from the enchantments of Circe

was the *alium nigrum* or garlic. Among the modern
Greeks and Turks garlic is regarded as the most powerful
charm against evil spirits, magic, and misfortune." (*Gipsy
Sorcery*, p. 52.) The rowan-tree was in like manner
esteemed to hold a great protective influence, and in the
olden times twigs of it were laid about the house till they
fell down, to protect the inmates from evil. Twigs of rowan
were placed about the byre to keep off murrain and all
evil. A piece of the Beltaine cake, supposed to hold great
virtue, was, as Pennant tells us, thrown to horses and sheep
to preserve them from disease and death. Even wassail
drinking and may-pole raising were esteemed as protective
agencies.

The worship of the hand amulet as a protector reaches
from Dongola to Ireland, and that of the paw or foot of
animal, bird, or the dead human in one form or other,
seems universal. Here it is the bear's paw, there the foot
of a wild bird, hare, or rabbit; even the claw or nail, or
merely the shoe that has been attached to a horse's hoof,
has in consequence of such association attained mystic
protective powers. Of the hand amulet we read it may be
made of gilded terra-cotta of carved bone, coral, or stone.
Some of the old Egyptian protective hands were clenched,
some open; some had the arm, whilst others had only the
first and second digits defined; many were only of glass.
They are met with in the viscera of mummies. Some pose
as the fingers of Greek and Latin priests giving the bene-
diction. Later on, some were made of bronze. It was
adopted by the Moslems, and hands of blue glass were
suspended about their dwellings, and attached to the
person. Some have a single finger cut from a corpse to
protect from ague. The virtue is greatly enhanced if the
finger is that of a Jew or Christian. The hand entire,
particularly if severed from the body on the gallows, was a
potent talisman. Such a hand made to hold a taper
rendered the light invisible to all but the burglar carrying

it, while it struck powerless any others to whom it was presented. The Etruscans used to carve in bone a right hand, the thumb thrust between the two first fingers, the wrist ending in a phallus. Hands with a crescent moon on the palm protected from the evil-eye. (*Jour. Arch. Assoc.* XXII. p. 294.)

Of the general use of protective charms, we will quote a few descriptions. Hesse-Wartegg writes: "Every Bedouin, man, woman, and child, wears either round the neck or arms, a number of charms, as a porcupine's hand-shaped paw. Even horses and geese have charms hung round the neck attached with cords. Their great fear is the evil-eye, and having tattooed a pretty design, they at once add to it two tiny squares, with a cross above them as a spell to prevent the design from disappearing." (*Tunis*, p. 253.) The same writer adds that "in all the houses there was the impression of an open bleeding hand on every wall of each floor. A Jewess never goes out here without taking with her a hand carved in coral or ivory; she thinks it a talisman against the evil-eye." (*Ibid.* p. 127.)

The old Egyptians had protective talismans, not only for use in this world, but after death. Lenormant writes: "Some of the most important chapters of the *Ritual of the Dead*, when written upon certain objects placed on the mummy, converted them into talismans, which protected the deceased with a sovereign efficacy, during the perils which awaited him in the other world." (*Chaldean Magic*, p. 91.)

The North American Indian's token was but an animal protective charm. Dorman writes: "The medicine-bags were constructed of the skins of animals, ornamented as suited the taste of each person; to it he paid the greatest homage, and to it he looked for safety and protection through life." It was a supernatural guardian on which he depended for the preservation of his life. At his death it was buried with him. That it did not depend on a will in the medicine is seen in the fact, that if a man lost his medicine-bag, he could replace it by capturing one in battle from the enemy; it was simply a protective charm—an amulet.

Schoolcraft, speaking of the American Indians generally, remarks: "Charms for preventing or curing disease, or for protection from necromancy, were the common resort of the Indians. These charms were of various kinds, generally from the animal or mineral kingdom, as bone, horns, claws, skulls, steatites, and other stones. They believed that the possession of certain articles about the person would render the body invulnerable, or that the power to prevail over an enemy was thus secured. A charmed weapon could not be turned aside. The possession of certain articles in the medicine-sack armed the individual with a new power, greatest when the possession of the articles was a secret. Charms might be thrown at a person—the mere gesticulation of the medicine-sack was sufficient." (*Ind. Tribes*, I. p. 86.)

Dorman describes the Eskimo as loading themselves with amulets dangling about their necks and arms. These were bones, bills, and claws of birds, which had a wonderful virtue to protect those who wore them from disease and misfortune. They were very anxious to get a rag or shoe of an European to hang about their children's necks, that they might acquire European skill and ability. For this purpose they requested Europeans to blow upon them. The kayak was often adorned with a dead sparrow or snipe, or the feathers or hair of an animal, to ward off danger. (*Primit. Super.* p. 157.) He also writes: "The natives of Yukon wear bears' claws and teeth, sables' tails, wolves' ears, porcupine quills, ermine skins, beavers' teeth, and the bright green scalps of the mallard as amulets. The Haidahs used small owls and squirrels as amulets. Amulets, made of the tusks of some animal akin to the mastodon, were found in graves in Tennessee. The New Mexicans

8

wore feathers of birds, antelopes' toes, and cranes' bills as charms. The Abipones wore crocodiles' teeth, and believed they would protect them from the bites of serpents." (*Ibid.* p. 158.) The Mexicans thought themselves perfectly safe when their bodies were anointed with an unction composed of scorpions and spiders. (*Ibid.* p. 156.) With the Peruvians, "If a person found anything that was of peculiar colour or figure, it was a canopa; and the bezoar stones were popular canopas—they descended from father to son. Each Peruvian might have as many fetishes as he pleased; they were images of llamas, vicunas, alpacas, huanacas, deer, monkeys, parrots, lizards, &c." (*Ibid.* p. 161.)

Sir George Grey describing the Australian aborigines, writes: "They use the Marramai, a round ball, as a talisman against sickness, and it is sent from tribe to tribe hundreds of miles. It is a quartz substance wrapped up in opossum fur and woollen cord. They swallow small crystalline particles which crumble off, as a preventative of sickness. Another stone appeared to be an agate, a third was a species of cornelian wrapped up with a fragment of chalcedony, and a fragment of crystal of white quartz." (*Jour. of Discov.* II. p. 342.) Of other protective charms used by the aborigines Smyth, in his *Aborigines of Victoria*, writes: "They seem to have had a belief in the efficacy of charms. One anxiety with them was to possess a bone from the skull or arms of their deceased relatives, which, sewed up in a piece of skin, they wear round their necks confessedly as a charm against sickness and premature death. The bones were worn by people in health, and they lent them to others of their own tribe when ill, who wear them as charms round the neck." (II. p. 398.)

There are many charms used to protect animals. Thus, to protect a horse put nine-fold grass and hairs from his mane and tail into a hole in the tent with earth scraped from his left fore-foot; in another, a hog-stone with a hole in it tied to the key of stable-door to protect the horses therein.

Again, a cow's abortion buried in the gateway of a close that other cows passing over may not cast their calves.

Anything may become a charm and be used as an amulet. Leland says: " All through many hands even in the heart of Africa the Maria Theresa silver dollar is held in high estimation for magical purposes. From one to another the notion has been transferred." (*Gipsy Sorcery*, p. 233.)

The Moslems have amulets to protect horses and mules, fruit-trees from being blighted, plagues of flies, the croaking of frogs, many of which are verses from the Koran. In Russia, oikons of saints are protective; in Spain, relics, medals of the Virgin, the cross of Caravaca, the holy countenance, and rosaries. For the same purpose the Chinese have various mystic charms with words and figures; and the Siamese depend on the supernal attributes ascribed to gold and silver beads and cords blessed by the bonzes. Amulets of various kinds are esteemed as protective by the Japanese, as inscriptions and figures, impressions of a black hand, sacred spoons, garlic and herbs.

Primitive man not only needed supernal protection; he was exposed to so many diseases and accidents, whose origin he could not account for, many of which seemed due to the mystic powers he recognized in things, that he readily ascribed to counter forces supernal powers of healing, or that which caused the ill in like manner by some mystic change became the minister to health. Thus, tertian fever was relieved by a root of nettle, the head or heart of a viper, a burn by exposure to fire; hydrophobia was cured by a slice of the liver of the dog by which the person was bitten. The skin of a snake, a portion of a viper, or the rattle of the rattlesnake, were esteemed as cures for their respective bites.

In a large number of cases the cure is ascribed to some sympathetic action attached to the remedy. It may be colour, as when wine is used to cure jaundice; or its form as a mandrake, a remedy for a man. It may be due to local association, as an otter's bladder a cure for gravel; and in the United States snake-root was a remedy for the bite of a rattlesnake. Heart-disease was to be cured by a piece of lead in the shape of a heart; erysipelas by a piece of scarlet cloth, or the herb Robert. Some remedies were crudely symbolic, others due to suppositions, animal affinities, assumed powers in words and actions, or some natural preservative virtue in the object, as in arsenic, salt, in wells, in wheat, &c.; but by far the most numerous were those to which, by fetish combination or the adscription of fetish powers, curative virtues were affirmed.

Mystic curative powers were attached to animals and parts of animals, these from the constant observation of by savage men, and the using of them for food, would easily suggest associative influences. Our own folklore shows how much power of various curative kinds were attached to moles, mice, otters, bears' grease, goose grease, fish brine, fur and hair of rabbits, hares, cats and dogs, feet of moles, mice and hares, soup of dried snakes, a live frog in a chimney corner, swallowing preparations of moles and mice, spiders, and wood-lice. So in like manner various other animal cures were presumed to be effective. In one a snake was drawn along a swollen neck, then bottled and buried, and as the snake died so it was presumed the swelling would perish. There were many often very disgusting cures to be effected by worms, toads, and spiders; and beetles and hairy caterpillars were worn as charms. The fathers of the old races of men found virtues in anything that was once animate—gall and blood, urine, spittle, the ordure of animals, or any part like the feet, claws, teeth, and paws, that had been most expressive of their passions; even the brains of a rabbit cured a fractious child, and spiders put in nuts, then wrapped in silk, were supposed to cure the ague. Good old Elias

Ashmole said he took a dose of elixir and hung three spiders about his neck—"which, by the grace of God, drove my ague away"—but whether the holy exorcizing virtue was the elixir or the spiders, or the fetish combination of both, he fails to expound. Still more difficult would it be to unravel the true anodyne Pope Adrian wore, which we are told by Smedley consisted of a sun-baked toad, arsenic, tormentil, pearl, coral, hyacinth, emerald, and tragacanth. (*Occult Sci.* p. 347.)

As with animal, so with the mystic virtues in herbs, many of these may have had their virtues discovered by preglacial man, and our rustics have inherited them through untold ages. To this class belong the curative powers in the rowan-tree, the aspen, the elder, and mistletoe; not a wild herb the eating of which had mysteriously excited or affected him, but contained some fetish power. Virtues of this character were ascribed to the poppy, the monkshood, the marigold, wormswood, sage, mint, galbanum, and so forth. Of the special powers thus esteemed to be present in animal or vegetal substances, Cockayne, in his *Leechdoms*, gives us many an insight. Thus pæony was more marvellous in its many virtues than Holloway's pills. It not only cured most diseases, blear eyes, spasms, rheumatism, and sterility, but it laid ghosts and nightmares, cured family discord and indifference to wives, barking of dogs, hydrophobia, and effeminacy; all that was required to obtain these many virtues was to pluck it when the moon was in Gemini. Special virtues were held in special parts. One swallowing a mole's heart, fresh and palpitating, would become an expert in divination. A crazy fellow would recover his senses if sprinkled with a mole's blood. Democritos described a root which, wrought into pills and swallowed in wine, would make the guilty confess; but we have never heard of this being applied under the eye of judge and jury. Curing tertian fever with the root of a nettle seems to anticipate the great law of Homœopathy, and there is a touch of cannibalism in some, as Xenocrates wrote of the good effects obtained by eating human brains, flesh or blood, or drink infused with burnt or unburnt human bones and blood. Surely the old Pelasgians were antediluvian New Zealanders. The amulets recommended by Alexander of Tralles, carry us back to the great stone age, and European man a wild savage among savage animals. One of his remedies consists of the dung of a wolf and bits of bone, another is the sinews from a vulture's leg, another was the astragali of a hare taken off the living animal and only of virtue if the animal lives, another was the bone cut from the heart of a living stag. These old medicine-men must have been experimental vivisectionists, for Marcellus, as late as A.D. 380, recommends as a cure for eye disease, catch a fox alive cut his tongue out, let him go, dry the tongue, tie it up in red rag, and hang it round the sick man's neck.

Of most of our old folklore charms, owing to their universal character and common-place asseverations, it would be difficult to trace the origin; many indicate neither time nor place, and are as new and efficient in our modern civilization as in the old savagedom; others on the contrary have the imprint of their status and local origin in the material or the philosophy of the charm. Cockayne affirms, "Some of the prevailing superstitions must have come from the Magi, for we find them ordering the modern feverfew (*pyrethrum parthenium*) to be pulled from the ground with the left hand, and the herbalist must not look behind him. Pliny says the Magi had many foolish tales about the sea-holly, and they ordered the pseudo anchusa to be gathered with the left hand, the name of the one who was to profit by it being uttered. They were the authors of the search for red and white stones in the brood nestlings of swallows." We may affirm somewhat the age of some charms by the materials used in them or the modes

in which they are applied. When we are told to stop
inflammation by a clean sheet of paper having a written
charm on it, we know that this must date after the
invention of paper. So when we are bid to write or mark
a figure on a thin plate of gold with a needle of copper, we
may presume the charm dates after the arts of working in
copper and gold were known and before the metallurgy of
iron and steel. So the use of unwrought flax refers to the
period when it was, at least, used for thread, if not for
linen.

We have seen that some spells must date from the period
when men were cannibals and criticised the choice parts of
the "human pig." Most probably of the wild-animal
charms date from the time when man was a hunter and
had to prey on all kinds of animal produce. Among the
remedies recorded by Sextus Placitus we have boar's
bladder and brains, wolf's back, the right eye of a wolf,
its head, its flesh, its spoor, its marrow, and milk. So of
hounds we have as cure-charms its milt, suet, milk, tongue,
shank, and dung. Of harts, the marrow, horn, shank,
cheek and shorn; and of bulls, the horns, blood, gall,
marrow, and dung. The last might refer to wild cattle or
tame, but when we read of barleycorns and ears of wheat
as charms we know that when they were enounced man had
become a cultivator of the earth. One charm carries us
back to the time when, like the Bushman and the
Eskimo, the prehistoric man tore open his victim, and
plunging his head in the still palpitating carcase, gluttonised
on the ebbing blood. "If a man drink a creeping thing
in water, let him cut instantly into a sheep and drink the
sheep's blood hot." (*Leechdom*, II. p. 115.)

The old nature-worship still lingers in innumerable
forms of charms and ceremonies attached to animal and
herb spells, or mystic customs. There it is a well endowed
with an occult virtue to cure a special complaint only, it
may be insanity, skin disease, ague, or the complaints of
women; it may be something taken in the moon's increase

or waning, or the full moon, or kneeling with the bare knees on an earthfast stone. A very early form of water-worship may be recognized in the charm for a woman who cannot rear her child : she was to take milk from a cow of one colour in her hand, sup it in her mouth, then go to a running stream, spew the milk therein, and after this offering, with the same hand she was to ladle up a mouthful of water, saying a word-charm. (*Ibid.* III. p. 69.)

In some cases we have strange mixtures of the old forms and customs of Paganism and Christian rites and usances. The moon-worship blended with that of the Virgin, Pagan charms drunk out of a church-bell, and masses sung over a wort concocted of a solution of herbs, animal ordure, or brains. Runes were crossed with Alpha and Omega, or T for Trinity made doubly potent a Norse-word charm. Many of the rites and ceremonies are mimicked in charm forms. We read of holy water being sprinkled to cure a sick pig ; a young man being cured of fits by being taken to church at midnight, when he was to take a handful of earth from the newest grave. With some, if a man, to be effective it must come off a woman's grave, and if a woman, from a man's grave. Confirmation is with some esteemed a cure for rheumatism, and some have sought the remedy a second time from the bishop's hands for after complaints. So rings consecrated on Good Friday cured cramp, and fretfulness in children was cured by baptism, and there were many forms of cure by making crosses or repeating incantations to Christ, the Virgin, or the Trinity, and there were curative virtues in repeating Ave Marias, Paternosters, and the Creed. We might quote the cases of occult virtue in sacramental money or bread or wine.

As associated with the church, we may note the many charms that are made from skull, bones, or grass from a churchyard, and to get a dead hand from a grave one possesses a most potent charm. We read in the *Journal of American Folklore* : "In Washington, the graves of paupers are not infrequently violated for the purpose of obtaining a hand or arm. Detached portions of the dead hand are quite commonly used for some lucky influence they bring " (I. p. 83).

In the evolution of charms into principles of supernal power omens served as the stepping-stones to prophecies. To see a sign readily led to affirming as a fact the advent of the change. This occurs every day now, not only in weather-lore, but in forms of sickness. In fact, the impression, the portent, the monition, the omen, and the prophecy, glide imperceptibly into each other. Often what we wish we affirm that we see, and the man or beast fore-spoken is already foredoomed. We have seen that the tendency to prophesy may be organic naturally with regard to the weather and general appearances; it is instinctive, assuming the character of our feelings and impulses, more especially under certain mental states or influences. Hence the inspirations of ecstatics, the weird prophecies induced by toxics, and the mental conversion of occult dreams into the present realizations of the mysteries of the future.

All and every form in which the future is rehearsed in the present, perceptibly or mentally, is by men accepted as a supernal intimation, and which may not only come as an occult intimation from the object itself, but may be divined through the occult powers possessed by men. Thus divination in its many forms are parts of the same chain of causes and effects we have recognized in premonitions and prophecies, and alike imply the vast influence that supernal sentiments have evolved in the human mind.

Many assumed forms of prophecy only intimate the scientific explanation of the necessary associations and timal changes in things, whether denoting atmospheric influences, the motions of the heavenly bodies, the course of disease, or alterations by growth. The distinction in this respect between the philosopher and the savage, is one of education rather than principle: the one sees objects and events present to his perceptive powers through the medium of his emotions, feelings, and previous imaginings; the other tests such presentations by the known laws of their formation, and the connection therewith deduced by his judgment; hence the change which the one affirms as the natural sequence of organic relations the other recognizes as a manifestation of occult power, and the range of these deductions marks the progress of man, and the decline of the belief in supernals whether in the form of divination or prophecy.

There is much in weather prognostics as true to the savage as to the scientific man. Like conditions always resolve into like results. Hence, the halo round the moon indicated coming rain to the savage in the past and present as well as to the observant farmer. Both might equally note the toad coming out to look for the rain, and the bees going home to avoid it; but their deductions from these special habits differed essentially. What one recognized as instinct, may-be acquired knowledge, was seen by the other to present the influence of an occult power working on the toad and the bee. That the presence of such powers should endow rooks and various beasts and birds .with prophetic powers or the capacity to divine the future, and present such an interpretation as an omen to men readily occurred to the one, while the other only read their various volitions as their natural movements under certain atmospheric conditions. There were many natural appearances incipient science could not explain. Need we wonder, then, that savage man when he had evolved the ghost-spirit saw in the supernal personalities, thereby educed, a ready explanation of cloud-forms, eclipses, and thunder-forces? Nothing was more easy than for the spirit-power which rode on the dust-column, hurled the lightning, or vainly devoured the moon, to intimate the courses it intended to manifest in the clouds or through the monitions of birds and beasts.

Of prescient powers in or possessed by animals we have

many intimations. Some, no doubt, are spirit manifestations, or deemed such, as when dogs are said to see ghosts, and cocks to see evil spirits; even the pig to see the wind; but the crowing of a hen or the howling of a dog before a death, no more indicates spirit influence than does the production of hens if the eggs are set when the tide was ebbing, or cocks at a rising tide. We are all familiar with the knowingness of a dog, but we can scarcely admit that he eats grass to tell us that it is going to rain. Still less can we ascribe to a ghost the assumed power in an egg if broken on the edge of a glass, holding a little water to indicate by the flowing of the albumen the prognostics of the diviner's future life. We can conceive of such invisible ghost-forms as Juno and Minerva in the Iliad warding off the weapons of assailants from their mortal friends, but we cannot see a present spirit-power in the position the point of the sickle takes when the reaper divines by it after throwing it over his left shoulder. Surely we need not ascribe to a spirit the prophecy that a child born feet first would live to be hanged, or that a ghost has anything to do with divination by cups drawing lots the direction a crumb of bread falls, or that in which a thrown staff lies. The occult sentiment present in any of these contingencies exists only in the operator's mind. What has a ghost to do with the protective or prescient powers in garlic, in stones, in an iron nail or horse-shoe; where is the ghost presence in a sign, a mark, a look, in the blood from the tail of a black cat, or in the charm concocted of many ingredients?

We may trace in some cases the history of the evolution of charms; and from these we feel assured that the oldest, the most numerous, and those asserted over the largest area are wholly impersonal objects, times, or seasons which appealed to the occult sentiment of the canny or uncanny in the human mind. The child sees the canny and the uncanny long before it personifies objects, and speaks to

the sun and animals and toys as if they were endowed
with the same faculties as itself; so it is with the savage;
and there is no concept of ghost present to his mind when
he endows the sun, moon, and stars, the dog, cat, bird, and
plant, with the same powers that he recognizes in himself
and fellows.   The folklore animal, or sun, river, or moun-
tain-fable, long antedate any mystic tale that assigns to
them spirit attributes. Here is one illustration of the
evolution of the ghost theory from the nature personality.
Pettigrew in his *Medical Superstitions* writes: "Melton
says the saints of the Romanists have usurped the place of
the zodiacal constellations in the governance of the parts of
a man's body. Thus, St. Ohlia keeps the head instead of
Aries; St. Blasius governs the neck instead of Taurus;
St. Lawrence keeps the back and shoulders instead of
Gemini, Cancer, and Leo. St. Erasmus rules the belly
in place of Libra and Scorpius " (p. 86). In like manner
every known disease controlled by a spell or nature-power
was taken under the curative charge of some saint, and the
virtues once possessed by a holystone, a topaz, or heliotrope,
a snake, or toad-stone, were dispensed by a saint. The
spirit may even take the form of the snake, toad, or other
animal that personified the healing-well or stone of power.
Thus at the holywell near Carrick-on-Suir, the trout no
doubt were the original potent agents, as only when they
were present did the waters hold the healing virtue; now
it is the holy saints Quan and Brogwan who become little
fishes to give the waters their virtue. (*Ibid.* p. 40.)

In tracing the output of charms and spells we note that
they are universal among men in the present as in the past,
and that faith in their protective agencies preceded the
differentiation of spirit sentiments; we are assured all the
old great religions of the world are founded on spells and
charms, and cognate supernal ideas. We can trace these
curative, protective, and prescient powers as well as all the
supersensuous powers as applied at first as impersonal

influences, and subsequently associated with the after
evolved ghosts, spirits, and gods. We detect in all the
fetish nature rites and ceremonies, in the sacrifices, in
the forms of adoration, in the customary dances, tabus of
food and concepts of pollution and purification, the presence of the early sentiments regarding charms and spells.
The conception of supernal impersonal induced disease is
present in the earliest and lowest human associations, and
as impersonal powers to injure they are blended in all the
old faiths with the spirit-induced disease, and that even
may be cast off by impersonal spells. All phallic worship
in its incidence represents charms and spells; so with the
customary relations of the sexes, and the organic changes
they present.

The sacred books of Iran, the sacred books of India,
teem with evidences that tell us they were preceded by a
religion of charms, spells, and impersonal fetish concepts.
The powers exhibited by the earliest priests and Brahmans
all affect the low supernal attributes of the modern medicine-
man in his lowest fetish character. Fear of the uncanny,
dread of pollution of a material nature, the enforcement of
charm purifications, and bodily and food tabus are general
as now with savage races. In the Gatha's, the Zendavesta,
and the Bundahis, we have many direct and more indirect
affirmations of their conceptions of mysterious powers and
principles; even in the modern customs and mental expressions of the Parsees we have as it were the fossilized
records of primary thoughts, the then highest supernal
aspirations of the Iranian soul.

Before the spirit sentiment was evolved, the various
impersonal powers and fetish concepts were evolved—the
doctrines of spells, charms, and divination. These must
have become of a very defined nature or we should not
have had them combined with the after evolved spirit-idea,
and these impersonal sentiments prominently characterize
modern Parsee faith. The rolls of buresma rods used in

their rites and ceremonies, and formerly invoked in their wars with the Turanian savage Danus, were not spirit-powers, but impersonal spell-powers, so were all the fetish concepts of pollution from women, from dead bodies and dead dogs. The powers of purification presented are charms, not spiritual cleansings. As spell-compounds the Visparad refers to the preparation of sacred waters, the consecration of certain offerings by fetish spells as the sacred bread, the branches of homa, the branch of the pomegranate endowed with mystic powers, the Parahoma, fruits, butter, hair, fresh milk, and flesh, which by being carried round the fire as a spell become endowed with supernal attributes. The fetish sacred formout Homa, long before it became a god spirit, was only a mystic impersonal spell. At first it was repudiated by the semi-moral Zerdushta, as we read in the Gathas, the fathers of the families could not but repudiate the excesses it produced; but when the spirit Homa appeared to Zerdushta in a dream, he accepted it as a source of material as well as supernal influence. Then he praised it in its branches, its juice, the clouds and rain that made it grow, the mountain which formed its body, and the earth that bore it. Fire, too, before it became a god, was an impersonal fetish power. It had five spell-attributes: one, that of burning; another as the good diffuser, which enters into men and aids digestion; that of the Aurvazist, which gives growth and special power to plants; and that of the Vazist, which produces motion and form in the clouds. It was by a mighty spell that the primary Medicine Archangel Ameродad produced the many species of plants. He pounded the small plants then on the earth together in a mortar, mixed them with water, after which Tistar, the great star, poured them as rain on the earth, on which plants sprang up as thick as the hair on a man's head. One of the most singular fetish spell-powers described in the Vendidad is that affirmed to be contained in the parings of the nails of the fingers and the toes, the hairs that cling in the comb or in the lather after shaving, to allow them to come within twenty paces of a fire, thirty of water, or fifty from consecrated bundles of barosma, was a grievous charm. "Look here, O Ashozusta bird, here are the nails for thee; may they be for thee so many spears, knives, bones, falcon-winged arrows and sling-stones against the Mazainya Daevas." (*Sac. Books East*, IV. p. 188.)

There are contained in the Vendidad and in several of the yasts many references to the primary faith in charms and spells. It would appear that in Iran all evil influences on the output of the spirit-sentiment were gradually transferred to the then conceived evil spirit, the fiend Drugs. Yet not only are there texts, which are spells to coerce these spirit-powers, but we also have spell-forms of the most primitive type, both curative and protective, in which no concept of spirit-influence is presented, and others in which the power of the medicine-man is presented to work the charm and the counter-charm through the attainment of supernal power of an advanced character, acquired by unremitting fetish austerities. The whole of the sacred writings of Iran are permeated by the fear of uncanny impersonal dreads, and the appeal to spells to withstand them. Disease, death, and pollution are always treated as spells; they are counteracted, influenced, or expelled by charms. In some instances we have spells enacted as crude as any now presented by savage races, and mystic fetish impersonal objects are as powerful as the after developed spirits and gods. In the Bahram Yast we read, " If I have a curse thrown upon me, a spell told upon me, by the many men who hate me, what is the remedy for it ? " Ahura Mazda answered, " Take thou a feather of that bird with feathers, the Varengnan (raven). With that feather thou shalt rub thy own body ; with that feather thou shalt curse back thine enemies. If a man holds a bone of that strong bird, or a feather of that strong bird, no one can smite or turn to flight that fortunate man. The feather of that bird of flight brings him help." (*Sac. Books of the East*, XXIII. p. 241.) James Darmesteter shows, in the accompanying note, that a similar spell is recorded in the Shah Namah. When Rudabah's flank was opened to bring forth Rustem, her wound was healed by rubbing it with a Simurgh's feather. Rustem, also wounded to death, is cured by the same charm feather.

Among all savage and semi-savage races all the changes in a woman's secretions, all the incidences of childbirth, are esteemed as denoting the power of spells; she and the child are ever considered as under the influence of fetish impersonal spells which have to be counteracted by purifying charms. Spells and charms for this purpose are so highly esteemed in the Zendavesta that we find them repeated twice in the Vendidad (*Ibid.* IV. pp. 226 and 227), and in the Vistasp Yast (*Ibid.* XXIII. p. 341). "Thou shalt keep away the evil by this holy spell. Of thee, O child, I will cleanse the birth and growth; of thee, O woman, I will make the body and strength pure. I make thee a woman rich in children and rich in milk, a woman rich in seed, in milk, and in offspring. For thee I shall make springs run and flow towards the pastures that will give food to the child." The commentator, James Darmesteter, writes that the spell refers to the cleansing and generative powers of the waters. The spell was probably pronounced to facilitate childbirth. Of another spell it is said, "Let not that spell be shown to anyone except by the father to his son, or by the brother to his brother from the same womb, or by Athravan to his pupil in black hair." (*Ibid.* XXIII. p. 51.)

The Ardibehist Yast terms the invocation or prayer to Airyaman as, "It is the greatest of spells, it is the best of spells, the fairest of spells, the fearful one amongst spells, the firmest of spells, the victorious amongst spells, the best healing of all spells." (*Ibid.* XXIII. p. 44.) Another general reference to spells:—"Ahura Mazda answered, It is

when a man pronouncing my spell, either reading or reciting
it by heart, draws the furrows and hides there himself."
(*Ibid.* XXIII. p. 50.) There are various other references
to the power of spells in the Zendavesta.

There are many illustrations of spell sentiments in the
Laws of Manu. Burnt oblations during the mother's
pregnancy, the ceremony after birth, the tonsure, and the
tying of the sacred girdle of munga grass, are all forms of
spells. (*Sac. Books of the East*, XXV. p. 34.) So also is
the naming of the child on a lucky lunar day, in a lucky
muhurta, under an auspicious constellation. (*Ibid.* XXV. p.
35.) Another form of spell is, "having taken a staff, having
worshipped the sun and walked round the fire turning his
right hand towards it." (*Ibid.* XXV. p. 38.) Again, "his
meal will procure long life if he eats facing the east, fame if
he eats facing the south, prosperity if he turns to the west,
truthfulness if he faces the north." The following are
charm forms:—"Let a Brahman always sip water out of
the part of the hand sacred to Brahman, or out of that
sacred to Ka, or out of that sacred to the gods, never out
of that sacred to the manes." (*Ibid.* XXV. p. 40.) And
in "seated on Kusa with their points to the east, purified by
blades of grass, and sanctified by three suppressions of the
breath, he is worthy to pronounce the syllable Om." (*Ibid.*
XXV. p. 44.) The syllable Om itself is a spell, so is the
daily reading of the Veda according to rule, which, among
other charm-powers, will "ever cause sweet and sour milk,
clarified butter, and honey to flow." (*Ibid.* XXV. p. 49.)
All the early religious ordinances were spell forms. Thus
"an oblation duly thrown into the fire reaches the sun,
from the sun comes rain, from rain food." (XXV. p. 89.)
In this there is no expression of a personality. In the
following we have offerings to the early ghosts as well as
to impersonals. "Let him throw Bali offerings in all
directions of the compass, proceeding from the east to the
south, saying adoration to the Maruts, adoration to the

waters, adoration to the trees. At the head of the bed he shall offer to fortune (luck), at the foot to Bhadrakali, then he is to throw up into the air a Bali for all the gods and goblins; all that remains is to be thrown to the cranes." (XXV. p. 91.) Diseases are the result of fetish evil, so the stealer of a lamp will become blind, the stealer of clothes will have white leprosy, a horse-stealer become lame, and an informer will have a foul-smelling nose. (*Ibid.* XXV. p. 440.) Here is a spell that might be matched in any rustic village. "A student who has broken his vow shall offer at night, at a cross-way, to Nirriti a one-eyed ass." (*Ibid.* XXV. p. 454.) In another he is to go begging to seven houses, dressed in the hide of a sacrificed ass. (XXV. p. 455.) Even at that early period cross-ways were places for powerful spells to be performed, and the fetish virtue is enhanced if the material of the spell is obtained from many sources. As a sample of the many modes by means of which fetish pollutions may be removed, we quote the following:—"By muttering with a consecrated mind the Savitri three thousand times, dwelling for a month in a cow-house, and subsisting on milk, a man is freed from the guilt of accepting presents from a wicked man." (*Ibid.* XXV. p. 470.)

We may note that sacred stones were common in Upper Assyria and in India, but none are specified in the Vendidad; so, in like manner, animal totems are not commonly referred to. The early division of the animal world into pure and impure, clean and unclean, are indications of totemism. So the ten incarnations of Verethraghna in the Bahram Yast are totem incarnations.

We have seen that man, under the inspiration of the doctrine of charms, had evolved and defined a vast series of virtues, in things curative, protective, and prescient; more, all that we know or conceive of the transcendental had their origin in this stage. Nothing is more common in the principle of charms than to transfer an attribute, a power or principle, good or bad, through some form or virtue; in stone, or leaf, or combination of objects, the present state of the attribute is withdrawn, and it is cast definitely on some other person, animal, or thing, or left, in the chance medley of the earth's waste products to be consciously or unconsciously appropriated by some other object. Out of this capacity of transference was evolved the doctrine of transformation if one attribute could be cast off and assumed by other than its original possessor so could all attributes. Hence the doctrine of transformation became a power, and all kinds of charms had power to transform sun, moon and stars into men or animals and birds, and other animals into other animal forms, stones, stumps, waters, anything and everything. In all these animal transformations so prevalent in myth and fable, there is no presence of a ghost, no spirit is yet eliminated. It is only in the after tales conceived under a new inspiration that men portray the ghostly powers of change. The real old-world literature knows no ghost.

We have defined the transcendental powers as the elimitation of time and space, the capacity to become invulnerable and invisible, the permeability of substance, supersensuous powers—that of thought transmission, and these more or less combined under ecstatic forms. All these states of being are induced by charms; many we have already expressed, and the reader will recognize most of them in common charms. These make invulnerable and invisible like the quartz stone; they can permeate the body of the Australian aborigine, and, in the form of toxics, induce supersensuous states and powers.

CHAPTER IV.

The Differentiation of the Medicine-man.

It seems a necessary consequence of the diverse range of the individual faculties in men that they should differentiate in diverse directions, and as their various powers became more fully evolved and their results accumulated, each successive series of manifestations became specialized. It was so when individuals first came to recognise the uncanny; it was so when the individual reduced them to special forms of manifestation; and it is so in the stage we have now to consider, in which, owing to the many supernal presentations and the wide results deduced from their influences, general man remits to a special class of visionaries the consideration of the forms and control of the various supernal manifestations. First, we were aware of faith in the unknown, then of faith in the seeming; now we have the birth of faith in men devoted to occult ideas and sentiments. These men very early stand out in every community among every isolated group, and they all affirm that not only are there supernal virtues in things, but that they, as men, are endowed with supernal attributes. Ordinary men look with awe on the medicine-man, the shaman, the wizard, the priest; they are not as other men; they may not, like the Pope, hold the keys of heaven, but they hold the keys of the human soul and thereby lead them as they list.

Before describing the modes by which such power is manifest, we have to consider its nature and origin and enunciate the forms it assumes among various races of men. We are not aware that the subject in its fulness of character has ever been considered; local and isolated magical and spiritual claims have been described and explained, but the common nature of the supernal influence or accepted influence has never been presented. Yet it follows, as we have seen, that powers one man affirms others may affirm, and the supernal presentations one now recognizes may, under other forms, be the common attribute of a like class of men in far distant communities.

That some men claim the possession of supernal powers that other men know nothing of, is a common assertion. We have it in various forms in every advanced community, and there are few but come across individuals who assert such pretensions. Among some races these mental characteristics are accounted for by the presence of a distinct supernal power—a personal virtue may-be—that enters and influences the minds of those who have in various occult ways been prepared for such presentations. Even with so low a race of men as the Australian aborigines, the medicine-men have generally ascribed to them the possession of a special power to read, manifest and control all occult things and occult influences. This power is known as boylya, and a man may become possessed of it by means of the many ascetic observances that in other countries produce like neurotic conditions, and the sentiments thus induced in all cases raise in the mind pretensions of magic powers and the capacity to influence whatever supernal conditions that have been evolved amongst them. Among the Australians some believed that a man became a wizard by meeting with Ngotje, who put quartz crystals in him; since then such an one can pull things out of himself and others. Some were instructed by the ghosts which took them up into the sky. One said, "My father is Yibai—

the Iguana. When I was quite a small boy he took me from the camp into the bush to train me. He placed two large quartz crystals on my breast, and they vanished into me. I felt them going through me like water. After that I used to see things mother could not see: these were ghosts. After the initiation rite when the tooth was out, my father said, 'Come with me,' and I followed him into a hole leading into a grave where there were some dead men, who rubbed me over to make me clever and gave me crystals. Then when I came out a tiger-snake was pointed out as my *Budjan*. Then my father as well as myself got astride two threads and went through the clouds." Another said, "I had some dreams of my father. He and the other men with him made me a cord of sinews, swung me about on it, and carried me over the sea. Then my father tied something over my eyes and led me into the rock, and I was in a place bright as day. After I was taught to make things go into my legs and pull them out, and to throw them at people." One man became a biraak by having dreamed three times he was a kangaroo; after that he heard the ghosts speaking. The wizards were supposed to have the power of throwing men into a magical state by pointing at them with the yertoug. They are believed to walk invisible, to turn themselves at will into animals, stumps or logs of trees, or go into the ground out of sight. They could draw the victims to them by the magic of their enchantments. They could make rain, raise storms, by squirting water out of the mouth in the direction the rain comes and shouting. They could heal by sucking the stone out of the patient's body, and by charms. They claimed the power of being carried up into the sky. All these capacities arose from the mystic boylya power that they had obtained. (*Jour. Anth. Inst.* XVI. pp. 30-51.)

This same mysterious power, though with them nameless, is claimed by the Andaman Okopaids, and the Peaimen of Guiana. In Melanesia, where the claim to it as an acquired occult power is general, it is known as Mana. This supernatural power exists in stones; snakes and owls possess it, and men acquire it; and they can even transmit the power from one stone to many. If a man dives to the bottom of a pool and sees nothing strange; to sit for an instant at the bottom will give him mana—supernatural power. (*Jour. Anth. Inst.* X. p. 277.) This supernatural power may be manifested through the Tamatetiqa ghost shooter. This was a bit of hollow bamboo in which a bone, leaves with whatever else would have mana for such a purpose was enclosed. Fasting on the part of the person using these charms added much to their efficacy; when he lifted his thumb the magic power shot out and whoever it hit would die. Cannibalism imparted mana. (*Ibid.* X. p. 284.) In order to obtain mana, boys and young men will spend months in some canoe-house, separate, where they sacrifice, or some one who has mana does so for them. This mana is neither a person or thing, but a power which may be in a person or thing; in the islands further west the Florida people suppose a stronger mana to prevail than among themselves. Heads are preserved in chiefs' houses as they give mana to it, even reflecting mana on the dead chief in whose honour they were obtained. They also give mana to his successor by his holding possession of them. A new war canoe is not invested with due mana until some man has been killed by those on board her. (*Ibid.* X. pp. 303-314.)

This mana was imparted by the medicine-man to the charms he made use of, and like the old sympathetic mana that Sir Kenelm Digby loved to discourse upon, it caused a mystic influence to exist between a weapon and the wound it had caused. Thus, when a man was shot by a poisoned arrow the possession of the arrow-head went far to influence the result. If the shooter regained it he put it in the fire; if the wounded man retained it he put it in

water, and the inflammation was violent or slight accordingly.   (*Ibid.* X. p. 314.)

   The North American Indians recognize this mysterious
power, this boylya or mana, in the word wakan.   Schoolcraft says, " This word signifies things generally which a
Dakotah Indian cannot understand; whatever is wonderful,
superhuman, or supernatural, is wakan.   Of their gods,
some are wakan to a greater, others to a less degree; some
for one purpose, some for another; but wakan expresses
the chief quality of them all.   Medicine-men pass through
a succession of inspirations till they are fully wakanized;
they are invested with the invisible wakan powers of the
gods—their knowledge and cunning, their influence over
mind, instinct, and passion, to inflict and heal diseases,
discover concealed causes, and impart the power of the
gods." (*Indian Tribes*, IV. p. 646.)

   To explain the origin of this mysterious wakan power,
Schoolcraft writes :—" The blind savage finds himself in a
world of mysteries oppressed with a consciousness that he
comprehends nothing.   The earth on which he treads teems
with life incomprehensible.   It is without doubt wakan.
In the springs which never cease to flow, and yet are
always full, he recognizes the breathing places of the gods.
When he raises his eyes to the heavens he is overwhelmed
with mysteries, for the sun, moon, and star are so many
gods and goddesses gazing upon him.   The beast which he
pursues to-day shuns him with the ability of an intelligent
being, and to-morrow seems to be deprived of all power to
escape from him.   He beholds one man seized with a
violent disease and in a few hours expire in agony, while
another almost imperceptibly wastes away through long
years and then dies.   He finds himself a creature of a
thousand wants which he knows not how to supply, and
exposed to innumerable evils which he cannot avoid; all
these, and a thousand of other things like these, to the

Indian are tangible facts, and under their influence his
character is formed. He hails with joy one who claims to
comprehend these mysteries. The wakan men and women
to establish their claims cunningly lay hold of all that is
strange, and turn to their own advantage every mysterious
occurrence. At times they appear to raise the storm or
command the tempest."

A power more or less akin to the boylya or wakan,
though often nameless, is recognized by all races of men.
Here it is obtained by charms and spells, there by many
ritual observances; now it comes by the laying on of
hands, breathing over the face, or by mesmeric passes.
Some obtain it by spells that command spirit appearances,
others by fetish ceremonies, magic, and incantations. It
is often earnestly sought as the reward of great austerities;
penance can command it, or as a divine influx it comes in
inspiration. It may come in cloven tongues of flame, or
descend like a dove on the devotee. We have no name
for this mystery of mysteries fuller than that of glamour,
which rather expresses the effect on the mind of the trans-
cendentalist than the nature of the power he is supposed
to obtain. But ever the man so recognized is in his own
and others' estimation separated from his fellows, capable
of knowing and doing all things, not only of controlling
the nature and virtues in things, but the relations of all
living things. The qualities they are assumed to hold
they can endow others with, and they ever maintain
intimate and special relations with ghosts and spirits and
all the exuberant creations in spiritual idealisms. All
the transcendental powers attached to material forms and
principles they transfer to the ghosts and spirits they
embody, and as they advance in the conscious knowledge
of nature and in higher human relations, they endow their
mystic mind-creations with corresponding attributes until
the poor abused ghost advances to be the master spirit in
heaven.

The many phases in which this wakan power is present among the various races of men wo will now illustrate. Of the Shamans of the Salish wo are told that they "are able to see ghosts, their touch causes sickness, they make violators of the tabu mad—their touch paralyzes men. They know who is going to die, and approach the villages in the evening to take the souls of the dying away. They drive away the ghosts by making a noise and burning the incense herb. They have a spell language handed down from one to another; they used it to endow men or parts of the body or weapons with special power. He becomes a shaman by intercourse with supernal powers, sleeping in the woods until he dreams of his guardian spirit who bestows supernal power upon him. He cures the sick, blowing water over him, and applying his mouth sucks the diseased place, then produces a piece of deer-skin or the like sucked from the body, the cause of the illness. He causes sickness by throwing a. piece of deer-skin or the loop of a thong, or he obtains the man's saliva or hair and causes sickness; he can harm one by looking at him." (*Report Brit. Assoc.* 1890, p. 582.)

We recognize the assumption of this wakan power among the Kaffirs, not only in the smelling out of a witch causing and controlling disease, making rain, and in various ways defining the action of the nature forces, but in that subtle prescient power of intimation described by Dr. Callaway, "When a thing is lost which is valuable, they begin to search for it by an inner power of divining. Each begins to practise this inner divination and tries to feel where the thing is, and not being able to see he feels internally a pointing which says if he goes down to such a place he will find it. At length he feels sure he shall find it, then he sees it and himself approaching it. If it is a hidden place he throws himself into it as though he was impelled by something. Some boys have the power more than others; some never have it at all. Some have it so strong that they are looked up to by their fellows." (*Jour. Anth. Inst.* I. p. 176.)

We might pause to describe the manifestations of supernal power, more or less of a like character, by medicine-men, magi, and priests, but we will be content to show some of the dogmatic claims that have been asserted in old world faiths and in modern spiritualism. All are familiar with the many pretensions made by priests and rishis of the power of exorcizing and anathematizing of capacity to redeem souls from hell and purgatory or to consign them to perdition; of communing with saints and gods, summoning angels and spirits, healing the sick, raising the dead, punishing the sinner both in heaven and on earth. The penances of a Brahmin can command even Mahadeva, and, as Elkins says of the Chinese Buddhists, they claim that the prayers of the *Hoshang* have the power to break open the caverns of hell. Nor are the pretensions of the occultist as to the power he has obtained by initiation less than those of the medicine-man and the priest. The power ascribed to the Akas and the Mahatmas is a form of mana unproven and unprovable; by it they claim to have power to transport objects to a distance, disintegrate them, convey their particles through solids, and reintegrate them. The adept in occultism can summon spirits and present them in materialized forms. He can consciously see the minds of others; he can by his soul force his wuken power, act on external spirits; he can accelerate the growth of plants, alter the natural action or quench fire; he can subdue wild beasts; he can send his soul to a distance and there not only read the thoughts of others but speak to and touch them, exhibiting to them his spiritual body in the likeness of that of the flesh. More, he can from the surrounding atmosphere create the likeness of physical objects.

Nor is the existence of this complex supernal power alone an attribute of man and spirit. Long before men had acquired the art of using it, or the ghost was elevated to a spirit-power, this mana was an integral attribute of things. Luck, fate, and destiny are but forms of mana. Mana is the presiding power, the ever present actuating force in things. By it they prognosticate the future, they command the present, they inform us of the past; by it they manifest every transcendental attribute—cure, protect and divine. It exists unconsciously in the animal, and the relic of a saint, the stone in the brook, possesses it; it is present in the herb and sea. The stars above, the mountains and the rivers, pour it out upon mortals. They even manufacture this power, endowing weapons and utensils with it, the water of baptism, the wine and bread of the sacrament. Nor is this a mere modern symbol. The old Chaldean ascribed the same power the Catholic recognizes in the host, to the unknown mamit of his devotions, the treasure which presented to the sick healed them, the treasure which never departeth, the one God who never fails. The old Peruvians had a divine food of the nature of the host in the sancu, that cleansed away all sins.

The earliest form of mana presents it as an attribute in things or appearances, denoting an omen or a curative or protective virtue. It may only signify luck. Then when men come to test these powers and to manufacture them they advance into abstract powers the result of the com-bination of several objects or of influences created in them by times, conditions, or words. Then it is that transcendental attributes or abstract qualities pass from the observer or the spell and influence, other personali-ties, other powers. We have many expressions of this secondary power influencing others than the immediate agents, and this leads to the evolution of it as a distinct supernal principle, and the after conversion of those devoted to supernal studies into medicine-men.

Of the working of this abstract power through animals

and material objects we may find examples in the folklore
of most people. Of simple forms in which this mana is
presented in things, we may note the luck induced in a
new boat by launching it with a flowing tide. Wild
animals must not touch milking vessels or the cow's udder
would fester. All forms of transferring diseases implies
the passing of evil mana from one to another. A form
of abstract mana passes into the dog who shuns people
about to die, or into the mole whose burrowing at a house
intimates a death therein. So the bridal bed made by
a woman giving suck, or there would ensue no family.
The Salish say if a beaver's bones are not thrown into
the river the beavers will no more go into the traps. It
is singular that the same people ascribe the same form of
mana in the structure of a beaver that is so often ascribed
by many races of men to a human structure, that is, that
to give stability to a building it must be founded on a
corpse. Most people are familiar with many home legends
of incidents by which this supernal power was obtained.
So the Salish say, when the beaver is constructing its dam
it kills one of its young and buries it under the dam that
it may become firmer and not give way to floods. (*Rep.
Brit. Assoc.* 1890, p. 644.)

All the forms of tabu are upheld by the supposition that
the power in the mana is made to have an evil influence
on the violator of its ordinances. So, in like manner, all
the supernal sentiments expressed through the fetish
customs of initiation, male and female, at puberty, those
regarding a woman's courses, childbirth and death, also
those of the couvade and a widow's practices, are the
abstract workings of the mana. Among the innumerable
illustrations of this working of the mana, one instance will
suffice. With one of the Northern Indian tribes in British
Columbia, the father and mother after a birth are not
allowed to go near the river for a year or else the salmon
would take offence. (*Rep. Brit. Assoc.* 1880, p. 837.)

Among the same people the girl at puberty must not only fast, remaining alone and unseen, for a fortnight, but as the mana is working in her then she must not chew her own food, for, if she desires afterwards to have boys, men must chew it for her—if girls, women. (*Ibid.* 1889, p. 886.)

The Salish also ascribe a special supernal mana as influencing twins. The mother of twins must build a hut on the slope of the mountains, and live there with them until they begin to walk; if she went to the village with them her other children would die. The mana in twins is affirmed to be so great that they can produce rain by allowing water to percolate through a basket; they can make clear weather by throwing a flat piece of wood attached to a string in the air. They can produce storms by strewing the ends of spruce branches, and their mother can tell by their play when children if her husband, though distant, is successful in his hunting. (*Ibid.* 1890, p. 644.)

The principle of sympathetic influence in persons and things is but one of the many forms in which mana is supposed to be presented. In Lord Bacon's description the power is supposed to be worked into a science. He writes:—To superinduce any virtue or disposition in a person, choose the living creature wherein that virtue is evident, of this creature take the parts wherein the same virtue chiefly exists. Thus to superinduce courage take a lion or a cock and choose the heart, tooth, or paw of the lion, and take these immediately after he has been in fight, so with a cock, and let them be worn on a man's heart or wrist. With this special mana power Sir Kenelm Digby is said to have cured a wound by applying a garter having blood from the wound upon it, to the weapon that caused the injury. In another case, the axe which caused the cut was dressed with a salve, wrapped up warmly and hung in a closet. The injured carpenter is said to have been at once relieved, and all went well for a time, when suddenly the wound again became painful, and, on examining the closet, it was found the axe had fallen from the nail, and, of course, when placed secure the man was soon sound. (*Pettigrew Medical Superstit.* p. 160.) We have seen that in one case it was customary so to treat the arrow-head, and of the same mana influence we read that only weapons that have taken a life are fit for the warrior's use. So Roderick Dhu affirmed the influence of a supernal mana power when he said, "Who takes the foremost fooman's life, that same shall conquer in the strife." The Salish say that "an arrow, or any other weapon which has wounded a man, must be hidden, and care taken that it is not brought near the fire until the wound is healed. If a knife or arrow still covered with blood is thrown into the fire the wounded man will become very ill. (*Rep. Brit. Assoc.* 1890, p. 577.)

Mystic mana powers were not only present in things generally on the earth, they were also present in the heavens. The sun and moon and stars, through the mana in them, influenced men and women, animals, and all things on the earth. In general, through the great development in later times of spirit influence it has been assumed that men have always conceived the supernal powers in the heavenly bodies as due to the action of spirits, but we feel assured that the primary concept regarding them was as with children, mere wonder at their brightness, and in the case of the sun its heat-producing power. Long before it even became a person it was a power, and the supernal influence of it as expressing mana only exist, to this day, in many spells and charms. Besides this stage in sun and moon lore, we recognize another, in which, as with children, they are personified, they are beings like men and women in their material aspect; no sentiment of their being controlled by a self-contained ghost or spirit-power is entertained. In many representations of the sun as a personality, its material nature is expressed by a disc with human features, its power by lines as rays. In other cases, as with the races of Northern Europe, it was a wheel, and its power represented by its revolving. This wheel form, or disc face, it was that held the mana men recognized in the sun, moon and stars. It was no angel or demon, no Prometheus, who then brought fire from heaven; there is no supposition of spirit influence. When the material fire was needed it was kindled in the same way as the presumed wheel-power of the sun produced it. The fire was kindled by the friction of a wooden axle in the nave of a waggon wheel by a rope pulled to and fro with great speed. The revolving of the wheel, whether in Carinthia or Scotland, drew down mana from the sun, and the need fire thus evolved cured men and cattle by passing over or through it. Kelly, in his *Curiosities of Indo-European Tradition* writes:—"In 1767, in the Island of Mull, in consequence of a disease among the cattle, they carried to the top of Carnmoor a wheel and nine spindles of oak wood. They then extinguished every fire within sight of the hill. The wheel was turned from east to west to produce fire by friction. They then sacrificed a heifer. Words of incantation were repeated by an old man from Morven, who continued speaking all the time the fire was being raised" (p. 52).

Though somewhat differing in arrangement, the same mode of obtaining mana from the sun was induced by a like instrumentality of fire in Carinthia. "Each house delivers a sheaf of straw on the top of the Stromberg, a huge wheel is then bound with the straw in such a manner that not a particle of the wood remains visible. A stout pole is passed through the wheel. At a signal the wheel is kindled with a torch and set rapidly in motion; the wheel is then rolled down the hill to the Moselle." (*Ibid.* p. 59.)

In some places the old prehistoric flint and steel were used in place of the discarded wheel to draw down fire from heaven, and with the mana of the sun both for healing and protecting. The writer we last quoted says, "At Lechrain, in Bavaria, the Easter Saturday fire is lighted with flint and steel in the churchyard. Every household brings to it a walnut branch, which, after being partially burned, is carried home to be laid on the hearth fire during tempests, as a protection against lightning" (p. 48).

Appeals to the mana present in the material sun meet us in many old customs and old spells. "The inhabitants of Colonsay, before any enterprise passed sunways round the church, and rowed their boats about sunways, as is still done in the Orkney Islands, nor do the Shetland fishermen consider it safe to turn their boats unless with the sun, as is marked of the Icelanders. A procession in this direction attended the baptism and marriage in the county of Elgin, thus was the bride of a Highlander led to her future spouse, and the waters of a consecrated fountain approached, in observance of the sun's diurnal course. The herdsmen danced three times round the fire, in Beltane, and in this direction did the bearers at Dipple churchyard encircle the walls of a chapel with a corpse." (*Dalyell, Dark Supersti.* p. 456.)

Sunway observances are known in many places. With the Salish, women, when drinking for the first time after being married, must turn their cups four times in the direction of the sun. Even a well may have mana relations with the sun. The well of Sindar, Isle of Lewis, foretells if sick will die: a wooden trencher floated on the water turns sunway if the patient will recover, the reverse direction if he will die. Lochsiant well, Skye, cures many complaints; the patient for that purpose goes thrice round the well, sunways, drinking the water. (*Brand, Popular Antiq.* III. p. 13.)

The moon's mana is supposed to influence men in almost innumerable modes; in most cases it acts simply as a material object having a healing, protective, or prescient virtue; it has scarcely advanced to a personality, much less a spiritual manifestation. In most cases its various phases expressed diverse mana powers, and the influence depended not on any personality or presence of a spiritual character, but on the quarter it was in, whether it had horns or was full, and whether it was ascending or descending. Cockayne writes:—"When the moon is one day old, go to the king; ask what you will; he shall give it; go in at the third hour of the day or at high water. It is good to buy land when the moon is two days old, or to take a wife. A new moon on a Sunday betokens in that month rain and wind and mildness, on a Monday diseases, on a Tuesday joy, on a Wednesday friendship, on a Friday good hunting, on Saturday fighting." (*Leechdoms*, p. 181.) So, every day of the moon's age had a different power. The new May moon cured scrofula. One attacked by sickness when the moon was one day old was in peril, at two days old he would soon recover, and so a different influence for every day.

Pettigrew writes:—"The Druids had many superstitions connected with the moon. Animals were killed, seeds were sown, plants were gathered, timber was felled, voyages were undertaken, new garments were worn, and the hair was cut only at particular periods of the moon. It was good to purge with electuaries the moon in Cancer, with pills the moon being in Pisces, with potions when the moon was in "Virgo," and so on. (*Medical Supersti.* p. 20.)

Through the layer of faith in spirits that now overlays the primary faiths of mankind we may still detect the old impersonal ministrants of the oldest supernal manifestations. Ralston, in his *Songs of the Russian People* clearly presents to us the three stages of supernal development we have been pointing out. He writes:—"The oldest zagadki seem to have referred to the elements and the heavenly bodies, finding likenesses of them in various material shapes, as the sun a dish of butter, for the world the crescent moon, a crust of bread; the moon, a golden ship crumbling into stars. In some the sun, the moon, the thunder, the stone, are likened to human beings; the dawn, Zarya, is a fair maid, the moon a shepherd, and the stars his sheep. Fire eats and is never full, water drinks and is never satisfied, the earth plays and is never tired out." Even in the blending of spirit mana with the primitive material possessing mana virtue, we have survivals of the old-spell faith. Thus, "to this day the Russian peasant, when he sees the new moon, will say, 'Young Moon, God give thee strong horns, and me good health.'" The addresses to the elements, the celestial luminaries, and the various forces of nature, which were of old the prayers with which the heathen Slavonian worshipped his elementary gods, and which were spoken on the house-top, are now whispered as spells. The peasant of to-day says, "Dost thou hear, O sky; dost thou see, O sky? O ye bright stars, descend into the marriage cup. O thou free sun, dawn on my homestead. Mother Zarya, as ye quietly fade away and disappear, so may both sickness and sorrows in me fade away. I take a bee, I place it in the hive ; but it is not I who place thee there; the white stars place thee there, the horned moon places thee there, and the red sun " (pp. 360-364).

In some of the Raskolniks the new and old faiths are blended as, "Forgive me, O Lord. Forgive me, O holy mother of God. Forgive me, O ye angels, archangels, cherubim and seraphim, and all ye heavenly host. Forgive, O sky. Forgive, O damp mother earth. Forgive, O sun. Forgive, O moon. Forgive, ye stars. Forgive, ye lakes, ye rivers and hills. Forgive, all ye heavenly and earthly elements." (*Ibid.* p. 365.)

A like conversion of a mere material personality into a spiritual being is seen in the old transfer of the mana once affirmed as manifested by the constellations to the saints. In *Medical Superstitions* we read : "Melton says the saints of the Romanists have usurped the place of the zodiacal

10 *

constellations in their governance of the parts of the human body. Thus Saint Otilia keeps the head instead of Aries; St. Blasius governs the neck instead of Taurus; St. Lawrence keepeth back and shoulders instead of Gemini, Cancer and Leo; St. Erasmus rules the belly in place of Libra and Scorpius; and St. Burgarde, Rochus, Quirinus and St. John govern the thighs, feet, shin, and knees" (p. 86).

At the present day we have the blending of the two distinct conceptions, material more or less anthropomorphic representations of the heavenly bodies as personalities, and their being possessed by a spirit power. Dorman writes: "In early philosophy throughout the world the sun and moon are alive and, as it were, human in their nature though they differ in the sex assigned to them. Among the Mbocobis of South America the moon is a man, the sun his wife. Among others the moon is wife of the sun. Among the pre-Incarial tribes the primitive conception of the sun being animated prevailed. The Haidahs think the sun is a shining man walking round the fixed earth, wearing a radiated crown. The Olchones of California worshipped the sun, but considered him the big man who made the earth. Many of the natives of Guiana thought the sun and moon were living beings. The Kioways pointed out the Pleiades as having the outline of a man, and said it was the great Kioway who was their ancestor and creator. The Guaycurus thought that the sun, moon and stars were men and women that went into the sea every night and swam out by the way of the east." (*Primitive Superst.* p. 326, &c.)

In these several instances we can trace the development of the supernal mana in the higher concepts entertained of the heavenly bodies. At first like the stone, the sun, moon and stars only express the possession of a supernal virtue, and this only varies in the different appearances that at times they present; some are curative, others protective, others prescient. Afterwards, through these supernal presentiments, they advance to personalities and are endowed with human attributes; then when heroes, chiefs and ancestors came to be set out as having possessed supernal mana more than the average of their fellows, they conceived their ghost-spirits to have a future destiny far beyond the ghosts of ordinary men. These might waste away in the grave, or wander in the woods, but they conceived of their great ones a higher destiny—they became the mana powers in the heavens and on the earth. Thus, as Dorman informs us, "The first mother of the Potawatomies was translated into a star, the male ancestor of the Ottawas became the sun, their mother the moon. The Housatonic Indians believe the seven stars were translated to heaven. The morning star with the Cherokees was once a sorcerer. One of the guiding spirits of the Zunis became a star, being shot into the skies. The Algonkins say the evening star was formerly a woman; and the fox, lynx, hare, robin and eagle had a place in their astronomy; even a mouse by them was seen creeping up the rainbow. The Greenlanders held the sun and moon to be man and woman, and the stars were Greenlanders or animals." (*Primitive Supersti.* p. 329.)

It is questionable whether there are any people who have not passed through the three grades of evolution we have designated. Their folklore always has evidence of the material mana only. Then in their folk rhymes and legends, their tales of animal, sun and star being animated, talking and thinking as men and animals, we have the exposition of them as being living personalities. Lastly, even in the barbaric human phase they recognize that every great natural presentation and force, in addition to presenting a physical aspect, are moved by the mana in its ghost-spirit, the same as are men and animals. Thus the Indian said the "sun was the wigwam of a great spirit." (*Dorman,* p. 347.)

The whole concept of a spirit-world and the diverse forms of mana that animated spirits could manifest arose everywhere from the differentiation of the medicine-man. So long as men only recognized mana as an individual supernal attribute in things, so long no one object possessed all kinds of supernal virtues. But when men gradually took up the roll of the wizard and severally in their supernal claims assumed all the prerogatives heretofore affirmed only of different things, then they attained the capacity to assert the possession of powers till then unknown both of good and evil. Thus the clerical and the laical elements were differentiated.

The medicine-man or priest who depends upon the ghost he can call up, the spirit whom he can evoke to do his bidding, is a being entirely distinct from his fellow who affirms he works his will on his victim with the *yulo* the throw-stick, a bit of quartz, or a combination of weird objects in which some portion of what once belonged to the man was attached. A spirit-will acting for evil or good is absolutely of another order from the charm ingredients concocted by a revengeful man or a crafty and cunning priest. As an exposition of thought from its association and continuity we feel assured that the ghost is not merely the revival of a mental image, but the evolution of a distinct state of the mind. The child, so untaught, fails to conceive a ghost. It is an acquired faculty whose origin we will endeavour to trace.

Among the various characteristics of the human mind one of the now most influential is the power of symbolizing. This is a developed faculty to the young child all is real; there are no symbols and the lower intellects in all communities take little or no account of types or symbols; they fail to generalize and judge of each object or event by its own apparent merits. The history of the human intellect is a history of the development of this capacity to symbolize and typify, and its after reduction to law. All

institutions, all customs, all supernal ideas, the language of
gesture and the language of words, all are founded and
dependent on the use of symbols; so is all registered
knowledge, all recognized thought. Luck itself was a
symbol, and all charms and spells are but symbols that the
crude mind accepts as facts. All forms and all the scenes
in the memory are symbols, so the ghost and the after-
spirit presentation was but the symbol of the man. And
what was that? Look at the rude representations of him
by the savage and thereby gain some insight into the
nature of the presentation of the man his mind symbolized.
Do not from the enlarged and defined image in the cultivated brain picture its semblance in the mind of the savage
or child. With both, the instant the reality is removed
from perception, it ceases to exist in the mind, or it is of
the lowest vague character according as the retentive
power is developed. Hence we can suppose a time when
it was never continuous in the mind, then that it existed
rather as a name than a figure, and that consequently it
was a long time, or ever the perceptive impression of a man
remained as a recognizable symbol in a human sensorium.
Hence there could have been races of men who never knew
a ghost, who had no idea, sentiment or feeling that
expressed spirit-beings.

We may in the sayings of children and the narratives of
savages, in cases like that of Caspar Hauser and Laura
Bridgman, and wild children, easily perceive that it is
possible for human beings to develop without having any
ghost sentiment. The researches of Francis Galton and
others have shown us how far the visual faculty can be
cultivated; but even their investigations fail to carry us
back to the time or state in which the power to recall
mental impressions of a perceptive nature exhibit the
incipient characteristics of the child and savage. Yet in
such mental states the ghost perception of a man was born;
it was at best a vague symbol of the warrior he saw but

yesterday. Such symbols in the prepared sensorium may be the expositions of thought, itself a variously developed faculty, or they may come in dreams, and these as they have been presented to us are often of the most vague and incipient character. With one they may be absolutely distinct presentations, to another they are only the vaguest symbols of the objects he conceives them to represent. The Psychical Society have enabled us to realize even in cultivated minds how diverse are these presentations: one person not only distinguishes the features, the colour, the contour of the hair and other personal attributes, but tells us the colour of the various articles of dress, the specialities of the costume and every little adjunct to the picture of the ghost; but with another all is simply a lady in white; may-be brass buttons are noted or the peculiar movement of a limb; with others, the figure has no parts, no accompaniments, there is but the vague impression of a shadowy form which is assumed to have represented a special individual. These, whether real ghosts or images revived in the memory, matters not to us now; we have to accept them as the highest symbols of certain forms the individual minds could present.

Now it is notable that all the savage and crude presentations of ghosts come to us as the vaguest concepts of men and women. They are shades, mere reflections, shadows; they are expressed as symbols by the terms, mist, air, smoke; they manifest no substance, and the forms are often so vague they may be taken for drapery, for men, for animals, for mere glints of light. All the explanations collected by Dr. Tylor, of the ghost, demonstrate that they are the first vague growths of the human symbol in the human mind.

The ghost as yet holds a very limited and uncertain status in the mind of the Australian aborigine and it is very questionable if the incidents in which the ghost or spirit is affirmed have not been derived from the whites. It is

probable that having familiar domestic animals was an
intermediate stage in the evolution of the ghost theory—all
savages accept the possibility of men becoming animals,
and that these animals associate with men and women and
become their familiars or instruments of evil. The witches,
cat, owl, snake, monkey and so forth are the means of
vengeance that succeed the charm spell, and the familiar
animal gives place to the familiar spirit. How these ideas
arise we know by many cases in our witchcraft annals in
which old women living solitary have made companions of
their cats until the weird supposition through some trifling
incidents arises that the cat is something more than a cat.
Here are two incidents of the origin of the same supernal
concept in the minds of the Australian aborigines. "One
of the Bratana clan had a tame lizard in his camp,
and his wife and children lived in another camp close by.
The lizard accompanied him wherever he went, settling
on his shoulders, and people believed that it informed him
of danger, assisted him in tracking his enemies, and was
his friend and protector. They also believed he could
send his familiar lizard at night to injure people in their
camps while they slept." In all this we have no ghost-
power expressed. In another case an old Bidweli woman
was much feared because she had a tame native cat
which she carried about with her, and which was believed
to injure people in sleep at her wish. (*Jour. Anth. Inst.*
XVI. p. 34.)

It is by the use of charms that the Australian wizard
expresses his power, by charms he brings diseases and
injuries, by charms he makes ill; the only means he uses
to control the nature powers is by the use of spells and
charms. He calls on no spirit, he invokes no ghost. If
he would bring rain he squirts water out of his mouth
in the direction it usually comes, chanting a spell. In
a similar way he throws a stone into his enemy's body

and draws it out chanting a spell, and by like means he
changes himself into a kangaroo or the stump of a tree,
or becomes invisible. By the same means he becomes
transcendental, goes up into the sky; and he uses the *yulo*
and the throw-stick, as well as lizards, brown snakes, and
iguanas to work his charms. In his system the ghost is
a modern invention; it can do nothing; and where it is
mentioned we often read it only in the white man's interpretation, calling the ancestral totem animal a ghost. They
ascribed transcendental powers to animals; so no wonder,
when one dreamed he was a kangaroo that he heard
their ghosts speaking. When the old wizard at the
initiation ceremony told his son the tiger-snake was his
budjan, ever after that would become a mystic power to
him. But the magical powers have nothing to do with
the ghosts of men nor the crow, or night jar omens, or
the crackling sounds probably caused in the earth by the
fire upon it, and supposed to be the ground giving warning.

The Shamans among the north-western tribes in America
like the Australian wizards, can bewitch their enemy by
throwing the magic cause of disease, a feather or thong,
at him, or by putting magic herbs in his drink. Ground
human bones mixed with food make the hair fall off the
person who eats it, and sympathetic charms may be fatal.
Thus, part of a person's clothing placed in contact with
a corpse will kill the owner. (*Reports Brit. Assoc.* 1890,
p. 647.) We meet with the same concept of the ghost or
soul of a living person going outside the body and performing
various actions independent of the body, among the Salish,
as among the Australian wizards; the living spirit of one of
the last was supposed to go in the night and see his victim
in the grave; so the Shaman sends his soul out to discover
game, and then informs the hunters the way they should
go. (*Reports Brit. Assoc.* 1890, p. 646.)

It is notable how similar are the modes of producing

mana, whether for good or evil, in all parts of the world. We have shown the charm forms in use among the Australian aborigines and the American tribes, and in the following it will be seen that similar customs prevail in Melanesia. Thus "the *Garata* was charming by means of fragments of food, bits of hair, or nails, or anything closely connected with the person to be injured. The *Talamati* was a charm composed of bone, a bit of stone with certain leaves tied up together, with incantations and prayers to a Tamate. This set in a path, the first who stepped over it was smitten with some disease. The *Tamatetiqa* (ghost-shooter) as we have said was a bit of hollow bamboo, in which a bone, leaves, or whatever else would have mana for such a purpose, was enclosed." (*Jour. Anth. Inst.* X. p. 284.)

The modes in which medicine-men express the power of the mana in them differs according to their stage of evolution, and that of their instruments. The early charm and spell medicine-man depends upon spells and charms to work his evil as well as good manifestations, the herbs containing special virtues he knows little of, and he is far from having conceived the possibility of calling to his aid any ghost or spirit. Between the spell-using medicine-man and the medicine-man who depends upon his power of controlling ghosts and spirits there intervenes a class of doctors, wizards, or priests, who, more or less, depend on all these various modes of inducing good or evil. They have not yet foregone the old occult charms and spells, and the spirit-power with them is yet in embryo; they may conceive of ghosts and spirits, but they have not yet endowed them with their higher semblances and modes of action.

In reviewing the general status of the wizard doctor or medicine-man among all the more developed races of men we should greatly err if we were to take the highest type of doctor or priest as representative of the class. He may have the highest concepts of spirit-nature and the relations of men with the Divine beings his mind conceives, but throughout every civilized community we have not only a low class of priests whose souls dwell only on the respective powers of good and evil spirits, but those who only appeal to the evil powers may be through charms and forms, or, at best, hope to buy off their malignity by reverence, words, and offerings. Yet lower than these, lower even than those lower medicine-men who appeal to the presence of the nature powers when they collect their charm herbs, are those wise men and wise women who only appeal to the lowest fetish charm-objects and have no concept of higher powers.

The vulgar witch or wise woman of to-day appeals not to a ghost nor summons a spirit; her power is the primitive fetish spell. In the *Folklore Record* we read:— "Numbers believe in the might of magic spell and in the power of witches and wizards to work them ill. There lived till lately a woman in a village near Chichester who was never spoken of but as the witch. All appeared to dread her power, and every sudden misfortune was ascribed to her. A groom assured his master that if she willed that he should sit across the roof of the stable all night 'she'd have me there in an instant, and nothing could bring me down till she gave me leave to come down.'" (I. p. 23.)

What was this wise woman and the means she was supposed to possess? Harsnet described the witch as an old weather-beaten crone, having her chin and knees meeting from age, walking like a bow, leaning on a staff, hollow-eyed, untoothed, furrowed in the face, her lips trembling with the palsy, and mumbling through the street,—one that has forgotten her paternoster yet hath a shrewish tongue, and can say pax, max, fax for a spell.

If any of your neighbours have a sheep sick of the giddies, or a hog of the mumps, or a horse of the staggers, or a knavish boy or an idle girl, or a young lamb in the sullens, teach them to roll their eyes, wry the mouth, gnash the teeth, startle in the body with hands still, and if old Mother Nobs has, by chance, called her idle, or bid the devil scratch her, then, no doubt, Mother Nobs is a witch, and the girl is owl-blasted.

Reginald Scot recognized divers powers in the witches. He writes:—"One sort can hurt and not help, the second can help and not hurt, the third can both help and hurt. Among the hurtful witches there is one which usually devour and eat young children. They raise hail tempests and hurtful blasts, they procure barrenness in man, woman and beast, they can throw children in the waters as they walk with their mothers, and not be seen, they can make horses kick till they cast their riders, they can pass in the air invisible. They can bring trembling in the hands and strike terror. They can manifest things hidden and lost, and foreshow things to come. They can kill whom they list, can take away a man's courage and power of generation, make a woman miscarry, even with their looks kill men and beasts, &c." Among these heterogeneous powers which are the general types of a modern witch, Reginald says they can bring to pass that churn as you will no butter will come; then gravely adds, "that may happen if the maids have eaten up the cream, or no butter will come if a little soap or sugar were added to the cream, so the witch-finder would have no difficulty to bring that result about if he so willed."

Whether we go among the Australian aborigines, the American red men, in Melanesia or Polynesia, the same class, whether men or women, have the power to project stone, bone, earth, or wood, or skin missiles into the bodies of those they would injure, or by concocting a charm of something once belonging to the individual and fetish ingredients, they can waste away by fire and water or other baneful means the assumed representative object, and with its decay the life of the victim will pass away. These are the great universal spells which bring disease and kill, whether they arose in the pre-glacial period, and since, as folk-charms descended to all men, or whether they have sprung as corresponding malignant wishes among the various races of men, we have no means of judging. Even in a new race of isolated men it is probable like sentiments would necessarily arise as the exposition of their malignant wills.

Van Holmont describes the mediæval witches as injecting into the bodies of their victims darts, thorns, pins, pricks, chaff, hairs, sawdust, small stones, egg-shells, pieces of pots, hulls and husks, insects, pieces of linen, and so forth, all of which are ejected with direful pains. In one case, a piece of ox-hide had been injected as large as the ball of a man's hand, in another an artificial toy, a young girl vomited a mass of pins, with hairs and filth, another had shavings and chips of wood, others a woman's coif, pieces of glass, three pieces of a dog's tail, a tobacco pipe, and stones. No wonder, to preserve themselves from such unpleasant guests the good folk hung pentaphyllon in the house entry, valerian vervain, palm, frankincense, branches of the rowan, and ash-trees, nor that a wolf's head, or horse-shoe, was nailed at the door. Even an ointment of potent virtue, made of the gall of a black dog and his blood, was smeared over the door-posts like that of the sacrificed sheep by the Jews, as a protective agent.

Such sentiments still linger in the old world, and they travelled into the new world with the Spanish knights and the pilgrim fathers, and even now bear the same malignant fruit. In *Florida Breezes* we read that Delia, a young country girl, when about eighteen, began to droop and grew most heartrending in her depression of spirits and

enfeeblement of body, and finally, without giving a sign,
died. After death the nurse brought to her mother a
packet of dingy cloth, in which was wrapped two or three
rusty nails, a dog's tooth, a little lamb's wool and a ball
of clay. Trembling with awe, she said, "This is what
killed Miss Delia. I know as how she was conjured." On
inquiry it was found she was a cause of jealousy to a
companion, who had made threats to her. All knew the
power that was at work upon her, but dared not break the
spell (1883, p. 181).

Sometimes the assumed death agent is, as in the case of
Sir George Maxwell and others, images made of wax or
clay, and the semblance tortured by pins inserted in it,
or burned at the fire. In the case of Erephan M'Calzeane
the accusation was that she had formed a waxen picture of
the King of Scotland, and had mixed storms at sea to
hinder his return from Denmark. Another witch was
charged with preventing George Sandie's boat from
catching fish, a third took the disease from her husband
and transferred it to his nephew, and to perform this feat
she buried a white ox and a cat alive, throwing in with
them a quantity of salt.

In all the cases we have given, and in all we shall now
refer to, the primitive wise woman or wise man only obtains mana by spells and charms, and when in addition to
using these means they refer to ghosts or spirits in a loose
and indeterminate manner as with some Australian wizards,
we may be sure the sentiment that influences them has
been newly acquired and it will be noted that practically
they depend on the strength of the charms they use and
their own mana power to concoct them. The materials
used for the purpose may vary in different countries, but
the fetish power relied upon in the material is the same in
all countries.

We will quote a few cases illustrating the charms used
by witches. Chalmers describes the magic treasures of a

sorceress at New Guinea as some seeds, a crystal stone, small shells, bamboos, black basalt stones inserted in the cup like spongiole of a pandanus root, other stones and a piece of quartz. Some were for incantations, some brought children, some caused death; and those objects were esteemed as male and female and used accordingly. (*Pioneering in New Guinea*, p. 316.)   Dorman describes a medicine-woman as concocting a medicine to cure internal wounds caused by a grizzly bear, consisting of a collection of miscellaneous weeds, chewing tobacco, the heads of four rattlesnakes, worn-out moccasins, sea-weed, petroleum and red pepper, and the patient was directed to take a pint of the mixture every half-hour. (*Primitive Supersti.* p. 359.)   In the Bahamas the wise woman or man ascribes some ailments to a beetle or spider in one of the limbs. This, like the quartz stone or a chip of wood is extracted by sucking the part, and producing the offensive article from the mouth of the sucker.   Obeah charms are used to protect stores in vessels from depredations.   This is usually a ball containing rusty nails, pieces of rushes, &c., which is laid on the door-step, a carved head on a tree guards the fruit grove or a horn with a cork in it full of pins.

In Western Africa, according to Rowley in the *Religions of Africa*, men and women encumber themselves with fetishes; some are for the head, others for the neck, others for the heart, the arms, the stomach and back, and every part of the body has its appropriate fetish or charm. These fetishes are generally simple things, the reeds of certain plants, the roots of certain trees, the horns of diminutive deer, the claws and teeth of lions and leopards, slips of wood fantastically notched, knuckle bones, beads, and a kind of white stone.   To detect a witch, a charm is used; a cock's feather is thrust into the tongue of the accused, or a red-hot wire is drawn through it, or the juice of acrid plants is squirted into the eyes, or certain ordeal tests have to be endured (p. 161-166). In Western Africa though mainly dependent on charms both to kill and cure in a less degree the appeal to spirits is known. They have charms for every kind of fear, as of ghosts, of an enemy, of thunder, snake-bite charms, sickness charms, love charms, all of which whatever their name are merely protective spells.

Im Thurn shows how much, while a Guiana Peaiman acknowledges the presence of spirits, he is under the domination of spells and charms. To gain mana he has to endure long fasts, wander alone in the forest, houseless, and unarmed, and only living on such food as he can gather, at the same time he has to drink large quantities of tobacco water. He has to train a command over his voice for all sounds, and acquire the capacity of working himself into a frenzy of convulsions. He has to learn the legends of his tribe and gain an acquaintance with the medicinal and poison plants. (*Ind. of Guian*, p. 334.) He describes the modern Indian as blowing away the evil spirit from the sick man. From Roth's description of the sick man and the doctors among the old Hispaniolans, the custom would appear to have been to blow away the disease, not a spirit; this appears to have been the initiary stage of the disease spirit, the following description shows it to have been material. The medicine-man first gives his patient a vomit as if to dislodge the disease, then rubs the man down, drawing down to his feet as if he would pull something off, then goes to the door and shuts it, saying, "Begone to the mountain or the sea, or whither thou wilt" at the same time giving a blast as if he blowed something away, and then draws in his blast and sucks the man's neck, stomach, jaws and breast. This done, he coughs and makes faces as if he had eaten something bitter, at the same time pulling out of his mouth stone, flesh or bone, saying, "See how I have taken it out of your body for your Cemi has put it in you because you did not pray to him."

(*Abor. Hispan*, p. 10.) The ceremony in this is the same as is the common fetish charm of sucking out a disease. It is caused by a spirit, but is removed by a spell.

As in the last case the disease spell was a stone, a piece of bone or flesh, so among the Onondaga Indians in North America the victim has been killed by the presence of a foreign substance that has been introduced into his body, and the cure is wrought by removing the missile or charm. At times the afflicted part is bandaged and on the removal of the bandage the witch doctor finds a few gray hairs, a bit of shawl fringe or a small piece of coal neatly sharpened at both ends. (*Jour. Amer. Folklore*, II. p. 277.) In another mode a slight incision is made, the place is sucked with a horn having a hole at the end and the doctor produces a whitish stone and some yarn thus drawn from the patient's body.

Turner in his *Nineteen years in Polynesia*, writes :—"The real gods at Tanna may be said to be the disease-makers. There are rain-makers, and thunder-makers and fly and mosquito-makers and a host of other sacred men, but the disease-makers are most dreaded. It is believed that these men create disease by burning nahak or the refuse of food. If the disease-maker sees the skin of a banana, he wraps it in a leaf and wears it round his neck. People stare and say he has got something. In the evening he scrapes some bark, mixes it in the leaf in the form of a cigar and puts it close to the fire to singe. Presently he hears a shell blowing. He says to his friends that is the man whose rubbish I am burning, he is ill. The horn blowing means to implore the person burning the sick man's nahak to cease. Then a present is arranged, pigs, mats, beads or whales teeth. If the man the next night has another attack another present must be sent, if not, the rubbish burns out and fear finishes the man " (p. 90).

Hardwick says:—" Healing witches are more prominent nowadays than baneful ones. Margaret Gordon was a Scotch witch of this class. She firmly believed to her dying day that she possessed power to remove or avert the ills and ailments of both man and beast by means of various incantations, ceremonies, and appliances as cuttings of the rowan tree, some of which she always carried about her. She would carefully place so many of these before and so many behind the beast she meant to benefit. Another of her charms was holy water from a holy well, this she sprinkled in the path-way of those she designed to bless. She would go round the dwellings of those she wished to serve, carrying a long rowan rod at an early hour in the morning. She also believed she was transmutable and was changed by evil wishers into a pony or hare, and was hunted by dogs. (*Traditions, &c.*, p. 275.)

In the transition to the ghost supernal manifestation we have spoken of the passage from the fetish foot or claw to the totem animal, we have seen that it may be the link that attaches the fetish sentiment through the guardian animal to the guardian penates or ghost. So, in like manner, the votive offering to a god of a hand or foot curing the sick may have arisen from the custom Lansdell now ascribes to the Gilyaks of wearing amulets in the shape of the diseased part as a wooden arm or hand. Possibly they considered the disease might be transferred to the wood model.

In concluding this part of our investigation we may note that not only may a man become possessed of mana by rites and ceremonies intentionally observed for that purpose, but he may manifest it through neurotic development. Thus, on the Congo, the power of the Ndochi is supposed to be inborn, it may exist without the knowledge of the possessor and even produce its effects without his knowledge. To detect if a man is a ndochi, the bark of a leguminous tree called *nkasa*, is ground to powder and a dose administered to the suspected person; like many other toxic principles, it acts variously, as an emetic purge or a toxic, in the last causing death by coma. (*Jour. Anth. Ins.* XVII. p. 222.)

Tylor tells us that among the Patagonians, patients seized with falling sickness or St. Vitus's dance were at once selected for magicians as chosen by the demons themselves, who possessed, distorted, and convulsed them. Among Siberian tribes the Shamans select children liable to convulsions as suitable to be brought up to the profession, which is apt to become hereditary with the epileptic tendencies it belongs to. (*Primitive Cult.* II. p. 121.)

CHAPTER V.

The origin of Ghosts—Human and Animal.

In passing from impersonal supernal assumptions to the assumptions of ghosts and spirits we enter upon a field of enquiry, vast in its dimensions and one that has engrossed the higher faculties in men to describe and account for. The ghost whether of the man or the animal has ever been esteemed as another self, capable of residing in the organic body which represents it or of holding an independent existence and in that state may be able to enter the body of another man or animal when its own ghost is absent, or when present coercing it by the greater mana power it is possessed of. Separate from its ghost the body perishes, but the ghost lives with some, perhaps, for only a short period, with others it is immortal. In the latter condition it becomes a spirit having no mortal attachment.

All spirits however are not esteemed as having been originally ghosts possessing a dual nature, there are spirits single, either *per se* representative or generated, without having been enclosed in a mortal husk. More, there are natural objects which are held to be personalities without possessing a dual ghost nature, and this we hold to have been the intermediate concept that anticipated the birth of the ghost theory. Children and savages now methodically personify any object that to them seems to possess life, without endowing it with an indwelling spirit. With the savage in his lowest state, the partially imbecile, and the child, every object as well as person is an independant actor, what it does or is done through it are questions of conduct, it has responsibility and is subject to penalties. The deodand was demanded of the stone on which a man fell and was killed, of the tree whose branch self-breaking caused his death. The savage and child immediately execute judgment on the unconscious floor on the fetish that fails to protect. They suppose that the powers they are conscious of in themselves are common to all things, with them nothing dies and any fragment contains the whole. Hence the broken horse, the headless doll are cherished, the child sees no incongruity in talking to a battered and misshapen figure or in putting the rag doll without head senses or parts comfortably to bed. Every attribute of the personal object to the savage as well as the child expresses the absolute nature of it. In the lowest mental states the thing is a personal self-existent being, its living powers are its common nature, and there exists no concept of a will separate from the object itself.

The child's imagination scarcely reaches to the fetish concept of the advanced savage, who, without having worked out a dual ghost power, conceives the man, it recognises in the uncanny object as something distinct from the object itself. Hence, there is no hitch or failure in belief, no conception of incongruous power or association. The child accepts any quality its toys seem to possess and any tale that is told to it. So the savage accepts at once his medicine-man's assertion he had climbed into the sky; the same as the child gives full credence to the adventures of Jack up the beanstalk, neither the one nor the other noting the physical impossibilities of the feats. Herbert Spencer says of primitive man he accepts what he sees as animals do; and so it is with the child whatever it sees has every attribute it seems to possess. The doll lives and has the same living nature as itself, it can do wrong and the doll can equally do wrong. The child knows nothing of the distinction between the spiritual and the material, to it all things and powers are material.

What its doll and other toys were to the child the tree, the sun and stars, animals, rocks, rivers, and mountains were to the primary savage. He did not distinguish them as self-existent generated or transposed. One and all were self-contained personalities, the will being consonant with the structure. The river, the rock, the sun, the moon are the same living entities as are the bear, the tiger, the snake, they may be transformed men, they may be men who have gone up into the sky, and who, as with the Australian aborigines, are the sun, moon, and stars themselves not their indwelling spirits. In all low mind presentations whether animal or inorganic they are simple personalities, as we have seen all objects are to young children.

The dream origin of the human ghost has often been affirmed, but as the evidence on this subject is now more complete than formerly, and, as we observe the phenomena from a new standpoint, believing the concept to have been preceeded by a long period in which much lower supernal ideas prepared the way for its assumption, we will again consider the dream origin of ghosts. We have recognised a power in the higher animals to dream, but that by no means implies ghost presentation, only the concept of the uncanny. Besides we have to observe that other than actual sense perceptions, as concepts of time, relations, influences and powers are presented to the mind in dreams of various kinds, in allusions produced by intense attention, in illusive states resulting from organic or mental disease, in suggestive illusions of thought induced by others or produced in the mind by special external conditions, internally by the food eaten or the medicaments taken into the stomach.

We will first pass in review the general expression of

dreams, as the various origins of the personal presentation
are by no means explained in many of the incidents we
shall quote. The Andamanese held the concept of the
dual nature of man, and they conceived that the soul takes
its departure through the nostrils and then appears to
the sleeper, this is to them the ghost form seen in dreams.
(*Jour. Anth. Ins.* XII. p. 162.) Among the Australian
aborigines the Kurnai believe that each human individual
has within him a spirit called Yambo, during sleep it
could leave the body and confer with other disembodied
spirits. These spirits of the living are supposed to be
able to communicate with other spirits, either those of other
sleepers or of the dead. Thus the spirit of one dead
appeared to his comrade in sleep and took him up a rope
into the sky. Their dreams Mr. Howitt writes, are to
them as much realities as are the actual events of their
waking lives. (*Ibid.* XII. p. 186.) One of the Kurnai
asked if he really thought his Yambo could go out during
sleep said, "it must be so for when I sleep I go to distant
places, I even see and speak with those that are dead."
(*Ibid.* XII. p. 189.)

Even among so undeveloped a race as the Kurnai, the
fetish personality thus evolved in dreams presents the
same supernal characteristics as those of much more
developed people. Thus, the existence of the ghost once
enunciated, all the varied powers possessed by the medicine-
man arise as a matter of course from the outer mental
attributes that are always present in some men, as the
origin of his boylya power, and the special capacity not
only to work spells but to call up ghosts in waking
visions and even foretell the future by them. These
attributes will be noted in the following observations,
"Sometimes a man dreams that someone has got some
of his hair, or a piece of his food, or of his opossum
rug. If he dreams this several times he feels sure of
it, and calls his friends together and tells them. (*Ibid.*

XVI. p. 29.) Anyone could communicate with ghosts in sleep, but only wizards during waking hours. (*Ibid.* XII. p. 191.)

The boylya powers that obtain among all wizards are not identical in mode of action although in principle. Thus at the Nicobar Islands the people have the idea that "some wizards have the power to cause a person's death by merely thinking of it, and should a villager dream so, there is no means of escape for him but by going immediately to another island. The greater part of the persons seen in the islands where they were not born have been compelled to leave their own on this account. If the dreamer mentions his dream to no one but the heads of the village, the sentence is passed and the eaters of men are taken and fastened to a tree close to the village and left to perish, no relative would give them anything to eat." (*Jour. Asia. Soc. Beng.* XV. p. 352.)

Im Thurn speaking of the Indians of Guiana writes: "the dreams which come to him in sleep are to him as real as any of the events of his waking life. He regards his dream acts and his waking acts as differing only in one respect, that the former are done only by the spirit, and the latter by the spirit in the body. When the Indian just awake tells the things which he did whilst asleep his fellows reconcile each statement by the thought that the spirit of the sleeper left him and went out on its adventures." Not only in death and in dreams but yet in a third way the Indians see the spirit separate from the body. Visions are to him when awake what dreams are to him when asleep, and the creatures of his visions seem no way different from those of his dreams. Innumerable instances of natural visions are recorded. Artificial visions are produced. When the medicine-man prepares himself for his office by fasting, solitude, the use of stimulants and narcotics, his object is to separate his own spirit from its body.

The Indians of Labrador place implicit faith in dreams, and visions of the night as Hind informs us, and these often lead them to commit shocking crimes. They follow their dreams with the utmost precision. Speaking of the Ahts, Sproat writes: "they imagine the soul may wander forth from the body and return at pleasure, it may pass from one man into another and enter a brute. Dreams are regarded as the movements of those vagrant souls; they often dream they are visited by ghosts." (*Savage Life*, p. 174.)   In like manner Reade in his *Savage Africa* describes the Negroes as saying the words they hear and the sights they see in dreams come to them from spirits (p. 248). The New Zealanders held that during sleep the soul left the body, and that dreams are the objects seen during its wanderings.

Speaking of the natives of Natal, Callaway observes that they believe in the real objective presence of the person of whom they dream. Many imagine the spirits of their ancestors come to express their displeasure. The same writer gives the case of an illusionist, after an illness, passing in his dreams from place to place seeing elephants and hyænas, lions and leopards. Not a day passing but he saw such forms when he slept, at the same time he heard internal voices calling to him at night. We know such perceptions are common in fevers and mental disorders, but the inference the Zulus deduced from these phenomena was that the power of divination which they attach to their medicine-men was being developed in him; thus, as in other instances, affirming the fetish association of dreams, ghosts, and the mana powers of the medicine-man. (*Jour. Anth. Inst.* I. pp. 165-174.)

The dreamer is not amenable to any of the ordinary restraining powers that influence the sensitive organism; time, space, size, and quality are nothing to him, he can waft himself from Indus to the Pole, or sail away on a summer's sea to the Islands of the Blessed. Though old he may become young again, live once more in the lost presences of departed friends; faded and worn out with the burthen of the day, he may become fresh as the lark; or, his enthusiastic aspirations may not only blend his soul with the past and the far distant present but reveal the unborn results of actions not yet in the womb of time.

Need we then wonder that men in all ages have from like concepts developed other existences than those of the substantive world about them, that they should have realized a state and condition of being other than those of the living world of nature. What other doctrine could the rude savage entertain than that in the dream hunt when he and his fellows chased and fought with the kangaroo, the jaguar, or the lion, that a something, an actuality, had gone out from them and achieved the midnight adventure? So, when in a dream the savage saw bodily before him the form of a friend whose body he had himself helped to bury, or may be that he had seen apparently annihilated on the funeral pile, he could not but have realized the idea that his friend had a dual existence, have been both a substance and a ghost. And the idea of the still living ghost would become thoroughly impressed on his mind; in as much as his fellows would in may instances have seen the same form, and many circumstances in the life of the savage conduce to bring about a suitable bodily condition suggestive of that evolved in dreams, more especially after a death. The funeral is always followed by a feast in which animal food, often only half-cooked, forms the substance, and this eaten to repletion brings on a plethora of dreams. But in some cases, as if this is not sufficient to recall the image of one over whose fate they may have been brooding for days, they seek by mental pressure to evolve the dream illusion. Thus some wear as personal ornaments bones of the dead, some widows have to carry their dead husband's remains about with them, and sleep upon them, and these objects

would be present in the lurid light of the camp fire at
night as they fell asleep. In other instances we read
of the living sleeping on the graves of their dead relations
for the very purpose that they may hold converse with
them in dreams. So strong in time becomes this belief
in the life of ghosts that a man whispered in his dead
wife's ear, among the Motus, not to be angry with them
because they could not give her a share of their feasts, and
when they should go inland hunting, or to sea fishing,
that she should watch and protect them. (*Jour. Anth.
Inst.* VIII. p. 371.)

Necessarily, as so much of the life of the savage is spent
about hunting wild animals, and as their images under
various emotions would equally appear to him in dreams
as those of his fellow men, it readily followed that he
attached ghost relations to animals, and in dreams confused
the two impressions until he realized the ideas of possession
and transformation.

Dreams do not only present to the sleeping mind
the actual images of absent or dead friends and of animal
forms, but they present incoherent monstrous or aberrent
images. The medicine-man or mystic priestess who after
a long process of wild howlings, chantings, incantations,
dances, and extreme physical rites, imbibes some strong
organic principle, some tobacco, coco, kava, or decoctions of
berries bark and leaves, and thus produces a wild feverish
and ultimately an exhausted state in which the whole
nervous as well as blood systems are highly excited, while
the physical stamina demands sleep. These, then, in their
agitated and incoherent dreams or visions, blend, and
confuse the multiform images in the memory until they
evolve inchoate idealisms, monstrous multiples of diverse
real existences, gorgons and hydras and chimaeras dire.

Thus the supernatural world became inhabited, not only
by human and animal ghosts and feverish monstrous forms,
but spirits in the similitude of every organic and inorganic

entity; and, more a series of higher beings evolved from the
practical workings of social institutions, and the inner
idealities of the higher mind forces into spirits, demons,
genii, angels, and gods.   Nor is it only the incipient
human mind that cannot separate the apparent from the
real in dreams, the more highly gifted build up spiritual
systems from the rhapsodies of dreams and neurotic
hallucinations.   In all ages the piously inclined accept
these experiences as the interpositions of their gods.   So
Job in his controversy with the Deity cried out, "Thou
scarest me with dreams, and terrifiest me through visions."

The origin of dreams has often been treated upon.   Dr.
Cappie defines sleep as caused by the pressure of venous
blood on the brain, and dreams come when the pressure is
lessened.   He writes, "the special molecular agitation
which conditions consciousness is not entirely suspended,
but the lines of vibration are contracted.   The sphere of
activity is localised, and the mental correlation is correspondingly narrow.   The long past becomes mixed up
with the present, and locality and objects and actions change
without any respect for the claims of physical possibility.
Consciousness is helplessly passive."   (*Causation of Sleep*,
p. 126.)   Of the physiological causes of dreams Dendy
gives several references; thus, if cramp has attacked any
of the limbs, or the head has been long confined back, the
dreamer may be enlivened by some analogous tortures.
Hypochondriacs express themselves convinced of having
frogs, serpents, a concourse of persons, or demons pent up
within them arising from flatulence, dyspepsia, or spasms.
Again persons affected by nostalgia are frequently presented with visions of home in their slumbers.

Dreams of a special character, and often manifesting
supernal attributes, may be induced by the nature, quantity,
or time before sleep when the dreamer partook of certain
foods.   A writer in the *Journal of Psychological Medicine* gives the case of a man who, after eating a supper

of halibut, had a dream of sliding down a cliff on the sea shore, and being saved by holding his niece's hand.— Another after a hearty fish supper dreamed of poisonous serpents. Even food retained in the mouth may give a character to the ensuing dream. A lady having a slight cough put a piece of barley sugar in her mouth and fell asleep whilst sucking it. She then dream that she was a little girl at a party, happy and enjoying herself, with all kinds of childish sports. After a long period had seemed to elapse she awoke with a smile to find the dream cause still in her mouth, and that only a few minutes had elapsed. (XI. p. 579.)

There are various self-induced causes of dreams with a special tendency of development. We have referred to the custom of the Australian aborigines sleeping on the new-made grave that they may dream of the presence of the dead and hold converse with him. So Gaule in *Visions and Apparitions* shows other cases of like dream presences being induced. He writes that it was a common practice after expiation and sacrifice to lie down in the temple at Pasiphae that they might have prophetic dreams, also others in the Temple of Æsculapius who was noted for sending true dreams. The Calabrians consulting Podalyrius slept near his sepulchre in lamb skins (p. 248).

Dr. Maury had a series of experiments made on himself in sleep to test how far dreams were induced by the influence of present external perceptions on the all but quiescent senses. In this state he dreamed of suffering a horrible punishment while a person tickled his lips and the point of his nose with a feather. From the striking of a pair of shut scissors with a small forceps at some distance from his ear he dreamed of a bell sounding, so Cologne water induced at first the dream of a perfumer's shop, and this after changed to scenes in the East.

In both visions and dreams which may thus be read as subjective the excited imagination when pre-disposed to accept the supernal holds the appearance as a reality, with the same full confidence as we have seen was customary with the most undeveloped savage. Phantasms utterly meaningless appear every day to numbers of individuals, not only when in a morbid state and under conditions specially apt to induce them, but even to the normal mind strongly affected by some person or incident, or by the attention being continuously directed to the same object.

Mr. Rushton Dorman found that the doctrine of spirits had its origin in the primitive conception of human ghosts, souls seen in dreams and visions. A Wionebago Indian thus saw a phantom woman who beckoned him to come and be her husband, and he pined away in the sure belief of meeting her in the spirit world. Hence the phenomena of apparitions. These are presumed to appear for the most varied purposes now appalling the criminal by the direct action of "God's revenge against murder," now as warning of coming danger, sometimes in the form of guardian angels, at others as threatening demons. Some in allegorical or mystic puzzles evince future events, others occur for very secondary purposes to renew friendships, explain mistakes, discover hidden treasures, wills, or even to show the whereabouts of lost sheep, a runaway daughter, or a mislaid book. Often there is no practical purpose derived from the dream.

Boismont shows that some presentiments are only the result of more than ordinary acute sensitive powers. Thus a girl had the capacity to hear a storm long before it came, and in the open country detected the tread of a horse hours before the traveller arrived. He remarks that facts demonstrate there are natures so impressible that they discern long before others changes about to take place in the air, and these, according to Maury's experiments, might come in dreams and denote supernal manifestations. Boismont suggests a simple explanation of some supernal

illusions. Thus a man in a dream saw the figure of a
relative many years dead, who in the usual way announced
that he would die the same day. He was a man of strong
mind and he told his dream, saying, if it were to be so, no
matter; but, doubting that it was only an illusion induced
by the way he had lain, he followed his ordinary occupations,
of course, without any unpleasant catastrophe, but, as he said
in so many cases of others, if he had been weak enough to
believe the dream, and give way to the emotion, he would
really have died as the men recorded by Procopius. In
another case, a lady dreamed that her mother appeared to
her in a dying state, the next morning she told her dream,
and her uncle, in whose house she was staying, said it was
true her mother was dead. Afterwards she found a letter
thrust into a corner which contained all the special incidents
of her dream. The inference was that she had seen the
letter which her uncle the evening before had put out of
sight, being unwilling then to disturb her with the
mournful news, and, that in the strong emotions on awaking
from her sleep, she had forgotten the exciting cause.
(*Rational Hist. of Hallucinations*, p. 196.)

All we have yet described have been simple natural
dreams, however supernal may have been the deductions
from them, but there are other classes of dreams arising
from physical disorder, mental aberration, and the action
of toxics. The ghosts presented to the mind under
these organic states are of the most varied character and
endowed with most extraordinary attributes. Haohshish
and opium, the delirium of fever, mania in its many forms,
and religious ecstasy, realize the most extreme characteristics of spirit agency. The ghost advanced to a spirit
at first is always evil. The ghosts recognized by the
medicine-men in all the lower races of men is by nature evil,
even though the individual's ghost responds to the wishes
of his tribesmen. Essentially among them the spirit natures
are pre-eminently malignant; whether they are the spirits of

enemies or their own discontented ghosts or the like spirit natures they recognize in animals and natural forces.

Evil as we have seen was at first due to the uncanny impersonal power in things; it was only ill-luck as distinct from good luck; but when the human mind had realized the power of ghost possession and spirit presentation, then the evil attributes of things were transferred to the evil actions of ghosts and spirits. Men in that social phase accepted whatever came as good to denote only luck, while all that was evil were ascribed to spirits. In the early state of all people we only read of wicked spirits, disease spirits, the ghosts of enemies, and the ghosts of their own neglected dead as causing all the direct evils that happen to them. These evil ghosts whose advent we have depicted. are at first general sources of ill, causing disease, killing, obstructing the men in hunting or fishing, and in various. ways putting obstacles in their way. Afterwards they are distinguished as manifesting special powers of evil.

Thus the home legends and folklore of every people abound with tales of the misdeeds of ghosts, and everywhere they are described as evincing malicious characteristics. In India they are known as Bhutas, devils, ghosts; they are of human origin, malignant, discontented, or savage beings; some the ghosts of enemies or of men in other districts or villages, many originating from the souls of those who in life were either at war with their fellows or who doomed they were aborted or degraded or injured by their kin. Some originated from the souls of those who had died an untimely death by neglect or accident, by being hung or beheaded, or who had been born deformed, were idiotic or insane, subject to the falling sickness or the many hereditary maladies men inherit. The Preeta was the ghost of a child dying in infancy or of one born imperfectly developed or monstrous, and it became a misshapen distorted-goblin which cursed and injured well-formed mortals on whom it looked with an envious eye. The Pisacha was the ghost of a madman; he was treacherous and violent tempered. The Bhutas were the spirits of those dying in an unusual way by violence, accident, or suicide; they haunted the living at home or abroad, made pitfalls so that they might fall, caused them to fall from trees or drowned them when fording a stream. They sometimes came in the form of snakes and stung them, or of savage beasts and tore them to pieces. The death of an exceptionally bad character was always followed by the presence of a Bhute or demon who afflicted human beings by entering their bodies and feeding on the excreta, or they possessed the living soul and caused family dissensions and hatred.

We find cannibal ogres, evil spirits, devils, and demons of various kinds either as living ghosts or folklore evil spirits in the domestic legends of all people. The Mkun of East Africa believe in the existence of harmful spirits who rove about among the living, and they attribute to them all evils such as sickness, drought, and death. The Bechuanas people the invisible world with ghost and goblin demons, and ovcatrums like the Rakshasas of the Hindoo, and Banshees, Phookas, ghouls, and Afreets of other races. At the Solomon Islands if a person is sick in any way, that shows it has been done by a ghost belonging to some unfriendly tribe; they therefore call upon some powerful ghost on their side by the medium of his mana or spells to attack the other who has done the mischief. The two ghosts are supposed to fight, but mortals only know the result as one of the adversaries' clients becomes sick or dies. (*Jour. Anth. Inst.* X. p. 300.) This may be accepted as one of the first attempts to conceive of a good spirit. As a rule, as we have seen, spells were the only available means to expel the intruding ghost.

The Motu of New Guinea are described as living a slavish life of fear of the evil spirits. At the death of a friend they will sit up all night and keep striking the

drums to drive away the spirits. The coast tribes most
fear the inland tribes. All calamities are attributed to the
power and malice of the evil spirits. Drought and famine,
storms and floods, disease and death, are all supposed to
be brought by Vata and his hosts. (*Proc. Roy. Geo. Soc.*
II. p. 615.) Most of the malign spirits or Ingnas of the
Australian aborigines are the souls of departed black men
who from some cause have not received the rites of
sepulture and in consequence are constrained to wander
about the place of their death. Such as are slain in fight,
and their bodies left to rot in the sun or to be devoured by
the wild dogs, are immediately transformed into Ingnas;
while as a natural consequence the spirits of all men not
of their own tribe are enrolled in this ghastly army. A
number of these Ingnas haunt all graves. (*Trans. Eth. Soc.*
III. p. 237.) These ghost spirits kill their victims in a
variety of ways. Thus the Beechairah is killed by an
invisible spear, the point of which is nearly cut through.
It is thrown without being felt or making any wound; then
the point breaks off, but, ignorant of the injury he has
received, the man goes on hunting; but at night when he
has returned to the camp the evil develops, he becomes
delirious, and dies. (*Jour. Anth. Inst.* XIII. p. 203.)
Sometimes these mysterious causes of death are explainable
from natural causes. The Australian savage is as commonly exposed to ruptures by any violent action as is the
white man; he might in a similar way feel the snapping of
the inner membrane like a cord, but ignorant of the nature
of his own organization he formulates the theory that one
of the invisible spirits of evil had entered his body, tied up
his intestines, and that the snapping he felt was the
breaking of the confining cord. This is described as
occurring when following an opossum from tree to tree;
he jumps down to catch it, and then when suddenly
alighting on the ground, or during the violent exercise, he
feels the string break in his inside. "Hallo!" he says,

12 *

"some one has tied me up." He goes home to the camp;
the usual result of a rupture follows, but with his supernal
theory of evil he loses all hope and dies. (*Jour. Anth. Inst.*
XIII. p. 293.)

The Fijians believed that the spirits of the dead appeared
frequently and afflicted mankind, especially when asleep.
The spirits of slain men, unchaste women, and women who
had died in childbirth, they held most in dread. They
have been known to hide themselves for days until they
supposed the spirit of the dead was at rest. (*T. Williams,
Fiji*, I. p. 241.) The Fijian peoples with invisible beings
every remarkable spot—the lonely dell, the gloomy cave,
the desolate rock, the deep forest. Many of these unseen
spirits are on the alert to do him harm. In passing he casts
a few leaves to propitiate the demon of the place. These
are demons, ghosts; the spirits of witches and wizards and
evil-eyes all alike possessing supernatural powers. (*Ibid.*)
All through the Polynesian Islands the same sentiment of
evil-disposed ghosts prevails; the spirits of the unburied
dead, as in classical times, haunt the survivors of his family;
without a home, without hope, they utter the mournful
wail "I am cold! I am cold." (*Pritchard, Samoa*, p. 151.)

Im Thurm describing the Indians of Guiana says: "There
are, the Indians think, harmless spirits and harmful. It
may be said that all the good that befalls him the Indian
accepts either without inquiry as to its cause or as the
results of his own exertions; but on the other hand all the
evils that befall him he regards as inflicted by malignant
spirits. He has no inducement to attract the goodwill of
spirits, but he acts so as to avoid the evil will of others."
(*Ind. of Gui.* p. 368.) According to Sproat (*Scenes of Savage
Life*, p. 174), the Vancouver Indians hold that when the
natural soul goes out of the body in dreams, when asleep,
that an evil-disposed ghost enters during its absence and
vexes and torments the man; and as owing to the quantity of
indigestible food that they eat, they are always dreaming

that ghosts continually visit them in sleep, and they live in constant danger from the unseen world.

Looking back through the æons of time to that primitive epoch, when incipient man was crudely welding the inchoate elements of thought, action, languages, and institutions, the concepts of nature, the vague perceptions of his own inner being and all that now constitute the great civilization with which we are endowed—we cannot forbear pausing for a moment to note the vast mental schemes that have resulted from his first supernal concept of luck and his after elimination of the dream ghost. In those original conceptions lay hid all the possibilities of the spiritual world—fate, destiny, the spirits, the godheads, heaven and hell, all the religions of the past, all supernal schemes for the future, every test power to divine the unknown, every evil influence that crushes humanity, every transcendental power, a lost world, and a saved humanity. So august, so grand a conclusion from such small premises may well cause us to be cautious of the inferences we draw from slight causes, and may make us doubt whether we have yet reached the ultima thule of the geography of the soul powers and passively await the evocation of other forms of supernal personalities, other mystic worlds.

Of the great Egyptian faith, how small now seems the heritage of humanity, and the thunders of Jove and the cognate Olympian deities exist as mere school-boy rhapsodies. So all the great mental forces that have been expressed in dynasties, empires, faiths, now remain as mere blotches on the escutcheon of time. There has been nothing eternal in human thought save the early fetish deductions man made from his supernal concept of luck and the presence of the dream ghost. These early deductions of the mystic are ever living, men conceive and re-conceive them, and to most men they have the same nature and express the same sentiments as when the pre-glacial man bowed in awe before the silent concepts of his own soul. From their long persistent immortality we are bound to expect they will outlast all the divine schemes that now encumber the human soul.

Yet among a limited class we know that fate and luck are mere words, and faith in the personality of a dream, trust in ghostly visitors and ghostly possessions, are only known as the aberrations of disordered or undeveloped minds, and between these two classes of mind-powers we read ten thousand supernal concepts ever rising higher and more varied in their expression and leading men to more universal concepts of being, higher expectations of the illimitable, until each supernal fiction emerges into radiant law. It is this vast series of expositions deduced from the primary human ghost that we have now to follow and show how, step by step, every supernal entity, every doctrine of every faith has been worked out of the successive evolution of new forms of social relation among men and the customs and sentiments that from them have arisen.

It is not in the nature of the human intellect to rest satisfied with its first essays in thought or action. If it was possible for a ghost spirit to exist of man, why not ghost spirits of animals, and ghost spirits in every important object in nature? Who could limit the capacity of ghost? That which could enter other men might enter animals, dwell in trees and plants, and make a home in a river or rock, exist in cloud and star, in short in everything. Such sentiments were slowly evolved. There are only a few objects to the Australian that have souls or spirits. We find more among the Red Indians; while with the Fijian and the Hill-man in India all things have their presiding spirits.

Many of the North American Indians, as the Nasquapees of Labrador, believe in the future shadowy existence of every material thing. (*Hinds' Labrador*, II. p. 103.) So the Indians of Guiana, according to Im Thurn, hold that not only many rocks, but also waterfalls, streams, and natural objects of every sort are supposed to consist of a body and a spirit. (*Ind. of Gui.* p. 855.) The ancient Peruvians, as Markham informs us, held that every created thing had its *mana* or spiritual essence. (*Cuzco*, p. 129.) And in *Mariner's Tonga Islands* we have the doctrine fully enunciated as prevailing among the Fijians, who held not only that the souls of men, women, beasts, plants, stocks, canoes, houses, but all the broken utensils of this frail world, tumble along over one another into the regions of immortality. (II. p. 122.) The same conception of the double nature of all substances was entertained, according to Captain Cook, in Tahiti. In the early barbaric times of the Finns the same doctrine prevailed; all nature was regarded as animated—the sun, the moon, the earth, the sea —each was a living thing. More, we have the same sentiment expressed by the ghost-seer in all countries. The ghost comes with every necessary accompaniment of ghost clothes, ghost weapons, and betimes ghost furniture, boats and so forth. Again, the universal expression of the same sentiment is to be inferred from the custom of burying or burning all kinds of objects with the dead for his use in the after-world, and it culminates in the Chinese faith that even the paper semblances of money, furniture, houses, and horses, in the new life, will be transformed into their realities.

The natural effect of working out the common duality of all objects was to make it possible that the spirits of the different existences might interchange their relations with material things; thus the spirit of an animal might enter the body of a man, more especially if it found that the proper ghost thereof was absent, or being more powerful it might either oust the native ghost altogether or only take up a residence with it in the same body. It is evident that when this new psychological system was created, a new world of phenomena were rendered probable. This was the first stage in the evolution of a god power, and introduced all possible combinations of the human and the animal. To it we owe all the animal myths, the fable *séances*, and the entire basis of customary folklore.

Not the least remarkable result of this belief was the creation of a certain class of affinities between animals and men which led to the evolution of the totem system. This, which Mr. Spencer only conceived to have arisen from the misinterpretation of nicknames derived from animals, and which Sir John Lubbock derived from that custom, has a far wider significance. We have only to take cognizance of its influence on the life of man and the origin of institutions to be assured that it never could have been derived from mere accident, but expresses the natural yearning of the human soul for some unexpressed want. We showed that the first dependence of man—his first deduction of help, the very birth of faith—was due to his recognizing in the uncanny, protective agencies. The doctrine of luck defined a new power in things to help and protect man. Charms and spells told him how to induce these powers, and all after forms of faith are but the expressions of higher protective powers whether present in the totem animal, the ancestral ghost, a tutelar deity, or a supreme godhead. Man at first sought help in the hidden mysteries in things, then he sought to secure help by interchange of relations with his fellow-man, and the human brotherhood was established by the fetish charm of sucking or imbibing each other's blood. But man not only stood in immediate relations with his fellows; he not only required to establish amicable associations with some men to secure himself from others; he also required the aid of some animals to secure himself from others. We see in the domestication of animals one of the modes in which this law as food protective worked, but its far more individual application was the taming of familiar animals. These are common all over the world, more especially among savage races, but in the highest civilization we

observe the same law at work, and, however strange it may
sound, we hold there is a blending of the mana of the
man with that of the animal. There is here no need
of any blood ceremony, the soul in each works out the
result.

The doctrine of the totem recognizes the presence of the
spirit in the animal. It has all the fetish attributes for
protection that we once noted in things. It is a general
power whose concept is gradually evolved as a social
institution, and, when higher sentiments of supernal protection are induced, it gradually decays. In its full
expression it enters as a guiding principle in all social
institutions, it regulates the status of the tribe, the clan,
the family, the individual, the sex. It affects birth and
puberty, marriage and death. Its origin is seen at the
present day in the relations that ever subsist between the
pet and its owner, and the birth of the individual totem,
before it has become a social custom, may be seen in the
instances we quoted of the Australian lace lizard and
native cat and in many instances of snake charmers, sacred
reptiles, and witches and wizards having familiar animals
of various kinds.

To develope different totems implies distinct likings of
animals among men. It is so in the selection of pets,
nowadays they are as various as the varieties of animals
attainable by men. In the savage state they are restricted
to native birds and beasts, and when men are more
developed, and new clan groups are formed, other natural
objects than animals become totems, the grass, the tree,
the rock, the sun; but when these are selected we may be
assured that men held that these objects possessed a dual
nature, these in their lower manifestations were only the
primary charm-objects endowed with the now common
spiritual nature.

It would lead us too far to enter into the consideration
of the various developments that followed the introduction

of the individual totem and its growth into the family and clan totems. These are fully described in Fraser's *Totemism*, a work which generalizes all the known aspects of totemism. But we may note that the individual totem like the ghost is usually acquired in sleep, and, of course, the objects that a man dreams of are those he is apt to think of, and in which he feels most interest. The Australian usually gets his individual totem in a dream; it was so with the American Indian, the animal came to the initiating lad in a dream and he went out and killed one of the same species, and made his medicine bag of its skin. In some cases the totem was selected by a process of divination, as at Samoa, and by the Indians of the Panama Isthmus.

In the early ghost state we question if any kind of worship obtained, like the Australian aborigines, men feared the ghosts of their living fellows, and avoided all contact with them. They were rather passive than active agents of evil; but, as soon as it was possible for a man to take an animal form or an animal spirit enter a man's body, the spirit-power became vastly extended. The tiger possessed by a man's soul with a man's knowledge of his fellows and their habits and re-sources, was a much more formidable opponent than the mere maneater who depended alone on his savage animal instincts. The northern nations worshipped the boar, before they killed it, in some measure to appease it, and thus prevent its spirit subsequently injuring them. Among the Florida Islanders snakes that haunt some place sacred to a *tindalo* are themselves sacred as being his property. There is one at Savo which causes the death of every one who happens to see it. Alligators are also sometimes supposed to be tindalos; a man will fancy one is possessed by the ghost of some friend, and will feed it or even sacrifice to it. Such an alligator will become an object of general reverence and even become tame. (*Jour. Anth. Inst.* X. p. 306.) Monkeys on the Gold Coast found near graves are supposed to be

animated by the spirits of the dead. The crocodile is sacred
at several places; snakes at Benin; sharks at Bonny. The
spirits of the dead, the Indians of Guiana hold, may pass
from the bodies of their owners into those of any animals
or even inanimate objects; and so prevalent is this opinion
that they are careful not to look at certain rocks or uncanny
objects. They avoid the flesh of certain animals because
they might contain malignant spirits, and in passing by
sculptured rocks, striking monuments, or shooting a cataract,
the Indians to avert the presumed ill-will of the local
spirits rub pepper in their eyes not to see them. (*Im
Thurn*, p. 368.)

As showing that token worship once existed in White
Russia, the Domovy is called a Snake, and this House Snake
brings all sorts of good things to the master who treats it
well. And, at the present day, the snake-totem compact is
not extinct, the peasants consider it a happy omen if a
snake takes up its quarters in the house: thus the totem
sentiment, after having arisen from mere luck to a spirit of
goodness, returns again to the pristine omen of luck.—
(*Ralston Songs*, p. 124.)

Totem worship is thus described in South Africa by
Arbousset. The phrase, " those of the Porcupine is applied
to the Baperis. When they see anyone maltreat that
animal they afflict themselves, grieve, collect with religious
care the quills if it has been killed, and rub their eyebrows
with them saying, ' They have slain our brother, our master,
one of ours, him of whom we sing.' Other Baperis
worship a species of monkey, others swear by the baboon.
At the new moon they stop at home, acting in this respect
like those who sing the sun. Those of the Sun, when the star
of day rises in a cloudy sky, say, it afflicts their heart. Like
all the other natives of this country the Malekutus venerate
their ancestors almost to adoration." (*Tour in the Cape*,
p. 176.)

The totem relation of the man and the animal having

arisen from that of the familiar animal was after evolved
into the form of ancestral and spiritual guardianship and
the assumed tutelar compact between man and his god.
We may read the evidence of the totem compact in the
principles which influenced the man's mind in relation to
his totem. First, the man reverenced and honoured his
totem. He might not kill it, or he could only kill it under
exceptionable circumstances, and then he might eat his
god-guardian. Often he asked its pardon for killing it, and
then treated some portion of its remains with honourable
distinction. The worship of the animal in some cases was
so far advanced that sacrifices were offered to them, and
various spell rites and incantations made to them.

To work out the system of intercommunion so necessary
between the totem and its worshippers, and all beings in
the same brotherhood, a telepathic power was conceived that
linked all the members of each group and enabled them
individually to communicate with their fellows. We have
already seen that transcendental powers were claimed for
the spell and charm; therefore, the savage saw no incongruity in the escaped fish warning its fellows all through
the sea, of human wiles, or even the skin of the slaughtered
totem informing its kin that certain tribesmen had broken
the implied compact, or, that before setting out on a hunting
expedition, permission should be invoked from the assembly
of bear or elks souls to kill them by their worshippers. It
has been assumed that the telepathic intercommunion of
souls was a new spiritual manifestation when it is in its
nature identical with the sympathetic virtues present in
charms and spells, which bring into the desired affinity
objects or persons however distant. This is the universal
mana power that encompasses all things and all personalities in the universe.

Of its special actions in the relations of the totem and its
worshipper, we will now speak our illustrations thereof we
have chiefly drawn from the mass of descriptive facts

presented in Frazer's store-house of supernal information the *Golden Bough*.

The semblances of the spell-powers were affirmed in the evolution of all the nature personalities, and the relations of man with the totem. The characteristics which express each animated power are evolved from the charm significance, whether as fire and energy in the sun, brightness and fickleness in the moon, procreative nature passing from the phallus to animate Adonis, or the symbols of Nature's changes as ever depicted and rendered continuous year by year in the symbols of the Corn Spirit, the Corn Maid, the Harvest Mother, the Mother of Maize, the Mother of Cotton; even in the symbol of the Carrying out Death, and the spring festivals of the Renewing of Life. So the institution of the totem was a spell—a spell affecting all that might be eaten, and its removal was an appeasing spell out of which grew the purification of the sacrament, the eating the flesh of the totem animal, and after, of the sacrificed god.

Necessarily from the character of the assumed totem relationship was educed the honour and respect offered to the animal in the hunt and after at the sacrifice. Primarily it was the totem animal that was sacrificed, and to the universal spell and mana power the totem animal was offered. It was so with the old Aryan races; with them it ever was the goat, the sheep, and the ox. It was the same with the Semites, and now the same doctrine is affirmed by sacrificing tribes. The Zuni offers the turtle to the general Turtle mana, the Aino, the Yakut, and the Gilyak the bear to the common Bear mana. In Africa, from the old Egyptian to the modern Kaffir and Malagassy, the crocodile was offered to the Crocodile god. Everywhere we meet with the evidence of honour and sacrifice—sacrifice in the hunt or on the altar.

Reverence to the wild beast itself, or the semblance of a spell to appease the mana of its totem race, are general.

The Aino and the Shaman honour the bear in the hunt. The Dyaks will not kill a crocodile until he has killed a man and broken thereby the implied compact. It is so with the hill tribes in India, only the man-eating tiger may be slain. The Malagasy tribesmen make a yearly proclamation to the crocodiles, announcing that they will revenge the death of their friends by killing an equal number of crocodiles. Though associated in the totem compact, the spirits of the animals are treated as a tribe distinct from their fellows, and the same law of a life for a life is exacted from the spirit tribesmen as the human tribesmen. The same feeling influences the American Indians: they spare the rattlesnake, because they say its ghost would excite its kinsmen to take vengeance on any redman.

Even when necessity causes the slaughter of the totem animal, it, and its fellow ghosts ill-will, must be turned aside, or honours must be accepted as compensation for death. Thus the Kamschatkan will apologise to the bear and seal he has killed, and excuse his act in various ways, offering to him nuts to forego future vengeance. The bear's head is honoured, after they have feasted on his flesh, with presents, so as to make it gratified by the notice it receives; for, like some Chinese heroes and heroines, it is more honoured in death than life. When the Ostiaks have killed a bear, they cut off its head and hung it upon a tree, with mystic honours, ascribing its death not to their own hands but to the Russian axe, and the skinning of it to the Russian knife. Then they honour the skin as a guardian god.

When the Koriaks have killed a bear or wolf they dress a man in its skin and dance round him saying it was the Russians who killed him. When they kill a fox they wrap it up in grass, and bid it go to its companions and tell them how hospitably it has been entertained, and that it has got a new cloak for its old one. The Lapps went a

step further, and thanked the bear for not injuring them
or breaking their weapons. (*The Golden Bough*, II. p. 112.)

Before setting out upon a bear expedition the North
American Indians offered expiatory sacrifices to the souls
of bears slain in previous hunts, and besought them to
be favourable to the hunters, and assume the character of
the decoy elephant to their wild living fellows. When they
had killed a bear they begged its ghost not to be angry,
and to gratify it they put a lighted tobacco pipe into its
mouth, and blew in the bowl to regale the ghost of the
dead animal with the smoke. The Otawas told the bear's
ghost it was glorious to be eaten by the children of a chief,
and probably a like sentiment explains the many instances
of family cannibalism in which the kin more or less
partook of the bodies of their own dead friends. The
Nootka Indians put a chief's bonnet on the slain bear and
powdered its fur with down, even provisions were set before
it and it was invited to eat. After being thus honoured,
surely no reasonable ghost could bear malice against those
who thus served it. (*Ibid.* II. p. 113.)

When the Kaffir hunters were in the act of showering
spears on an elephant, they call out "Great Captain, don't
kill us, don't tread upon us, mighty chief;" and when it is
dead, they make excuses to it, pretending it was an
accident and to gratify its ghost they bury the trunk with
much ceremony, crying, "The elephant is a great lord, and
the trunk is its hand." As treating the living animals and
the spirits of their dead as being in associate confraternity
with men in West Africa, they try the tiger who has killed
a man, so the negro who has killed a leopard is bound to a
tree; he is then tried by the chiefs for having killed one of
their peers, but he defends himself on the plea that he was
a stranger; then the dead leopard is set up in the village
and honoured by nightly dances. (*Ibid.* II. p. 114.) In the
many cases on record of the exorcisings as well as trials of
various animals for offences committed on human beings,

we may see the survival notions of the primary compact with the totem animal.

The telepathic spiritual power is always at work, and not only may the living animal communicate with the ghosts of its fellows, but the same virtue remains as in charms in every fragment of its body. When the Guiana Indians have killed a tapir and roasted its flesh on a babracot, they take good care to destroy the fireplace, or they say the friends of the tapir, if they came that way, and saw what they had done, would follow them to their sleeping-place and serve them the same. The savage Stiens in Cambodia beg an animals pardon after they have killed it, leat its soul torment them. (*Ibid.* II. p. 114.) Small animals, unless totems, are treated with contempt when killed. A certain amount of reverence is shown to sables and beavers. Alaskan hunters are careful that the bones of both are kept from the reach of dogs; so with the Canadian Indians, sables have been supposed to take it as an insult that live sables have been taken to Moscow. All through the animal world a sympathetic telepathy is assumed to be disseminated, it passes through the clouds, it penetrates the earth, it is diffused through the sea, and outwits the telephone and the telegraph in its universal presentation, not only through the spirits of the dead and the living, but in the charm activities present in all things.

The remains of deer and elks were treated by the North American Indians with the same punctilious respect: their bones might not be given to the dogs or thrown into the fire, because the souls of the dead animals were supposed to see what was done to their bodies and to tell it to other beasts, and as a result they would not allow their kin to be taken either in this world or the next. A sick man would be asked by the medicine-man if he had thrown away some flesh of deer or turtle, and if he had the reply was that the soul of the deer or turtle had entered the sick man and was killing him. The telepathic sympathy was universal: the Canadian Indian would not eat the embryo of the elk, less the mother elks should hear of it and refuse to be caught.

The Indians of Peru adored the fish they caught. The Ottawa Indians believed that the souls of dead fish passed into other fish, and they never burnt fish bones for fear of displeasing the souls of the fish, and they would no longer come into their nets. The disappearance of the herring from the sea about Heligoland was ascribed by the fishermen to two boys after ill-using a herring casting it into the sea, when it informed its fellows and they avoided that coast. The Thlinket of Alaska call the first halibut of a season chief, and give a festival to its honour. There are many evidences of the honours bestowed upon the heads of deer, wolves, lions, bears, foxes, and so forth; may not the honouring of the Yule boar's head and decorating it with fruits and spices be the remnant of honouring the soul of the dead boar, and the cherishing and displaying of the fox's tail a sacrifice to the spirit of its ghost, after transferred to its captor or the one first in at the hunt?

Among the vagaries of human belief arose the supposition that the spirit might locate itself in any special part of a human being—in the head, the bowels, the limbs; he might produce pains in those parts only. A singular modification of this belief prevailed among the Samoans: they inferred that at the instant of birth as well as its own, the spirit of its tutelar deity, or of some animal, found an entry. Sometimes one took up its abode in the loft wing of a pigeon; another in the tail of a dog, the right leg of a pig, a shark, a cocoanut, a banana, bonita, or an eel. Each of these objects then became sacred to the individual whose god or totem it embraced.

At this early stage of psychological evolution we may not, we must not infer that men had learnt to idealize a spiritual immaterial soul, a something that could combine

with matter, act on matter, and yet preserve its own series
of special attributes. Far from this, man was only
acquainted with matter in its several conditions and their
variations, he knew it as a solid, as a flexible substance, as
a fluid, and in the gaseous state. It was in the most
attenuated of these conditions, the one most likely to
manifest the various changes, that he noted the relations of
man's dual nature, that he inferred the nature of the two
principles in man. He had seen the steam rising from the
boiling geyser, the vapour rising from the waterfall; the
mist creeping along the hill-side may be ascending into the
heavens in clouds;—he had also seen the smoke of his own
fire, and of the sacrificial fire, even the greater portion of
the solid body of the victim, rising in long wreaths, and
gradually becoming more attenuated until it was lost in
the blue of the sky; more, his own breath, in general
unobserved at times, passed out of his body in a distinctly
marked vapour. These states of matter were as present to
his perceptive powers as were the solids and fluids, and
uniformly the ghost was this same vapour; it might be
visible as the human breath, or it might be invisible as
betimes was the same. Such was the primary ghost, such
is the ghost or spirit of the lower races of men everywhere
in the world, and even such is the vulgar apparition among
the more advanced races; like the human breath it may be
visible or invisible. There ultimately came a period when
this ghostly substance became more sublimated, and was
esteemed of a so-called spiritual nature, but so impossible
was it for the spiritual idealists to separate it from the
common attributes of matter that under the most transcendental conditions it is described as glory, light, fire, or
flame equally material attributes.

While in the general ordinary course of material relations, man became cognizant of the physical and mental
differences in substances and of the varied relations he had
with the animal and vegetal world about him, he also

recognized relations in things of a more marked and impressive character. He had seen the—in general—quiet brooklet become a roaring raging flood, the usually narrow river overflow its banks and lay regions of the neighbouring country under water; the sea usually only laving the sands, changed into a vast onsweeping wave, or bursting into perilous breakers; so high overhead where the sun coursed along his daily arch, black clouds rolled, the thunder roared, and the lightning flashed. These and many other forms of natural force must have been ever present to his perceptive powers as denoting greater forces, distinct modes of action having few or no affinities with his ordinary sublunary conceptions of the relations of things and beings.

Yet the one series of forces differed only as one man differs from another; one animal from another; an animal from a plant or stone; though the distinctions were vastly greater. Ordinary earth and water he could associate with the plant and the stone, but the mighty natural forms and forces stood outside the ordinary habits of things; he could scarcely associate them with all that was common to him in the ordinary course of things. He knew only of the two great dualistic natures of beings, and these were all that he could utilize in distinguishing the heavenly and earthly bodies, and the great powers they evinced. He recognized the same set of relations between the living and the sleeping man, the raving and the quiet beast, as he saw in the placid river and the raging torrent, the serene sky and the wild tornado. It was the ghost spirit in the man, in the animal, even in the fetish stone that gave it all its active principles, so he could not expect other than a like ghost-power in the sun, the moon, the thunder, the wind; they possessed the same dual natures, the same passions, the same wills as all terrestrial beings. So as men fought with men, animals with animals, and men with animals, ever producing various temporary supremacies, so was it in the great outer world of nature. In the sky he became conscious of the same antagonisms as on the earth, ever he saw allwhere the independent actions of many varied kinds of organisms, each acting under its own temporary impulses, and all discordant disintegration being replaced by a like varying series of heterogeneous individual forces.

As it was customary for the rude savage to ally himself under certain circumstances with the inhabitants of the neighbouring caves or wigwams, to repel the assaults of tigers, wolves, or bears, or to resist a like action by other associated men, he acquired the capacity to conceive of spirit or ghost help. So among the vast series of dual existencies, men had to select those whom they could hold communion with, and by some apposite circumstance those who would enter into spiritual affinity with themselves. We may in speaking of this relation use the word totem spirit or god, but everywhere the association is of the same nature a reciprocal interchange of obligations, the basis of all forms of religion is the assumed necessity for supernal help.

Hence when man passed from the consideration of, and dependence on charm spells, his soul went out into the Kosmos about him, and according to his local surroundings were the nature of the powers on which he learnt to depend. The individual selection of a protector would naturally precede that of a group, and the supernal protector of the man who became a tribal leader, or who was noted for his mana, would be more apt to be selected by the young during the initiation rites, and as the impersonal worshipper selected various spells to strengthen his fetish aims, so the spirit worshipper enlarged the circle of his protective relations; thus we find many protective totems in the medicine-bags of many Indians, and ever in the tribes when one divine power fails to reply, another is appealed to. Thus humanity passed from the concept of spirit-power as indifferent, or only evil to the realization of beneficent

service and the evolvement of mutual good relations
between man and spirit, whether of human or nature
origin.

We have incidentally referred to the derivation of the
sentiment of the familiar animal as preceding that of the
familiar spirit out of which the sentiment of evil spirits
as the agents of human malignity has been evolved. In
treating on totems we showed how general has been the
concept of human derivation from animals and of animal
origin from men and women, and in this transfer of
attributes and the mystic nature of the changes induced we
detect the stepping-stones as it were of the development of
the familiar animal to a familiar spirit animal, and then
when the ghost sentiment was evolved, the concept of the
familiar ghost spirit. The witches' cat thus became a
mystic animal possessing supernal powers and able to aid
its mistress not only in her malignant devices but to
accompany her through the air in her transcendental
manifestations. In the old witchcraft of Europe such
fetish powers of help were ascribed to hares, dogs, owls,
and so forth, and when ghosts and imps were conceived
they might come in the forms of snakes, toads, rats, and
other animal shapes. Jenkinson describes similar ideas
as being expressed by the Zulus. "Diagaen said the
witches went out in the dead of the night carrying a cat;
they sent this cat into the house of the person whom they
meant to bewitch. The cat brought out a bit of hair or
something else which the witch deposited under the floor of
her house, and in consequence the object of her dislike soon
became sick. There were five animals they used—the cat,
the wolf, the panther, the jackal, the owl." (*Amazulu*, p. 116.)

Whether the cat familiar of the Zulus was of native
origin or derived from the Boers we cannot say, but the
sentiment of men ghosts entering and possessing animals
is common among them. Livingstone writes:—"It is
believed that the souls of departed chiefs enter into lions

and render them sacred. A hungry lion came attracted by meat, and Mokoro, imbued by the belief that it was a chief in disguise, scolded him roundly. "You a chief, eh? You call yourself a chief, sneaking about in the dark trying to steal our buffalo meat! Are you not ashamed of yourself? You are like a scavenger beetle; you have not the heart of a chief! Why don't you kill your own beef? You must have a stone in your chest and no heart at all." (*Zambesi*, p. 161.)

Jenkinson says the witches and wizards "go about at night accompanied by familiar wild cats, leopards, and baboons, and lay poisons in the path for people to step over, and on the threshold and in the fields, to destroy the crops." Like many other African races they saw a supernal power in snakes, and if one is found in a hut the people move out and wait patiently till it leaves. The owner will say it is perhaps the spirit of one of his ancestors come to visit him in this form. (*Kaffir Folklore*, p. 22.) We have noted that the same idea of an ancestor coming in a snake form was known in India and in the East. In New Zealand it took the form of a lizard, in West Africa it comes in the form of a snake or crocodile, and elsewhere in other animal forms. Rowley writes of the Hottentots that they "had a spirit who came in the form of a butterfly." In Scotch witch trials we read of the witches' imps coming to them in prison in the form of flies. The Hottentot insect spirit was the *Mantis fausta;* they sang and danced while it remained. If it entered a kraal the inhabitants were in a transport of devotion. They threw to it the powder of the herb *buchu* and offered a fat sheep as a thanksgiving. They believed that it brought them favour and prosperity and that all past offences were buried in oblivion. If it alighted on a Hottentot he was a man without fault and sacred, so if it alighted on a woman she was a sanctified person. If one of these insects were killed their cattle would perish by wild beasts and themselves die. (*The Religion of the Africans*, p. 64.) In *Africana* we read of

the bewitcher becoming a leopard or carrion crow.
(I. p. 210.)

Possession among the North American Indians could not
have primarily been that of men ghosts, it was that of
animals. Schoolcraft describing the Dacotahs writes:—
" Their idea of the pathology of diseases is that the spirit
of something, perhaps a boar, deer, turtle, fish, tree, stone,
worm, or of some deceased person, has entered into the sick
and caused his illness. The effort of the medicine-men is
to expel this spirit by incantations and ceremonies and the
aid of the spirit or spirits he worships, then by noises,
gestures, and sucking." (*Ind. Tribes*, I. p. 250.) The same
writer in his *History of the Iroquois* writes: " The witch had
power to turn into a fox or wolf, run swift, emit flashes of
light, or transform into turkey or owl. Onondaga said one
day he stepped out of his lodge and immediately sank
through the earth into a large lodge in which three hundred
witches and wizards were assembled" (pp. 130-141). We
know there were Walpurgis nights on the Brocken, in churchyards among Scotch witches, and in India the rakchasas
and apsara bhutes assemble on a set day on the mountain-
side; so it would seem the same worthy confederates
had their mystic assemblies underground in America.
In Copway's *History of the Ojibway* we are informed
that the witches and wizards " are believed to fly invisibly
from place to place and to turn themselves into bears,
wolves, foxes, bats, and snakes; they do so by putting on
the skins of those animals and imitating their cries "
(p. 145).

In Europe we hear of demon cats, dogs, foxes, and cock-
headed devils. The demon weasel is common in Japan, and
besides possessing men and women it maliciously injures
them by causing them to fall. Conway says "the devil-
worshippers of Travancore to this day see the evil power in
the form of a dog." With the Navajos Indians the coyote
is the possessing animal. With the Ainos and the north-

eastern Asiatics the bear was the mystic animal, and in other places serpents are the possessing animals.

One series of depositions in the old witch trials of the witches of Huntingdon will suffice to show the nature of the supernal powers attached to animals. "Frances Moore deposed that eight years since she received a little black puppy from Margaret Simpson who had it in bed with her. Margaret Simpson told her to keep the dog all her lifetime and said if she cursed any cattle and set the dog upon them they would die. Also one good wife, Weed, gave her a white cat telling her if she denied God and pricked her finger in affirmation thereof—which she did, the cat licking the blood—that about six years since William Foster would have hanged her children; on which she cursed William Foster and set the white cat on him. He fell and died. About five years since in a dispute about cows she cursed Edward Hull's cow, which shortly swelled and died. She said she killed the cat and dog a year since, but after a like cat and dog haunted her and when she was apprehended they crept under her clothes and tortured her" (p. 6).

In the European Folklore we read of the souls of men going into the owl, the cuckoo, the stork, robin, woodpecker, and swallow, as well as into the witch animal, and in the various animal vampires. Among several races of men we have statements of the souls of men after death entering into birds, as those of North American chiefs into singing birds. Tylor quotes several cases of the souls of the dead warriors and chiefs becoming birds in Africa as we have seen chiefs become lions, in some places snakes and crocodiles, while cowards become lizards and frogs; but as most of these peoples have, besides various abodes for souls, some sort of shadowy Hades, we look on these animal and bird presentations as poetical estimations of class and character worth out of which the concept of successive incarnations or re-births was formed. More, as these sentiments imply that the attributes while living decide the condition of the soul in a future state wizards become powerful spirits, and murderers, suicides, lepers, abortions, and women dying in child-bed malignant spirits.

Side by side with this concept of animal possession we note the higher sentiment of ghost and spirit possession. The invisible animal that entered the human body gave place to the malignant ghost of a man or a nature spirit. These possessing ghosts might be as vindictive and savage as the demon animals whose places they supplied, or they might represent the first exposition of supernal good, as the African with the headache who considered his departed father was in his head scolding him. (*Livingstone*, p. 521.) These good spirit agents imply a higher stage of development and will be considered in our next chapter. Spencer writes that the Veddahs look to the shade of a dead parent or child to give success in the chase; then they have arrived at the worship of good ancestor spirits like the East African.

The first concept of a ghost or spirit-power always represents it as malicious or vindictive; it may injure by charms only, it may act through animal forms, it may come in its own ghost or spirit nature, but ever it essentially represents an evil impulse or power. This primary ghost-power at first is only to be restrained by the same spells and charms that characterize the earliest supernal concepts. Afterwards the evil action of one ghost is supposed to be restrained by the intervention of another ghost or spirit through the instrumentality of the medicine-man; it is then ever evil warring with evil. As the primary savage only at first endeavoured to change or coerce the presumed supernal evil that affected him by amulets, mystic ceremonies, and the virtues he acknowledged in weird substances, so when the medicine-man had presented his assumed powers over ghosts and spirits, he became the ready means to overthrow at first the malignant spells of other ghosts or their presumed possession. Ever at this stage as we have seen the good influence extracts the evil influence as a material substance in the form of stone or organic waste; but when an ancestor ghost is evolved, we have the commencement of the contest of spirit with spirit, ghost with ghost, the ancestor spirit against the devil spirit, whatever its nature.

If we endeavour to work out the primary evolution of evil spirits, devils, we can always do so by recognizing it in man, animal, or nature power which manifests vindictive attributes. Hence we ever, according to locality, meet with the wolf, the dog, the tiger, the bear, hyena, snake, or crocodile devil. Hence the cognomen, devil, applied to the ghosts of ancestors; hence the devil in the tree that, falling, killed the man; in the eddy which capsized the canoe, the blast that caused a death. To each other the warring tribes of old Aryans were devils; if one conquered they became giant demons, ogres, or genii. The evil spirits of the Australian aborigine were his dead enemies; it was so in the contests of Britons and Picts, Teutons and Sclavonians. As Conway shows, the devil at Mozambique is the wicked white man, Muzongu Maya, and we doubt if a worse devil ever existed than the merciless Arab slave-hunter. If the Yakuts say there is a devil in the body, they mean an enemy.*

Of the supernatural beings acknowledged by the inhabitants of Sindh Burton writes: "They believe in the Jinns or genii, in Bhut ghosts, in disembodied spirits, in ghoul or demons of the wilderness, in Peri, fairies in Dew Rakas and Pap, powerful fiends. The Dakkan is the same as our witch; she has the power of turning men into beasts, killing cattle, flying to any distance by reciting a magic formula, and mounting a hyena. The Bauble are frightful beings,

---

* Dorman shows that the devils were educed from enemies. Thus Ercono was the devil of the Moxos, their racial enemies the Conox tribe. The devils of the Tacs were Tupas, their enemies the Tupis. Chelul Patagonian devil, their enemies the Choloagos. (*Prim. Super.* p. 27.)

half-female, half-hellish. They live in the hills and jungles where they frequently appear to travellers; they are covered with hair like bears, and have large pendant lips. The Shir is a creature that partakes of the Satanic nature; he lives in the burial ground." (*Sindh*, p. 175.)

Of actual ghost possession we have many records even in our own witchcraft annals. In the palmy days of witch power the possessing ghosts were as demonstrative as spirits now are at *séances*. Holland in his *Treatise against Witchcraft* writes: "There was a poor woman in my country named Jacoba, out of whose belly I myself heard the voice of an unclean spirit. It was small indeed, and yet as oft as it listed it was both a distinct voice and very intelligible. Many others heard the same, and noble men, affecting predictions, greatly desired to hear and behold this pythoness whom, therefore, they sent for often and stripped her of all her apparel that no secret fraud might be hidden. If a man did ask him of the most secret things, past and present, he answered ofttimes most strangely, but concerning future events he always erred" (p. 12). No doubt the sly Jacoba, or a confederate present, was a skilful ventriloquist.

Witch narratives are so common that we need not dwell on this form of possession which is, with insignificant variations, general among most races of men, with some it is an evil spirit as with the Arab, the Negro, the Indian, who buried his dead secretly that the Mulasha might not get them. Throughout Asia, as well as formerly all over Europe, possession by ghosts and evil spirits were supposed to be every day events, and such ideas are still maintained by the rustics in various parts of Europe by the Dyaks and the Hill Tribes in India. Wherever we observe possession expressed for good purposes, as for prophecy, enunciation of laws, and the declaration of rites, we may be assured a new mental force is being created, and that the sentiment of divine goodness is being evolved, and the spirit guardianship developed. Yet, though the greater power of the doctor ultimately exorcises all that is evil, for a long time the contest of the good medicine-man, the priest, is only exercised in using more powerful charms to expel the evil spirit of disease in its many forms.

The Malagassy holds that disease is caused by evil spirits, and to get rid of them pieces of white wood are put on the housetop pointed and painted, and 3 ft. from the door is planted a forked branch like horns, and twice every day a dance is performed by the household, and charms are brought into the courtyard and placed on the rice mortar, the sick man is dressed in a curious fashion, and drums and bamboos are beaten and hands clapped to drive the spirit away, this ceremony is repeated two or three times a day until the patient dies or recovers. (*Folklore Record*, II. p. 46.) Burton in his *Zanzibar* shows that, as with the Jews, the spirits, not to be homeless, might be cast into unclean swine; so the African medicine-man, more sympathetic, attached some article to the sick man's neck, a charm object into which the expelled demon might find a home. (II. p. 88.) Cockayne in his *Leechdom* shows the transition stage to the powerful mana exorcism, when *Alpha and Omega* were added to the old rune charm, with its powerful medicaments, bramble, lupins, and pulegium put under the alter, and nine masses said over them, then the ingredients made into a drink to expel the disease fiend. No doubt the old hedge priest was at home in these Druidical incantations. (II. p. 185.)

The Melanesians held that "when a man went out of his mind it was supposed that a ghost was possessing him, and wonderful things were thought to be done by one in such condition. To recover such a person if he could be caught, a fire was made of strong smelling herbs, and the patient held in the smoke. The names of the dead were called, and when the right name was given, the possessed man would confess it, and the power of the ghost would fail." (*Jour. Anth. Inst.* X. p. 85.) According to Pocqueville the Moslems described the plague as an evil spirit. "It was seen to glide along their roofs, a decrepit object covered with funeral shreds, he called by their names those he wished to cut off." (*Pettigrew*, p. 66.) More definite is the action of the Hindoo Bhuta spirits, these "are believed to afflict human beings by entering into and possessing them. They seat themselves in the lower part of the abdomen and feed on the excreta. They cause fits, paralytic strokes, temporary aberrations, outbreaks of madness, cramps, rheumatic pains." (*Jour. Anth. Inst.* V. p. 410.)

The low class Brahmins who are medicine-men to the village Hindoos, by various spells and mantras draw out of the patient's body the possessing Bhute, and then to prevent its return to the patient or its entering into another member of the family they endeavour to buy its good will. For this purpose in every house a cot is provided for the Bhutes, they are not only fed with rice and sundry good things, but flowers are laid on the cot, and perfume burnt before it, and certain ceremonies are performed to make the half-domestic spirit comfortable. It is almost advanced to the status of the house god of the Russian peasant.

Captain Falconer of the Bombay Artillery was of a different temperament to the Bhute worshipper. He had a servant who appeared wasting away, for a long time he would not tell his ailment, at last he said a Brahmin had bewitched him with his revenge, and that he was now eating up his liver. The Captain at once rode to the Brahmin, and with his whip lashed him severely for bewitching his servant, on which he roared he would release him from the spell. On the Captain coming back home, for no doubt the news had spread by the fellow servants, he found the man much better. (*Zoist*, VII. p. 5.)

Even many rude tribes of man have adopted the Captain's mode of expelling the possessing spirits, or have used equally as efficacious spells to remove the evil from among them by exporting the devils and ghosts wholesale. Bancroft tells us the Nicaraguans have a ceremony by which they expel them from their dwellings. (*Bancroft,* II. p. 785.) The Mayas of Yucatan had evil spirits driven away by the sorcerers, they fled when the fetishes were exposed. The Peruvians had a long religious rite in which all the mana of the priests were combined, these in a band advanced from north, east, south and west, driving, like wild fowl, the evil spirits into the river, which were then borne by its current into the ocean.

When the time arises for the annual expulsion of the ghosts and demons from the Nicobar Islands the priests, to produce sufficient mana, fast for a long time beforehand, and by constant potations and mysterious ceremonies they work themselves up to an excited pitch, and then commence their conjurations. They are daubed over the face with red paint and rubbed with oil over the body. In deep bass voices they sing a doleful dirge, and rush wildly about. On the beach lies the small model of a boat for the spirits, adorned with garlands of fresh leaves. The priests try to catch hold of the spirits, and they coax, scold, and abuse, and rush after their invisible antagonists, the women howling all the time. After great trouble the Iwi are safely brought on board and seated on the skiff. Young men in boats then tow the craft so far out to sea that it will not be brought by the wind and tide back to their village, it is then set adrift, and the young men return to feast and rejoice. Even should it be borne back a screen is erected between the village and the sea, that the spirits may not see it. (*Calcutta Rev.* LXII. p. 193.)

A somewhat similar precaution to get rid of the ghosts of foemen is undertaken by one of the tribes at New Guinea. "The Motuans had killed many Soloans at the entrance of a channel, since which the Solo spirits have been troublesome there detaining the boats. To drive them away from

the boats entering the sound, they were brought right up,
then the chief took his nephew by the hand, handed to him
two wisps of cassowary feathers, and he stood in front of
the vessel shaking them with a peculiar motion of the body,
then all shouted as if driving something before them, and
by this incantation the ghosts were driven away." (*Chalmers
New Guinea*, p. 29.)

CHAPTER VI.

The Evolution of Ancestral Worship and the sentiment of Supernal Goodness.

As no step in progress is ever induced but by the manifestation of tentative stages, even as the leaper who makes a backward movement so as to gain impetus, so we read the evidence of rude preliminary anticipations of the principle of goodness among some tribes who have only rude concepts of the attributes of the spirit powers they would fain appeal to.

In the primary mental stage man only recognizes luck, the vague and uncertain conditions resulting from chance; there is neither the intelligent presence of good or evil, all influences express unrestrainable impersonal fate. Then, when man conceived of the powers in charms and spells, the result depended on the power or mana in the charm or spell, and it was good or bad only as it affected the inflictor and the victim; it was equally impersonal and devoid of principle, the same action expressing severally each sentiment. When the man possessing mana, and as a necessary consequence the medicine-man was evolved, then the charm power became more defined, and good and evil influences, not mental selective attributes, were attached to the impersonal objects depended upon in spells. These powers were worked by the medicine-men, and through their constant application schools of charm spells were generally evolved. Both for good and evil purposes, besides rites and ceremonies, they appealed to the natural virtues as well as the presumed mystical virtues they recognized in objects. Hence the first real concepts of good, as distinct from evil were the attributes which affected humanity found in plants, but also equally ascribed to other things.

When the dual nature of man and animal was evolved, then the ghost in reality represented the medicine-man of the day, and as his charms, whether to bring disease or cast it off, represent ill to some one, so the primary spirit always expresses evil.

The Australian aborigines have evolved many evil spirits, not only the Ingnas, the same ghost-demons of evil mou that are recognized by all the lower human races, but other nature evil spirits derived from rivers, hurricanes, beasts, birds, and reptiles, as the Bunyipa, a monster that dwells in the swamps and rivers and devours men. With some it is a mystic emu, with others a giant kangaroo. The Myndie is a great snake. Whirlwinds are caused by a giant magpie. One, an animal near Western Port, resembles a human being, but his body is as hard as stone. The river Murray was made by a snake's spirit. Nargon is a ferocious monster who dwells in a cave; he is all stone, he seizes black fellows and drags them into his cave; some liken him to a huge frog. Kootcher is an evil spirit who causes death and disease, and to charm away his influence they take red ochre, human bones, and clay. Some say he is a black fellow, others a snake. (*Abor. Vict.* I. p. 457.)

The Okopaid of the Andamanese is described as communicating with the invisible powers; he ascribes epidemics to evil spirits whom he attempts to control with a burning brand, or by planting charm stakes. (*Jour. Anth. Inst.* XII. p. 110.) He is in fear of the evil influence in the sun and moon, he ceases his work when the moon is declining and does not begin it again until it is once more enlarging; so he is afraid to work at sunrise lest he should offend the sun. Storms denote the anger of the cloud spirits, earthquakes

are caused by ghosts. All the evil influences the Andamanese recognize due to ghosts and spirits, they appear to
have no concept of supernal goodness.

According to Sir John Lubbock there are many races of
men which only recognize spirits of evil, malignant beings
of the same nature as the Christian devils, the Moslem
Ginns, the Hindoo Bhutes and the Chaldean demons. Of
these he instances the Hottentots, the Bechuanas, the
Mosquito Indians, the Abipones, Coroados and other South
American tribes, the Bougoos in Africa, and generally the
North American Indians and Tartar hordes. We are afraid
that many of the peoples he refers to are wrongly estimated
by the travellers he mentions, and that in many cases the
more prominent fears of the vulgar (for there are vulgar
minds even among savages) have been accepted as denoting
the general concepts of the tribe. Only the other day we
read of the natives of New Guinea that they hold the spirits
are all malignant, and they do not seem to grasp the idea
of a beneficent spirit, and that they have to be overcome by
force of arms, blessings, or cursings, but are most effectively dispelled by fire. (*The Popular Science Monthly,*
XXXVII. p. 859.) On the contrary Chalmers the Missionary, reports that they recognize the ghosts of men as good
and bad, kind and vindictive; they recognize spirits in pigs
and wallabies, in frozen fish, in most natural things;
thunder is an angry spirit, and Koitapu sends death and
and sickness, and he is to be bought by offerings. All
objects possess spirits, they worship the sun, the moon,
stones, rocks, mountains, and dead warriors, and these
without having evolved an active spirit of good, imply the
grateful acceptance of the good in nature and the incipient
beginning of ancestor worship. (*Pioneering in New Guinea,*
p. 169, &c.)

Even the Veddahs, as described by Herbert Spencer, are
not wholly devil worshippers, however much they may
dread the spirit ministers of evil; if they look to the shade

of a dead parent or child to give success in the chase, they have arrived at the preliminary stage of ancestor worship. The Araucanian saving fairy, also referred to by Spencer, implies spirit-help; and the mixed character of the spirits for good and evil among the Ashantees, the Amazula, the old Chaldeans, and all the Aryan races, imply the gradual growth of the sentiment of goodness.

Essentially among all races of men in the past and in the present, the most prominently expressed monition is that of fear, and its effects last longest in the mind. The good in nature, goodness in our kindred, are accepted without thought; we at first accept it, and after, if withheld, demand it. Evil in every form always denotes an enemy, one to be shunned, feared, and, at best, prevented injuring us by submission, entreaty, and offerings. Goodness begins in the most trivial recognitions of interest, service and duty. All men cannot see all things under the same aspects; to the hunter there is little or no natural goodness, he is indifferent to sunshine or rain, and the river which carries his bark or skin canoe is no more thought of than the earth on which he walks; but if in the eddies of the rapids he sees his fellow's frail bark upset and himself engulphed in the waters, an evil spirit has seized him and carried him down, probably he had broken some tabu or failed to offer some leaf, stick, or stone, and thus excited the malignity of the usually placid spirit. To the earth cultivator the universe bears another aspect, sunshine and rain are equally necessary to him, and therefore he learns to recognize the nature-powers under their double aspects of good and evil and thereon builds up the lower forms of the divine nature. Also he becomes more dependent on his fellows, and this sentiment he carries into the after-life, and thus natural goodness and human goodness build up spirit goodness, more especially when he carries the kin soul into bird and beast, into sun wind and rock.

The origin of the whole of the totem systems begin with

the hunter. They are most evolved in that intermediate
state in which man is an incipient cultivator, and depends
chiefly on the wild products of nature. They gradually
cease or evolve into social institutions, affecting class
position and influence, when men settle in permanent communities.

The mode of the totem evolution is everywhere similar,
though the mediums differ. When the kin ghost was
recognised, and the sentiment of goodness as an active
attribute was being evolved, men sought to associate themselves with some of the supernal forms denoting goodness
that they recognised. All natural physical existences, all
material forms of power, all kinds of animal life were
endowed with soul-spirits like men. They might differ in
nature, as one animal differs from another; but as one man
now entered into blood-relations of brotherhood with another
man, so might the soul of man enter into a brotherhood of
mutual help and service with any of the like spirits it
recognised in its spiritual kosmos. It has to be remembered
that in all human associations men most desire to associate
with those of a different temperament, having another class
of emotions even of opposite characters. Hence, we can
understand how the Indian hunter esteemed the cunning of
the coyote, the subtlety of the snake, the strength of the
alligator and tiger. In like manner, the all-piercing eye of
the sun, the power of the storm and thunder appealed to
some men, while others sought association with the soul in
the corn, the winds and waters.

Because of the commonness of animal totems, the whole
totem system has been conceived to be that of animal
relationship. This is an error. Animal totems are most
common because animal objects are most common, and the
special animistic attributes of animals most appealed to the
instinctive nature of the hunter, or were specially attractive
to the individual. We have in this way seen how the
familiar animal became the familiar spirit, and so evolved

into the totem. Of course, when it was supposed the
medicine-man went into the sky, it was possible for some
ancestral ghost to have ascended into the sky, or some sun
star-spirit to have descended on the earth ; and thus the
ancestral spirit of goodness might have been evolved from
any material form or force, or from any animal association.

We may express this evolution of the spirit of goodness
as ancestral worship, we may describe it as totem worship ;
in all cases it implies the bond of a common brotherhood,
kinship and mutual service, whether manifested to men by
an animal totem, or sun, star, or other nature spirit. Animal
association or spirit association may arise in dreams, in
waking visions, in every abnormal state, toxic or otherwise,
in which mental aberrations may be excited. As proving
the protective association is mutual, the totem worshipper
affirms the totem will not injure him ; and if the snake or
lion kill him, or the lightning burns him up, his fellows cry
that he has been false to the assumed compact. Thus in
Senegambia lions and crocodiles discriminate their votaries,
scorpions in the East, snakes among the Moqui, the Jaguar,
the Peruvian Indian, even the cattle in Madagascar, the
child of their owner. So general was this idea that one
bitten by his totem animal in some instances has been
expelled from the tribe as disowned by his totem.

The nature of the totem to a certain extent implies the
social state in which it was accepted as the divine guardian.
Many animal totems express their origin as being in the
hunter state. Many as sun, moon, and star totems may
have been accepted at any time : scattered tribes, like the
Australian aborigines, conceive the moon and stars were
once men and women. Many totem relations are manifested
by spells, and probably had their origin in the spell era,
when the status of the medicine-man was established.
Thus the general small bird and reptile clans of the Omahas
express the era of corn cultivation, when men depended not
so much on one animal protector as on a class of pro-

tectors.   Frazer writes :—" In harvest time, when the birds eat the corn, the small bird clan of the Omahas take some corn, which they chew and spit over the field.   This is thought to keep the birds from the crops.   If worms infest the corn, the reptile clan of the Omahas catch some of them and pound them up with some grains of corn which have been heated.   They make a soup of the mixture, and believe that the corn will not be infested again, at least for that year.   During a fog the men of the Turtle clan of the Omahas used to draw the figure of a turtle on the ground with its face to the south.   On the head, tail, middle of the back, and on each leg were placed small pieces of a red breech cloth with some tobacco.   This was thought to make the fog disappear.   Another Omaha clan, the Wind people, flapped their blankets to start a breeze, which will " drive away the mosquitoes." (*Totemism*, p. 24.)   In all these instances the power of associative goodness is appealed to through charms and spells.

We have ample evidence that the American totems represent ancestral forms, and we will again refer to the great mass of evidence that Mr. Frazer has so industriously collected.   " The Turtle clan of the Iroquois are descended from a fat turtle, which gradually developed into a man.   The Bear and Wolf clans of the Iroquois are descended from bears and wolves respectively.   The Crayfish clan of the Choctaws were originally cray-fish.   The Carp clan of the Ontonaks are descended from the eggs of a carp warmed by the sun.   The Ojibways are descended from a dog.   The Crane clan of the Ojibways are descended from a pair of cranes transformed into a man and woman.   The Buffalo clan of the Omahas were originally buffaloes.   The Osages are descended from a male snail and a female beaver ; to do so, the snail burst its shell, developed arms, feet and legs, and became a man, and the beaver became a maid, then he married her.   The Iroquois, in their respective clans, are descended from the eagle, pigeon, wolf, bear,

elk, beaver, buffalo and snake. The Moquis say the great
Mother brought from the west the clans, deer, sand, water,
bears, hares, tobacco plants, and reed grass, and turned
them into men. The Californian Indians are descended
from the coyote. The Lenape clans were descended from
the wolf, turtle and turkey. The Kutchin say once on a
time all beasts formed only one class, birds another, and all
fish a third. So the Arawak tribes came from an animal,
a bird, a plant. Some aboriginal tribes in Peru came from
eagles, others from condors." (*Totemism*, p. 3, &c.)

In like manner other totem races Mr. Frazer shows had
like origins. The West Australians are descended from
ducks, swans, and other wild fowl. The Santals have a
wild goose clan. In Senegambia there are hippopotamus,
crocodile, scorpion, and so forth clans. The people in
Ellice Island, in the South Pacific, say they are derived
from the porcupine fish, the Kalungs of Java from a transformed dog. The clans of the Indian Archipelago from
trees, pigs, eels, crocodiles, sharks, serpents, dogs, &c.
The snake Moquis say a woman gave birth to snakes.
With the Bakalai of West Africa a woman is said to have
brought forth severally a calf, crocodile, hippopotamus,
monkey, and wild pig. The Aino ancestor was suckled by
a bear.

Though most numerous, animal totems are by no means
the only ones. The old Aryan races deduced men from
the gods through demigods, human ancestors. In Australia
we read of the Thunder, Rain, Star, Hot-wind, and Sun
clans, also of Honey, Clear-water, Flood-water, and
Lightning clans. So in America there are the Ice,
Thunder, Earth, Water, Wind, Salt, Sun, Snow, Bone,
Sea, Sand, and Rain clans. In Africa Sun and Rain, in
India a Constellation and the Foam of a river, in Samoa
the Rainbow, Shooting-star, Cloud, Moon, and Lightning
tribes. More, we have clans denoted by colours as the

Red, Blue, and Vermillion and by the soul in manufactured articles as a Net and Tent.   (*Totemism*, p. 25.)

We discover the presence of one influence in all these human evolutions of the supernal; these and all the forms of supernal manifestation we have before treated upon, and all we shall have yet to unfold in multiple supernal aspirations have but one object, one purpose.   Man conscious of his own powerlessness in the presence of the vast living and material forces in the universe, seeks as in human brotherhoods for a supernal protector. We have seen that he essayed to find this soul of goodness in the mystic power of luck, then he sought for it in spells and charms, and when the medicine-man was evolved he hoped to paralyze all evil influences by the might of his mana; he then sought help from a like mana power which he recognized in all personalities, the sun, the thunder, the tiger, the snake, until through various successive stages he created the spiritual world. Then the horizon out of which the good his soul craved for became infinite, the ghost became a spirit, the spirit a god, and all we have now to show is the mode by which this mana power of the primary ghost has been step by step amplified to a Supreme Deity.   This was brought about by the necessity of evolving the spirit power in accordance with human evolution.   In all cases and allwhere this spirit of goodness is the embodiment of the stage of moral goodness in human nature, and the divine institutions and powers recognised are only the reflection of the social and political conditions among men.   As it was in the long past so is it in the living present, the soul still craves for that mana of unchanging goodness that all faiths have failed to supply to their most ardent votaries.

We cannot conclude the subject of totemism without referring to the important social results that accrued from the recognition of human kinship with animals. Of these one of the most notable was that of the domestication of

the local totem in various countries and by many distinct
tribes of men.   The evidence we have is by no means
complete, nor do we as yet infer that every totem tribe
domesticated their kin animals, but, we have so many
illustrations of |that being the case, that we may rest
assured that the nature of the animal or local circumstances
would have been very detergent to prevent such a consum-
mation.   Of course, owing to the special characteristics of
each species of animals, the advantages derived from
domestication would vary, the Negroes of Senegambia who
may for many ages have tamed the crocodile and kept
numbers of them in their sacred pools, and the Moquis in
New Mexico who also have tamed snakes by hundreds so
that they can wind them round their arms and necks
unscathed, have not, and could not, have made any profitable
use of their animal totems.   Not so, however, when the
selected animal possessed qualities that gave it an intrinsic
value, as the cow, sheep, goat, mare, and other milk-
producers or those whose hair and wool, as the camel and
sheep, could be applied to many domestic purposes.

We infer that the totem selection of protective animals
took place when man was a low-class hunter, and lived on
the smaller game and vegetable productions of his native
woods and plains, then any animal that he could kill was
suitable for food; but when, by the growth of supernal ideas,
he conceived that he was akin to his totem, the tabu of
its flesh was instituted.   If there were several animals in a
district, each of which was selected by some of the scattered
denizens, it would follow that those of the same ilk would
be drawn into association, and, as the primary sentiment of
attachment in each group was the totem, general customs
and rites affecting it would be introduced.   Of course, the
histories of these supernal associations are lost in the lapse
of time, and the barbarism of the savages who instituted
them, but we have one living example of a totem race
where the totem custom seems to have been continuous

from primitive times, and, in which it is said even traditions
of its origin appear to linger.   The Toda race in the
Neilgherries since attention has been called to their peculiar
institutions have ever been considered an interesting and
unique subject of study.   We, in their sacred relations
with their herds, are carried back to the time of the calf,
Apis sacrifice at Thebes; that of a bull at Athens; a cow in
Cyprus; and a bull calf at Tenedos.   Egyptian paintings
and Egyptian sculptures as well as Assyrian cuneiform
inscriptions illustrate that as now among the Todas so then
through Greece, Asia Minor, Chaldea, and Egypt, herds
of the special totem animals were kept in the temple
precincts.

The one effect of this religious custom was to make them
well acquainted with the points in their own totem animal;
if they detected none serviceable of course no further
development through them could ensue.   We can well
understand that observation of the milk-bearing herbivorous
totem animals would make them, unless restrained by some
tabu prejudice, desirous of utilising it as an article of food,
and those most productive would be most esteemed; no
doubt human selection was then at work, yet it probably
took ages to evolve constant milk-giving herbivora.   We
have to remember that in those times no totems were kept
simply as food-giving animals, as a rule the totem was
never eaten but as a sacrifice and at a religious feast, both
as a brother and as representing the totem.

The Todas have a tradition that formerly they lived
exclusively on the milk of the buffalo with such herbs,
roots, and fruits as the forest produced, though they now
use wheat, barley, and other grains.   (*Trans. Eth. Soc.*
VII. p. 242.)   Then, when little better than the lowest
savages now are, their totem habit had brought them in
direct relations with their totem animal, and its value as a
milk-giver converted the religious habit into a pastoral
institution.   Now, as then, the buffalo is not kept for its

flesh, the dairy itself is the temple and the milkman its priest. A glamour is thrown over all the early institutions in classic lands, but once their priests were herdsmen, the oxen, sheep, and goats were sacred, and their flesh only eaten as a sacrificial rite. Even now among the Todas the flesh of the buffalo is only eaten, as we have said, as a sacrifice, the herd is always sacred, and when the house chief dies all his herd are slaughtered, not eaten, but burnt in the dairy temple pyre that their ghosts may ascend to their totem kindred in the sky. That such totem customs were once general in India, the national abstinence from the flesh and reverence for cattle, implies. We see in other places horses, asses, and goats specially honoured and specially kept for their milk, the same was the primitive custom with the llama and vicuna in Peru. In all cases it appears the flesh was only eaten at the festival sacrifice, it is even now a religious rite to slaughter animals for food, with the Jews their conservative spirit still retains the custom, but in classic lands, and the east generally, the lamb's flesh might be presented to a guest, or the kid soothed at even the domestic festa, until the flesh of all herbivora became esteemed as common food.

Professor Robertson Smith traces from totem relations with herbivorus animals the output of the social customs of fosterage and adoption. He writes: "It would appear that the notion of kinship with milk-giving animals through fosterage has been one of the most powerful agencies in breaking up the old totem religions, just as a systematic practice of adoption between men was a potent agency in breaking up the old exclusive system of clans." (*The Religion of the Semites*, p. 336.)

We may note that primarily the totem relationship is more than is expressed by mere kinship, it is supernal, the totem is part of the man's self, it embraces, as it were, in one entity not only all of the same totem on earth, human and animal, but all in heaven that came of the same stock, man or beast. This is seen in the following, when a Colombia Indian has injured himself, that is not only a loss to him, it is a loss to his clan, and he has to pay blood-money to the clan, this goes to the mother's clan, but the father's clan claim tear money, friends, sorrow money; with them association or being contributory alike requires compensation. If a man is thrown by a borrowed horse or mule then all relations ask compensation, not from the rider, but the lender of the mule. The liability may extend to everything sold, exchanged, or lent. (*Pro. Roy. Geog. Soc.* VII. p. 790.)

Under the primary matriarchal association in which man and woman only cohabited temporarily, when the home was only the occasional lair of the woman and her child, the association dissolved as soon as the semi-brute became self-dependent, and so, in the heterogenous home of the human horde, when sex was common, and man never knew a father, there could have been no concept of ancestors, mothers might be recognized, but father was an unknown cognomen. So, in the mixed associations that afterwards intervened, and irregular groups associated under every possible marital arrangement, the definite common idea of father was unknown. Under such supposititious conditions every possible idea of animal or divine origin might well have birth, and all the concepts after evolved of animal lore and legends have origin.

Society must have been somewhat advanced when the family group was evolved, and men and women recognized that they had grandfathers and grandmothers, all beyond them was lost in the unrealized memory of the past, and, accepting the legends of transformation then common to each group, they read in the unknown past a totem origin, the descent from sun, moon, or stars, transformation from trees or stones, or the output of humanity from holes in the earth, the sea, or descent from the clouds. In the family group, whatever its nature, if permanent from the ghost concept the ancestral spirit was evolved, and to it, whether sun or cloud, bird, beast, or man, the new power of spiritual goodness was attached.

In principle there is no essential difference in the supernal and human association affirmed in whatever character the ancestral ghost is conceived. Ever it represents mutual interest, mutual help, according to the respective natures of the parties forming the compact; on the one side reverence, worship, offerings, and the acknowledgment of dignity as chiefs, on the other, help in difficulties and dangers, material and supernal, and help in the hunt and against enemies, in all respects they became partizans, looked for good for themselves and cared not for anything beyond.

This aspiration for union with the supernal must have began in the mind through the birth of new desires, the craving for a good man failed to find in the life of nature. How the primary search for happiness began we may never know, but the autobiographies of many men and women even now prove that the desire, the struggle, the hope of supernal protection is still an unsatisfied aspiration of the human soul. Faiths innumerable have endeavoured to supply this want, but the many struggling consciences, the accessions, the grasping at faiths, as drowning men catch straws, intimate the never ending character of our aspirations and the vanity of the supernal illusions. Generation succeeds generation and race follows race, yet, the mists and the shadows still build up illusions, still delude the human soul; these may vary but their effects are ever the same, the maya of delusion ever draws our souls to the horizon of time, and still as ever unsatisfied we glide into eternity.

The Hidatsa Indian, the Australian aborigine, go forth into the world of nature, living and inorganic, and in the solitude of the wilderness, the solitude of the night, enduring the pangs of toil, hunger, and anxiety, present their craving souls to the spiritual supernal influences they recognize in the mystery of being. To them the tree, the stone, the mountain, the star, and the animal were not such as we now hold them, but that each and all possessed intelligences like their own, and that these powers and presences might visit them in the visions of the day, or command their souls in the nightly dream or that their own souls could pass out in sleep and seek association with other souls.

As it was in the ancient days, so is it now, like forms of spirit association and spirit influences still retain their prestige, and claim the reverence of like fears and like superstitious rites. We may even follow the derivation of races by these husks of old faith-forms, with a much greater probability of success than in any laboured interpretation of the affinities of words, the one code of records is fragmentary and often evanescent, but the other has a persistent vitality without break, often without change, for thousands of years.

Thus it follows that in the highest civilizations however lofty, and abstract may be the god conceptions of the most intellectual minds, however great the attributes applied to the god-power in common acceptance, practically each man and woman by the tendency of their devotional acts testify to the nature of the Supernal relations most in accordance with their religious instincts. Some never advance above fetish worship, they believe in the mystic power in the amulet itself, in dog or crow, they feel the presence of a self-contained supernal power, and, if from habit or accustomed surroundings, in theory they acknowledge a presiding deity, their souls ever cling to the concrete spiritual goodness in fetish forms and fetish words.

During the primary evolution of the family when so many spiritual natures were being conceived, it was possible that the soul help, at first restricted to the medicine-man, might be attached to any object the man supposed possessed.

mana, and, therefore, capable of supporting or protecting him; hence the diverse nature of the mana existences, the fetish of one man might be an animal, of another a tree, of a third a star or rock.   At first we infer their spirit natures only, supplied the place they held in the charm, and they were worked as by the Australian aborigines, by the power of spells, but the co-ordinate evolution of the family and the ghosts led to the attachment of the individual concept of supernal goodness to ancestors, and the consequent sentiment of animal, sun, tree or star descent.   The one sentiment would naturally become prominent in the continuous presence of the father, the sense of their dependence on the strength of his arm, and on the food he supplied. While the goodness of the mother early ceased to influence the child, and soon passed out of its memory, that of the father, manifest at a more developed period, become continuous, and blended with, and become associated with, the tribal protection.   Under such conditions the family and even tribal totems became continuous, but in addition every individual had his own totem, even as previously he had his own amulet.   Usually the influence of the individual totem ceased with the life of the individual, but the family totem and when present the tribal totems were continuous, the son accepting it from his father or mother and carrying it on from generation to generation.

In the usual course of savage life ancestral memory is only continuous for a few generations, at every step the memory of the progenitors become more and more atrophied until it ceases altogether.   It is then myth comes in to supply the place of memory, and, as the only continuous idea is that of the family or tribal totem, and the universal power of transformation recognised by undeveloped man, the primary ancestor was evolved from the totem spirit, be it the sun, animal, bird, or rock,

At the same time that the family totem was being evolved in one wigwam, other totem spirits were in like manner being evolved among other groups, whether friends or enemies, and myth in these instances stepped in to evolve the status of the generally acknowledged ghosts as in the family.   Legends were evolved for tribal associations, and, differences, and other legends, converted the spirits of their dead enemies into evil and malignant beings.   Out of these and the malignant powers in nature came the great force of evil spirits, but, usually in early society the most baneful were the ghosts of their own tribe, men, women, and children, by some fatal chance converted into enemies.

As illustrating the dependence for supernal goodness on ancestors we quote the following: Macdonald in his *Africana* writes : "The spirit of every deceased man and woman becomes an object of religious homage.   The gods of the natives are nearly as numerous as their dead, they cannot worship all, each turns to his immediate ancestors.   Thus, the village chief will not trouble himself about his great-grandfather, he will present his offerings to his own immediate predecessor and say, ' O father I do not know all your relations, you know them all, invite them to the feast with you.'   In giving an offering the man regards himself as giving a present to a little village of the departed which is headed by its chief." (I. p. 68.)   Of the Sumatrans Marsden says, "They made Anitos of their deceased ancestors, to which they made their first invocations in all difficulties and dangers.   They still continue the custom of asking permission of their dead ancestors when they enter any wood, mountain, or cornfield for hunting or sowing."   (*Sumatra*, p. 256.)

Mr. Howitt writes that the Kurnai and other tribes of the Australian aborigines believed that the spirit of the deceased father or grandfather visited the male descendant in dreams, and imparted to him charms against disease or witchcraft.   They also had men who professed to communicate with the spirits of the dead.   (*Kamilaroi*, p. 278.) In this case we have the preliminary concept of the dead ancestor as supplying the place of the medicine-man, and it was nearly the same among the Melanesians. Codrington writes of prayers being addressed to the recently dead, but to call this worship of ancestors is hardly correct, it may be doubted whether any dead person is appealed to by one who has not known him alive. More, they are not invoked simply as benevolent spirits. The help asked is very often to do mischief. Of course we could expect no other in this early state of ghost development; it is not endowed with any moral principle—only, like the inquirer, a mere tribal partisan.

The totem worship and the worship of ancestors began with the first offering of food and drink to the dead, and the association of the first beast, bird, or insect seen at, or on the grave, may be attracted by the exposed food with the spirit of the departed. We know that the doctrine of transformation must have long preceded that of spirit; it was probably evolved in the era of spells, and certainly fully developed in the era of the medicine-man, nor is it yet still extinct in the souls of human beings, as witness the white bird spirit assumed to have been seen by Lord Lyttelton.

The spiritual association thus induced by the incidental or occasional offering of food by a more than sympathetic tribesman grew to be a general custom and at last a religious rite. Of course it could not have been conceived without the theory that the dead man had become a living ghost, and in his new life needed the same sustenance that he had found necessary in this life. The dead, as the Chinooks affirm, go out at night to search for food. What more pious service could his children, or those of his own household perform, than supplying this need? All human institutions grow, so the supplying the ghost with food ended in supplying it with clothes, arms, wives, animals and attendant ghosts, all that it had been used to when living. These were so universally buried or burnt with the dead body, that we may well spare the reader any illustrative details.

Naturally, reciprocal benefits were expected in return, and these were severally expressed in the divine help that was accorded to the worshipper by the totem or other ancestral spirit. We may even note, as Spencer shows, that the term for god is, as with the Tanna, only that of "dead man." That food was, and is, supplied to the dead, we have almost universal evidence. We read of it in Egyptian annals, it comes present before us in Lycian tombs, on Spartan steles and Etruscan monuments. Not an European race, whatever its origin, but has some survival form of the offering of food for souls; and the All Souls' feast to the Dead is presented from the shores of the Mediterranean to the coast of the Yellow Sea. We only need peruse the works of any traveller among savage or barbaric hordes to be equally sure it prevails generally among the lower races of men.

That which had its origin in personal sympathy grew into a habit, and from a habit into a law expanding at every stage until with the advance in the spiritual nature of the ghost it became converted into a sacrificial rite, and the honours to the dead became ancestral worship. This in various forms is manifested by the native tribes in both the old world and the new; with many it is to the immediate ancestors, with others it is restricted to the higher ghost spirits of chiefs, heroes, and medicine-men. Generally, the sacrifices in this stage of evolution are to the family spirits, or may be to the village or clan chief's ghost. In all cases, however exalted may be the after gods evolved, the penates and household divinities are educed from the family association continuing as a supernal compact with the ghosts of its dead members.

Ancestral goodness was primarily represented by the goodness men presumed they received from their dead warriors, medicine-men, or successful leaders. Long before

the ancestor spirit was recognized the groupal hero was
known, and the tie of blood brotherhood brought into
affinity the souls, whether living or dead, of those who, by
some spell rite, had been made spirit brothers.   Hence in
various ways, and through diverse classes of ghosts, tribal
supernal goodness was established, and this, when special
marriage rights were instituted, and the family relations of
the sexes defined, evolved into the worship of ancestral
ghosts and family penates.

As among the Australian aborigines so with most races
of men in the olden times, and now there are legends of
men being taken up into the sky, and becoming the sun,
moon, or stars, or a mountain or river. These natural
personifications or transformations give origin to hero protective spirits, and, ultimately, ancestral protective spirits;
all is a process of growth or elimitation, and, according to
the differentiation of the social institutions, are the forms in
which it is presented.

The supernal relations thus induced are well affirmed
by Ralston in his *Songs of the Russian people*.   There
can be no doubt about the belief of the old Slavonians that
the souls of fathers watched over their children and
their children's children, and that, therefore, departed
spirits, and especially those of ancestors, ought always
to be regarded with pious veneration and sometimes be
solaced or conciliated with prayer and sacrifice.   The
cultus of the dead was connected with the fire on the
domestic hearth.   This accounts for the stove of modern
Russia having been considered the special haunt of the
Domovoy or house spirit, whose position in the esteem of
the people is looked upon as a trace of the ancestor worship of olden days " (p. 119).   "In some districts tradition expressly refers to the spirits of the dead, the functions
attributed now to the Domovoy, and they are supposed to
be careful in keeping watch over the house of a descendant
who honours them and provides them with due offerings.

15 *

So the non-Slavonic Mordoins, dead men's relations, offer the corpse eggs, butter, and money, saying 'Here is something for you': Marfa has brought you this; watch over her corn and cattle, and when I gather the harvest do thou feed the chickens and look after the house.'" (*Ibid.* p. 121.)

In the earliest phase of ancestor worship the ghost of the father lives in the memory of his immediate descendants, and he becomes a house spirit to them or he reposes in the family tomb and his own immediate wants are supplied by his living kin who retain kindly remembrances of his social virtues; but when, after many generations of these kindred associations, the early ancestor may be associated with some mystic animal, itself becomes a myth, then by slow stages the gift of food becomes converted into the general sacrifice to ancestors, and the local animal, or the animal symbol of the family, is the object sacrificed; it may begin in a convenient custom, become a habit, and end in a permanent religious rite.

It is notable that ever in totem groups it is the sacred totem animal that is sacrificed at the totem feasts. Thus, as Frazer shows with the Zunis in their respective clans, it was the divine buzzard or turtle, with the Negroes of Issapoo the sacred cobra, that, as they say, the children may be initiated and introduced to their totem. For the same purpose the Ainos and Gilyaks sacrifice the bear; there is the sacrifice of the lamb at Uganda, and by the Semitic Arabs, with the Todas that of a calf, the Bhils and other tribes, of a goat. Sometimes the custom degenerates into a symbolic sacrifice as in the dough image of the Mexican god, and other cake and bread eating as symbolic of the totem eating.

We must not infer that when the remote ancestor became a totem and an object of sacrifice that the earlier worship of the immediate ancestor ceased; far from it, the two forms of association were continuous and food was put in the tomb by the old Etruscans, by all the Aryan races; at the same time as the devoted animal was offered at the family or communal altar. The offering of first-fruits of anything choice at the feast, the pouring out of libations, is general, as we have shown, not to the long past mythical dead, but to the ancestors whose family protective acts are held in grateful remembrance. It is so at Tanna now, it was so in Polynesia, with the Zulus and many other African races; whether the totem progenitor was the sun, a lion, or snake, ever with its worship we observe the more humble family gifts of food for the dead, even to the living mother dropping the milk from her breast on the grave of her dead child.

Another result from the establishment of ancestral worship was the special development of guardian angels having special charge of their individual descendants. This has been a general concept through the whole of the Aryan world. Classic history is surcharged with incidents concerning guardian spirits; the introduction of Christianity converted them to angels, but they still influence the supernal concepts of many millions in India as the souls of the dead kin looking after individual living descendants. Every Karen still has his "guardian spirit" walking by his side, whom he has to appease by unceasing offerings to preserve his life and health. These Le come into the world with the individual man and remain with him unto death. (*Asi. Soc. Beng. Jour.* XXIV. p. 297.) We read of these guardian deities at New Caledonia and Tanna, at Tonga and New Zealand, among the Malays and Malagassy, the Zulus and various Negro tribes, in all classic writings, and from Ceylon through China to Japan.

Another circumstance that marks the social nature of the family and totem association both in this life and in the ghost state are the incidents which mark the personal introduction of each individual and rank him as either kin or friend. At every burial the spirit of the newly deceased among the Malagassy is introduced to his long departed relatives by name, and they are entreated to respect him as a friend. (*Ellis, Mad.* I. p. 237.) Frazer in the *Golden Bough* shows that in many cases it was even necessary to introduce even a visitor to the house spirits before according hospitality to him. Thus, at Laos, before a stranger is admitted the master of the house has to offer a sacrifice to the ancestral spirits or they would take offence and send disease among the inmates (I. p. 151). So visitors must in some cases obtain passive protection of the house guardians by something symbolic of the family being offered to him, and thereby linking him in communion with the home spirit. Among the Malays this introduction may be through the ornament taken from a child's hair being held by him for a time, or, like Captain Moresby, they may be inducted to the tribe by the waving of palm leaves over the head by the medicine-man, or by a green twig being put in the mouth; by these charm means the evil spirits of enemies are kept out and the good know whom they may trust. Dodge describes how the North American medicine-men in like manner keep away the evil spirits of their enemies when strangers visit them. According to Crevaux a stinging ant served as the medium of introducing him and his party to their ancestral spirits. With the Eskimo the strange visitor becomes a friend by receiving and giving a blow and then embracing. Ever ceremonies of introduction are needed to make a man free of the household. So in returning after absence or a long journey a man wants purifying to clear him from the spirits of enemies which may linger on him. (*Golden Bough*, p. 152, &c.) We might also refer to blood brotherhoods and the totem habit of exchanging names as other supernal modes of totem alliances.

CHAPTER VII.

The Evolution of Human Ghosts and Nature Powers into Tutelar Deities.

THE myths of the institution of human culture by a prehistoric divine presentation have long delayed the inquiry into the home evidence of the growth of local ideas on the original relations of the fathers of the tribes with the spirit powers their crude supernaturalisms had evolved. Everywhere men sought for a supreme God, and as to each man and each tribe the one it reverenced was the Great One they saw in individual fetishes and local tutelar spirit powers the signs and semblances of the Great Unknown. Men whose cultural capacities had never passed beyond the conception of a present and immediate force, a mere local impulse, were supposed capable of comprehending an abstract entity whose manifestations were concurrent in every place, implying those lofty conceptions of deity which are only the result of the highest culture in modern times and were wholly unknown even to the fathers of the Vedic hymns, the old Egyptian priests, and only vaguely idealized by the loftiest thought powers of Greece and Rome.

Another class of poetic dreamers read the myths of spirit and God powers not as evolutions from the concrete aspects of nature but as the figurative idealisms of devotees and bardhic rhymesters when social culture admitted of class leisure and the amenities of a pastoral or simple agricultural life, and thus spread the sentiments present in

human manners over the physical attributes of nature.
These god-tales and spirit adventures, these solar and
lunar myths, varied by animal legends and quaint stories
supplied the place afterwards filled by the mystic histories
and romances of later times and the novels of the present
age. More, the ideal exponents of sky symbols and visionary
changes beheld the whole supernatural world through the
charm transcendental spectacles the same as the modern
spiritualist.

It is symptomatic of the changed direction of human
thoughts and the more careful investigations of modern
times that men unhesitatingly now deduce all arts and
social appliances and all the known expositions of nature
and thought from the happy primary concepts of original
thinkers, and the same doctrine is now being applied to all
human concepts of a spiritual world.

Among those who have expounded the natural evolutions
of supernal ideas we quote the following :—Mr. Lang, in
Customs and Myths, says the experience of the savage
is limited to the narrow world of his tribe, and of the
beasts, birds, and fishes of his district. His philosophy,
therefore, accounts for all phenomena on the supposition
that the laws of the animate nature, he observes, are
working everywhere. But his observations, misguided by
his crude magical superstitions, have led him to believe in a
state of equality and kinship between men and animals and
even organic things. He often worships the very beasts
he slays; he addresses them as if they understood him; he
believes himself to be descended from the animals and of
their kindred. These confused ideas he applies to the
stars and recognises in them men like himself or beasts like
those which he conceives himself to be in such close human
relations. There is scarcely a bird or beast but the Red
Indian or the Australian will explain its peculiarities by a
myth. It was once a man or a woman and has been
changed to bird or beast by a god or a magician. Men,

again, have originally been beasts in his philosophy, and
are descended from wolves, frogs, serpents or monkeys.
The heavenly bodies are traced to precisely the same
origin, and hence, we conclude, come their strange animal
names and the strange myths about them " (p. 138).

In searching for the origin of one of the higher forms
of faith, Mr. Rhys Davids comes to the same natural
evolution of supernal ideas. In his *Lectures on the
Growth of Religion*, he writes: "The beliefs of the
remote ancestors of the Buddhists may be summed up as
having resulted from that curious attitude of mind which
is now designated by the word 'Animism.' They had
come to believe, most probably through the influence of
dreams, in the existence of souls, or ghosts, or spirits
inside their own bodies, and they had not yet learned to
discriminate in this respect between themselves and the
other animals and objects around them which seemed to
be possessed of power and movement. The Vedas, though
they are our earliest records, show us only a very advanced
stage in the beliefs resulting from this simple faith, so
widely diffused among all races and ages of mankind.
The more powerful ghosts, supposed to dwell in various
external things, have already become in the Vedas objects
of greater fear than the rest; they are endowed with higher
attributes, are surrounded by deeper mystery, and have
been promoted to be kings as it were among the gods.
These were chiefly the spirits supposed to animate the sky
and the heavenly bodies, and the promotion of the spirits
had so dimned the comparative glory of the rest, that
the animism had become in the Vedas what we call
Polytheism.

"But the newer stage of belief was no contradiction of
the older—it was simply a further advance on the same
lines, and resting on the same foundations. The lesser
spirits, or at least most of them, survived as Naiads and
Dryads, spirits of the trees and the streams, demons,

goblins, ogres, spirit messengers and fairies, good or bad;
and the old belief in magic, in sorcery, and in charms of
various kinds" (p. 14).

The theory that Professor Max Müller so fondly developed, of a pristine religion in which the bright powers
of morning and spring are opposed to all the dark powers
of the night and the winter, and out of which the conflicts
of good and evil were evolved, represent a form of gene-
ralization not pregnant in the soul of the rude savage. He
could not aggregate and compare a long series of diverse
ideas, and from them idealize an abstract conception, much
less evolve a graceful and poetic series of similitudes,
harmonizing and accounting for the seeming antagonisms
in nature. True to the primitive ideas resulting from his
individual relations with other individual men and the
individual forms about him—animal, river, stone, sun and
storm, each was, like himself, a personal power—he never
conceived of them as genera and races, but ever spoke of
them in their individual capacities. It is a well-known law
in the development of languages that the lower the race
the less use is made of abstract or even adjective terms, so
that where we meet with two or more terms from one root,
yet distinct in their expressive application, we may rest
assured that the form which implies a substantive existence
is the oldest and the parent of its after modification into
an attributive or abstract character.

Primarily men recognized their own individuality and
the individuality of all objects, and when they conceived
of ghost and spirit powers they were equally individual in
their attributes. All were isolated supernal forces, differing only in their natures, even as men and women differ.
But there came a time when the crude balance of these
heterogeneous forces was no longer to be retained; men
themselves could not always continue to act as individuals,
only they combined in temporary unions, they associated
as groups, they aggregated as families. So the animal and

concrete natural affinities, which had been only manifested
in isolated acts, became associated in both individual and
tribal affinities between the souls of men and the spirit
forces they had conceived in the animal and physical
worlds. Then individual terms alone did not suffice to
express the altered character of Kosmic relations ; generic
and distinguishing terms thus evolved a new philological
phase.

We can only conceive of the soul of humanity being
awakened into this new life by the outpouring of new
thoughts in the mind of an individual man. He desired
then a more entire intercommunion with his fellow-man.
He purposed to evolve new relations with the living organisms and the concrete nature about him, and this could
only take place through the medium of the ghost forms
he affirmed as common to all existences, and it could only
become a permanent institution by the souls of his fellows
having advanced to the capacity to entertain those relations
when he presented them for their approval. How many
such may have failed before any accepted scheme of human
and supernal relations became the characteristic of a social
group we may never know; untimely enthusiasts pass
away and leave no record, but the expression of a felt
want becomes an eternal word. So at last it came to pass
that men sought relations of a more intimate nature, not
only with their fellows, but with all the world-forces of
which they were cognisant.

In tracing this affinity of man with the supernal beings
human thought had evolved, we have to remember that the
undiscriminating mind of the rude savage saw not a tree, a
stone, a mountain, or star, or animal such as we now conceive it, but that each and all possessed like intelligences as
himself, that they had spirit forces like his own soul, which,
like his own soul in dreams, could wander forth. So there
were not only spirits in all objects, but that allwhere on
the land, in the water, among trees and hills, in clouds

and throughout the air disembodied spirits moved and had their being.

Man ever, as we have shown, yearning for supernal protection when he had learnt how he might come into affinity with these many spirit-powers as he now had with his fellows in brotherhoods, would cultivate the means of so doing. Accordingly, we find allwhere this alliance of human thought and spirit-power, and ever the various germs of nations and races severally selected their own classes of co-ordinate spirit influences, out of which they subsequently evolved their local god-forms. These from the beginning have been continuous, there is no crushing out these primary concepts of spirit-powers any more than it has been possible to cast off the concepts of charms and spells; like them they have, as it were, become part of the nature of every human being once initiated into their mysteries. They survive all the after evolved higher forms of faith, and hold their place under every doctrine that has usurped position in the world. In the local phases of every Buddhist, every Moslem, every Christian belief, we find a substratum of supernal ideas that carry us back to the primary supernal instincts of the human soul. The old lower pagan belief everywhere in classic lands underlies the faith in Christ and the Madonna. So the might of the midnight spectres reigns in the north. Even in the New World, among the descendants of the Quichuas and Aztecs, the old low spirit-powers still carry on the very old rites. There is not a Polynesian isle blessed with the Christian faith but preserves intact not the great gods of its chiefs or its partially supreme after developments, but the primary spirit forces its fathers endowed with vitality and brought into unison with their own souls.

So it is in China, in Burmah, in Japan, among all the distinct races, who, in their many millions, acknowledge Buddha. The fetish still lives, and the Obi mysteries are still rehearsed, though the black devotee raises his hands in pious acknowledgment of the blessings he receives from Allah, or worships with the white man in the Methodist communion. The same cry comes from the missionary to the Zulu, from the remote shores of Patagonia, from the humble teachers of the Eskimo in Greenland or Labrador; even the attentive and pious Australian aborigine maiden, scarce from her birth out of the higher influence, flies from the greater civilisation to revel in the bora associations.

As it was in the ancient days so is it now; like forms of spirit influences still retain their prestige, the gods of the vulgar never die, they still claim the reverence of like fears, and like superstitious rites, as when they were the only known local supernal powers. We may even follow the derivation of races by these husks of old faiths with a much greater probability of success than in any laboured interpretation of the affinities of words.

As the associations of men became enlarged, and many definite institutions were evolved, the inter-relations of men became more extended and of a higher grade. Distinctions of rank and position created varied ideas of worth, systems of personal relationship were introduced, and custom defined the nature of law and the range of rights. It could not be expected that these important changes would take place among any community without evolving corresponding reactions on the nature, relations, and influences of the supernal powers. We have seen that, at first, there were only men ghosts, spiteful and malicious, individual in their actions, in fact the primary spirit world was a mere chaos of ghostly individualities. As the wigwams became households, and a feeble exhibition of power was maintained by the elders of the small group, the headman, or those who utilized the primary crude supernal ideas, gradually evolved a class of more powerful ghost-powers, the spirits of the heroes, medicine-men, and fathers of the small community. As a necessary consequence of these enlarged supernal ideas, sundry of the ghost spirits entered into their system of myths, they from living men became associated by tradition with the great phenomena of the heavens, that men, heretofore, had only looked at with wonder and dread.   The early association of men with the nature powers were grossly anthropological, they only differed from their own savage fellows in the possession of some few supernal attributes, and these were often ascribed to their living medicine-men.

When men grew into clans, and from clans developed into tribes; when by the cessation of indiscriminate converse with the women the family was evolved, and following that patriarchal rights and property qualifications; when, therewith, dependence was systematized, and not only slave labour created, but the power of headmen and chiefs extended; and when, on seeking the presence of the leaders, it became customary to present them with gifts; then, at the same time, the old relations of men with the supernal powers were marked with the same characteristics.   Then sacrifices took the place of food offerings; and as there were ruling chiefs, war leaders, and powerful necromancers among men, so were there among the spirit-powers.   In supernal relations the family group was represented by the ancestral family spirits, and men then took no note of the possible, but accepted a fanciful attribute or supposed influence as sufficient to account for any change.   Thus fetish powers, essentially personal and individual, became in many cases associated with animal forms and other definite objects in the natural world, and from being the accepted medicine of individuals they became the totems of families, so that the sentiment expressed through the fetish was in time transferred to all progenitors, and the service offered and accepted from the family emblem became the attribute of the group.

A large class of the spirit forces evolved in this discriminating age are not only the family representative dead; there are the great spirit powers of heroes, of medicine-men, of anyone who might become notable, not only in the tribe, but whose worth had reached neighbouring tribes, and with these were associated the great natural forces in their spiritual aspects. Often the embodied ghost-powers of a lower state were endowed with higher attributes by the enlarged concepts of their descendants, as the sun-god of the Peruvians, the heaven-god of the Chinese, and several of the old Hindoo nature-gods, many of which can be traced to a condition that implied no higher attributes than men ascribed to their medicine-priests.

With the differentiation of the power or influence of the elders in governing the camp and restraining the relations, food, and habits of the more youthful members the conception of the nature of the spirit and ghost forces were correspondingly modified. Like the actions of the elders, so the ghost forces became aggressive; they coerced individuals, by force they entered men's bodies, torturing and destroying them, and were only to be restrained by submission and gifts, the universal modes of deprecation to superior powers. Naturally the most vigorous of the spirit forces in each class, either as representing strength, immensity or subtlety, became the leading manifestations. Thus the crocodile, the serpent, the lion, tiger, and bear became the most prominent objects of supplication in the animal world, and the sun, moon, thunder, and fire in the world of the physical forces. Usually these great natural powers became more immediately related to the tribe or the chiefs, and the humbler members of the community found their fetish or totem protective supernal powers in birds and the lower animal and physical manifestations.

The more notable of these spirit forces, like the headman in the clan or tribe, becomes the chief, and ultimately the tutelar deity of the tribe or locality; but as the chief spirits are generally the supernal property of associated tribes, one spirit will be selected as tutelar guardian by one group and another spirit by a neighbouring group. In some cases the tendency was to select the clan or tribal protecting totem or tutelar spirit from the great personations of the sun, the blue expanse of heaven, the storm cloud, the hoary mountain; others again were content to appeal to the gentler influences about them—the tree or waterfall, the river rolling on in its course, or the ever-living sea bringing supplies of food to their shores. Those were all self-personal powers, the animal exhibiting animal combined with human instincts, the physical manifesting human attributes may be in some cases only animal powers.

Of the diverse supernal powers that may be accredited by low-class neighbouring powers we will refer to the evidence on the subject given to a Select Committee of the Legislative Council of Victoria in 1858. They, in a formal manner, took the evidence of many witnesses, many of whom said the natives had no religious ideas, some that they only believed in a spirit that thundered; one spoke of a good and evil spirit, another of evil spirits and the offerings made to them; others recorded their beliefs in water spirits and land spirits; some affirmed the sun and moon were held by them to be spirits, and that the stars were once black fellows, who were for good acts taken up into the sky. (*Abor. Vic.* I. p. 423.) As illustrating the nature of the aborigines' concepts of the supernal powers in the sky and on the earth, Smyth writes: "The progenitors of the existing tribes, whether birds or beasts or men, were set in the sky and made to shine as stars if the deeds they had done were such as to deserve commendation. The eagle is Mars, the crow is a star and smaller ones his wives; the moon before he was set in the sky was very wicked, according to some it was the native cat. The spirit or power in Venus is a sister of the sun spirit. Nearly all animals they suppose anciently to have been men, who transformed themselves into different animals and stones"

(*Ibid.* I. p. 431.)   "Thilkuma and Whaigugan, two of the gods, appear to have been the leaders of two tribes who fought about their respective boundaries.   Saturn was a bird, the Southern Cross a shrub with an emu; other stars were cockatoos, lizards, green parrots, kangaroos, and night cuckoos; the Hyades was a man, others were owls and iguanas." (*Ibid.* II. p. 274.)

As all the ideas that men express regarding supernal beings and states can only be derived from external objects, their own feelings, and the narratives of [their fellows, they can ascribe to them no other attributes than those presented thus to their minds.   It is impossible for an Australian who never heard of or saw any other structures but rude bark wigwams to conceive of palaces in the clouds, or idealize a ghost-spirit other than a man or animal form.   He could not ascribe to these beings mental conceptions or expressions more elevated than he heard expressed by his mates and before society had established practical realizations of the voluntary submission of men to the authority of leaders and headmen; he could have no conception of divine government, nor until custom had evolved law could it be possible for him to conceive of moral obligation and social order.   As the elements of government differentiated among the tribes, so would the conception of supernal government be evolved and the morals of the spiritual groups would be in accord with those of human groups.   As far as supernal attributes were concerned, his highest conception thereof would be similitudes of the physical forces of their best warriors, and the powers exercised or claimed by those select men of the tribe who were set apart as medicine-men.   The transcendental assumptions, they affirmed, were only delusive presentations or the adscription of the faculty in one animal or object to something of a different nature, as when their priests claimed the power of ascending into the sky from observing the flight of birds.

. We may fully realise the origin of an Australian aborigine's supernal concepts in the narrative of the wizard who got through the sky vault, and there saw the so-called god Baiame as a great old black man with a long beard, sitting with his legs under him in his camp, certainly a bark hut like those of his fellows.   On his shoulders extended two great quartz crystals, the wizard's only idea of untold wealth and power; and about him were a number of his boys and his people, their pet birds and beasts. (*Anth. Inst. Jour.* XVI. p. 51.)   This was the highest conception the wizard could form of his god and ministering spirits.   It is nothing more than a native camp, its master lounging idly at the entry, no doubt his ginn behind preparing his food, while the young blacks sport about the clearing, or amuse themselves with the dingoes, tame jays, crows, and opossums this embodiment of exalted savagedom by their aid has been enabled to associate with his household.   If he goes forth like the wizard, he may fly down to the earth to attain any purpose, and like him may assume the form of bird or beast, and he uses the same crystal and fetish charms to attain his object as the medicine-man.

The fact is, these so-called gods are but the ghosts of men or animals in constitution; none of them are advanced to that state of animism in which the material ghost-nature passes into that of the spiritual; they but represent the full development of the dream-image as controlled by the will of the medicine-man.   Many of them, like the wizards of alien tribes, are evil ghosts, such as Neulam Kurrk, the malignant spirit of Fiery Creek, who, in the form of an old woman, steals children and eats them.   Colbumatum Kurrk comes in storms and kills people by throwing great limbs of trees upon them.   A demon, Winniung, resides in winter time on a hill in the Darling range, but in summer he dwells on the other side of the river, because he cannot cross it when flooded. (*Abor. Vict.* II. p. 268.)   Wangun dwells in a large brown snake.   The Sun Koen is an old woman, because the women collect and carry the fire sticks.

She traverses across the sky all day, carrying her fire-stick, and at night goes down under the earth to gather fresh fire-sticks for the next day. (*Ibid.* I. p. 424; and *Bonwick, Tasmanians*, p. 192.) Another of the sky-ghosts is Os rundoo, a big black fellow in the sky, whose two wives were always quarrelling, so he drowned them in the two lakes, Alexandrina and Albert. (*Angas, Austral.* I. p. 97.)

All nations have passed through the same primitive supernal stages, and all have the prototypes of these Australian god-powers. In our own legendary myths they laid in wait for children, they killed wanderers, they acted against men and women in various supernal ways; they could pass over the land in their seven-leagued boots, they could ascend to the upper sky by beanstalks, and by trickery and horseplay they circumvent the giants, or in animal shapes outwit the lubberly human-like monsters.

Not even with the Australians were the spirit powers all evil. The totem system that prevails among them intimate their aspirations for the same good influences of a supernal nature that all men appeal to. The so-called native bear of Australia, like the true bears from the Lapps to the Ainos, and from the last to the North American Indians, is an object of fetish reverence. It is " the sage counsellor of the aborigines, and the men in expeditions seek help from it; it is revered, if not held sacred, and has an influence over the water supply." (*Abor. Vic.* I. p. 446.) To account for the human semblances that give a weird character to many animals, the natives say they were once men; but in the totem relation the animal through its own ghost comes into affinity with the tribe or clan. Of this mutual relation Sir George Grey says: "A certain mysterious connection exists between the family and its *kobong*, so that a member of a family will never kill an animal of the species to which his *kobong* belongs." When a native was asked how his *kobong* would protect him, he said:

16 *

"Were I going along and saw an old man-kangaroo hopping straight towards me I should know he was giving me notice of enemies about." In this case the kangaroo was the man's *kobong*. (*Jour. Anth. Inst.* XVI. p. 45). We may in this instance trace a connection between an omen and the evolution of totemism.

The same crude similitude of spirit and human surroundings is expressed by the Andaman Islanders, as by the Australian natives. With them Puluga lives in a large stone house that is a rubble beehive, but such as they sometimes make; he has a large family, all but one girls; he eats and drinks, passes much of his time in sleep; he is the source of animals, birds, and turtles, and when they anger him he comes out of his house, growls, and hurls burning faggots (lightning) at them; during the rains he descends to the earth to provide himself with certain kinds of food like the natives. Like them, with opposing tribes he has no authority over evil spirits. He is merely the representative of a human tribe with the same rude impulses as men; in capacity he is no more elevated than their own medicine-men, the Okopaids or dreamers. They hold also that certain ancestor spirits vanished from the earth in the forms of animals and fish. They have the totem custom of abstaining from certain kinds of food, either from the animal having manifested its power, or by selection. (*Anth. Inst. Jour.* XII. p. 354.)

The believers in human ghost monsters only, and who fail to form concepts of higher natures, are the lowest of the low hunting tribes, those unfortunate beings who have never aggregated into communities, but wander about the lands they know so little how to use, and live indiscriminately on its wild produce, and the low animal life of the locality which they have acquired skill to circumvent. These are the small game, seed, and bulb eaters of Australia, the Andaman Islanders, the Fuegians, and some small and degraded or undeveloped inland groups as the Shoshones of North America, the Kubus of Sumatra, and the lowest of the scattered Bushmen tribes, and the wretched fragments of small people dwelling here and there on the waste lands of Africa, Asia, and the Indian isles; the partial tendency of these to form small scattered groups alone saving them from the lowest of all states of debasement, that of solitary root-grubbers.

We have seen that among these lowly denizens of the earth the search for goodness has passed beyond dependence on fetish charms and dependence on the supernal acquisitions of the medicine-man; they have evolved the concept of ghosts, they have realized the presence of some kinds of spirit natures in things, and they have in various ways brought them in ghost and totem relations to express forms of protection and other manifestations of supernal goodness. But beyond those broken races of men we have more defined groups associated in clan and tribal communities, men whose main sources of subsistence are the wild game of their districts, the fish that periodically visit their shores and rivers, and in some cases a partial rude cultivation of the soil. Most of those tribes of men have formed more or less organized social groups. They have learnt to acknowledge headmen and the patriarchal ancestors of the groups. They have in some measure exhibited submission to authority, and as they admit distinctions of status in their tribesmen, so they recognize distinct powers in the spirit and ghost conceptions of supernals. Such are the higher class hunters in North and South America, associated fishing clans as the Eskimo, the Chinooks and the Innuits on the North American Atlantic territories, rude tribes of low class herdsmen as the Bechuanas and some of those scattered hillside tribes in various parts of Asia and Africa, and who eke out the year's subsistence by a rude system of cultivation. As these various races differ much in their modes of life, the resulting concepts they entertain of spirit natures consequently are most diverse.

The spiritual natures that these more developed races took cognizance of, were the same physical and totem ghosts we have described, but all their attributes were considerably advanced and brought into parallel modes of expression with their own human institutions. The idea of sex is only as it were incidentally expressed by the lower tribes in their ghostly spirits of evil, but now it is a dominant sentiment, and what man now endows with spirit or god-power, must either be male or female, and all their developments must be the result of such unions. Thus it happens that Sun and Moon became husband and wife, though they may differ in their affirmation of which is masculine, and their attributes are universally deduced from the habits and modes of life of their creating worshippers. With the Greek and Hindoo, the sun-god was a fiery warrior driving his steeds through the sky; the Eskimo sun-spirit is a young woman carrying, as is her wont, the fiery moss for their lamps; the Australian sun-power is a native ginn holding aloft her fire-stick as she lights the way for the men in the great sky path. In like manner among some of the South American tribes, the sun is feminine; it was also the inferior power among the Caribs, Ahts, Hurons, and generally among the African tribes. The Agachemen of California held that heaven and earth were brother and sister; they had a numerous offspring, first earth and sand, then rocks and stones, trees, grass; those were followed by animals; at last Oniot, the great captain, in some unknown way had children who became men. (*Bancroft, Pacif. States*, IV. p. 162.) Out of like elements the myths of the spirit races of all people were evolved.

One of the elements out of which a chieftain spirit may be evolved, is the father of the family, but in most groups of men this source of a presiding spirit is of a low type, and the living father must have had more than homo influence for his prestige to continue beyond the next generation. When the father of a family is a more notable character, his influence passes beyond the household, it encompasses the clan or community, it extends to the limits of the tribe, may be even continuing as a persistent expression of power among other groups. When he dies the memories of his deeds become more or less persistent, and his spirit is correspondingly enhanced. This hero status may be derived from the spirit of a ruling chief, a notable fetish man, or a brave warrior; it may be that of any man who won position, influence, or power, and this does not cease at death, for as long as the memory of their deeds remain, their prestige is preserved, yet when this ceases, like all other notables, their work is lost in the lethe of the departed, and some more recent spirit hero succeeds to their apotheosis.

Occasionally some more or less mythic hero becomes a persistent groupal spirit, and this once accepted, he becomes typified as the founder and father of the race, the spirit-god, the tutelar genius of the tribe may be the being who instructed them in the arts, gave them a faith, or blessed them with their customary social rules and institutions. Such were the Menes and Manoo Capacs of the great races of the earth, or the more modest spirit-powers of the hill-tribes of India, as Mithu Bukia the ancestor god of the Banjari, Madjhato of the Rewari, Alha and Wendul of the Blundel, Rai Das of the Chamars, Lal Guru of the Bhangi, and in modern times Nanak of the Sikhs. (*Calcutta Review*, LXXVII. p. 379.)

The supposed gods of the Guiana Indians, Im Thurn describes as really but the remembered dead of each tribe, and where there is mention of one great spirit or god, it is merely the chief traditional founder of the tribe. (*Ind. Gui.* p. 366.) Among the rude aboriginal tribes of the Hima-laya region, we read of several mortals, whose history is scarcely yet forgotten, being worshipped. Thus, Gogah, a chief of the Chohan tribe, was killed when fighting against the first Moslem invaders; he has his shrine and his seer, and is worshipped with the same rites as the Deotas. (*Contemp. Rev.* XXXII. p. 415.)

The only term applied to spirits by the Caribs and Arawaks express one who lived a long time ago, and is now in skyland, the maker of the Indians—their father. (*Im Thurn, Ind. of Gui.* p. 366.) Burton, in his *Abbeokuta*, writes:—"The Egba deities are palpably men of note in their day" (I. p. 191). Hale describes the deities worshipped in Southern Polynesia as only deified chiefs, the memory of whose deeds were lost in the efflux of time. So, referring to the inhabitants of the Solomon Islands, it is said :—"The Ataros of the previous generation are superseded by their successors. Men must remember the power of the Ataros when they were alive ; hence, as they die off, and new Ataros are appointed, they take the place of the forgotten spirits. Individuals, families, and sets of neighbours will have some ghost of their own, to whom, as an Ataro, they will apply." (*Jour. Anth. Inst.* X. p. 300.)

A few illustrative examples will best show how the local chief, the great warrior, the mystic medicine-men were advanced to tribal or tutelar deities. Mr. Macdonald, in his *Africana*, gives us an exemplification of how the local chief was associated with the locality in which he dwelt, and ultimately became a tutelar deity. He writes :—"Man deifies the powers he sees around him ; he is ready to fall down and worship the mountain whose lofty summit is clothed with the rain-cloud, or the lightning that springs from the cloud. He looks back to the days of his youth ; he remembers a grandfather who told him how he fled from the face of an oppressor, how he had built up his home far up, near the mountain top, and there brought up his family in safety. By-and-by, as danger passed away, this ancestor moved further down the mountain, gradually he increased in power, and in his old age found himself the chief of a clan ; yet he never forgot the days of his adventure, and ever pointed proudly to the spot where he had first found a

shelter; and his children's children, as they listened to the
old man's tale, counted the ground holy. The days come
when they can see the old man's face no more. But does
he not still exist? Yes; did we not hear his voice, as we
listened to sounds that played about the mountain-side?
Did we not see him, though but for a moment, sitting beside
his own home, as he used to sit long ago? Did he not
appear to us in dreams? Yes; he is living on the old
mountain still, he is taking care of us; he knows when we
need rain, and he sends it. We must give him something.
When we had no corn, he always gave us. We will give
him food, we will give him slaves, and he will not forget
us" (I. p. 78).

A hero-god may be evolved in various ways, according
as the local sentiments find something of a spiritual and
commanding nature in an individual that specially distinguishes him from his fellows and the usual capacities
that men exhibit. Lyall, in his *Asiatic Studies*, gives the
following cases:—An Indian tribe, much addicted to high-
way robbery, who worship a famous bandit who probably
lived and died in some mysterious way. M. Raymond, the
French Commander, who died at Hyderabad, has been
canonized there, after a fashion; and General Nicholson,
who died in the storming of Delhi in 1857, was adored as
a hero in his lifetime (p. 19). Yermac, the conqueror of
Siberia, was so highly exalted, even in the conceptions of
his enemies—they could not but admire his prowess, his
consummate valour and magnanimity—and when he perished
in the river Irtish, the Tartars proceeded to consecrate his
memory: they interred his body with all the rites of Pagan
superstition, and offered up sacrifices to his manes. (*Dillon's
Conquest of Siberia*, p. 24.)

Describing the various human personalities whose dead
spirits have been apotheosized, Lyall writes:—" We have
before us in Central India the worship of dead kinsfolk and
friends, and then the particular adoration of notables recently

departed, then of people divinely afflicted or divinely gifted, of saints and heroes known to have been men. Next, the worship of demi-gods ; and finally, that of powerful deities, retaining nothing human but their names and their images. It is suggested that all these are links along one chain of the development of the same idea, and that out of the crowd of departed spirits whom primitive folk adore, certain individuals are elevated to a larger worship by notoriety in life or death. The earliest start of a first-rate god may have been exceedingly obscure; but if he or his shrine make a few good cures at the outset his reputation goes rolling up like a snowball. Of wonder-working saints, hermits and martyrs, the name is legion. There are some potent devotees still in the flesh who are great medicine-men, others very recently dead who exhale power, and others whose name and local fame have survived, but with a supernatural tinge, rapidly coming out. Above these we have obscure local deities, who have entirely shaken off their mortal taint; and beyond these again are great provincial gods." (*Asiatic Studies*, pp. 23-24.)

In vast countries, in which the races of men have become more or less homogeneous and distinct, tutelar districts are not specialized, the tutelar character of the deities fail to be distinctly defined, and the worshippers of each canonized god become scattered into small unaggregated groups. In China these saintly deities are manufactured by the State. One decree speaks of a deceased statesman's spirit which has manifested itself effectively on several occasions, and has more than once interposed when prayers have been offered for rain. In another we have the intimation that the Dragon Spirit of Han Fan Hien has from time to time manifested itself in answer to prayer, and has been repeatedly invested with titles of honour, in gratitude for the provinces which, after prayers, have been visited with much rain. (*Ibid.* pp. 187-189.)

On the evolution of the Hindu gods Lyall observes :—

"At first we have the grave of one whose name, birthplace and parentage are well known in the district. If he died at home his family set up a shrine, instal themselves in possession, and became hereditary keepers of the sanctuary. If the man wandered abroad, settled near some village or sacred spot, became renowned for his austerities, and then died, in the course of a very few years, as the recollection of the man's personality becomes misty, his origin grows mysterious, his career takes a legendary hue—his birth and death were both supernatural. Four of the most popular gods in Berar, whose images and temples are famous id the Deocan, are Kandoba, Vittoba, Boiroba, and Belaji. These are now grand incarnations of the Supremo Triad; yet, by examining the legends of their embodiment and appearance upon earth, we obtain fair ground for surmising that all of them must have been notable living men not long ago." (*Ibid.* pp. 22, 23.)

Of the various modes by which the personified forces in nature were advanced to local tutelar deities, we have various modern examples. The power recognized, though human in its character, is of the highest grade that rude man can conceive; it is that of a chief, it is that of one noted for his mana, and he represents the solar and lunar forces—the power in the thunder, the might of the wind. Thus Shango, the Jupiter Tonans of the Yorubas, became the stone caster, and the old stone hatchets picked up in the fields are called his thunderbolts. Shango was a mortal man born at Ifeh, he reigned at Ikoso, was translated to heaven and made immortal. (*Bowen, Central Africa*, p. 317.) His younger brother is the River Ogun and the symbol of war. We have seen that the name for a ghost was that of a *dead man*; so when on the Congo we read that Erua, the term now applied as god, is also that of the sun, we cannot fail to notice its source. (*Jour. Anth. Inst.* XV. p. 11.) More especially when we recognize the same origin for other like terms. Thus among the

Kitaveita *Zuwa* signifies both sun and god, and among the
Gallas *Waka* means indifferently god and sky, with the
Masai *Engai* means both god, sky, and rain. (*Ibid.* XV.
p. 12.)

Mr. T. Hahn in his *Tsuni Goam* collects several of the
old reports on the Hottentot nature gods, more especially
of the sun, moon, and thunder. Kolb reports that they
believe in God a good man, who does them no harm, and
they dance to the new moon. Schmidt, more explicit, notes
that on the return of the Pleiades mothers lift their little
ones in their arms to show the friendly stars, and teach
them to stretch their little hands towards them singing,
" O Tiqua, our Father above our heads, give us rain that the
fruits may grow, that we may have plenty of food." Hop
says their religion chiefly consists in the worship of the
new moon; the women clasp their hands and sing that the
moon has protected them and their cattle. Moffat says
that their god, Tsuni Goam, was a notable warrior of great
physical strength, and in a desperate struggle with a neighbouring chief he received a wound on the knee. Alexander
describes them as making offerings to snakes, to water
spirits, to the spirit of the fountain, saying, "O great
Father, son of a Bushman, give us the flesh of the rhinoceros,
the gem-book, the zebra, or whatever we require." Krapf
says they see the powers above as the shades of the dead.
These they say are at one time in the grave, then above the
earth or in thunder and lightning as they list. Bosman
describes the natives of Guinea as worshipping snakes,
lofty trees, and the sea. (*Pinkerton*, XVI. p. 494.)

Much of the same character was the rude sun and moon
worship of the old Lapps as described by Scheffer, and
they, like the Negro tribes, were crudely developing from
the nature forces, as fetish conceptions of independent
supernal powers. The inhabitants of Ancitum island, one
of the New Hebrides, according to Mr. A. W. Murray, held
that the sun and moon originally dwelt upon the earth, that

the sun went up into the heavens and told the moon to
follow; they had sacred dances to the moon singing songs
in her praise. (*Mis. to W. Poly.* p. 26.) At Aneitum,
Nugerain, the chieftain spirit, produces a host of minor
powers, gods of the sea and land, of the mountains and
valleys, gods of war and peace, of diseases and storms.

Direct sun and moon and star worship underlie all the
old-world faiths. Men, as with the Australian wizards,
crept up into the sky and came forth as sky-powers, and
when higher social affinities were evolved in the tribes,
then these ghost sun-and-moon men grew into spirits,
forces, and presided in the sky, as their chiefs presided on
the earth. The genius of one race gave lofty consideration
to its war-god, that of another to the storm-spirit, in some
cases the memory of a great chief or warrior overshadowed
the nature forces, but ever we may trace the survival form
or evidence of the earlier spirit forces and some relics of
the ghost gods, the nature gods, the earliest concepts of
mystic powers which still remain among all developed
races. Thus we know that sun-gods and storm-gods, spirits
of mountains, forests and rivers, as well as hero gods and
supernal attributes derived from animals, influenced the
tone of feeling and the every-day acknowledgments of
supernal action among the progenitors of the great Aryan
races. The classic Saturn and Jupiter were the modified
concepts of a much earlier and more human sky deities.
Underlying Brahminism, Buddhism, and even the relics of
the old Vedic faiths; Dr. Stephenson, of Bombay, found
Diwars still cherished the remnants of the ante-Brahminical
religion, and Sir H. M. Elliott recognized in the south of
India traces of worship not of Hindu origin, and carrying
the mind back to a period when that great land was
parcelled out into mere village communes, temporary and
isolated, as is now the case over a greater portion of
Central and Eastern Africa and in New Guinea. (*Hist. of
Races N.W. Provin.* I. p. 243.)

Sproat found sun-worship and moon-worship still lingering among the Ahts of Vancouver's Island, though the great Quawteaht is gaining a more spiritual ascendency among them. We may note, where sun and sky worship has never ceased among an advancing race, how gradually the incense of the soul to these supernal forces has been elevated in its spiritual attributes as in the sun-worship of the old Peruvians and the supremacy of heaven with the Chinese. All the nature gods and spirit forces of the primitive races have but limited powers, and each only rules in his own tribal district or forest lands. They vary in power and in the nature and extent of their jurisdictions, but all their arrangements are moulded on the system evolved in their own social states, and they carry back the memories of events for only a few generations; all beyond is the mystic long ago.

We have given one illustration of the similitude of the Australian's heaven to his own camp. We will now quote another of the Dyak's application of every-day earth-life to his sky existences. The Rev. W. Lobscheid in his *Religion of the Dyaks* describes the sky-world, where the great spirits dwell, as being a region having all the characteristics of the earth, with mountains, valleys, rivers, and lakes, and like the earth as known to them in Borneo, parcelled out into petty districts, each under the control of the rajah or headman. So in the sky-world rivers form the boundaries between the local jurisdictions; they have not yet evolved a head sultan, but each spirit is independent of the other sky-spirits and governs his own district. Nominally one takes the lead as in every like state on the earth, and these spirit-powers associate in the same sexual relations as the Dyaks. Their chief spirit has a wife, who, like the wives of the earth chiefs, may be dismissed at pleasure, and then he may select another. In these, as in all other social groups, the Divine nature and the Divine attributes are but the mystic representations of their ordinary sentiments and actions. (*Relig. of Dyaks*, p. 2.)

In tracing the progress of tutelar development, we must

not look upon it as simple growth in a homogeneous tribe; that probably seldom occurs. A family may grow into a clan, and a clan possibly evolve into a tribe, and ultimately expand into a nation; but more commonly it aggregates by outward adhesion or absorption. Sometimes the growth may take place in many directions, or there may be alternate disintegrations and aggregations. Increase may arise from adoptions, through intermarriages, by voluntary association, by submission and absorption. Now every separate independent group, whether a clan or commune, will have its set of gods, some family, some individual, and one the special tutelar clan god. As a general rule most of these gods would be common in the same district of a country, but any one of them, whatever its origin— from a dead man, an animal, or nature totem—might be the tutelar head of the group. If one group is conquered by another group, they impose their tutelar god on the dependent people, or they, from the result of the contest, accept him as their communal tutelar deity and give their own local god a secondary place. When, among many small clans, diverse changes of the nature we have indicated take place, then the same tutelar deity acquires many phases; for if three or four groups have taken the same god as their tutelar deity, or if they are aggregated together through any circumstances, they can only distinguish themselves by a secondary characteristic.

Probably in no part of the world did such interchange and blending of the status of the gods take place as in pre-Vedic and Vedic India; hence the many attributes and natures of their gods. Thus the same god is broken up in regard to position and action; he is Agni, he is Vayu, Indra, or Surya; he is, moreover, multiplied through his relations with the Asvins, the Maruts, and others. So the same name may imply diverse powers. Thus Aditi is the sky, Aditi is the earth; it is the firmament, it is the mother, it is the father. Or Varuna is Mitra, and Mitra Varuna.

With some Daksha sprang from Aditi, with others Aditi sprang from Daksha. In other heaven systems, Light and Darkness become broken up into many tutelar powers; they do not create other forms, but they express the same power in many names. Thus arose the many Jupiters, the many names of Zeus, the endless forms of the Osirian myth. Thus the god-evolving Maoris, through their many temporary aggregations, multiplied the nature powers of Light and Darkness, and gave them the seeming consistency of many forms, as Hanging Night, Drifting Night, and Moaning Night, and from the light of day they gave personality to the Morn, the Abiding Day, the Bright Day, and the fair expanse of space.

In like manner Rhys, in his *Celtic Heathendom*, shows that the Celtic Zeus was split up into several characters; may we not rather read it that the Celtic Zeus blended in his nature the combined attributes of various local deities of a similar type? These sky-gods, like the sky-gods of most races, were derived from men. Thus Conchobar was the son of an Ulster chieftain; Cormac was the grandson of Conn the Hundred-fighter; and Conaire the Great appears to have been a local chief who first gave his name to his tribe and then to the sun, and was afterwards one only of the sun powers. Rhys notes that the sun-god was partly of human descent—"and this," he writes, "carries us back to the pre-Celtic stage of culture when the medicine-man of the tribe claimed the sun as his offspring." In Ireland we find stories which mention several births of the sun-god. Cian represents the light of the sky-god. Lug, another sun-hero, was the son of Cian. Lug, re-born, was known as Cúchulainn (possibly the new year's sun). Kulhwch was another sun-god, and possibly there were as many sun-gods among the various Celtic races as there were Apollos among the Pelasgians.

That communal tutelar deities were common among the Celts, as with all races in a like stage of progress, Rhys writes:—" Every Gaulish city and British too, probably, had its eponymous divinity, under whose protection it was supposed to be. Nemausus, Vesontio, and Vasio were the tutelar divinities of Nîmes, Besançon, and Vaison respectively." (*Celtic Heathendom*, p. 100.) Each tutelar god had his wife; like mother deities were also general among the Chaldean tutelar local gods and the many Aryan tutelar deities, and universally we may say among all the semi-barbaric races of men.

The range of special tutelar gods began in family and tribal relations, as men specialized in their pursuits, their customs, and affinities. Thus every acquired attribute, every applied purpose had its special tutelar spirit. There were gods of hunting, of war, of fishing. In some cases there were dairy gods, and gods of riding, gods and goddesses of grain, of agriculture, of rice, of the palm tree and the palm wine, of cava, of soma, of pulque. Bacchus belonged to the same agreeable fraternity; even some went so far as to deify drunkenness. There is not a vegetal dedicated to the service of man, but has its tutelar protector. Thus there came to be a god of yams, of the tara root, and of many medicinal plants. So it was with times and seasons in Egypt: every month, every day, every hour, had its presiding deity. In most instances these were deified mortals specialized as limited supernal powers.

We need not dwell on these various manifestations of special and limited supernal tutelar powers; they have little or no connection with any of the forces out of which the greater gods of humanity have been evoked. These, in all cases, are found to have been local or tribal tutelar gods, and the sense of the enlarged power is always derived from the amalgamation of districts or tribes.

Among the various semi-barbaric races, whose aggregations we can follow during historic times, one or other of these modes of supernal agglutination may be perceived; so if we investigate the origins of any of the great races

of men on the earth, we ever trace the growth of their
national deities from district or tribal gods. Thus
Pritchard, writing of Samoa, notes that "the tutelar
district gods, who presided over the various political
divisions, were incarnate in birds and fishes, one in the
rainbow, another in a nation. There were, besides, the
lower class of tutelar gods, each having supremacy over
his special village or small township, and looked up to by
the local inhabitants as their special protectors, defenders,
and advocates, with the more exalted supernal powers
whose tutelar jurisdictions included many townships, an
ample extent of country or even whole islands." (*Poly.
Remin.* p. 111.)

Among the Maoris, whose supernal relations were not
connected with the land on which they settled, but with
the great chiefs who brought them there, and the special
tutelar attributes they themselves evolved, we accordingly
notice a corresponding evolution of tutelar powers. Naturally the great natural features of the country, as Polack
informs us, had their Atuas and Mawi, and Toaki, the great
volcanic mountain upheavers, formed the land. Specialized
powers were common as Irawari, the god of animals;
Otuma, the god of the fern-root; Pain, the god of the
kumara; Papa, god of earth and rivers; Pape, the god of
butterflies and moths; Potiki, of infants; Rehua, of the
sick; Rongomai, of war, &c., &c. Po Rangi, Papa, and
Tiki were invoked by the whole Maori race; they were
their common ancestor chiefs; at the same time every
Maori tribe and family invoked independently each its
own tribal and family ancestors. (*Shortland, Maori Religion,*
p. 8.)

Of the Fijian tutelar deities Erskine in his *Islands of
the Northern Pacific* writes:—"They have superior and inferior gods and goddesses, more or less general and local
deities; some were always gods, others once were men.
Any great warrior is deified after death, their friends are

also sometimes deified and invoked. The different tribes attribute their origin to different gods " (p. 246). Mariner describes a like series of tutelar gods at Tonga as we have seen evolved in other Polynesian races. There are the original Atuas, then the various classes of tutelar gods of the first division; we have the heaven god Tooi Fowa; Bolotoo, the chief of all Bolotoo; another who assumes the title of chief of Bolotoo, probably a successful chief who combined some of the districts, or claus. Then we have the usual sea and wind gods of maritime people, the god of artificers, of war, and probably a very modern creation, the god of the iron axe. Some of the tutelar gods are special to the different islands, others represent the chieftain families, and some of a lower rank were the tutelar deities of the moas, or common people.

In Tahiti, as elsewhere, the various islands had their tutelar gods as Tane of Huaheine, besides, every chief and family of rank had its own tutelar deity. There were the special tutelar spirit-powers of physic, surgery, husbandry, and, so far was the system carried, that they had gods of ghosts, and gods of thieves. (*Ellis, Poly. Res.* p. 339.) We might illustrate the evolution and amalgamation of the god-powers in other Polynesian groups, but they are all based on the same elements, and more or less follow the same progressive lines, starting from nature and fetish-powers, then adding thereto hero-gods and gods representative of new social differentiations, until, from an extended group of heterogeneous individual powers, they coalesce into local groups and simulate the improved social arrangements among men.

The Madagascese are one of the most advanced of the African races, they have been enabled to work out their exposition of the supernal forces in their own way with little or no influence from without. Their whole religious system appears to be of native growth, for, whatever may have been its basis, its present attributes enable it to stand

17 *

on the individuality of its founders. We cannot perceive
any absolute links assimilating it with the vast array of
fetish and nature-god communities in Central and Western
Africa, nor is it in affinity with the Amazulan or Hottentot
expositions of the supernal. Much has been written on
its lingual association with that of the Polynesian races,
but we meet with no more similitudes in supernal character
therewith than might naturally arise in the primary conceptions of each race. They could not as men but begin
with ghost and spirit forces. They could not fail alike to
eliminate the mysterious powers of nature, and endow
them with self-evolved or human spirit forces; but their god
system is of native origin, the very term for supernal
intelligence is known nowhere else. And, though fate or
destiny is universal, and men everywhere conceive of
impersonal powers, and the possibility of piercing the
mysteries of the unknown future, the Malagassy have solved
the problem in a manner unknown to other races of men;
even what they have of sacred mana influence is an original
manifestation.

The Malagassy have no ancient civilization, they have no
remnants, philological or traditionary, of an advanced past.
Their religious formulæ carry us back to a still lower
phase than that now manifested. So recent is the growth
of sovereign power that they have not evolved its presumed
prototype, but deduced representatives in the heavens.
They know nothing of a sovereign god, they never had a
sky-chief, their nature gods rather express the lower
powers than aspire to the majesty of the greater powers in
the heavens. Hence, when they began to conceive of a
common supernal power, a mana that expressed the supernal element in ghost and spirit, and every occult attribute,
they could not give it a tangible name, they could only
express it by vague terms of excellence that equally applied
to the sun, the star, the sky, a chief, the principle affirmed
in their divinations and ordeals. We cannot conceive that

this multiple term expresses what is affirmed in the word god, for then even silk, and rice, money and the reigning sovereign would be gods. All the term implies is that the objects to which it is attached hold some mysterious principle of excellence and are endowed with a sacred attribute and mana; tabu or fetish more express the many meanings of Andria manitra than that of god. Mr. Ellis truly says that the Malagassy have no knowledge of "Him who created the heavens and the earth, and who clothes Himself with honour and majesty." (*Madag.* I. p. 390.)

It does not appear to have been many generations since the Malagassy were mere rude nature-worshippers, without any defined system, and reverencing various mysterious fetish powers and evil ghosts. Some few hero-gods with limited local influences had been evolved with various family penates, but the national gods had then no existence, any more than the nation itself. We even seem to be present at the birth of what, had their civilization been left to home development, might have become the Jupiters and Apollo's of a Southern Olympus.

Mr. Ellis writes :—"The whole system of the national idols appears to have sprung up in comparatively modern times and long subsequently to the prevalence of the worship of the household-gods. Imploina, the father of Radama, did repeatedly convene the population to witness the consecrating or setting apart of several of the present national idols. Imploina is said to have acted thus solely from political motives, having their foundation in the conviction that some kind of religious or superstitious influence was useful in the government of a nation." (*Hist. Madag.* I. p. 396.)

It is evident that, in Madagascar as elsewhere, the god-powers aggregated as through various circumstances the people aggregated, and that they grew from family-gods to be clan-gods, then tribal and ultimately district-gods. Mr. Ellis says there are in the immediate neighbourhood

of Tananarivo twelve or fifteen principal idols, these belong
respectively to different tribes or divisions of the natives,
and are supposed to be the guardians and benefactors of
these particular clans or tribes. Four of those are considered superior to all others, and are considered public and
national. There are throughout the country many others
belonging to the several clans or districts; every province
and every clan has its idol. Every house also, and every
family its object of veneration and confidence. (*Hist.
Madag.* I. p. 395.) That some missionaries should, like many
writers in other countries, conceive that the occult mana
formerly recognized as pervading all fetish objects implied
a mystic concept of a supreme deity as once recognized, but,
such a conception has always collapsed in the consciousness that it ascribes to men in a low state of development
the capacity to generalize the highest class of abstractions.
Mr. Ellis gives us a more plausible tradition, that a king,
or rather chief, followed the custom of the people; each
family had its own ancestral penates, and he, in like
manner, instituted tribal, or possibly district tutelar
gods. (*Ibid.* I. p. 897.) The dii penates were a very
ancient institution, of whose origin there is no tradition.
(*Ibid.* I. p. 400.) The references to the chief tutelar
deities imply from their fady or tabu attributes that
they express the combinations of several family or clan
totems in the aggregation of a tribe. Thus one of the
most powerful of the enlarged district gods is Rakelimalaza;
and pigs, onions, a shell-fish, a small animal, the goat,
horse, cat, and owl, are fady to him, and imply the
coalition of as many small clans of which they were the
totems. Another of the chief idols is Ramahavaly, and
besides certain domestic animals the serpent is fady to his
devotees, serpents are also said to instinctively cling around
this idol's guardian and attendants, and also kill all who
break his fady. (I. p. 409.)

It is a singular fact that in Madagascar we have no

evidence of the development of a class of priests or even medicine-men. This seems to have arisen from the power to make charms never having left the fetish idols. Like Micah's teraphim, whoever had possession of the idol held all power over the charms it could express. This, as we have shown, is the survival form of the old charm worship; for whoever held the mana, the fetish spell object commanded all its supernal powers. All the idols are representative of the powers in charms and spells through the mediation of their guardians; but " Rapakila is the great seller of charms;" whether a charm against the fever, the measles, the leprosy, the dropsy, or other diseases, whether charms against crocodiles, scorpions, and venomous insects, or charms to obtain their desires, Rakapila will supply. (*Ibid.* I. p. 413.)

As explanatory of the late development of a central authority in the country from which the idea of the higher god-power would have been evolved, it was the father of King Radama who reduced the fifty distinct tribes each under its own presiding chieftain, and amalgamated them into one state. (*Ibid.* I. p. 118.) At that period the system of local tutelar gods was fully developed, and each of the tribes was under the protection of its special divinity. By the fusion of the tribes, the fifteen most influential tutelar deities were formed into a sort of Olympian conclave among which four, as dispensing the greatest benefits and guarding the interests of the sovereign and the kingdom at large, were considered public and national. (*Ibid.* I. p. 395.) There was but one more move necessary—that of selecting the heavenly Radama.

In endeavouring to unravel the steps by which the great supernal powers have been evolved, it is most important that we have thus presented to our investigation the evolution of a supernal system based on the same general progressive laws as have marked the growth of other Theogonies. What happened in Madagascar a

hundred or more years ago was but a repetition of the
process by which the gods of Egypt, Chaldea, Greece, and
Rome had ages before come to the supernal front. The
tutelar gods of the tribes or districts became amalgamated,
the conquering line becoming the supreme head. The same
submission of the other local tutelar gods took place when
the victorious Cuzcoans conquered Pachacamac and the
lands he divinely governed; so it was with the Aztecs, and
many of the neighbouring gods were held in honourable
captivity in the temples at Mexico.

In some cases the growth of a god's power had other
and more agreeable origins. Thus Apollo, as Mueller shows,
had his supremacy extended by a growing nation sending
forth colonies and establishing trading stations, and by the
virtue of its genius, may we say mana, influencing cognate
minds. Originally only a Greek god, unknown to the old
Romans, at Sparta, the national idol to whom its chief offered
sacrifice, his influence extending with his victories over
the earth ruling monsters; thus he gained Tempe, he
presided at Delphos; thus he went with the Greek traders
and soldiers to Asia Minor, to Crete, and Thrace. When
the Dorians took possession of the temple at Olympia as
the patron and guardian deity, he acquired the title of
Thermius. This name, originally derived from that of an
old nature sun-god, was blended with the attributes of
other local sun-gods, as at Corinth, Rhodes, and Athens.

We have seen how general, throughout the vast regions
of Negro Africa, fetish charm worship abounded. That and
a low form of nature worship appears to have continued
through untold ages to distinguish the low class supernal
powers her sons evolved. Witchcraft, charms, and the
indefinite dread of evil, are the prevailing sentiments. A
man may claim to be a living god, but his slight supernal
powers end with his life. There are few hero-gods, prophet-
gods, self-evolved tutelar deities known in negro lands. Poet
and artist are alike of no effect, and only vague, natural,

tutelar gods become differentiated.   In the more advanced groups a low brutal fetishism, rarely advancing to a local or aggregate power, supervenes; in which the family ancestral system, appealing as it does to the social affections continued in another life, is only here and there superseding, by their guardian care, the dependence on mere fetish charms.

The African terms that have been assumed to embody the idea of a godhead are most vague, and they in no instance can be considered as other than representing low spirit or human ghost-powers. Many are merely the native terms for sky, sun, and rain; some signify human ghosts; but none have any attributes assimilating them to the higher god-powers, much less that of an abstract deity. Doff Macdonald, in his *Africana*, forcibly illustrates the process by which, under the dispensation of the missionaries, the change is brought about.   He observes that in translations they use the word *Mulungo* as synonymous with God; but this Mulunga, according to the natives, is the spirit of a deceased man—that is, a mere ghost—yet it is taken as signifying the God of the Christians. (I. p. 59.) In the same way others have misapplied *Erna* the sun, *Masai Engai* the sky, and *Mtuoa* the sun, and have used those terms in Scripture history and doctrine as synonymous with a supreme intelligence. *Not* only by such misrepresentations will the native mind be confused, but a false presumption becomes affirmed of a highly evolved god-power.

Even among the Ashantees, the chief god-powers are nature forces, some of which are general, others are tutelar to the rulers, the towns or districts, or the cabooeers. Thus the rivers Tando and Adirai are tutelar deities to the King of Ashantee, that of Sekim is tutelar to Akrah, and the lake Echiu is the guardian deity of Coomassie. We have previously spoken of the local tutelar influence of certain totem animals at the chief towns on the Gold Coast, but nowhere is there any attempt to evolve a conclave of national gods and found a new Olympus.

More advance has been made in the direction of family ancestral worship. Chieftain worship has obtained in many places; thus we are told that among the Marutse "when a member of the royal family was ill he was taken to the grave of one of his ancestors, the king then knelt at the grave and prayed to the deceased: 'You, my grandfather, who are near to N'yambe, pray to N'yambe that the disease may be taken from this man.'" (*Pro. Roy. Geo. Soc.* II. p. 262.) Reade in his *Savage Africa* writes: "In times of peril and distress they will assemble in clans on the brink of some mountain brow or on the skirt of a dense forest, and extending their arms to the sky, while the women are wailing and the very children weep, they will cry to the spirits of those who have passed away" (p. 249). Of the passage of dead ancestors into tutelar chiefs, Macdonald writes: "Some say that every one in the village, whether a relative of the chief or not, must worship his own forefathers, otherwise their spirits will bring trouble upon him. To reconcile these authorities, we may mention that nearly every one is related to the chief, or if not in courtesy is considered so." (*Africana*, I. p. 65.) So "a great chief who has been successful in his wars may become the god of a mountain or lake, and may receive homage as a local deity long before his own descendants have been driven from the spot. When there is a supplication for rain, the inhabitants of the country pray not so much to their own forefathers as to the god of the mountain on whose shoulders the great rain clouds repose. The god of Mount Sochi is Kangomba, an old chief, who when defeated, instead of leaving the country, entered a cave on a mountain, from which he never returned. The conquerors honoured him as the god of the mountain, and betimes ask the members of his tribe to aid them in their offerings and supplications." (*Africana*, I. p. 71.)

We have but a confused account of the original religious notions of the inhabitants of the Philippines. That the universal belief in the spirit forces presiding in natural things prevailed we have ample evidence. Thevenot's account, as given in Marsden's *Sumatra*, and which appears to have been the basis of both Sir John Bowring's and De Morga's narratives, speaks of both sun and moon worship, of the spiritual attributes ascribed to the rainbow, and the usual adoration of the supernal powers contained in rocks and streams. That fetish, animal, and tree worship abounded extensively all affirm. The creator god Bathala, probably originally the spirit of an ancestral chieftain, was worshipped in association with his totem, a blue bird; the crow was called the lord of the earth, and, as with the tropical negroes the alligator was addressed as grandfather, offerings were made to it, and they prayed that he would do them no harm. That the usual rude tutelar deities were evolved both special to occupations and tribes we note: thus one was the god of harvest, another of fishermen, one expedited the growing crops, another was the native Esculapius. We also meet with the huntsman's god, the god of eating, and sundry others with only local influence. The wild Indians at the present day still worship the nature forces, and the natives in their ceremonial rites still with uplifted hands cry, "O thou god, O thou beautiful moon, O thou star!" (*Bowring, Phil. Is.* p. 177.) They also still retain their local tribal tutelar gods, as Cubija of the Altabans and Amanolay the special god of the Gaddens. They have local gods of the mountains and plains and cultivated lands, and without having evolved the family ancestral system, they have both chieftain and ancestor gods, these termed Anitos or Monos were worshipped both in the field and the house. All these were crude individual god-powers, without an Olympus; and as they have very few affinities with the gods of other races, such supernal ideas as they entertained appear to have been of native origin. Thevenot (*Marsden's Sumatra*, p. 256) says: "They made Anitos of their deceased ancestors to which they made invocations in all difficulties and dangers. They also reckoned among these beings all those who were killed by lightning or had violent deaths. They still continue the custom of asking permission of their dead ancestors when they enter any wood, mountain, or cornfield for hunting or sowing."

Another race of men favourably disposed to evolve on independent lines were the residents of the extreme south of the American continent, who were little influenced by foreign or adventitious modifications. It is true that the equally self-contained god systems of Cuzco and Quito might have influenced the Araucanians, but the antagonisms of the races prevented the little intercommunications that they held with one another having any special effect on the national sentiments; on all sides the satisfaction with their own supernal powers prevented any friendly amalgamation, and no conquest on either side supervened to bring a forced association.

Of the early nature worship we still note some indications. "They say the stars are old Indians, and that the milky way is the field where the old Indians hunt ostriches, and that the southern clouds are the feathers of the ostriches they kill." (*Falkner's Patagonia*, p. 115.) "They have a multiplicity of deities, each of whom they believe to preside over one particular family of Indians, of which he is supposed to be the creator, as the lion, tiger, guanaco, ostrich, &c. They imagine that these deities have each his separate habitation in vast caverns under the earth." (*Ibid.* p. 114.) Of their more national god-powers, one has a name signifying the governor of the people; another presides in the land of strong drink; a third bears the cognomen of the "Lord of the dead;" another is "the wanderer."

Since Falkner wrote his narrative the Araucanians, probably profiting in some measure from information derived through the modern Peruvians, from isolated tribes mostly unsettled, have formed pastoral and agricultural communes on an original system, that reminds us of the process of national amalgamation now going on among the Afghans. Naturally warlike, and confident that their safety from aggression will be due to union, the country has been divided into districts, each under what may be termed its own feudal lord. But while each Toqui is independent in his civil government, they are confederate for the general good. In like manner they have evolved a like chieftain, if not feudal, government in the heavens. "The Supreme Being, whom they call Pillian, is at the head of a universal government, which is the prototype of their own. Pillian is the great invisible Toqui, and has his Apoulmenes and Ullmens, to whom he assigns different situations in the government. Meulen, the genius of good, and Wennuba, that of evil and the enemy of man, are the two principal subordinate deities." (*Stevenson's S. Amer.* pp. 1-55.) According to the *Journal of the Anthropological Institute* (I. p. 202) nature worship still prevails : they salute the new moon, the spirits of the rocks and rivers, and their devotions are directed to propitiate the tutelar powers presiding over them.

The full history of the development of the tutelar from the nature and ancestral gods, is worked out in connection with the development of the supernal system in each great race of men. In these several expositions of the development of national and racial gods we describe, first, the earliest form of faith that we can discover they expressed, and we then trace the evidences their history, traditions and other forms of survival convey of the stages of supernal development that they passed through, up to the highest manifestation that each presented.

CHAPTER VIII.

The differentiation of King-Gods in Egypt.

THE social evolution of human races depends upon locality
and progress, and progress itself depends upon locality.
The configuration of a country influences the capacity of
its inhabitants to aggregate and the forms of aggregation
that may ensue. The inhabitants of icy regions are
absolutely precluded from forming confederacies that in
their various expositions tend to advance their members,
and corresponding deterring conditions permanently mark
the status of the denizens of rocky and desert lands.
Thus the Eskimo and the Fuegian make no advance; as
they were in the olden times so they continue now to
present mere isolated family groups; they never group into
communities. In Australia sandy deserts and barren
lands resulting from long-continued droughts resulted in
producing somewhat like conditions, and kept the small
clans which simply represented great families from
aggregating into amalgamated tribes. So if we take note
of the Arabs, the Moors, and the Tartars of the desert
regions we may recognize that like detergent local conditions ever restrain the capacity for men to aggregate. They
may betimes be influenced by the neighbouring cognate
races, whose natural conditions are more favourable for
inducing the confederation and coalition of tribes, but when
this external influence is withdrawn they always break up
again into their simple integers.

As the social state of men so are their supernal ideas,
and the Arab of to-day, though he may nominally assent to
the God of the Koran, knows Allah only as a man-spirit of
the same *genre* as the ghost of the wely or neby at whose
tomb he leaves his simple offering.   Our presentation of
religious and social development among the Bedouins is
fully confirmed in the observations of Professor Robertson
Smith. He writes: "The progress of religion followed that
of society.   In the case of that of the nomadic Arabs shut
up in the wilderness of rock and sand, nature herself barred
the way of progress.   The life of the desert does not
furnish the material conditions for permanent advance
beyond the tribal system, and we find that the religious
development of the Arabs was proportionally retarded, so
that at the advent of Islam the ancient heathenism, like
the ancient tribal structure of society, had become effete,
without having ever become barbarous." (*The Religion of
the Semites*, p. 35.)   What Allah is to the Bedouin has been
shown by Sir John Lubbock in the curse on him by the old
Arab woman suffering from the toothache, and Spencer, in
a quotation from Palgrave, shows that the only possible
concept the Bedouin could form of Allah was that of an
Arab Sheik presiding only in his encampment.   On his
being questioned "What will you do coming into God's
presence after so graceless a life?"   "What will we do?"
was his unhesitating answer, " Why, we will go up to God and
salute Him, and if He proves hospitable, gives us meat and
tobacco, we will stay with Him; if otherwise we will mount
our horses and ride off."   To the Arab, Islam is but a form
and a name, and for all practical purposes nature worship
and hero worship still prevail; they comprehend local and
tribal supernal powers as they did in the days of Mohammed,
and continue now to make gods of the class we have seen;
they esteem Allah, of every wely or neby who exhibits
mystic powers.

No man can ever conceive the nature of a god other than

by the symbols of power present to his soul in the world about him, and in his own social institutions. The god of nature represents at first not the real force and immensity present to his perceptive powers, but the low class deduction thereof he is able to conceive. As his concepts advance so does the sentiment of the god he entertains. So it is with the personal attributes of the Deity formed on the human model; he can only represent the highest standard thereof present to his mind. He may, like the totem man, idealize it from his favourite animal; he may, like the Greek, conceive of it as a more powerful athlete; it may be to him an ancestral ghost, the head of a family; it may be a village chief or the chief of a tribe: in more advanced communities, the tutelar god of a community, a town, a group of confederate or subdued tribes, or the sovereign of a more or less extended state, built up of many aggregate elements even up to the imperial suzerainty designated by the epithets Lord of Lords, and King of Kings.

In all cases if we analyze the sentiments a man's god expresses we may demonstrate the conditions which have surrounded a man or which have formed the elements of thought out of which he has embodied his divinity. We have illustrated several such embodiments of a low class character in which the divine nature is only that of his human compeers as seen through the glamour of the medicine-man's ideality. But while the individual's standard of deity is usually that of his tribe, it often happens that his mental perceptions being of a low character only advance to his tribe's lowest fetish or even charm concepts of the supernal, for no man can conceive of supernals beyond the organic evolution of his own mental powers. So in like manner the man with great original thought-power naturally takes a more august comprehension of the relations of the nature forces, and he may even anticipate the capacities of human society, though unable to integrate them in the forms they afterwards assume.

We have made these general observations preliminary to our investigation of the development of the higher class religions, as they account in some measure for the divergences they present. In every upward manifestation of the supernal the possibility of branching off on distinct lines becomes apparent; there could be only minor distinctions in the character of charms, spells, and magic powers; but when the ghost-spirit was invented the varieties thereof became most numerous, but after conceived as confederacies under leaders, like the tribes of men they become organized on as many systems as are apparent in human societies.

In considering the development of each of these special supernal systems we have first to show they had their origin in the same elements as the lower class sentiments of the supernal we have treated upon, and that their higher manifestations were due to their surrounding conditions and the racial aspects of their own mental powers. In all cases we shall have to recognize special attributes and special results though founded on the same intrinsic principles of development.

From the days of the Father of History to those of Rawlinson and Brugsch, the ancient Egyptian race has ever been held up as one of the most remarkable expositions of natural religious sentiments—uncontrolled by external relations, uninfluenced by the enthusiasm of the ascetic, ignorant of the wild supernaturalisms of the medicine-man, nor urged to ferocious manifestations by the rhapsodies of prophets and seers. Mildly contemplative, intensely devotional, they recognized the spiritual attributes and supernal influences present in all things—not alone in the grand phenomena of the natural world, but in all the infinite forms of life, more especially in their fellow-men, in kings, heroes, and priests. The world to them was overflowing with the expression of supernal power; the gods were allwhere—in the air, in the stars, in the thunder and in the cataract; they saw god in all life, in bird and beast and

creeping thing; mortality to them was but a semblance
enwrapping the deity.   Hence, they breathed and moved
and had their being, as it were, in a supernal world; when
they ate and drank, when they rose up or laid down, it
was in the presence of the gods, and this sentiment of
divinity moulded, as it were, their forms of thought and
their habits of life.

As Lenormant says, all Egypt bore the impress of
religion; its writing was full of sacred symbols and of
allusions to sacred myths, so that its use beyond the land
of Egypt became impossible.   Literature and science were
but branches of theology.   The fine arts were only employed with a view to religion and the glorification of the
gods or deified kings.   Each province had its special gods,
its peculiar rites, its sacred animals.   It seems that the
priestly element had presided even over the distribution of
the country into nomes and that these had been originally
ecclesiastical districts.   (*Ancient History of the East*,
p. 817.)

It is the origin of this faith and its progress among this
ancient people that we have now to consider.   It was one
of the most autochthonous of religions; its gods, its ghost-
powers, its rules of life and aspirations of the future were
self-created; the Greek, the Roman, the Hindu faiths,
might be traced to a far earlier cult in some unknown
region, and to this parent of religions even the rude
Slavonian and the primitive Celt may have been indebted
for the foundations of their faiths.   So the Chinese, the
Japanese, even the Mexican gods, may have been first
present in the skies of Mongolia and in the bitter cold of
the far north; but the gods of Egypt had nothing in
common with the gods of other nations, save in the fact
that many of them were educed from the physical presentation of the same natural phenomena.   In their essence, in
their characters, in their influence on men, they were a
special creation, and as they began so they ended, hey

were never the cults of other races, they gave forth no successive foreign dynasties of gods, but were content to remain the sacred and inherent heritage of that great and archaic race who instituted that special form of worship on the banks of the ever-mysterious Nile.

Nor was this singular faith only the work of yesterday—we have to unroll a vast cycle of ages to discover its birth. When Greece was the home of the shaggy bear and the wolf and the wild cave-dwelling savage, before the mud huts of Erech and Bel sheltered the humblest of communities, the dwellers on the banks of the Nile had become many states. Before Terah had honoured his racial gods, or ever Jahveh had selected his chosen people, a series of god dynasties had been evolved in the souls of the Egyptians. The Greek had some faint inkling of bygone dynasties in the heavens, some vague myths of the reigns of Ouranos and Chronos in his Olympus, but the Egyptians had known many successive epochs of sun-gods. In the historical period we only know of the evolution of the worship of Serapis, as of Krishna in India and Apollo in Greece; but before the advent of Serapis we have in Egypt those of Horus, and Osiris, and Seb, and before them, in a series of antecedent cycles, the long duration of the heavenly sovereignties of Amun, Thoth, Ra and Ptah, the mighty and venerable father of the gods. Yet before the first of these great gods was conceived, the Egyptians had built up the more primary faith the evidence of which survives in the fetish records of animal supernal manifestations and the ghost forms of dead humanity, that gave origin to the faith in the after-world that had so prominent and intimate relations with the subsequent development of the gods and their general unity of action.

We feel assured that the old Egyptian faith, like the primary religions of other races, must have been preceded by the usual archaic supernal ideas. Animal totem fetishes were as reverently honoured and feared in Egypt as in

18 *

modern times in Western Africa. There are as many totem gods recorded of the Egyptians as of the North American Indians. These fetish animals were recognized by special marks or signs of which the priests took cognizance. Hence, when one died, the cult was not complete till his successor, like the Dalai Lama of Thibet, was found with the emblems of his sacred character and high position. The marks denoting the holy Apis were a triangular white spot on the forehead, white spots on the back in the shape of an eagle, and bicoloured hairs on the tail; there was also a fleshy growth under the tongue in the form of the sacred beetle of Ptah.

Instead of being a centralized state at this early period, or even consisting of binary combinations in the local worship of the totem animals, we recognize various distinct tribes, each having its own local centre, both of worship and influence, and in which it was the tutelar guardian. Thus the cat-totem centre was Bubastis, that of the hawk at Buto, the ibis at Hermopolis, the hippopotamus in the Papremis nome, the crocodile at Thebes, the bull Mnevis at Heliopolis, and the bull Apis at Memphis.

In the magical texts published in the *Records of the Past* may be detected, not only the actions and assumptions of the medicine-man, but even that adscription of power to many of the substances used in incantations that denote the appeal for protection to spells and charms of the lowest kind, the waste of animal and human bodies. Thus: " Shu takes the shape of an eagle's wing; he makes a lock or tress of sheep's wool to go round this god's neck. He makes his body protected, &c." Again: "Tefnit resists; he prevails against the wicked ones by the hair of a cow passing yesterday; carrying to-day the blood of the mystic eye, the skin of the head of ursus serpent, the eye of a dwarf." Another: " A circle of a green herb, a drop of well water with the following objects therein :—The heart of a jackal, the nostril of a pig, the urine of an ape, followed by a

plate of beaten gold, wherein an eagle's wing is figured."
(*Records of the Past*, VI. p. 110.)

In the following we have spells which imply the age of
totem evolution and the medicine-man :—

> " May they cry out for me, Lala, my good mother,
> Closing the mouths of the lions, of the hyæna, the heads of all animals
> Having long tails, who live upon flesh and drink blood.
> To fascinate them, to snatch away their ears, to cause darkness,
> To prevent light, to cause blindness, to prevent visibility
> Every moment during night.   Up, bad dog !
> Come, I command what thou must do to-day.
> Be thy face like the gaping sky ; the aspect of thy mane
> Like that of metal rods.   Do not set thy face against me.
> Set thy face against the animals of the land ; repel thro' fascination."
>
> (*Ibid.* X. p. 156.)

In the following incantation and case of possession we
are presented with the same low-class spirit manifestations
that so generally prevailed in Europe during the Middle
Ages :—

> " Oh Spirit of the Heaven protect thou !
> Oh Spirit of the Earth protect thou !
> Oh Spirit of the Lord of Lands protect thou !
> Oh Spirit of the Lady of Lands protect thou !
> Oh Spirit of the Lord of the Stars protect thou !
> Oh Spirit of the Lady of the Stars protect thou !
> Oh Spirit of the Lord of Light and Life protect thou !
> Oh Spirit of the Lady of Light and Life protect thou !"
>
> (*Trans. Soc. Bib. Arch.* VI. p. 539.)

Possession by evil spirits was an early doctrine in
Egypt. An inscription in the Bibliothèque Nationale at
Paris records the case of. an Asiatic princess married to
one of the kings, who was supposed to have been troubled
by the intrusion of an evil spirit.   The royal priest, unable
to cope with the spirit that troubled the princess, had the
image of the god Chonsu sent in his ark accompanied by
a talisman of the same god to exorcise the evil one.   We
are told the spirit yielded to the superior supernal power of

the god, and retired from the body of the princess, a sacrifice at the same time being offered to propitiate the evil genius, and thus prevent it inflicting further injury.

In the long history of the Egyptian dynasties we have present to us the sovereignty of the local triads or the local councils of the gods. At an early period the concept of an evil principle and the doctrine of evil spirits feared and worshipped by men, and which precedes the adoration of benevolent and superintending deities, prevailed. We have in the war between Osiris and Typhon the death of Osiris and the victory of young Horus, a traditional myth of the existence in Egypt of the worship of evil spirits. Therein we have the same monstrous forms and characters as those which gave origin to ogres and giants among most races of men, as the monster Typhon, of Nubi of Taouris, the feminine evil spirit of Bes, with a hideous cannibal aspect, a match for the archaic Medusa of the Greeks. These with Anubis, Amenti, Anset, Hapi, and many others evince that a form of faith like the old Bhuta worship in India prevailed in Egypt. An observation in Rawlinson's *History of Egypt* infers at one period the supremacy of the general worship of Bhutes in Egypt, and that inscriptions to Set and his emblems were common on the earliest monuments which were subsequently obliterated; this according to Rawlinson implied a serious change in religious opinion, the after ascendency of moral deities. (*Hist. Egypt*, I. p. 317.)

There can be little doubt but that nature-worship in various forms existed long before the suppression of the worship of evil spirits in Egypt. Indeed, it must have progressed through several stages, and been associated with the worship of men-gods and presiding principles before there could have been evolved the social institutions that superseded the primitive barbarism. According to Duncker, the day of Typhon became set apart as unlucky, and he himself was called the almighty destroyer; he filled the whole earth and sea with evils, and in some measure assumed the character of the Persian Ahrimanes.

That nature worship, more especially the worship of the sun, had progressed through several stages, we may well affirm. The boat of Osiris belongs to the same attempt of men to associate the motions of the heavenly bodies with human pursuits as the chariot of Phœbus and the carriage of Surya, but the living disc of the sun, and of the Peruvian Incas, personified the sun as a self-existent being, like the old Beltane wheel, having its own proper motion, and not dependent on a presiding totem. We have even the attempt to divest sun-worship of its anthropomorphic character, and honour it as a self-existent principle. We know nothing of the birth of Egyptian solar worship, yet in some of the old sun-gods we have but personifications of its aspects as expressed in the various local centres, the same as we found has existed among many like confederated states. Thus Kephro was sun-creative; Tum, sun-setting; Aten, the sun's disc; Shu, its light. Many of these occur as the presiding sun-principle, as Ra, Kephro, Tum, Shu, Mentu, Osiris, Horus, Harmaches, and Aten. So of the moon, we have Khons, Thoth, Seb, and Sabak.

The distinction between the two forms of sun-faith, the worship of it personified as a man-god, and that of devotion to it as a sublime spiritual principle, is manifest in the diverse forms in which it is addressed, as recorded in the inscriptions. Rameses II, speaking to his father, the Osiris King Sati, says: "Awake, raise thy face to heaven, behold the sun my father Mineptah, who art like to God. Here am I who make thy name to live. Thou restest in the deep like Osiris, while I rule like Ra among men, and possess the great throne of Tum, like Horus, the son of Isis, the guardian of his father. Thou hast entered into the realm of heaven, thou accompaniest the sun-god Ra. Thou art united with the sun and the moon. Thou restest in the deep, like those who dwell in it with Umofer, the eternal; thy hands move the god Tum in the heavens, and on earth like the wandering stars and the fixed stars." (*Brugsch, Egy.* II. p. 41.)

To Ahmenhotep IV, as to the Peruvian Incas, the sun was not a man-god but a refulgent disc in its own special form taking its course through the heavens. He discarded its many personalities, its various aspects, its human characteristics; to him it was a disc of glory, the source of life and being. "Beautiful in thy setting, thou sun's disc of life, thou lord of lords and king of worlds; when thou unitest thyself with the heaven at thy setting mortals rejoice before thy countenance, and give honour to him who has created them, and pray before him who has formed them, before the glance of thy son who loves thee, the King Khunaten (Ahmenhotep IV). The whole land of Egypt, and all peoples, repeat all thy names at thy rising to magnify thy rising in like manner as thy setting. Thou, O God, who in truth art the living one, standest before the two eyes. Thou art He which createst what never was, which formest everything, which art in all things; we have also come into being through the word of thy mouth. Thou disc of the sun, thou living God, there is none other beside thee. Thou givest health to the eyes through thy beams, Creator of all beings. Thou goest up on the Eastern horizon of heaven to dispense life to all which thou hast created, to man, to four-footed beasts, to birds and all manner of creeping things on the earth where they live. Thus they behold thee, and they go to sleep when thou settest." (*Brugsch*, I. p. 450.)

Ahmenhotep was before his age, and it was not likely that his attempt to cast out the surviving fetishism in Egypt would succeed. The priests who essentially had subsisted on the many god-affirmations were against him, and the people were unable to sustain this phase of the divine. On the death of the king his sun monotheism

collapsed, and after a troublous period, the holy father Ai
became king. He returned to the old forms of faith,
sacrificed to Ammon, restored the old capital, and called
himself Prince of Thebes.

That the highest nature-gods of Egypt possessed nothing
of the omniscience of a supreme being, is apparent in the
Stele of the Coronation (Records of the Past). It may be
remembered that in the Iliad when Zeus makes a trip to
Ethiopia, he was ignorant of what then took place at Troy;
the telegraph had no existence, and consequently telepathy
was not invented. It was not until he returned to Mount
Ida that he became acquainted with the modes in which
the other gods had subverted his decrees; so, in tho
Egyptian inscription, Ra has gone out of heaven into the
land of Aukhet, his seat in heaven is empty, and the new
king, without his presence there, could not be consecrated
because Ra alone knew him. So they went down to Ra,
the god of the kingdom of Kush, and presented the brothers
to him that he might announce the selected one. The god
was no more than a human sovereign, and if a State
document required his signature, the State council had to
post to the Balmoral of the god.

It is most probable that before the Egyptian State was
consolidated, the sun was a general object of adoration, and
was represented in the various local centres or cities, under
diverse names and attributes. Like as in Assyria, there
were the local supernal powers separate and distinct in
each community, but kept to represent the one series
by neighbourhood and the inter-marriages that thereby
accrued. How many such centres obtained in Egypt we
know not, but many retained their distinguishing god-
attributes far into the historic period. The sun-god of
Heliopolis was Ra, of Thebes, both Amon and Tum, of
Abydus Osiris. Other local centres had for their totems
other gods, who, on the doctrine of each selecting its own
divine council of tutelar deities, became their local Olympic

councils. The Zeus or president of the council of gods at Memphis was Ptah, at Hermopolis Thoth, at Sais Neith, at Coptus Chem, at Dendera Hathor, at Syene Chnum, at Elephantine Sati. While these specialities marked the distinctive head-power in the communes, the basis of the faith was the common divine character of all the gods in the several groups of states. In each important centre the local god was the ruling, the feudal chief, not a supreme god; there were the family deities as well as the several clan deities, which constituted the distinct tribe. To this tribal deity it was the fashion to attach a wife and son, forming a family triad as at Memphis, Thebes and Hermothis.

That Egypt had its hero-gods we may well affirm. Menes, the tribal founder, was a man-god; so was Menta the war-god, Hapi the Nile-god, Aemhept the Egyptian Esculapius, Chepera and Horus, as well as Osiris and Tini. In later times, when the nomos were confederated into the states of Upper and Lower Egypt, it became the fashion to deify every king and sometimes the powerful priests. At what time the worship of ancestors was introduced we have no certain knowledge. In the ancient mode of burial, as observed in the oldest graves opened by Mr. Rhind, no indications of the adoration of the dead were manifest. After sepulchral chambers were built for special families, and in which oblations and libations were presented, as well as flower decorations, protective amulets, and other manifestations of reverence and affection to satisfy the presumed wants of the dead, and enable the new Osiris gods to compass the journey to the after-world.

The last stage in the evolution of god-powers in ancient Egypt was presented in the Horus myth; it embodies the concept of an universal nature and the sentiment of moral mediation between humanity and the retired majesty of a sovereign deity. Osiris represents the ruler of a great confederate state, formed from many principalities, whose august sovereign is only known by his edicts. He is the god of the two Egypts, whilst the sun in the name type of Ra is the great feudal conqueror who unites in his godhead the name types of the various nomes. We know there was a time when neither Horus or Osiris were cognomens of the sun, they never existed until there was an united Egypt. Before that time each nome, each city had its own tutelar sun deity. We suspect many of these were successful chiefs deified by their prosperous followers.

That the sovereigns at least were worshipped as gods after death we have evidence, and they had priests attached to their worship. (*Egypt from the Monuments*, p. 83.) Recorded instances are those of Amenophis I. and Aohmes. Thoth, the inventor of speech and writing, the god of wisdom, must be considered an abstract god; probably he was the deified introducer of the art of writing, and by the results thereof became characterized as the god of wisdom. We sometimes find the gods of two or more neighbouring cities, like their rulers, associated together, but in all cases the greatness or rank of a god depends upon the numerical strength of his worshippers, and we may not infer, as did Sir G. Wilkinson, that the minor deities were satisfied with presiding over towns of minor importance, but we rather hold that the size of the town itself and its population was the source of the dignity of the god. Surely Minerva as a village goddess and Diana as the tutelar deity of a small hamlet would have been much less dignified than was Pallas Athenæ and the great goddess Diana of Ephesus. Hence Amon became a supreme god because he was the chief of the gods at Thebes when it became a regal sovereignty, and at first Ptah, and after Osiris, holding the same position at Memphis, acquired a like ascendancy.

Among the philosophic priests of the later period the gods were comprised in two imperial dynasties or families,

that of the sun-god Ra and his family, and that of Osiris
and his family. These became imperial sovereignties, and
all the other god-powers were arranged in graduated ranks
below them, most having their special allotted offices in
the kosmos. The idea of an Eternal Self-existent God was
never evolved in the soul of Egypt.

We might add that in a learned article in the *Nineteenth
Century* (XXXII. p. 89, &c.), J. Norman Lockyer not
only shows the derivation of the Egyptian nature-gods from
star and animal totems, but that the special position of the
heavenly bodies then implies that the myth must have
originated 5000 years B.C., otherwise the constellation
Hippopotamus could not have figured in it.

CHAPTER IX.

The Evolution of the Gods of Assyria and Western Asia.

THERE is no primary exposition of the supernal, in which we are more personally interested, than that of the races we have now to consider. The special nature and the mythogonies of the god-powers in Greece and Rome are perhaps more familiarly referred to, but to us they are but cold poetic entities in whose being we feel no interest. Not so the vague embodiments of supernal force that succeeded the physical gods of Western Asia and the neighbouring lands. Out of these were evolved the only autocratic morally providential gods the wit of man has invented, and the exposition of whose attributes now engrosses the supernal impulses of the greater part of humanity. The various races we refer to may have had several origins, yet, at a very early period, they manifested the same general social instincts, and naturally they passed through the same successive stages in evolution as we have noted is general.

Dynasties of gods and men remarkable for their heroic characters are familiar to us, even among the rudest tribes, that we need not be surprised to note that like reverential records were either preserved or invented by the tribes who aggregated on the banks of the Euphrates and Tigris,

or made their homes in the rocky valleys of Syria and the
fertile oases and border lands of Arabia.   It is a pleasing
conceit of the isolated clansman to call himself a man, and
limit the designation of this distinctive term to his few
fellows, and to esteem their traditions of a few generations
as the great records of humanity.   Our Scotch brothers
carry forward even the features of their mythic heroes and
enrol them in galleries of paintings.

Modern science, discarding these puerile conceits first
assayed by philological semblances to work out the
primary characteristics, subsequently it analyzed the traditions into the physical semblances of human actions to
unfathom the mystery of the social beginnings.   These
modes of research have been applied to the peoples and
their racial aspects in the countries we are now considering
with such important results, that we not only seem to
relive the life of past greatness and the social attributes
of the old empires, but, passing over the heraldic emblazon-
ments, penetrate into their primary struggles for position,
and even trace their very origins.

Among these special researches, we will refer first to the
Survey of Western Palestine, in which the investigators
stayed not their searching explorations to the exposition
of majestic temples or the ruins of palaces, which in
their day emulated the glories of a Sargon, the might
of a Rameses.   Though they took record of great battle-
fields and traced out the lines of old city fortifications,
they failed not to note every rude wall, cairn, cave,
tomb, or other rubble work that denoted the early
structural constructions of men, with the result that we
now know the early arts and habits, and even supernal
concepts of the primary inhabitants of Syria and Phœnicia,
and from other like investigations we also glean that those
of Assyria were at least mere nomads wandering like
the father of the Hebrews from Chaldea to Egypt, and

pasturing their flocks by the wayside or in the unappro-
priated valleys, the great wealth of land as yet rendering
it an almost unmarketable commodity save where the
scattered hamlets had begun to aggregate.

We have ample evidence that savage man, not only in
Cappadocia, in Kurdestan, and in Armenia, once dwelt in
caves, but we know also that such must have been the
primary human status in Palestine, in Syria, and Phœnicia.
Beehive huts of rough rubble, just such as a man by
standing on tiptoe could raise with his hands only, the
earliest form of house where suitable materials abound are
common survivals, not only in the Shetlands and other parts
of the British Isles, but are to be seen at the present time
in Syria and Beloochistan. These, too, are accompanied
with flint flakes and flint arrow-heads implying that early
stage of human society when the use of metals was
unknown. Various survivals of this kind are described in
the *Survey of Western Palestine.*

Of the primary nomadic state of the Chaldeans, Sayce
writes that Aloros of Babylon, the first king, was called
the Shepherd, a title which we find assumed by the early
Chaldean princes and which proves the pastoral habits of
the people. He also notes "the evidence of language
shows that when the Semites first came in contact with
the civilisation of Accad, they were mere desert nomads
dwelling in tents and wanting the first evidence of culture.

At the earliest historical period throughout the extensive
region we are now considering, the doctrine of local
tutelar gods prevailed, and as the country was parcelled
out into districts under definite tribal or communal
arrangements, so was it allotted to distinct god-powers,
each of whom, singly in small places, but in connection
with other like tribal gods in larger groups, presided over
all the communal supernal manifestations in their special
districts. In some cases this supernal authority went with

the land; they were the inalienable gods of the country;
in others it applied to the people. Possibly the first class
of gods were nature deities and the second tribal or hero
fathers. In some cases these distinctions might be
abrogated, as by conquest, and the carrying off the local
gods; they were ousted from their jurisdictions; the
conqueror may be attaching the people to his god.
Several instances of the conquest and removal of the local
gods are on record, in some cases their restoration and
consequent renewal of authority, as was the case with
the Hebrews on their restoration after the Babylonian
captivity. Thus, Esarhaddon, in the inscription recording
his conquests, records that Tabua, "a young woman
brought up in my palaces I appointed to be their queen,
and with her gods to her land restored." (*Records of the
Past*, III. p. 115.) Samsivul, King of Assyria, besieged
and took Meturnal and two hundred other cities, when
besides seizing the people and their goods he carried off
their gods into captivity. (*Ibid.* V. p. 96.) In another
inscription Sargon restores the gods who are living there
to Kalus, Orchoe, Ur, Rata, Kullub, and Kisik. (*Ibid.* VII.
p. 25.) The same king is said to have taken from Musasir
the gods Haldia and Bagabartu, and also the gods from
Ashdod. (*Ibid.* VII. p. 40.) In another case, Yauteh, son
of Hazael, king of Kedar (Damascus), made submission to
Sargon for his gods which Sargon's father had carried off.
"I made him swear by the great gods and then restored
them." (*Ibid.* IX. p. 61.) Merodach Baladan, King of
Babylon, fled in the night from the attack of Sargon to
the town of Ikbibel; he assembled together the towns
possessing oracles, and the gods living in these towns;
to save them he brought them to Dur Sakin, fortifying
its walls; after the conquest he returned each god to
its town, restoring them to their sanctuaries. (*Ibid.* IX.
p. 15.) In some cases the gods, as a severe punishment,

were destroyed.   Thus Sennacherib, when he took the city
of Niti, broke up the gods thereof.   The most remarkable
case is that Maraduk nadin Ahi, King of Accad, carried
away Vul and Sala, the gods of Ekali; these in the time
of Tugulti Palesir, King of Assyria, were carried off and
brought to Babylon, and after the long period of 418
years, according to the Bavian Inscription of Sennacherib, he caused them to come forth and "to the temples—
I restored."   (*Ibid.* IX. p. 27.)

We have quoted these many instances of the restoration
of gods, because from them, and the still more extensive
series of instances in which not only were the gods but the
people also absorbed by the conqueror, we may form some
conception of the manner in which, under like conditions,
the series of local tutelar deities in any large homogeneous
country became blended and confederated.

The relation of the tutelar god and his worshippers was
that of an implied contract, and did not necessarily signify
more than a personal agreement which admitted of a new
selection.   Thus, Bel from the beginning was the tutelar
god of Babylon, yet, for certain personal reasons, Nebuchadnezzar esteemed Merodach as its tutelar god.   During
his sovereignty all his enterprises were undertaken in the
name of Merodach as the presiding deity in the Babylonian
supernal confederacy.   Rawlinson (*Five Great Monarchies*,
III. p. 26) writes: "Nebuchadnezzar devoted himself in
an especial way to Merodach, and not only assigned him
titles of honour which implied his supremacy over all the
remaining gods, but even identified him with the great
Bel, the ancient tutelary god of the capital. Nabonidus
seems to have restored Bel to his old position, re-establishing
the distinction between him and Merodach, and preferring
to devote himself to the former."   We have to remember
that each important personage, besides having his communal gods, also had his special individual guardian deity.

It might be his totem, his natal selected name, or the planetary power that presided at his birth that became his individual guardian. In the case of Nebuchadnezzar, at least two of these motives settled his supernal selection. Merodach was only second in rank among the tutelar gods of Babylon, and as the presiding star of his existence, he says, " The god Merodach deposited the germ in my mother's womb." (*Records of the Past*, V. p. 114.)

The apparent principle on which a local or an individual's god was selected was purely arbitrary. What the gods of Terah, the father of Abraham, were we are not informed; but from Genesis we infer that his god was not Yahweh, as Nahor, Abraham's brother, worshipped other gods, and as we read, these penates or totems were stolen by Jacob's wife from her father. The first intimation of the tutelar relationship of Yahweh and the father of the Hebrews, was God appearing to Abraham probably in a dream, as He afterwards did to Jacob.

We can follow the growth of supernal powers in the relations of the various tutelar deities in a district to one another, and when a people were enslaved and their god carried away into captivity, the god of the conquerors takes precedence over that of the captives, and, like the Hebrews under the Philistines, Baal was worshipped by them in conjunction with Yahweh. In a similar manner the various groups of gods had their origin through the combination of several local communes. That such was the case with the Babylonian empire and the Council of Babylonian gods will be readily perceived. Babylon, like Rome, was constituted of two communities residing on the opposite sides of the river, each of which had its original tribal tutelar god. On the one side Bel was honoured, on the other Merodach, and at an early period when the two were combined in one state, Bel, as representing probably the largest community, was accorded precedence. Other-

communes along the river bank had also selected their
gods, as Nebo by Borsippa, Nergal by Cutha, the moon-
god by Ur, Bettis by Niffer, Hea by Hit, Ana by Erech,
the sun-god by Zipparah. As Rawlinson says: "Out of
his own city a god was not greatly respected unless by
those who regarded him as a special personal protector."
(*Five Mon.* III. p. 28.)

Wheu by conquest, and probably in some instances by
voluntary amalgamation, the several cities we have named
became one political confederacy, then we find the local
tutelar gods were also brought together as a supernal
conclave. Thus, as a general rule, at Babylon Bel was the
chief of the gods, though often others are referred to as
chiefs of the gods. Probably, as a general rule, each god
was esteemed as chief in his own immediate jurisdiction,
and this may explain why we so often meet in inscriptions
with even secondary gods being named first and addressed
as great gods.

The same system of local tutelar deities prevailed in the
various communes that formed the Assyrian State, and they
differed both in the persons of the gods and in their reputed
rank in the supernal conclave at different periods. Assur
was the presiding deity of the city of Assur. Calah was,
during the continuance of the empire, the great god, the
father of the gods, the god who created himself. Nebo was
also a tutelar god in Calah, and Sin, the moon-god, at
Harran. Ishtar was tutelar at both Arbela and Nineveh.

Betimes, the tutelar god, like the offended ghosts of dead
kindred, becomes antagonistic to his kin or the land and
people of his adoption, and, like Yahweh, delivers them over
as a spoil into the hands of their enemies, as the Hebrews
to the Philistines. The Moabite stone declares that
" Omri, king of Israel, oppressed Moab for Chemosh was
angry with his land, 'but like Yahweh, Chemosh relented'
and had mercy and said to me, Go, take Nebo against Israel,

19 *

and I went in the night and fought against it, and I took
it, and slew in all seven thousand men. The women and
maidens I devoted to Chemosh, and I took the vessels of
Jehovah and offered them before Chemosh." (*Records of
the Past*, XI. p. 167.) It is singular that, like the medicine-
man, the tutelar god makes capital out of defeat or failure.
If the spell or charm fails it is due to some fault in the
worshipper; if the rain fails to come, some tabu has been
broken. So, when the people are defeated and their lands
harassed, it is due to the wrath of their tutelar god who
withholds his hand.

We have evidence through inscriptions on stone, coins,
cylinders, and bricks, that the same system of communal
tutelar deities prevailed from the shores of the Mediterranean to the Persian Gulf, and from Armenia to the
Straits of Hercules. We have affirmed the tutelar deities
of the Phœnicians, the Moabites, the Hittites, the Hebrews,
the Arabs, and the various peoples of Upper Chaldea and
the modern Mesopotamia, and there is great probability
that in time, through the efficiency of the researches, that
complete records of the several tribes and nations will be
affirmed and classified with the names of their successive
sovereigns, their conquests and guardian tutelar deities.
As it is, we know that the same system of combining
the worship of amalgamated gods and peoples prevailed
generally as we have shown in reference to Assyria and
Babylon. Even distant Aden had its council of gods, as
Athor, Hanbas, Il Makah, Yatha, Dhat Hima, and Dhat
Bádan. (*Trans. Soc. Bi. Arch.* II. p. 336.) Of the
general worship of tutelary gods in Arabia, the same work
notes that the "word patron, or tutelary god, frequently
occurs in Himyaritic." (*Ibid.* II. p. 340.) Duncker
informs us that the Benu Bekr worshipped Audh the
burning one, the Kinnana and the Benu Gatafaur
worshipped the goddess Uzza, and the Kafit tribe the

goddess Allat.   At Medinah the goddess Manat held sway, and the associated Koresh swore by Allat, Uzza, and Manat. Most of these are also referred to in the Koran.

Among the Canaanites and Phœnicians we meet with a series of tutelar gods assimilating in some respects with those of the Syrians, Accadians, and Chaldeans.   El or Il in various modifications is observed in several god-conclaves, also Itar or Astarte, and Artemis is familiarly known from the river of Jordan to the Euphrates.   Yav, so familiar as the Hebrew Yahweh, was a Babylonian god in the days of Nebuchadnezzar, and was the patron of agriculture at Borsippa; he was associated with the moon-god, and in one Assyrian inscription is described as the great ruler of heaven and earth.

Urukh is the first, as yet recorded, early military feudal king who brought several of the tribes and communes under one royal jurisdiction.   Rawlinson places this event B.C. 2286.   For such a coalition to have been workable, the civilisation of the associated communes must have been of an elevated character, and we find that architecture was considerably advanced, and that Urukh, probably in connection with the priests, caused new temples or shrine mounds to be erected in every city under his rule.   They not only knew how to make bricks, but had acquired the art of burning them, and applied them in various ways to buildings, drains, and walls.   More, they had elaborated a simple style of writing which they used in inscriptions on bricks and on cylinders, with figures of men and gods. We take it that the communes at Bel Nimrod, Mugheir, Warka, Calnah, and Larsa, must have been a long time in existence before they were combined to form the empire of Urukh, and that more primitive temple mounds must have existed in all those places to their several tutelar deities.

At the early period to which we refer, the general

system of god-heads, of whose after existence we read so
much, had been evolved, their nature, character, and myth
settled, though they afterwards may have been more
amplified. Throughout Western Asia the communes had
accepted their tutelar gods, subject only to necessary
political changes. Yet a vast period of time must have
preceded this era, in which the whole series of hero-gods
had been evolved, in which the god-myths and nature-
myths were conceived, and the nature-gods themselves had
passed from physical entities to personal deities, ghost
spirits had run through the cycle of changes embodied
in evil spirits, fetish powers, and ancestral penates, the
surviving forms of which still exist in the same countries as
they did in the days when Assor and Nebo, Merodach, Bel,
El, Yav, and Melkarth expressed the highest evolution of
supernal powers.

That the old Assyrians believed in the universal appearance of spirits or ghosts, and, as with the South Sea
Islanders and other races of men, held that men were of
a double nature, body and soul, so they held that all other
objects in nature possessed the same essential duality.
Professor Sayce writes: "The Accadians believed that
every object and phenomena in nature had its Zi or spirit,
some of these beneficent, others hostile to man, like the
objects and phenomena they represented. Naturally, however, there were more malevolent than beneficent spirits in
the universe, and there was scarcely an action which did
not risk demoniac possession. Diseases were due to the
malevolence of these spirits, and could be cured only by
the use of certain charms or exorcisms." (*Assyria, its
Princes*, p. 55.)

According to Lenormant, in the creed of the Chaldeans,
all diseases, as among savage races, were ascribed to the
malevolence of spirit demons. Diseases, death, anguish of
all kinds, are the direct actions of offended ghosts, either

those of relatives or enemies. The evil bewitchment, we
are told, may be the bewitchment of my father, or of the
seven branches of the house of my father, of my family, of
my slaves, of my free bondwomen and concubines, of the
living or the dead. Evil as the action of low-class spirits
is an early sentiment, but evil as moral punishment by the
deity for a crime or sin expresses a much higher state of
evolution. We have both phases expressed in the plastic
writings of the Chaldeans—more, we have an intermediate
phase present to us in the dramatic romance of Job.
Therein the tutelar deity plays with his worshipper as a
child plays with its toys. Job is twitted by the evil one as
being good, simply because it pays, on which his tutelar
deity relegates him to the influence of his enemy; he is
tried and not found wanting. The dramatic form of the
contest works out the assumed cause of Job's misfortunes;
he must have been false to his God, and the ills he endured
were the Divine punishments therefore. Of the direct
actions of the gods in punishing men, whether by removing
their protective agencies, as in several instances in the
Iliad, or by the thunderbolts of Jove, the arrows of Apollo,
and other examples in Greek mythology, we need only
refer to.

In the Chaldean inscriptions evil is presented to us in its
several aspects—now as the spirit of kin-revenge, then as
the spell of the medicine-man. An evil bhute may cause it,
or it may express the vengeance of the tutelar god, even
the punishment for moral sin. The primitive idea of
totem vengeance is affirmed by Lenormant of the Arabs,
when the soul, separating from the body, flies away in the
form of a bird, calling *hama* or *sada* and incessantly flying
around the tomb, or coming to the corpse and telling
the dead what his children are doing. If he had been
murdered, the bird cried 'give me drink,' and continued
to repeat the words until relations had avenged him by

shedding the blood of the murderer."   (*Anc. Hist. East*, II.
p. 258.)

Of low-class spirits as the cause of evils, we read :—

> "On high they bring trouble and below they bring confusion.
> Falling in rain from the sky, issuing from the earth,
> They penetrate the strong timbers, they pass from house to house.
> Doors do not stop them, bolts do not stop them ; they glide
> In at the doors like serpents, they enter the windows like the wind.
> They hinder the wife conceiving by her husband,
> They take the child from the knees of the man.
> They make the free woman leave the house,
> They are the voices which cry and pursue mankind.
> They assail country after country ; they take the slave from his place,
> They make a son quit his father's house."—(*Chal. Magic*, p. 30.)

Of the higher class of demons which rule on the wastes
of the earth, and the beneficent guardian deities which are
becoming tutelar, we quote the following : "The wicked
god, the wicked demon ; the demon of the sea, the demon
of the marsh, the demon of the desert, the demon of the
mountain ; the evil genius, the enormous *uruku*, the bad
wind. Spirit of the heavens conjure it, spirit of the earth
conjure it." (*Ibid.* p. 3.) Later on the demons had special
names and special powers. We read of the wicked Alat,
the wicked Gigim, the bad Tolal, the wicked god, the
wicked Maskim. These were most probably the tutelar
gods of the enemies. Special diseases were caused by
special demons. "The execrable Idpa acts on the head of
man, the malevolent Mautar on the life of man ; Unq on
the forehead, Alal on the chest, Gigim on the bowels, and
Tolal on the hands. Some evils are the effects of imprecations. 'The malicious imprecation acts on the man like a
wicked demon.' The voice which curses has power over
him. The malicious imprecation is the spell which produces the disease of the head. The voice which curses
loads him like a veil."

The gods of Assyria, like the gods of Olympus, may strike
direct.

> " May Ishtar strike him in the presence of the gods,
> May Gula pour inside him a deadly poison,
> May Rim inundate his fields, Sarukh destroy his harvests,
> And Nebo hurry him into incurable despair." (Ibid. p. 69.)

So the tutelar gods may directly intervene to save their
worshippers. Thus "the god Ztak (the Tigris); may he
penetrate his head for the prolongation of his life. He
will never depart from him." Of evil ensuing as the
punishment for sin Lenormant quotes many illustrations:
in one like Job the man knows not in what he has offended.
He is ill, but he cannot fathom how he caused it.

> " O Sun-god! thou that clotheth the dead with life,
> Supreme in mercy for him that is troubled.
> O father supreme! I am debased and walk to and fro.
> In misery and in affliction I hold myself.
> My littleness I know not, the sin I have committed I know not.
> I am small and he is great. O Sun-god! stand still and hear me."

We have in these ancient Babylonian magic texts expositions of all the early concepts of the origin of evil, they
represent also, in a series of successional developments, the
history of the social and mental progress of the race. We
expect that those expressing the most primitive ideas are
the most archaic, and that any references to physical or
mental anguish being punishments for sins are the products
of an advanced civilisation. It may happen that some
betraying archaic forms of thought are of later date, mere
survival sentiments among the vulgar of exploded concepts, but we feel assured that none denoting moral sin
will ever be presented in an archaic type.

On the early sentiments entertained by the races we are
now considering, Lenormant, who has fully perceived the
process of god-evolution in Babylonia, writes: "The system
was actually that of an adoration of the elementary spirits

as marked as among the Attai nations or in ancient
China. It was founded on the belief in innumerable personal spirits distributed in every part throughout nature,
sometimes blended with the objects they animated and
sometimes separate from them. Spirits everywhere dis-
persed produced all the phenomena of nature, and directed
and animated all created things. They caused evil and
good, guided the movements of the celestial bodies, brought
back the seasons in their order, made the winds to blow
and the rains to fall, and produced by their influence
atmospheric phenomena both beneficent and destructive;
they also rendered the earth fertile and caused plants to
germinate and to bear fruit, presided over the birth and
preserved the lives of living beings, and yet, at the same
time, sent death and diseases. There were spirits of this
kind everywhere in the starry heavens, on the earth, and
in the intermediate regions of the atmosphere; each element
was full of them, and nothing could exist without them.
A very distinct personality was ascribed to them, and we
see no trace of the idea of a supreme god, of a first principle with which they were connected and from which they
derived their existence." (*Chaldean Magic*, p. 144.) They
were simply a heterogeneous chaos of forces not regulated
by a superior power, not impelled to action by fate, but,
like the interactions of a miscellaneous crowd, their movements were balanced, though occasionally coming into
contact, by that indefinable rule of each for himself that
mortals call chance. This was the presiding principle in
nature: the eclipse, the storm, lightning and rain were
only occasional antagonisms in which the weaker force had
to give way, and the chaos of self-acting atoms proceeded
as before. Man held his position in this world of conflict
and individuality, not only by the prowess of his hand, the
strength of his limbs, but by his capacity to utilise all
other forces, and the physical substances, living beings,

and the supernal attributes were rendered subservient to his good.

The magic texts of the Babylonians not only define spirit action, but they convey to our minds the survival forms of the primary adoration of charms and spells, and that transitionary stage in which the indefinite spirit-powers are still worked by spells, and the spirit taking the place of the medicine-man gains his purpose, not by the mana-power of spiritual control, but is content to appeal to charms and invocations.

We recognize the primitive sentiments in the worship of holy fetish stones as the Caaba, of trees as the sacred trees of the Assyrians and the Arabs, of animal forms of all kinds, of fetish foods and the use of parts of animals, as symbols possessing sacred powers. Rawlinson writes: "Each god seems to have had one or more emblematic signs by which he could be pictorically symbolized. The cylinders are full of such forms which are often crowded into every vacant space. Thus a circle, plain or crossed, designated the sun-god; a six-rayed star, Gula; a double or triple thunderbolt, Vul, the god of the atmosphere; a serpent, Hea; a naked female, Ishtar; a fish Ninip. Of many others the significance is unknown; each of them represents a deity as well as the idol figure. The owner of the cylinder reverenced all the gods whose signs were contained on his cylinder, and one cylinder sometimes had eight or ten such emblems." (*Five Great Monarchies*, III. p. 82.) These were all fetishes as totems. Such was Kirub, a bull with a human face; Morgal, a lion with a man's head. Esarhaddon says: "May the guardian bull, the guardian genius who protects the strength of my throne, always preserve my name in joy and honour." In the illness of Izdubar the fetish "Manu-bain tree was angry." In the Fragments on the Seven Evil Spirits Merodach is ordered to fetch "the laurel, the baleful tree that breaks in pieces the incubi." The seven

wicked spirits themselves are but fetishes: the first is a
scorpion, the second a thunderbolt, the third a leopard, the
fourth a serpent, the fifth a watch-dog, the sixth a raging
tompest, the seventh a messenger of an evil wind.

Like fetish forms were attached to the later talismans.
Some were demon images with the heads of rams, hyenas,
and other animals, hair, feathers, and other parts of animals,
stones of various kinds, metal articles, anything strange
or mysterious. Some were sacred from their associations
and of immense power, like the host in the sentiment of
the Mediæval Catholic, was the mamit of the Babylonians;
others were sacred bands having texts and imprecations,
these were bound round the head, worn on the body and
in various ways attached to the person.

Dogs are fetishes in the omens of blue, white, spotted
and female dogs, also in the "hair of a cow passing yesterday," the "blood of the mystic eye, the circle of grass
herbs, the heart of a jackal, the nostril of a pig, the eagle's
wing, and the bird's beak." Portents are presented in an
endless variety of unexpected or irregularly appearing
objects, in the sky, on the earth, in the air, and in the
house whose portentous influence passes from the family to
the planetary bodies.

On the evolution of the Assyrian gods Lenormant observes:
"Certain of gods who did not differ essentially in their
nature from the other spirits were known by the same
name—Zi spirits. They possessed a distinct title only
because their power was thought to be greater and to have
a wider scope than the other spirits. As far as we can
see, the god differed from the simple spirit in that he was
less strictly localized and that he was regarded as animating
a great part of the world, many phenomena, and a class
of similar beings, each of which individually possessed a
spirit." (*Chal. Mag.* p. 148.) This simply describes them
as petty supernal kings, each having chiefs and headmen

under his jurisdiction. As yet there is no great king, as afterwards occurs. In the process of development M. Lenormant infers that the spirit of heaven and spirit of earth of the old invocations were converted into the ruling gods Ana and Hea.

Duncker (*Hist. Ant.* I. p. 355) shows that many of the gods were hero-gods. Thus, "when the highest fell in the conflict with wild beasts he was worshipped by his children with libations and sacrifices." Ninip is called the most powerful hero. Ur, the mythical King of Berosus, was reverenced as a god. There can be little doubt but that El, Bel, Dagon, said by Philo to have invented the plough, Moloch, Melkarth, Izdubar, and several others were men-gods. El is said to have built Byblus, in Phœnicia, and when he died a star was named after him.

Though neighbouring on Egypt, it is remarkable that family ancestral deities were never fully developed in Western Asia; this may in a great measure be accounted for in the vague conceptions they evolved of a future life; indeed, it is doubtful if the after-world cult was not derived from foreign sources, and though human spirits or the ghosts of the dead were conceived, like as with the Tonga islanders and some other people, these were only those of chiefs, heroes, and priests.

Some of the gods, probably of human origin, represented principles and attributes. Rimmon, the crowned hero, was lord of fertility; Dabara, the warrior, and Ninip, the son of Bel, was the great warrior. Hea was god of wisdom, Serakh the god of harvest, Manu the great Fate. Out of the various deities common in a locality each family, commune, or tribe selected, like Abraham, his own tutelar divinity. Some appear to have appointed the founder of the community, or a notable warrior or discoverer, as their supernal representative; others devoted themselves to the powers in nature. Some, as cultivators, appealed to the sun-god or

the rain-god and the special spirit of the harvest.   Others
appealed to the unknown manu in all things—the vague,
the incomprehensible.   They called it "the Strong One—
the Existing One—the Mighty One Tree—the Above."
Some of these terms are generic, and were applied indiscriminately to all conceptions having an exalted supernal
nature, mere chieftain gods.   Such were Ul, El, Eloah, Al,
Allah in its various local expressions of a supernal power.
This was used in the most general way by the Assyrians
and the other races for any of the various god-powers and
fetish idols.   As far as we can judge, there were ten or
more accepted gods in each local Divine conclave, but the
selected tutelar spirit of the place held the chief position
and presided in the assembly.   M'Clintock (*Cyclop. of
Bib.* III. p. 901) writes that Jerome and the Rabbis
enumerate ten Hebrew words as meaning God; each of
these probably represented a different manifestation of
supernal attributes.

In the smaller communes the one god-power does everything, but in the larger states each has his ascribed duties.
Sargon assigns diverse forms of help to each of his gods.
Samas made his designs successful, Bin afforded him
abundance, Bel El laid the foundations of his city, Mylitta
grinds the painting stone in his bosom, Anu executes the
work of my hands, Ishtar excites the men, Hea arranges
the marriages.   (*Bull, Ins. Khorsabad.*)   So, according to
G. Smith, Rimmon had charge of the canals, Ninip
destroyed the wicked, Samas was judge of heaven and
earth, and Nergal illuminated the great city Hades.

Naturally the apportioning of the gods to diverse duties
led not only to their classification but to the supremacy of
the most exalted.   As the chief god varied in different
places, nothing is more common in the inscriptions than to
find the same deity allocated to diverse positions in the
various lists.   That it was a common thing to abandon or

change the tutelar gods we have many exemplifications.
"Thus the anger of the great gods whose worship he had
abandoned—Ashur, the Moon, the Sun, Bel, and Nebo—
laid great affliction on him, and in the land of Elam slew
him with the sword." (*Rec. of Past*, III. p. 105.) The gods
of Carthage were originally Baal, Hamon and Tanith,
Melkarth and Eamun; these, under subsequent Greek
influence, were abandoned, and a temple of Apollo was
erected in the market-place, and the worship of Ceres and
Proserpine introduced. (*Lenormant, Anc. Hist. Ea.* II.
p. 279.)

We can best present the similitude of gods and men in
their attributes, actions and associations, by quoting the
"War of the Seven Evil Spirits," which is simply an ideal
delineation of a war between Assur and Babylon. "Against
high heaven, the dwelling-place of Anu the king, they
plotted evil. Bel heard the news, and took counsel with
Hea, the sage of the gods. They stationed the Moon, the
Sun and Ishtar, to keep guard over the approach to
heaven. These three gods watched night and day unceasingly. Those seven evil spirits rushed on the base of
heaven, and close in front of the Moon with fiery weapons
advanced. Then the noble Sun and Im the warrior, side
by side stood firm, but Ishtar with Anu entered the exalted
dwelling and hid themselves in the summit of heaven.
Bel saw the noble Moon in eclipse, and sent Peku, his messenger, to the deep to Hea. Hea, in the deep, bit his lips
and tears bedewed his face, and sent for Merduk to help him.
They are seven, those evil spirits, and death they fear not.
They are seven, those evil spirits, who rush like a hur-
ricane and fall like firebrands on the earth. In front of
the Moon with fiery weapons they draw." (*Rec. of Past*,
V. p. 165.) In all the particulars the conflict is essentially
that of human antagonists; heaven is besieged as a city is
besieged, and the defence is carried on by a similar distri-

bution of forces; external help is sought in the same manner by an ambassador, and the assailers and assailed exhibit the same courage and pusillanimity as human combatants.

The highest evolution of the gods in Chaldea partook of the division into gods of Heaven, Earth and Hades, as with the Greeks. The great source of associate power was a council of the gods. These councils in Olympus are several times referred to by Homer. So the gods in the war of the seven took council. Assur is described as the first of his peers, "king of all the assembly of the great gods." (*Rec. of Past*, III. p. 88.)

END OF VOLUME I.